Strength of the Heart

Carrie Carr

Yellow Rose Books
a Division of
RENAISSANCE ALLIANCE PUBLISHING, INC.
Nederland, Texas

ISBN 1-930928-75-0

First Printing 2002

9 8 7 6 5 4 3 2 1

Cover design by Mary D. Brooks

Published by:

Renaissance Alliance Publishing, Inc.
PMB 238, 8691 9th Avenue
Port Arthur, Texas 77642-8025

Find us on the World Wide Web at
http://www.rapbooks.biz

Printed in the United States of America

Acknowledgements

I want to thank the hardworking people who made this book possible: Barb & Linda, whose belief in my stories made all of this possible. Mary, whose dedication to detail makes the best damn covers. Day, whose tireless patience had to be sorely tested, but was always there to guide me though the editing process. Lori, whose unwavering support kept me sane. And last, but certainly not least, Cathy, for giving me the opportunity to make my dreams come true.

— Carrie Carr

This book is dedicated to—

My mom and dad, who have always been there for me with their love and support. I love you both dearly.

My brother, who is not only a great guy, but gave me a wonderful niece and nephew to spoil.

My daughter, Karen. Your smile and laughter always brighten my heart.

And, of course, my AJ. Your light outshines the brightest stars and beckons me home. Always and forever, my love.

Chapter 1

The light tapping resounded in the empty room as the young woman limped her way across the polished wood floor. The walking cast on her right leg was covered with a dark stocking and blended well with her knee-length black skirt. Amanda Cauble smiled at the young couple as they whispered together, the body language of the newlyweds decidedly familiar. When the husband's eyes met hers, Amanda's smile widened. "Would you two like more time? Since this house is older, not many people have shown an interest; so there's really no rush."

"Oh, no. We were just trying to decide where all of our furniture would go." He was not much taller than his wife, who was the same height as Amanda. "We love this place. How long will it take to get the paperwork completed?"

"Not long at all. Let's go back to my office, and we'll get started, all right?" Amanda tucked her clipboard into her briefcase and flipped the clasp closed. She didn't argue when her client gently took the briefcase from her, as his wife linked arms with her and helped her from the room. "Thank you. I can't wait until this blasted cast comes off." She locked the front door behind them.

He held the rear door of their car open, waiting until Amanda was settled in before closing it quietly. Opening his wife's door, he placed a quick kiss on her lips before racing around the light-gray sedan and settling in behind the wheel. "Amanda, Laurie and I would really like to thank you for finding this house for us. It's exactly what we've been looking for, isn't it, honey?"

Laurie nodded. "It sure is, Dan." She turned around in her seat so that she could meet Amanda's eyes. "We wanted something older that we can renovate ourselves. The newer houses just don't have the personality that the more established homes do."

"I know what you mean. My grandparents' house is about the same age as this one, and it's always felt more like home than the house my parents owned in California." She glanced out the window as the car headed back to the real estate office. "Thanks for driving, Dan. I'm afraid I can't get back behind the wheel until I can use my right foot. I'm sorry that Wanda had to leave the office early today. She really wanted the chance to show this house to you both."

"Not a problem. We love Wanda, but it was nice to have the office manager show us around." Dan pulled the car into the parking lot of Sunflower Realty, parking next to a green four-door pickup truck that dwarfed his sedan. He rushed around the car and helped both women from the vehicle, then let his attention focus on the huge truck beside them, his eyes lighting up as he checked it out. "Whoa. Now *that's* a toy I'd love to have."

His wife nudged him in the ribs with her elbow. "I don't think so, honey. Our new house would almost fit in the back of that monster."

Warm hands on Amanda's shoulders caused her to smile and turn around. "Hi, Lex."

"Hi, beautiful." The tall figure's face was partially hidden by the dark cowboy hat, but her teeth gleamed in the afternoon sunlight. "I was in the neighborhood, so I thought I'd drop by and see if you would like to go to lunch." Lex looked over at the young couple. "Unless I've come at a bad time. Hi, I'm Lexington Walters. That's my 'monster' you're parked next to." The green Dodge Ram was a larger version of the one that had been wrecked, and Amanda continually teased her friend about the noise the diesel made.

Laurie blushed. "Oh, my, I'm sorry. I didn't mean..."

"No, no. I'm the one who's sorry. I was just teasing you." She met the young man's eyes and winked. "You want to get a closer look? I can show you the interior and the engine."

"That would be great." Dan gave his wife a pleading look. "If that's okay with you, that is."

She nudged him with her hip. "Go on. I'll be inside with Amanda, starting the paperwork." Laurie linked arms with Amanda and tugged gently.

Amanda waved at Lex and allowed herself to be led into the

building. "I guess I'll be seeing you in a little while." She turned and waved before closing the front door behind her.

Lex waved back and opened the passenger side of the truck, showing off her relatively new toy to an appreciative audience.

"So," Amanda waved her empty fork at Lex, who was busy cutting another large bite from her own steak, "how's the work on the house coming along?" Their ranch house was in the final stages of rebuilding after Amanda's mentally unstable mother had burned it to the ground two months prior.

Lex swallowed the bite of food that she had been chewing and took a healthy drink from her glass of tea. "Pretty good, actually. We should be able to move in a couple of weeks from now." She placed her fork down on the edge of her plate and looked across the table. "Martha cornered me this morning down at the barn."

The fork that was almost to Amanda's mouth stopped, the contents forgotten. "What did she want?" Her confusion cleared as she realized what her partner was trying to tell her. "Oh, no. She didn't?"

"Yep. Said that she's made all the arrangements, 'cause she's getting tired of waiting for us to make up our minds." Lex leaned back in her seat and looked around. Satisfied that no one was listening to their conversation, she leaned forward again. "How does April twenty-third sound to you?"

"That soon? But that's only about a month away! I'll never be able to get everything done by then." Amanda grabbed Lex's hand and squeezed it. "We've got invitations to mail, clothes to pick out, decorations to decide on..."

"Hold on there, sweetheart. Martha's got all that under control. She's been plotting with your grandmother, and I think it's pretty much out of our hands. All we have to do is show up and recite our vows." Lex stood up and walked around to Amanda's side of the table, pulled up an empty chair, and sat down next to her flustered friend. "We have kinda been changing our minds a lot and putting things off. Let's let the two of them have their fun, okay? I think they both really want to do this. It's not every day that we get married, you know."

"I should hope not." She leaned into the sturdy body next to hers. "I guess you're right."

Lex was confused by Amanda's reticence. "Well, don't sound

quite so excited about it. Are you having second thoughts, or something?" Not caring where they were, she wrapped one arm around Amanda's shoulders. "If you're set against it, I'll call her right now and cancel the whole thing."

"No!" Amanda jerked back, realizing her attitude was hurting the one person she'd sworn she'd never hurt. "That's not it at all. I'm just..." Her voice trailed off, the last word unintelligible.

Lex tilted her head until she could see her lover's eyes. "You're just what, love?"

"Nervous." Amanda picked up her fork and swirled it through the leftover gravy on her plate. "I've never done this before."

"No, really?" Chuckling, Lex reached down and took the busy utensil away, placing it out of reach. "Well, Miss Cauble, contrary to public opinion, I've never done this before either." She twisted in her chair until their knees were touching. "Sweetheart, look at me." Once Amanda's eyes were locked with hers, she smiled and lifted both hands to frame the worried face across from her. "To tell you the truth, I'm a bit nervous myself. I don't want to disappoint you."

Amanda's eyes widened at the admission. "Really?"

"Yep." She cleared her throat and shook her head. "I'm scared spitless, if you want the truth. But I figure that we'll get through it like we always do...together." Lex almost leaned down and kissed Amanda, but the sound of a throat being cleared reminded her of where they were.

"You gals about done with your lunch?" The waitress placed the check for the meal on the table.

Both women laughed, and Lex stood up and brushed at the wrinkles in the legs of her jeans. "I am." Lex reached into her back pocket for her wallet, grabbed a few bills and handed them to their server. "Thanks, Alison."

The woman picked up the money and winked. "Thank you, Lex. Y'all take care, all right?" She walked back to the kitchen, humming a tune to herself.

"Alison? That wasn't—"

"Uh, yeah. It was." Lex helped Amanda from her chair and escorted her from the restaurant. "I didn't realize she worked here until she took our orders, and then I was too preoccupied to say anything to you about it." The waitress had been a childhood girlfriend of Lex's. The rancher hadn't seen much of the other woman since they were both fourteen and had lost a friend in a hunting accident.

Amanda nodded, linking her arm through her fiancée's. "Huh. She's a bit, uh, shorter, than I pictured her."

"Ya think? I thought she looked pretty good." Lex jumped when she felt small fingers pinch her stomach. "Hey! Watch it."

"You'd better *stop* watching it. I'll go kick her with my cast."

Laughing, Lex opened the restaurant door, allowing Amanda to exit ahead of her. "You've got nothing to worry about, blondie. I've only got eyes for you."

"You want another cup of coffee, Tray?" Lester asked, as he stood up and slowly limped over to the stove.

Travis shook his head. "No, thank you, my friend." He watched as the old cook stirred the boiling pot. "Why are you limping?"

Looking up from his stew, Lester shrugged his shoulders. "Old age, I'd imagine. I reckon I'll have to retire before too long. These old bones get creakier every year." He was almost back to the table when the large radio on the counter crackled to life.

"Base, this is Roy. Do you read me?"

Lester picked up the large microphone and squeezed the bar along the handle. "This is Lester. Go ahead, Roy."

"We've got an emergency, Lester. Me and a couple of the boys are on our way back to the bunkhouse. Better have an ambulance meet us."

"Roger that." Lester exchanged worried glances with his friend. "What's wrong out there?"

Roy's breathless voice echoed in the quiet bunkhouse. "It's Rawson. He fell off his horse, and we can't wake him up. There's no sign of a head injury, either."

The old cook rubbed his whiskered cheeks in thought. "All right. We'll get the ambulance on the way. How far away are you?"

"'Bout twenty minutes, I think. One of the boys is riding behind Mr. Walters, holding him up. We're trying to keep him as still as possible, since we don't know what's wrong."

Lester knew what was wrong, as did Travis. Rawson Walters had pancreatic cancer, and he had returned home a couple of months before to spend his final days with his family. Only the immediate family and Lester knew of his illness. "Just take it easy with him, Roy. We'll be here waiting for you." He set the microphone back down on the countertop and scrubbed his hand over his face. A strong hand squeezed his shoulder, and he looked up into the concerned face of his friend.

"I'll give Lexie a call on her cell phone," Travis offered quietly.

"Good idea. She needs to hear this from family, not from a hospital." Lester walked over to the phone that hung on the wall, picked up the handset, and dialed the ambulance emergency number that was posted on the nearby bulletin board. He watched as his friend took a small phone from his shirt pocket and hit the speed dial.

"And, believe it or not, I actually cornered Lexie this morning. Told her that we were tired of them fartin' around, and gave her a set date for the ceremony." Proud of herself, Martha poured fresh coffee into her mug and her companion's.

Anna Leigh nodded and picked up the cup. "Thank you. I'll bet that went over well. How did she take it?"

"Not too bad, really. At least, once she got over the initial shock." Martha chuckled as she remembered the look on Lex's face. "I tried to talk her into going on a cruise for their honeymoon, but she wouldn't hear of it."

"Well, after hearing all about yours, I'm ready to pack up Jacob and leave on one myself." They had been splitting their time between planning Lex and Amanda's wedding and reminiscing about Martha's own recent honeymoon. "It sounded so wonderful."

Martha smiled. "It certainly was. I knew Charlie was a romantic, but I never knew he was such a fine dancer. And seeing him in that tuxedo for dinner in the evenings..." She sighed. "It was the most perfect time in my life, I do believe." Although she had danced with the sheriff in the past, it had always been in the small local bars, not ballroom dancing like they had done on the cruise ship.

Seeing the dreamy, far-away look in her friend's eyes, Anna Leigh reached over and rested her hand on Martha's arm. "I'm so happy for you, Martha. You both deserve all the happiness in the world." Glancing at her watch, she shook her head. "Goodness. I need to get back to town."

"Hot date?"

"Not exactly. But there is someone I need to see."

"Well then, let me walk you out to your car." Martha linked arms with Anna Leigh and led her through the neat home. "Don't be a stranger, now." Martha watched as Anna Leigh slipped behind the steering wheel of the luxury car.

"Not a chance of that, Martha. You tell that handsome husband of yours I said hello." She waved through the open car window before putting the vehicle in reverse and driving away.

Martha waved until the car drove out of sight, then closed the front door. "What a wonderful lady." Back in the kitchen, she tied her apron around her waist and was about to start lunch when she heard the front door slam. "What on earth?"

A slender teenage boy raced into the kitchen, breathless. "Mada! There's a—"

Martha pulled the young man into a nearby chair. "Calm down, honey. What's going on?"

"I was up at the main house, watching the construction guys work, when I saw an ambulance go up the road to the bunkhouse. It was moving pretty fast, too. Their lights were flashing, but they didn't have the siren on. What do you think happened?"

"I'm not sure, Ronnie." Martha hurried over to the phone and dialed a number from memory. Allowing it to ring several times, she finally gave up and placed the receiver back in the cradle. "Something's going on, that's for sure. Lester always answers the phone up there."

"Easy now, fella's. Watch his arm, there," the old cook ordered. He was standing next to the medical technicians who were strapping Rawson down onto the gurney. The pale, gaunt form under the thin sheet bore faint resemblance to the robust man who had left the ranch so many years earlier. Lester looked back over his shoulder and saw Travis standing by the door to the bunkhouse. Deciding he was in the way more than he was helping the EMTs, Lester limped back over to where his friend was standing. "Were you able to get hold of Miz Lex?"

Travis shook his head. "No, not yet. Either she has her cell phone turned off or is out of range. I didn't want to leave a message on her voice mail."

"I can understand that." Lester studied Travis's face carefully.

"You all right?"

"Not really. I've never gotten along with Rawson, but I hate to see this happen. No one deserves to die like that."

"He ain't dead yet, Tray. Maybe this is just..."

Placing a hand on his friend's shoulder, Travis sighed. "No. We both know that his time is short. No sense in trying to kid ourselves." He watched as the paramedics placed the gurney in the back of the ambulance and closed the door. "We need to find Lexie, and let her know what's going on."

Lester followed the vehicle with his eyes until it disappeared from sight. He looked over at Roy, who was standing quietly by the horses with several other men. "You made good time, Roy. Thanks for all your help."

The ranch foreman dusted his cowboy hat against his leg. "No problem, Lester. Do you think he's gonna be okay? I've never seen a man fall from a horse like that."

"What do you mean?"

"Well," Roy walked over to where Lester and Travis were standing, lowering his voice so that the other men couldn't hear him, "I was right behind him, and it looked as if he was out before he hit the ground." He locked eyes with the old cook. "He's pretty sick, isn't he?"

"Yes, he is. But he didn't want anyone else to know about it." Travis's voice was barely above a whisper. "I'm afraid that Rawson doesn't have much time left, Roy. He wanted to spend what he could at home, without people pampering him. You can understand that, can't you?"

"Yeah, I sure can." Pulling his hat back onto his head, Roy spoke in a loud voice. "You tell the boss if she needs anything from us, to just let us know. We'll be around." He tipped his hat to the retired oilman and walked back over to where the other men stood.

"Good man."

"The best." Lester slapped his tall friend on the back. "Let's go on up to Martha's and see if she knows where that granddaughter of yours is. Maybe we can get in touch with her from there."

Lex smiled as she pulled in at Sunflower Realty and parked next to the new Cadillac. "Looks like your grandmother is here."

"Cool! You want to come in and say hello? I'm sure she'd love to see you." Amanda was unbuckled and had opened the door before the truck stopped rumbling. She turned back around to see an amused grin on her partner's face. "Well?"

"Hold on, sweetheart. Let me come around and help you out, okay?" Lex released her seatbelt and hurried around to the other side of the truck. She put both hands on Amanda's waist and easily swung her down from the tall seat, looking down into Amanda's eyes without releasing her hold. As the world faded around them, Lex leaned down and placed a tender kiss on waiting lips.

Amanda's hands slowly slid up the strong arms until they were tangled in Lex's hair. She leaned into the kiss, allowing her lover to prolong the contact for several seconds. The honk from a passing car finally broke the spell, causing Amanda to pull back slightly. "Whoa."

"Yeah. Um, what were we going to do?"

"I have several things on my mind, and none of them can be done here. But I think we were going to go inside and see Gramma."

Lex nodded. "Right." She reluctantly released her hold and closed the truck door. "Shall we?" She bowed with a flourish.

"Why certainly." Amanda linked her arm through her partner's.

They were both still laughing as they stepped into the real estate office. Several heads turned to see who had entered, and waves accompanied by scattered hellos greeted the couple.

Anna Leigh stood at the far end of the office, a fond smile lighting her patrician features. "Good afternoon, girls." She opened her arms and welcomed each woman with a firm hug.

"Hi, Gramma." After getting her hug, Amanda stepped back and wrapped one arm around Lex. "What brings you down here?" Although her grandmother still owned the agency, she tended to allow Amanda to run things without much intervention.

"Can't I come by just to visit my granddaughter? Or do I need a reason?"

Amanda shook her head and reached out with her free hand. "Of course not! I just meant..."

Laughing, Anna Leigh took the younger woman's extended hand. "Oh, dearest, you're so much fun to tease." She looked at Lex, who seemed to be enjoying the exchange. "Actually, I was hoping to catch Lexington."

"Me? What did I do?"

"You haven't done anything, yet. But there is something that I'd like for you to do, if you can spare the time."

Lex grinned. "Name it, Gramma, and I'll do it."

"You haven't even heard what it is."

"I don't care. If it's for you, then it's a done deal."

Anna Leigh smiled. "You're such a dear, Lexington." She winked at Amanda. "Must be the reason my granddaughter loves you." At Lex's blush, she reached out and enveloped her in an embrace. "One of the many reasons, I'm sure." She pulled both women into Amanda's office. Deciding that she had embarrassed Lex enough, Anna Leigh decided to broach the actual reason for her visit. "Have a seat, girls."

"Okay, Gramma. Now you've really piqued my curiosity." Amanda sat down in one of the visitor's chairs next to her lover. "What's going on? Is there something wrong?"

Anna Leigh perched on the edge of the large oak desk, gently swinging one foot back and forth. "No, nothing like that, Mandy. There's just a matter that I have to handle tomorrow, and I'd really appreciate Lexington's help."

"Sure. Just tell me when and where, and I'll be there." Lex grinned. "Although if you'll give me some kind of hint, I'll have a better idea of how to prepare myself."

"Goodness, yes. That would help, wouldn't it?" Anna Leigh shook her head, somewhat bemused with herself. "Some days I swear I don't know where my mind is." She leaned forward slightly, making eye contact with Lex. "As much as I hate to admit it, I need your...ah...muscle. Or, more truthfully, I need to make a show of force."

"You want me to break someone's legs for you?" Lex stood up tall and crossing her arms over her chest. "Cool."

Anna Leigh laughed, waving her hands in denial. "Oh my, no! Let me try and explain." She pulled at one earlobe nervously. "I have a meeting early tomorrow morning with Tanner Brumbaugh."

"Tanner Brumbaugh? What would you be meeting with that big goon for?" Amanda asked. "He's a—"

"Unsavory fellow. But he promised the Historical Society a donation last year before Christmas—a rather sizable one, actually. We gave him the receipt for his taxes in good faith, and he was supposed to turn over the deed to a parcel of land just east of town."

Lex bit her lip in thought. "Why are *you* meeting with him?"

"Because I'm the acting president of the Society, dear. It's my duty, so to speak." Anna Leigh waved one hand in a dismissive gesture. "I'm sure he'll listen to reason, so you probably don't *need* to come, if you'd rather not."

"No, that's not it at all. I said I'd be there, and I will. What's so important about this land, anyway?"

Anna Leigh sighed. "It's not the land as much as the principle involved. He's already taken a tax deduction for the donation. I'm just trying to get what rightfully belongs to the Society."

Lex nodded. "All right. I'll pick you up in the morning after I drop Amanda off at work, if that's okay."

Electronic strains of *Bolero* suddenly echoed in the large office. Lex grimaced as she reached for the cellular phone that was hooked to her belt loop. "Excuse me." Lex opened the small device. "Yes? When? Where are you now?" She listened for a moment, then jumped to her feet. "I'm on my way, Grandpa. Thanks." Lex looked down at Amanda. "I've got to go."

"What's wrong?" Amanda asked, also standing up. Seeing the distressed look on her friend's face, she reached out and placed one hand on the other woman's arm. "Honey?"

"That was Grandpa. Dad fell off his horse, and they've rushed him to the hospital." She turned to Anna Leigh. "I'm sorry, but I've got to..."

Quickly sliding from the desk and onto her feet, Anna Leigh embraced the shaken woman and stepped back. "Don't you dare apologize, dearest. Is there anything I can do for you?"

Lex shook her head. "No. But I'd better go." She started for the door but was stopped by the small hand hooked in her belt.

"I'm going with you." Amanda looked up into the frightened blue eyes.

One blink, and the fear was replaced with a sudden warmth. "Thanks." Lex looked over Amanda's head to Anna Leigh. "I'll call you when we find out something." She turned and escorted her lover through the door.

"Godspeed," Anna Leigh murmured, tears in her eyes. She knew of Rawson Walter's illness and feared that this news only meant the worst.

Chapter 2

The tall figure raced through the hospital doors, then suddenly stopped, rushing back to grab a smaller woman by the arm. "I'm sorry, sweetheart." Lex slowed her pace so that her injured lover could keep up.

"That's all right. I'm sorry if I'm slowing you down." Amanda limped as she tried to match her pace with Lex's. "Stupid cast."

Lex mentally kicked herself for being so thoughtless. She stopped in the middle of the hallway and looked down into Amanda's eyes. "Forgive me?"

"Lexie!" A slightly overweight, middle-aged woman scurried down the hallway, worry creasing her attractive features. "I'm so glad you're here." Three more steps, and Martha was enveloped in a bone-jarring hug.

"Mada." The gravity of the situation sinking in, Lex buried her face in Martha's shoulder and struggled in vain to fight back her tears.

The housekeeper gently rocked her charge for a long moment, rubbing the strong back comfortingly. "There, there, honey. We'll get through this, you'll see." She gave Lex a few more moments then, seemingly out of nowhere, produced a handkerchief. "Here. We were just waiting for the doctor to come in and tell us how your daddy is."

"Thanks." Lex wiped her eyes and quietly blew her nose. She slipped the used linen into her back pocket, reached out for Amanda, and was gratified when her hand was taken. "Is

Grandpa here?"

"He sure is, honey. He's in the ICU waiting room upstairs. I was just coming down to wait for you when you walked in." Martha led them down the hallway and to an elevator. "Lester's with him."

Lex waited until Amanda followed the older woman into the elevator, then stepped inside. "Lester?"

Martha nodded as the doors closed. "Yep. They were having coffee down at the bunkhouse when Roy radioed in. He's the one who called the ambulance."

Surprised by the news, Lex stood quietly until the doors opened again. She silently followed Martha and Amanda out into the bustling corridor. *I know that they are old friends, so I guess it just stands to reason that they'd spend time together. I just never imagined Lester leaving the bunkhouse.* Lex knew that the old cook sent either Roy or one of the hired hands to do most of the buying. The old man claimed that he didn't want to have anything to do with the "dunderheads" in town, but she figured that he was just getting too feeble for the long drive and the hours of shopping. *I'm going to have to see about getting him some sort of assistant. He's getting too long in the tooth to do it all alone.* Her thoughts were interrupted by her grandfather's voice.

"Lexie, Amanda. I'm glad you're both here." He hugged Amanda and then reached for his granddaughter. "The nurse was just in, and told us the doctor would be with us in just a few minutes." As Lex continued to struggle with her emotions, he felt the body in his embrace shudder.

A short, middle-aged Hispanic man in a white medical coat stepped into the waiting room. Pushing his wire-framed glasses back up on his nose, he peered down at the clipboard in his hand. "Is anyone here a relative of Rawson Walters?"

"I am." Lex pulled away from her grandfather and wiping her eyes with the back of her hand. "He's my father."

"Ah." The doctor reached out with his free hand. "I'm Dr. Martinez. And you are?"

"Lexington Walters." Accepting his hand, Lex squeezed it firmly and released it. She turned and motioned to the others in the room. "This is the rest of my family."

Dr. Martinez acknowledged the others with a nod of his head. "Very good. Ms. Walters, I'm not going to lie to you. Your father is gravely ill."

"I'm aware of that, doctor. How is he right now?" Lex hated the tremor in her voice. She clenched her fists at her sides until a small hand grasped the left one, squeezing it gently. The distraught woman gave her lover a thankful smile, then turned her attention back to the doctor standing in front of them.

"He's stabilized for the moment, but his prognosis is quite grim."

Lex swallowed hard and bit her lip."Grim? Are you saying—"

"I'm saying that he's lucky to be alive at this moment, Ms. Walters. In fact, if he has any other family, I'd suggest that you contact them immediately."

"How..." The break in her voice caused Lex to stop and close her eyes for a moment to regain her composure. "How long do you think he has?"

The middle-aged doctor reached out and clasped her shoulder in a comforting manner. "A few days, maybe a week. We'll do everything we can to make his final days as comfortable as possible. I'm sorry." He squeezed her shoulder one more time, then nodded to Amanda and left the room.

Tears filled her eyes as Lex watched the doctor walk away. "A week." She turned and took comfort in Amanda's arms.

The smell of antiseptic assailed her nose as Lex slowly entered the darkened room. She stood just inside the doorway for a long moment until her eyes adjusted to the gloom, the only sounds a raspy breathing and the beep of the heart monitor machine attached to her father. A small light shone on his bed, painting a starkly frail picture of the man she'd once thought of as invincible. "Aw, Dad," Lex whispered, trying to fight back the tears of despair.

The gaunt face turned towards the sound of her voice. "Lex? That you, girl?"

"Yeah, I'm here." Lex walked the rest of the way into the room until she was standing beside his bed. She reached down and brushed his hair away from his forehead. "How ya doin'?"

Fighting back a groan, he reached up and tried to swat her hand away. "Stop that. Been better, I imagine."

"Ornery old man." What had threatened to become animosity between the two quickly softened into a playful banter as they reconnected. Lex sighed and pulled a chair close to the bed. Sitting down, she leaned forward and touched his right arm, which was hidden by the bedcovers. "Is there anything I can get you?"

"How 'bout a ride home?" Rawson tried to reach across the bed with his left hand but was stopped by the intravenous drip that was attached to his arm. "Damned contraption." His arm fell listlessly to the bed, all his energy spent.

"Doesn't look like you're going anywhere for a while." Lex blanched when she realized the truth of the statement. "I mean—"

Rawson closed his eyes as the exhaustion overtook him. "I know what you meant, girl. Why don't you let me get a little rest, and we'll talk in a while?" The last words were almost a whisper as the dying man fell back to sleep.

Lex closed her eyes and nodded. "Yeah. You get some rest, and we'll talk later." She laid her head down on the bed and quietly began to weep.

Some time later, Amanda cautiously opened the door and peeked inside the semi-dark room. She saw the dark head resting on the edge of the bed, and her heart ached for her lover's pain. Quietly Amanda limped across the room, until she was able to kneel awkwardly beside Lex's still form. "Honey?"

"Huh?" Lex raised her head and looked at her father, who was still resting peacefully. She turned her head and glanced into the concerned face so close to hers. "Amanda? What are you doing here?"

"The nurse asked me to wake you. She came in earlier and saw you asleep." Amanda reached up and placed her hand gently against Lex's cheek. "How are you doing, love?"

Lex leaned into the touch and closed her eyes for a long moment. When her eyes opened, she turned and kissed the soft palm next to her lips. "Better, now." Suddenly realizing the position Amanda was in, Lex stood up and helped her to her feet. Nodding in the sleeping man's direction, she whispered, "I think he's out for the night. C'mon."

Amanda allowed Lex to lead her into the hallway. "Where to now?"

"Now we go home. I need to call Hubert and let him know about Dad's condition, anyway." Lex started down the quiet corridor, mindful of Amanda's limping. "And I want you to get that foot up. I'm sure it's killing you by now."

Knowing better than to argue, Amanda linked her arm in Lex's as they slowly made their way to the elevators.

The drive home was quiet, as Lex tried to gather her jumbled thoughts. She didn't know exactly what she was going to tell her brother, but she knew he had to be notified of their father's condition. As they drove down the street, she noticed a light on in his office. Startling Amanda, Lex executed a U-turn and parked the large truck in front of the small building where Hubert kept his accounting office.

Amanda looked at her partner carefully. Lex had turned off the engine and was silently staring at the smoky glass windows that covered the front of the building. "Do you want me to go in with you?"

Do I? Should she have to be subjected to my brother just because of me? Ignoring the childlike need that wanted just that, Lex sighed. "No, that's all right. This shouldn't take very long, and I can tell that your leg is bothering you." She opened the truck door and stepped out, but stopped before closing the door. "If I'm not out in fifteen minutes, better call for help."

"I love you."

Lex smiled gratefully. "I love you, too." She closed the door and hurried around the vehicle. With a slight wave at her watching lover, the rancher opened the door to the office and stepped inside.

"I'm closed," a deep voice yelled from the back office. "Come back tomorrow."

Lex followed the voice until she was standing in the doorway of her brother's office. "Hubert, we need to talk." She leaned against the doorframe and ran one hand through her hair.

Eyes the same color as hers glared up from a stack of papers, an ugly scowl marring the handsome features of the man sitting at the desk. "You've already got a restraining order against me. What the hell do you want now?"

To be an only child. Ignoring his hateful remark, Lex walked over and sat down in a visitor's chair. Leaning back and crossing one leg over the other, she met his glare with one of her own. "There's no easy way to say this, but Dad's in the hospital."

"So? You came all the way over here to tell me that?" He tossed his pen onto the desk and leaned back in his chair. "Am I supposed to send him flowers or something?"

Lex jumped to her feet and slammed her hands down on the desk. "Look, asshole. Can't you forget about yourself for one damned minute? Our father is lying in a hospital bed, dying, for

God's sake!"

Hubert jumped up as well and pointed a finger at his sister. "That son of a bitch has never been a father to us, and you damned well know it! Or have you conveniently forgotten how he deserted us?"

"He's made some mistakes, that's true. But—"

"But nothing!" Hubert stepped around the desk. Although not much taller than his sister, he easily outweighed her by thirty or more pounds. The accountant rarely exercised, and his expanding midsection was proof that he enjoyed what the good life had to offer. He pulled ineffectually at his pants. "I don't owe that old bastard a damned thing. I hope he dies slowly and—*urk*!" Hubert never saw his sister's hands wrap around his throat as she slammed him back against the top of the desk.

"Watch your fucking mouth, asshole." Lex looked down into the terrified face that was beginning to turn a dark shade of red.

"Lex!" Amanda had grown nervous waiting out in the truck and had just peeked in the doorway when she saw her lover pin the larger man down. She hurried over and pulled at the angry woman's shoulder. "Stop it! You're going to kill him."

"So?" But realizing Amanda was right, Lex loosened the grip she had on Hubert. "You're not worth the effort it would take to kill you, big brother." She shoved him and pulled away slowly.

Amanda could feel her heartbeat slowly returning to normal. *They really shouldn't be allowed to be in the same room without a referee. What if I hadn't come in when I did?* She reached over and gently rubbed Lex's back. "Why don't we go home?"

Lex watched with a satisfied smirk as her brother struggled to roll his large bulk off the desk. "Might as well. Got no reason to hang around here." Lex privately enjoyed the hateful look she received from Hubert.

"Bitch. I ought to—"

"You ought to what?" She moved closer and caused him to scramble so that the desk was between them. "Face it, Hube. You don't have the guts." Lex purposely turned her back on him and headed for the door. "I'll let you know if Dad's condition changes."

He threw a book at her, missing and hitting the wall next to the doorway. "Don't bother. I could care less what happens to the old bastard!" As soon as the front door closed, Hubert pulled up his pants and sniffed. "And stay out, you hateful bitch. Or next time I'll kick your ass!"

After getting Amanda settled, Lex sat down behind the wheel of the truck and closed her eyes. "I could have killed him." She struggled to control her shaking hands as they gripped the steering wheel. "If you hadn't come in when you did..."

"Shh." Amanda reached over and wrapped her fingers around Lex's forearm. "I don't think you would have, love. You just didn't realize what you were doing."

"No, I knew *exactly* what I was doing. And I was enjoying it." Lex's head dropped forward until it rested on her whitened knuckles. "I completely lost it."

Amanda unbuckled her seat belt and scooted across the cab until their bodies were touching. She wrapped both arms around Lex and held her. "I don't believe that for a moment. If you had lost it, he *would* be dead." Placing a soft kiss on the dark head, Amanda sighed. "I don't know how he's stayed alive as long as he has. The man is a complete butt nugget."

Unable to help herself, Lex chuckled. "He does seem to bring out the worst in everyone around him, doesn't he?" She turned her head and gave Amanda a light kiss on the lips. "Thanks, sweetheart."

"Any time." Amanda squeezed Lex tightly and pulled back. "Can I interest you in a nice massage when we get home?"

"Only if I can give you one, too. I think we both could use it."

"Deal." Amanda buckled her seatbelt and leaned back happily. "Let's go. Time's a-wasting."

Lex laughed. "Yes, ma'am." She drove off into the night, thankful for the gift of the woman by her side.

Although it was barely after seven in the morning, the well-dressed man sitting across from Rawson looked wide awake. He placed several papers into the expensive leather briefcase that was on his lap. "I'll take care of all the arrangements, Rawson. You don't have a thing to worry about."

"I really appreciate you doing this for me, Mr. Benton. Especially on such short notice." Rawson was sitting upright in bed, but his features wore a heavy weariness.

"It's no problem at all. You've always used our firm for your legal work, and I'm glad that I could be here to help you now." He could tell that the visit had exhausted the ill man and decided it was time to leave. "You have my card, and I've written my home number on the back in case you need me after hours." The lawyer stood up and shook Rawson's hand. "Just give the papers to the nurse, and I'll pick them up on my way home from work this evening. I don't want to disturb you if you're resting."

"Thanks, I will. Look out for my daughter, will you? I have a feeling she's gonna take this a lot rougher than that boy of mine."

The attorney nodded. "I certainly will." He turned and quietly slipped from the room without another word.

Thankful to finally be alone, Rawson struggled to ignore the pain that wracked his body. He looked down at the blank paper on the table in front of him and picked up a pen. Just as he was about to begin writing, a nurse stepped into the room with a syringe.

"Now that your guest is gone, how about letting me give you something for the pain, Mr. Walters? It's way past due." She reached for the intravenous bag hanging from the stand by his bed but was halted by a wave of his hand. "What?"

"Not yet. I've got a letter I want to write, and I don't want to be all doped up."

The nurse sighed. "Can't that wait until later?"

"No. This is really important, and I have to have it done before she gets here." He gasped as another painful spasm hit. "Please. Give me just a few minutes, will ya?"

Temporarily deterred, the young woman nodded. "All right. You have about ten minutes, then I'm coming back in here whether you're finished or not, okay?"

"Thanks, miss. I really do appreciate it." He flashed her a grateful smile and watched as she left the room. Looking back down at the empty paper, Rawson bit his lip for a moment and then began to write.

Anna Leigh was about to climb into her car when a large green truck wheeled into her driveway. She looked up in surprise as Lex jumped out of the vehicle. "Lexington? What are you doing here?"

"I thought you wanted me to go with you to meet with Brumbaugh," Lex replied. She reached Anna Leigh's side and gave her a quick hug. "That was this morning, wasn't it?"

"Well, yes. But your father..."

"Is resting comfortably. I called the hospital before I came over here. He was just given something for the pain, and the nurse said that he'd probably sleep until almost lunchtime." She kept one arm around Anna Leigh and guided her over to the truck. "I would have been here sooner, but I dropped Amanda off at the office first. She wanted to come too, but had to meet with some clients this morning."

Knowing that she had lost, Anna Leigh got into the truck and waited until Lex sat down beside her. She reached over and touched Lex on the arm. "I'm terribly sorry about your father, dear. I know this must be hard for you."

Lex cleared her throat to fight the rising emotion that simple gesture caused. "Yeah, well. It's not like we weren't expecting it, Gramma. But thanks." She carefully backed the truck out of the driveway. "Where exactly are we going, anyway?"

"I suppose that would help, wouldn't it?" Anna Leigh reached into her purse and pulled out a small piece of paper. "His office is over on Larson Street. Eight twenty-four, to be exact."

"Okay." Lex headed the pick-up in the proper direction without another word. As they drove past her brother's office, she noted with smug satisfaction that it appeared to be empty. *Guess ol' Hube must have slept in this morning. Probably had trouble sleeping.* She hoped that their confrontation the night before had something to do with his absence. *Serves him right. He had no call to talk about Dad like that.*

Anna Leigh covertly kept her eyes on Lex. She had noticed the tense set to the broad shoulders and feared that her granddaughter's lover could buckle under the strain. As the Dodge Ram pulled into the parking lot adjacent to the office building, Anna Leigh patted Lex on the leg. "Are you sure you want to do this, Lexington? I doubt he'll give me much trouble."

After turning off the engine, Lex twisted around and reached into the back seat for her black cowboy hat. "I'm not about to let you do this alone, Gramma." She pulled her sunglasses down on her nose and winked. "Let's go get that deed."

Moments later, both women entered the office of Tanner Brumbaugh. The young secretary looked up from her keyboard and smiled at the elegantly dressed older woman. "Hi. May I help you?" Her eyes widened at the grim figure standing in the background. Dressed completely in black with a black hat pulled low over her brow, the tall woman even had her eyes hidden by mirrored sunglasses. With her arms crossed over her chest, she looked quite intimidating.

"We're here to see Mr. Brumbaugh," Anna Leigh said. She saw the look on the young woman's face and turned around. "Lexington, relax. You're frightening the poor girl."

The scowling woman sighed but uncrossed her arms. "Sorry, Gramma."

"D-do you have an appointment?" the secretary stammered, still rattled.

Anna Leigh nodded. "Yes, dear. I'm Anna Leigh Cauble of the Somerville Historical Society." She gestured to the woman behind her. "And this is my granddaughter, Lexington Walters. Is Mr. Brumbaugh in?"

A reply was rendered unnecessary as a tall, heavyset man stepped from the other room and extended his hand. "Mrs. Cauble, so nice to see you." His oiled dark hair shone brightly under the florescent lights as he crossed the room. Although it was only a few minutes past eight o'clock in the morning, the dark shadow of his beard could already be seen on his face. "Why don't you step into my office? I'll have my secretary bring us some coffee." He snapped his fingers at the young blonde still sitting at the front desk. "Lor, hon, grab us something to drink, will you?"

Tanner Brumbaugh was reputed to have made most of his money illegally. Up until a few years before, he had run a trucking company out of Houston, but had sold that business and was now more interested in antiques. His paunchy body attested to his soft lifestyle, the expensive suit he wore straining at the buttons. He held out a chair for Anna Leigh and sat down behind the extravagant mahogany desk, not even bothering to acknowledge the somber figure with her.

"What's on your mind today, Mrs. Cauble? I was surprised when I found out that you had made an appointment to see me. Perhaps you'd like me to find you a rare antique?"

"No, thank you, Mr. Brumbaugh. I'm here strictly on business, I'm afraid." Anna Leigh pulled a folded sheet of paper from her purse and slid it across the immaculate desk.

He took the paper and opened it, frowning as he read it. "What's this?" Wadding the paper up into a ball, Brumbaugh tossed it back onto the desk. "Are you trying to waste my valuable time?"

Lex stepped forward and placed both hands on the desk, leaning forward until she was certain she had the man's attention. "I don't give a rat's ass about your time, Brumbaugh. We're here to pick up the deed that you promised the Historical Society last year."

Brumbaugh jumped to his feet. "Who the hell do you think you are, trying to intimidate *me*?"

A large hand planted itself on his chest and shoved him back into his chair. "Watch your language, asshole." Lex was around the desk before Anna Leigh could stop her. She grabbed the heavy man by the lapels of his jacket and pulled his fat body up out of the leather chair several inches. "I'm not asking you again, buddy. You tried to screw over the wrong people this time."

Anna Leigh hurried around the desk and grabbed at the younger woman's shirt. "Lexington, please! Let go of him this instant."

With a disgusted snarl, Lex did as she was asked. She lowered her clenched fists to her sides and struggled to control her heavy breathing. *What the hell is wrong with me? That's twice in less than two days I've attacked someone.* Lex could feel her heart pounding, and a part of her was happy to see the fear cross the man's face.

Brumbaugh sat up in his chair and shakily tried to straighten his jacket. "Why didn't you just say so, Mrs. Cauble? I had forgotten all about the deed." He reached down into a desk drawer and pulled out a piece of paper. Handing it to the older woman, Brumbaugh hated to see his hand tremble slightly. *Her granddaughter is a psycho. Must be adopted.* "Is this all you need?"

"Why yes, it is." Anna Leigh checked the paper before putting it away in her purse. She took Lex by the arm and started to pull her from the office. "I'm terribly sorry about all of this, Mr. Brumbaugh."

"Nothing to apologize for, Mrs. Cauble." The businessman stood up but stayed behind his desk. *Wonder if her granddaughter would like a job? I could always use someone like her.* He took another look at the tall woman, whose face was set in an expressionless mask. *Maybe not.*

"Come on, Lexington." Anna Leigh never released the hold she had on the dark sleeve as they left the office. Once outside, she stopped and turned to face Lex. "What on earth was that all about?"

Lex shook her head. "Nothing." She took off her hat and sighed. "I'm sorry, Gramma. I honestly don't know what's come over me. Every little thing seems to set me off." Embarrassed by her behavior, Lex couldn't even look the other woman in the eye. "I did the same thing to Hubert last night. If Amanda hadn't come in when she did, I could have killed him."

Anna Leigh could feel her heart breaking at the tone in Lex's voice. "Oh, dearest, I sincerely doubt that." She continued on to the truck and climbed inside, waiting until Lex was in as well. "You're worried and probably exhausted. Were you able to get any sleep last night?"

"Sleep?"

"Yes, honey, sleep. It's that *other* thing you do in bed." Not getting a response, Anna Leigh sighed. *Well, it was worth a try, anyway.* "Would you like some company at the hospital? I don't have any other plans this morning."

"Hospital?" Lex blinked, and then realized what was being offered. "Uh, no." Afraid of how that sounded, she hurried on. "I mean, thanks, but I'll probably spend the whole day there, Gramma. No sense in you having to do that, too."

Anna Leigh nodded but persisted. "Are you sure? Because I certainly don't mind, you know."

"I'm sure. If you don't mind, can I just drop you off at the real estate office? It's only a couple of blocks from here." Tired of conversation, Lex started the truck and pulled back onto the street.

"That's fine, dearest. Jacob and I were going to go out for lunch anyway, so I'll just have him pick me up there." Anna Leigh reached across the vehicle and grasped the nearest arm. "But remember, your family is here for you when you need us."

Lex glanced across the truck and smiled. "Thanks. That means a lot to me."

"You're a very important part of our family, Lexington. Don't you forget it."

Fighting back tears, Lex nodded. "I won't."

The afternoon passed quietly as Lex sat solemnly by her father's bedside. He had been asleep when she arrived at the hospital, so she spent the time watching the peaceful figure and reminiscing about happier times. A painful gasp from the bed caused her to sit up. "Dad?"

"Lexington, come here." Rawson reached out with one hand

to the woman beside the bed. "I need to talk to you, girl."

"What is it, Dad? Can I get you something?" Lex stood up and took his hand.

"Yeah, you sure can." He struggled to sit up further. "Help me get out of here."

Lex shook her head. "I can't do that. You're sick, and you need to stay here so that you can get better." The argument sounded weak, even to her ears.

He squeezed her hand and shook his head sadly. "We've gotten along a lot better since I've been back, haven't we? No sense in lying now, Lexington." Rawson grimaced as another strong wave of pain wracked his weakened body. "I ain't getting any better, girl. We both know that."

"Dad," although Lex knew it for the truth, she had trouble accepting his words, "we don't know that for sure."

"Yes, we do." His eyes took on a glint of their former fire. "I don't want to die in a hospital bed, girl. I know I haven't been the best father to you, but don't I deserve a bit of dignity at the end of my miserable life?"

Tears welled up in her blue eyes. "Yeah, you do. What do you want me to do?" Lex held her breath. She was afraid of what he might ask of her.

Rawson saw the tense set of his daughter's shoulders. It took him a long moment before he realized what she must have been thinking. "Hey, nothing like that." He pulled her down until she was sitting on the edge of the bed. "I'm not afraid to die, Lexington. But I'm willing to let the good Lord take me when He has a mind to, not take the matter into my own hands. And I'd surely never ask you to do that."

Lex slowly released the breath she had been holding. "Okay. So what *do* you want?"

"Get me out of this damned hospital."

"Where do you want to go? Is there someone you want to see, before..." Lex couldn't bring herself to finish the sentence.

He shook his head. "I'd like to spend my last days with you, girl. Maybe I can finally get a few things settled, before I go."

Lex nodded. "Okay. I'll bring you home with me."

"No."

"But you said—"

"I want to go back to the ranch, Lexington. I want to die under the stars, like I was meant to." His eyes filled with tears.

"Remember the first time I took you camping? We could go back there."

Swallowing the lump that had formed in her throat, Lex closed her eyes. "Yeah, I remember. I was about seven, I think." She opened her eyes and looked at her father. "Are you sure you want to do this? It's a long way from town, and you won't have a doctor readily available if you need one."

Rawson smiled. "I'm sure. Just get me out of this place, and I know I'll feel a lot better."

"All right." Lex squeezed his hand once more before standing up. "Let me go find the doctor so that you can tell him what you want."

When she got to the door, her father's voice caused her to turn back around. "Thanks, Lexington," he rasped, falling back against the pillows. Before he closed his eyes, Rawson smiled at his daughter. "I'm damned proud of you, girl." The frail form in the bed sunk back further and fell asleep, the smile still gracing his lips.

Lex bit her lip to hold back the sob caught in her throat. "I love you, Daddy," she whispered, before she turned away and left the room.

Chapter
3

Amanda stepped across the unfurled sleeping bag that stretched across the floor, setting the cup of coffee she'd brought for Lex onto the nearby table. The house that they were renting while the ranch house was being rebuilt was cozy, but there wasn't much space in the small living room. "Are you sure you don't want me to come with you?"

"Sweetheart, with that cast, you'd be completely miserable out there." Lex leaned over and brushed her hands over the nylon bag, folding it in half and then rolling it up. She tossed the tied bundle into the corner of the room, where it landed next to a growing pile of supplies. "Besides, we'll probably be out there for a week or two, and I know how busy you've been at the office lately."

"I don't care about the damned office." Amanda dropped onto the nearby sofa. When she saw the shocked look on her lover's face, she softened her tone. "I care about you, Lex. I hate to think about you out there all alone."

Lex stood up and crossed the room to sit down next to Amanda. She wrapped an arm around Amanda's shoulders and pulled her close. "I won't be alone. Dad will be there, too."

"But he's sick. What if he gets worse? Wouldn't it be better if you had some help?" Amanda tucked her head against Lex's shoulder and fought back tears of helplessness.

"Amanda, listen to me." Lex waited until she was certain she had her attention. "We've already talked about this, love. Dad wants to spend his last days out there. I won't be coming back until he's..." Her voice broke and tears trickled down her face. "God. I don't know if I can do this."

Amanda turned and wrapped her arms around Lex's body, trying as best she could to offer comfort. "Then don't." She ran her fingers through the dark hair as Lex buried her face against Amanda's chest and cried. "I hate the thought of you having to bring him back all alone," she murmured, not caring whether Lex heard her or not. *How can he ask this of his own daughter? Doesn't he realize how this will affect her?*

"I have to, Amanda. He's my father, and I've already given my word that I would honor his wishes."

"So? Just tell him what you've told me. Surely he wouldn't blame you for feeling this way," Amanda argued, even though she knew she had already lost.

Lex raised her head until their faces were bare inches apart. Her eyes pleaded with Amanda to understand. "I have to do this. All of my life, I wanted to do something that mattered to him. I made straight A's in school, but he didn't care. I gave up the piano because he said it wasn't necessary on a ranch. I lived, breathed, and slept for the damned ranch. Nothing. So, I began to follow him around, and tried to be the perfect daughter."

Amanda blinked the tears from her eyes and shook her head. "You don't have to—"

"He didn't want a daughter," Lex continued quietly as if she hadn't heard. "He never really told me *what* he wanted." She shook her head ruefully. Her blue eyes filled with the remembered pain of her childhood. "I learned to build fences, break horses, rope cattle...all in the hopes that I'd find something, sooner or later, that would make him notice me." Lex swallowed the lump that had suddenly formed in her throat. "But now, finally, he needs me. And I can't deny him that any more than I could deny the love I have for you."

"Oh, honey." Amanda reached up and wiped the tears that had fallen from Lex's eyes. She leaned forward and kissed the damp trail they had left, gently trying to heal her lover's pain. After she had covered Lex's face with soft kisses, she pulled back and nodded. "All right. You go take care of your father. I'll be here waiting for you when you get back."

The rancher bit her lip to keep from breaking down altogether. "Thanks," she rasped quietly. "I love you so much, Amanda. Don't you ever forget that."

"I love you too. Now, why don't you let me help you get things together, and we'll try to go to bed early. You've got a stressful time ahead of you." Amanda placed a final kiss on waiting lips, then stood up and helped Lex to her feet.

Lex glanced sideways to look at her father. Although he was dressed in his usual clothes, the denim shirt appeared to be several sizes too large and draped loosely on his thin frame. His pale face looked almost waxy in the early-morning sun, and his once-alert eyes were cloudy. When those eyes caught hers, she quickly turned her attention back to the road in front of them. They had left the hospital less than an hour ago, but she was already beginning to regret agreeing to this trip. *He doesn't look strong enough to get on a horse, much less ride several hours to a campsite. Maybe this was a stupid idea.*

"I ain't dead yet. Stop looking at me as if I was, girl." Rawson felt a momentary pang of regret, knowing full well what was going through his daughter's mind. He almost asked her to take him back to town, but his intense fear of dying in a hospital bed kept him silent. *At least this way, someone will be with me. I don't want to die alone.*

"I'm sorry, Dad. I didn't mean..."

Turning back to watch the passing scenery, Rawson sighed. "I'm the one who should apologize, Lexington. I had no call to jump all over you like that." He closed his eyes and leaned back against the seat. "I appreciate you going to all this trouble for me, girl. Lord knows I haven't done much to deserve it."

"You're my father. I'd say that entitles you to ask anything of me." Lex clenched her jaw and stared at the road ahead.

"Anything?" He turned his head and opened his eyes to study his daughter for a long moment. "You're quite a piece of work, girl," Rawson admitted ruefully, mindful of the years they had spent apart.

Driving past the construction on the new house, Lex parked the truck in front of the horse barn. "Why? Because unlike some, I take my responsibilities to my family seriously?" Angry, she turned off the engine and climbed out of the vehicle. "I'll get the horses saddled up. Why don't you just sit here and try to get a little rest."

Rawson flinched as she slammed the door closed. "Wonder

where she got that temper?" He pulled his hat down low over his eyes and followed her advice.

Lex stomped into the barn and slammed the heavy door behind her. "Damn it! Why do I always let him get to me like that? Ever since he's been back, we're always at each other's throat."

Several heads poked over their stalls as the horses looked out to see who had come in. The nearest horse, a dark stallion, whickered in greeting.

"Hey, fella." Lex rubbed his velvet nose. "Sorry I haven't been out for a few days, Thunder. Things have been pretty hectic lately." When the large animal nuzzled Lex's shirt, she reached around his neck and gave him a hug. "Thanks."

Wiping the tears from her eyes, Lex opened the door to the tack room and gathered up what she needed. She had decided to bring Amanda's gentle mare for her father to ride. The paint pony bobbed her head in greeting as the rancher stepped into her stall and began to place a saddle across her back. "You'll take good care of Dad, won't you, girl?" Not waiting for an answer, Lex continued to ready the animals for the trip.

Thirty minutes later, Lex had their mounts saddled and the supplies packed away on an extra horse. As she brought the last horse out of the barn, she yelped when she almost ran into a body that just happened to be heading inside at the same time.

"Goodness, Lexie! You startled me." Martha held one hand over her rapidly beating heart.

"I could say the same for you, Mada. What are you doing out here?" Lex looked over the housekeeper's shoulder to the cab of the truck, where her father appeared to be sleeping.

Martha placed her hands on her hips and glared up at Lex. "Were you going to go off without saying goodbye? I thought I raised you better than that."

The rancher tipped her hat back on her head and sighed. "To tell you the truth, I hadn't really thought about it one way or the other. How did you know that I was here?"

"Amanda called me a little while ago. She wanted to make sure I gave you this." Martha reached into the front pocket of her apron and pulled out one of the small handheld radios. "Just in case you need something and the cell phone doesn't work."

Lex took the device and shook her head. "You two are always watching out for me, aren't you?" But she tucked the radio into her shirt pocket without complaint.

"Every chance we get. Where will y'all be, just in case?"

"At the far north end of the property where the spring feeds into the creek. Roy knows where it's at." Lex stared at Martha and shrugged her shoulders. "Guess this is it. Better go wake him up, if we're going to get camp set up before it gets dark. I don't know how long it'll take us to get there."

Martha stepped forward and wrapped her arms around Lex. "You be careful, you hear? And give me a holler if you need anything." She leaned back and sniffled. "I'd even get on one of those beasts, if you'd like for me to come along and help."

Touched at the offer, Lex bit the inside of her cheek to control her emotions. "Thanks, Mada. That means a lot to me, but we'll be okay." She leaned over and kissed the housekeeper on the cheek. "Love you."

"I love you, too, honey." Martha reached up and touched Lex's cheek. "Be safe. You've got a wedding to attend next month, you know." She stepped back so that Lex could lead the horses over to the truck. As she watched, Lex opened the passenger side of the vehicle and helped Rawson to his horse.

Once they were on their respective mounts, Lex turned around and waved to Martha, who raised her hand in response. She motioned for her father to take the lead away from the barn while she pulled the pack animal behind them, not looking back for fear of losing her composure.

Two squirrels frolicked in the courtyard, playing tag under and around the concrete picnic table that sat beneath the huge oak trees. Amanda continued to stare sightlessly through the large window that looked out over the area shared by several small office buildings on the same block. Her partner had only been gone for half a day, yet the pain in her heart from the separation felt as if it had been much longer. Amanda was so involved in her thoughts that she didn't hear the light knock on her office door or the quiet greetings from the couple standing in the doorway.

"Mandy?" Anna Leigh tiptoed into the room, her husband following quietly behind. "Dearest?"

Amanda jumped and spun her chair around. "Oh, hi. Sorry about that." She stood up and limped around the desk to give them welcoming hugs. "To what do I owe the pleasure?"

Jacob kissed the top of Amanda's head before he released her.

"We just wanted to check up on you and see how you were doing, Peanut. A little birdie told us that you might need some company."

"This birdie wouldn't happen to be about six feet tall with blue eyes, would she?" Amanda asked. She sat down on the edge of her desk and ran her hands over her skirt. Tears sprang to her eyes as she thought about what her lover would be going through for the next few days. *That's just like Lex. More concerned about me than herself.* "When did you talk to her?"

"She called us early this morning," Anna Leigh replied. "I believe she said they were on their way to the ranch to get the horses." She sat down in the chair closest to Amanda and placed her hand on the younger woman's knee. "Forgive me for saying this, dear, but is Lexington up to doing this? She sounded so worn out when I spoke with her."

"To tell you the truth, no. She's been on such a short fuse lately, I'm worried about how her father's death will affect her." She stood up and angrily knocked a pile of papers from the desk. "Damn him! Damn Rawson Walters for what he's doing to her." She covered her face with her hands and started to cry, as both grandparents rushed to her side to offer what comfort they could.

Rawson sat up in his saddle, invigorated. "Damn, girl, I never thought that fresh air would smell so good. We going to that little place where the creek always runs deep from the spring?"

"Yeah. Thought if you were up to it, you might like to do a bit of fishing," Lex offered, gently pulling the packhorse behind her.

"Sounds good." He slowed his mount so that she could catch up. "Doesn't look like he takes too kindly to hauling that load. Do you think you packed enough?"

Lex felt her temper flare. "I wasn't sure what you'd be needing." She kneed her horse and moving ahead.

Shaking his head, Rawson followed. "Don't get your hackles up, girl. I was just making talk."

They traveled the rest of the way in silence, Lex not trusting herself to speak. She still had a lot of unresolved feelings where her father was concerned, and she hoped that this final trip would exorcise her childhood demons. She pulled the horses into a quiet clearing, then closed her eyes for a moment and enjoyed the quiet sounds of the running creek and the occasional bird-call.

After setting up the campsite, Lex brushed down the horses and staked them out. She watched as her father reached into his shirt pocket and pulled out a small prescription bottle. He poured several tablets into his hand and swallowed them dry, quickly slipping the container back into his pocket. Sighing heavily, she walked back over to the small campfire he had started and sat down.

"We never quite decided who'll be doing the cooking," she said.

"No, I guess we didn't." He looked into her eyes and grinned. "Did you ever learn your way around the kitchen?"

She laughed. "Um...no. Why do you think Martha has hung around all these years?" Lex tossed a few twigs into the flames. "I brought some canned stuff, just in case."

He wrinkled his nose. "Not that crap that we used to take camping? I thought it was banned by the government years ago."

"Nah. I brought some bread and some canned meats—nothing as sinister as that other stuff."

"Well, I reckon that's okay, then." Rawson grimaced and leaned back against the folded blanket that Lex had placed over his saddle. He was thankful for the two sleeping bags she had given him to lie down on so that the cold from the ground wouldn't seep into his body. "Never figured I'd be this worn out over such a short ride. Think I'll rest up a bit before dinner, if you don't mind."

Lex squatted down beside him and placed an extra blanket over his legs. "Sounds like a good idea. Are you warm enough?"

Weakened, Rawson didn't even feel like fighting her attention. "Maybe another log or two on the fire?" he asked hoarsely. "Can't seem to get warm."

"Sure, Dad. I'll take care of it." Lex reached behind herself and grabbed her own sleeping bag. She unzipped the thick material and gently covered the frail man. "You just rest." She fought back her tears as his eyes closed.

The evening progressed silently, and Lex continued to feed the fire in the hopes of keeping her father warm. Although the temperature had dropped to the low fifties, the heat from the blaze had forced her to strip down to her tee shirt hours ago. She looked up into the late night sky and sighed. *I don't know what to do. I must have been out of my damned mind, agreeing to bring him out here.*

Rawson moaned and rolled over onto his side, facing the fire. He pulled the thick covering closer to his face and curled up slightly.

"Dad?" Lex walked over to kneel next to him. Realizing that he was still asleep, she glanced at her watch. *Four o'clock in the morning. He's been asleep since we got here.* Concerned, she reached down and brushed her fingertips lightly against his forehead. The sleeping man's skin was clammy, even in the glow of the blazing fire. Satisfied that he was resting as comfortably as possible, Lex settled down beside her father and stared into the crackling fire.

Morning dawned clear but cool, and Lex was startled awake by the feel of something on her leg. She jerked up from where she had fallen asleep against her saddle and glanced around. Her father's pained eyes looked up into her own.

"Hey there, sleepyhead," he teased hoarsely. "Where's your sleeping bag, girl? You've got to be freezing in that getup."

Lex looked down at herself and shook her head. She was still garbed in just a tee shirt and jeans. "Uh, well..."

"Kids." The ex-rodeo rider rolled into a sitting position and removed most of the blankets that were piled on top of his body. "Part of this mess was probably yours, wasn't it?"

"Yeah." Lex stood up and grabbed her denim shirt. "I didn't think I'd be sleeping much, anyway. Thought you could use it more." She tossed a few more logs onto the dying fire and dusted off her hands. "Looks like it's gonna be a pretty nice day today. You want to see about doing a little fishing?"

Rawson appeared to think about the question for a long moment. *I don't think I can even get up off the ground. Maybe this wasn't such a good idea, after all.* "Nah. I think I'd rather just take it easy today. Maybe we can do some fishing tomorrow."

Not fooled by her father's words, Lex nodded. "Sure." She placed her hands on the small of her back and stretched. Several vertebrae popped and caused her to moan. "That feels a lot better. Would you like me to make you something for breakfast? I think I can handle that."

"I'm not very hungry, girl. But you go ahead and get yourself a bite to eat." He dropped back against the saddle and closed his eyes.

The rest of the morning went by uneventfully, although Rawson made it a point to stay close to the fire. Lex could see that he was growing weaker, and his already pallid complexion was turning frightfully waxen. She knelt by his side and tucked the blanket up under his chin. "Dad? Do you want me to get you back to town? You're looking really pale."

"No, girl. I'm doing just fine out here with you. Why don't you sit down with me for a bit?" He gasped in pain. "Grab those pills out of my pocket, will you?"

She pulled out the bottle and read the label. "This says to take one every six hours. You've been popping them like candy."

He nodded. "I know. And it's not doing a hell of a lot of good right now, either. Give me about four of them. I can't seem to work the bottle too good."

"But—"

"Lexington, please. It's not like I'm going to get addicted to them or something," he joked weakly. "I can't take it, honey. It's getting too bad." His voice faded on the last words, as he fell back against the padded saddle.

"Okay." She helped him swallow the four tablets, then looked into the fire. "Guess I'd better get a bit more wood, huh?"

Rawson shook his head. "Leave it be. I got some things I'd like to say to you, so just be still for a bit, all right?" *I know I ain't got much time, and by damn, I'm gonna get this off my chest.*

"You don't have to—"

"Hush, girl." He reached out and beckoned for her hand, which she promptly placed in his. "I know I've been a pretty sorry excuse for a father, and I'm not going to try and make up for it now with half-assed apologies." His hazel eyes were fogged with pain, but he continued. "It was never your fault, Lexington. I've always been so damned proud of you, but I never knew exactly how to say it."

Lex sniffled and cleared her throat, but didn't say a word.

"When you turned about ten or eleven, you looked so much like your mother it nearly killed me. I wasn't much, but I loved her with all I had." He looked up into his daughter's face, fighting back tears of his own. "I wasn't her first choice, but things worked out and she married me. When she passed on, I wanted to die too. But I had you kids to think about, so I did the best I could." Rawson paused for a moment to pull himself back together. "It got to the point that I couldn't stand to look at you, because you reminded me of what I had lost. I'm sorry for that, Lexington."

"Dad, please. It's all right." Lex could see that he was now fighting for almost every breath. "Rest for a while, and we'll talk some more later."

He shook his head vehemently. "I will, in a minute. Let me just finish this first, okay?" At her nod, he sighed. "I can't take the credit for how you turned out, girl, but I'm right damned proud of you. I know your brother has been giving you grief most of your life, and I'm sorry. I could never control him much, either." He lay back and closed his eyes, exhausted with the effort. "This may be late in saying, but I want you to know that I love you, Lexington. You're the best daughter a man could ever hope to ask for, and I hope that some day you'll forgive me for not being around for you more."

She pulled his hand up to her face and rubbed it against her cheek. "You're here now, Dad. That's the important thing." An errant tear fell from her eye as she watched him doze off. "Sleep now, we'll have plenty of time to visit, later."

Hours later, the late-afternoon sun peeked through the budding trees, its light tracing bright patterns over Rawson Walter's prone form. Lex sat next to him holding his hand, fearful of letting go. She had spent the entire day watching the slight rise and fall of his chest, afraid to look away. His eyes fluttered open and wearily found hers.

"Lex?" His voice was a bare whisper.

"Yes, Dad?" Lex had to lean down to hear him. "What..."

"I love you, girl," Rawson gasped, closing his eyes again.

The young woman leaned over and kissed his stubbled cheek. "I love you too, Daddy," she murmured. The hand she held went slack, and the sounds of his troubled breathing stopped. She gently released her grip and looked down into her father's face. For the first time since he had returned home, Rawson looked at peace. "Tell Momma and Grandma Lainey hello for me," Lex whispered as tears began to fall down her cheeks.

Chapter 4

"And so we return to this earth a good man and a loving father. Rawson Lee Walters, go with God, and join your beloved wife and son who went before you." The minister closed his Bible and turned to the somber figure standing alone on one side of the gaping hole in the ground. "May God watch over and comfort you, young man." He shook the quiet man's hand.

Hubert nodded. "Thank you, Reverend. I'm sure my father would have been pleased with the ceremony." He looked down into the ground where the casket lay. "I'm just thankful that he's no longer in pain." *Now maybe I'll finally get my hands on the ranch. I can't wait for the reading of the will.* He watched as the clergyman walked over to where his sister was standing. Her housekeeper and an attractive blonde woman flanked Lex, and several older people stood close behind her as she focused quietly on the casket.

The overcast sky appeared as if it would split open and rain at any minute, although the temperature on that April afternoon was almost sixty degrees. Amanda was thankful that she had listened to her grandmother and worn the outfit that she had. The simple black dress had long sleeves and dropped to just below her knees. Although her cast had been removed two days earlier, she was still favoring the leg that had been injured months before. She squeezed Lex's hand in sympathy, knowing that the past week had been extremely hard on her partner. The pancreatic cancer that ravaged Rawson's body had attacked with a vengeance the last week of the man's life.

Lex stood between Martha and Amanda, her blue eyes covered by mirrored sunglasses. She was dressed completely in black—boots, slacks, tab-collared shirt, and a new black duster which she had draped over one arm. Turning to Amanda, she looked down and studied her face. "Are you okay? Do you need to go sit down?" At the negative shake of Amanda's head, she smiled slightly. "Okay. But let me know the minute you need to, all right?"

"I will, love." Amanda watched as Lex stared at Hubert, who was now accepting the condolences of several of his friends. "Are you okay?"

"Yeah. Just thinking. I can't believe that he would have the nerve to show up here today, considering..." Lex bit back the rest of her sentence as the minister stepped in front of her, a serious expression on his wrinkled face.

The white-haired man looked pointedly at her hand, which still held Amanda's, and cocked his head to one side. "Lexington. I see you haven't changed much," he observed.

Feeling her lover stiffen, Lex squeezed Amanda's hand again and smiled. "Actually, I have. This is my fiancée, Amanda Cauble. Amanda, this is Reverend Hampton."

"Fiancée?" The clergyman smiled. "Well, then, that changes things." He extended one hand towards Amanda. "How do you do, Miss Cauble. I'm very pleased to meet you." Turning his attention back to Lex, he grasped her arm gently. "I'm really sorry about your father, Lex. If you need to talk, you know where you can reach me." With a quick squeeze of her arm, he was gone.

"What was that all about, Lex?" Amanda asked, watching the older man navigate through the crowd. "Nice man, though."

"He's been trying to get me to settle down for years." Lex stood up a bit taller as Hubert walked towards them. "Great." A warm hand on her shoulder caused her to turn around.

"Do you want me to take care of this?" Charlie asked. He had been standing behind Martha, quietly watching the entire ceremony. "He's supposed to stay away from you, thanks to the court order." Hubert was out on bail, awaiting trial for his part in the accident that had injured Lex and Amanda on New Year's morning.

"No. Let's just see what he wants first."

Hubert stopped in front of Lex and smiled. "Hello, little sister. You're looking well." He winked at Amanda and made a show of looking up and down her body. "Hey, babe. Nice legs."

Lex surged forward, barely held in check by the two women next to her. "Watch your damned mouth." She shook off the restraining hands and took a calming breath. "What do you want, Hube?"

"Nothing. Just wanted to see how my little sister was doing. There's no law against that, is there?" He looked smugly at the sheriff, who was standing behind Lex. "You're not going to enforce that stupid restraining order, are you? We are family, after all."

Charlie gently shouldered Lex aside to stand in front of her. "That's exactly what I'm going to do. You have exactly ten seconds to step back, or I'll arrest you right here."

The taller man held up his hands defensively. "Don't get your shorts in a wad, old man. I'm going." He blew a kiss at Lex, then turned and walked away.

Amanda glared at Hubert's back. "What a jerk. I wish that there was some way to keep him in jail. Preferably with a boyfriend called Bubba." Her head twisted around when she heard Lex's chuckle. "What?"

Lex shook her head. "Nothing." She leaned close and kissed the top of Amanda's head. "Could you do me a favor?"

"Sure. What do you need, honey?"

"Could you try and get Grandpa to sit down? He's not looking too good." They both turned to see Travis standing by the headstone for Lex's mother, his daughter Victoria. "I think this is bothering him a lot more than he's letting on." *And maybe if you're worried about him, you'll get a little rest yourself. I can see that your leg is bothering you.*

"Of course I will." Amanda patted Lex on the arm and slowly made her way over to where Travis stood.

Travis looked up when he heard quiet footsteps behind him. "Oh, Amanda. How are you doing, sweetheart?" He glanced over her shoulder at his granddaughter, who was accepting words of condolence from several people. "I thought that you'd be with Lexie."

Amanda wrapped her fingers around his arm and sighed. "Well, to tell you the truth, my leg is aching a bit. And I know that Lex needs to talk with people before she can leave." She looked up into his eyes. "I was hoping that you'd walk me to the truck so that we could sit down."

"Of course. Come on, my dear." Travis led her through the

sparse gathering until they reached Lex's truck. Opening the front passenger door, Travis placed his hands around her waist and partially lifted Amanda onto the seat. "How's that?"

"Much better, thank you." She gestured to the back seat. "Would it be too much to ask for you to stay and keep me company? *Watch out, Mandy. He's going to see through you, if you're not very careful.*

With a shake of his head, Travis opened up the back door and climbed into the truck. "Subtle," he teased, closing the door. "I almost fell for it, too."

Anna Leigh watched from her vantage point on the other side of the mourners as her granddaughter allowed Travis to escort her to the truck. She turned to her husband. "Do you think that Mandy is all right? I never thought I'd see her leave Lexington's side."

"I think she's just fine, love. But if you want, we can go over and check for ourselves." Jacob noticed the slight slump to the rancher's posture and nodded over in her direction. "Although I think that Lex is the one that needs us right now."

"You're right. Let's go see if we can rescue her from the good intentions of the crowd." Anna Leigh linked her arm through her husband's and steered him through the group of people surrounding Lex. "Excuse us, please."

Lex nodded her head. "Yes, ma'am. I'll keep that in mind," she assured the well-meaning matron in front of her. "Thank you for your kind offer." The woman was the owner of the rental house that Lex and Amanda were staying in temporarily while the ranch house was being rebuilt. She had assured the rancher that she would be glad to sell her the property at a very fair price if she wanted to keep a place in town. Lex looked up into the friendly faces in front of her. "Hi. Amanda's over—"

Jacob smiled. "We know, honey. We saw her and Travis head for the truck." He pulled Lex into a hug and whispered into her ear, "Why don't you come back to our place for a while? I think you could use the peace and quiet." He knew as well as Lex did that the Ladies Auxiliary had set up a covered dish dinner at the rental house, and that the small home would be swarming with well-meaning people.

"Thanks, Grandpa Jake. But I'd hate to disappoint the ladies, especially after all their hard work."

"Don't you worry yourself about that, Lexie." Martha had

been standing by quietly, trying to figure out how to steal the younger woman away. "Charlie and I will go over and take care of things, if you want. There's no sense in you wearing yourself out any more than you already have." She reached up and pulled the sunglasses from Lex's face. Her heart ached at the dark circles and pain reflected in the normally bright eyes. "Go on, baby. Let me handle this for you."

Lex felt her resolve crumble, and quickly replaced the glasses before anyone could see the tears filling her eyes. "Thanks, Mada." She leaned down and kissed Martha's cheek. "Will you come by later?"

The housekeeper nodded. "Of course we will. Just let us get things organized at the house, and we'll be over." She brushed the dark hair away from Lex's face. "Go on, now. I'll see you in a little while."

"Okay." Lex sniffled and walked to her truck, politely waving off well-wishers as she went.

Amanda stood at the kitchen window, looking out over the back yard. Her eyes followed every movement of the solitary figure that was clearing dead limbs from the newly budding trees. A light touch on her back caused her to gasp and turn around. "Gramma. You scared me half to death."

"I'm sorry, dearest. I didn't mean to startle you." Anna Leigh glanced through the window. "I see that she's still at it. Maybe I should go out and have a talk with her."

Amanda reached over and grasped her grandmother's arm. "No, I think she needs some time alone." She sighed and turned her attention back outside. "She's not been herself since her father died. I don't know what they talked about, but something's bothering her." Silent tears tracked down her face as Amanda continued to keep a watchful eye on her partner.

Anna Leigh put her arm around her granddaughter's shoulder and gently leaned her head against Amanda's. "You know her best, Mandy. Just know that if you need someone to talk to, I'm always here." She kissed Amanda's cheek, and regretfully stepped back. "Don't let her stay out there too much longer. I'm afraid we won't have any trees left." With a knowing smile and a slight wave, Anna Leigh left the kitchen.

"I wish I knew what was going on in that beautiful head of

hers," Amanda mumbled as her lover tied up another bundle of dead branches.

Lex was wearing a faded pair of jeans and a black tee shirt, with her battered black hat crammed down tightly on her head. The late-afternoon sun had broken through the clouds, and the humidity had caused her dark hair to paste itself to her damp skin. She stood up and braced her hands against the small of her back and bent until she heard the popping of her spine. "Damn, I'm out of shape," she grumbled, wincing at the tightness in her muscles. Lex gathered up the bundles of tree limbs and stacked them neatly in one corner of the yard. Her eyes were focused on one of the stacks of wood, while recent memories assaulted her mind.

Tears trickled down her face as she remembered her father's final wishes. Rawson had only lived for one more day after his discharge from the hospital, and Lex continually wondered if she had somehow inadvertently contributed to his sudden death. She angrily wiped her face on her shoulder as she continued to stack the wood. "I'm sorry, Dad. I guess I failed you somehow."

"I don't think so, honey," a deep voice from behind her answered.

Lex spun around to see her grandfather standing by the fence. "Grandpa Travis, what are you doing out here?"

He stepped forward and pulled a handkerchief from his pocket to wipe at her tear-stained face. "I was going to ask you the same thing, Lexie." Travis looked at the large pile of wood. "I hope you left a few of the trees standing," he teased.

"I overheard Jacob saying something about hiring someone to clear out all the dead limbs. Figured I could save him a bit of money."

"Uh-huh. And this had to be done today?" Travis wasn't convinced. "What's going on with you, Lexie?"

She sniffled and gently edged by him. "Nothing. You'll have to excuse me, Grandpa. I want to get these tools put up before I forget."

Travis watched his granddaughter walk through the picket gate. *Something's got to give, sooner or later. I hope we can handle it when she finally breaks.* He shook his head sadly and walked back to the house.

"Well? What did the judge say?" Hubert asked the man across

the table from him.

Kirk Trumbull shook his head. "He says that your confession at the church was more than enough to hold you over for trial." He took another bite of his hamburger. They were sitting in the back of the diner, his client having offered to buy dinner. "He also told me that if I disturbed him one more time before the trial, he'd have me locked up for contempt of court." Judge Packer had a very low tolerance level for the lawyer and had butted heads with him on more than one occasion.

"Obnoxious old fart," Hubert grumbled. "Doesn't he realize that I'm still in mourning over my father's death?" He smiled at his friend. "That should be good for a little sympathy, shouldn't it?"

"Not really. He's already postponed the trial because of your father's illness, although I think he did it more for your sister's sake than yours." Kirk waved a greasy french fry in the air. "I don't think you'll be looking at jail time, anyway. They weren't seriously hurt, and the sheriff hasn't found the truck or the men actually responsible for the accident."

Hubert nodded. "Good point. Have you heard anything back from my sister's lawyer? I thought you were going to try and get her to drop the charges so we wouldn't have to go through this whole fiasco." He leaned back in his seat and belched. "Now would be a good time to talk to her, since she's still upset about our old man."

Reaching for his glass of water, Kirk shook his head. "You're going to have to at least *act* a bit more upset, Hubert. You never know who's going to be on the jury. If someone hears you talking like that, it could really screw up our chances for an acquittal."

"Don't get your hackles up, Kirk old boy. I've got a few ideas on how to handle my sister. We'll come out of this looking like saints." He quieted as the waitress stopped at the table.

"Can I get you fellas anything else today?" Francine gave the two men her best "professional" smile. At the negative shakes of their heads, she scribbled the total onto the piece of paper in her hands and dropped it on the table. "Thanks for stopping in." She quickly left the area, feeling a chill run down her back at looking into Hubert's eyes. *He sure gives me the creeps. Not at all cute like that sister of his.* She raced for the kitchen, intent on washing her hands. Again.

"I don't know what I'm going to do," Amanda lamented quietly. Her eyes looked up at the ceiling as the knot in her chest tightened. "I'm feeling a bit out of my league here."

"You're not alone, honey. There's quite a few of us around that would like to help you, if you'll let us." Martha stepped into the dark den. The only light was coming through the windows from the setting sun, and dark shadows filled the room. She sat down on the sofa and patted the younger woman's leg. "Have you talked to her?"

Amanda shook her head. "No. Every time I try, she jumps up and finds something else to do. I haven't gotten more than a couple of sentences out of her since she brought her father's body back from the camp." With tears spilling silently down her cheeks, she looked over at Martha. "I'm so worried about her, Mada. I've never seen Lex so withdrawn before."

Martha pulled a handkerchief from her dress and dabbed at Amanda's eyes. "I swear, if the man wasn't already dead, I'd probably kill him myself for what he's put my girl through. He had no right to ask that of Lexie."

"Didn't he?" a strangled voice whispered from the doorway. Lex stepped into the room until she could make out the features of both women.

"Oh, baby. How long have you been standing there?" Martha started to rise, but stopped when Lex backed away.

"Long enough to hear what you said about my father." She moved over to the window and looked outside. "No one was more surprised than me when he walked back into my life," Lex murmured, almost to herself. "All I could think about was: what could I do to keep him from leaving me again?" She cleared her throat before she turned back around. "When he told me he was dying, I felt like someone had kicked me in the gut. He was gonna leave again, and there wasn't a damned thing I could do about it."

Amanda stood and walked over to Lex. "Oh, honey."

Lex held up a hand. "No, wait." She looked back at Martha. "When he asked me to take him out of the hospital, how could I refuse? I wouldn't want to spend my last days cooped up inside. I figured that maybe this was my chance to do something for him—something that he would finally love me for." Her voice broke. "For the first time in my life, I felt as if I mattered to him." She wiped her eyes with the heel of one hand as she searched the room. "I can't..." Lex hurried from the room, slamming the front door behind her seconds later.

"Lex, wait." Amanda chased after her, stopping at the closed door. She turned and looked at Martha, who was standing in the hallway with a sad look on her face. "I've got to go find her," she almost pleaded.

"I know, honey. We'll both go look for her. I know of a couple of places she might have gone."

"Hey there. Don't think I've seen you in here for quite some time." The blonde sat down on the stool next to the quiet woman.

Weary eyes took in the relaxed form, noticing how the tight sweater showed off the woman's considerable assets. "Been a while, Francine." Lex picked up her bottle of beer and took a healthy swallow. "You still trolling for playmates?"

Painted red lips formed a small pout. "I wouldn't call it that, exactly. We had some good times in here, didn't we?" She leaned in closer to Lex and ran a long fingernail down her cheek. "Wanna buy me a drink, for old times' sake?"

"Not particularly. I'd really like to be left alone, if you don't mind." Lex brushed the finger away from her face and studied her half-empty beer. *What in the hell are you doing here, Lexington? Do you think that running away solves anything? Amanda's probably worried sick about you.* "Shut up," she grumbled, taking another deep drink.

"C'mon, sugar. How about a run on the dance floor? You used to love to dance." Francine stood up and ran her hands down the strong back.

Lex spun around on the barstool and grabbed the buxom blonde's hands. "I told you to back off, Francine!" She pushed the woman away from her.

"What's going on here?" a man's deep voice inquired. "You girls having a spat?" Hubert had been sitting in the corner when he saw Lex come in. He knew of Francine's predatory ways, so he sat back and watched as she zeroed in on his sister. *I couldn't have asked for anything better than this.* When the waitress put her hands on Lex's back, he knew a fight was about to break out.

"Why don't you mind your own business and crawl back under your rock?" Lex spat, her nerves already on edge.

He raised his hands defensively. "Now, now. No sense in getting all riled up, little sister. Did you and your little girlfriend have a fight? I never thought I'd see you back in here."

She eyed her brother suspiciously. "No. I just needed some space, that's all."

"Ah, well. I can understand that. It's probably a little rough on you, knowing that you killed our old man, and all."

"You bastard!" Lex lunged forward and punched her brother in the face. She tangled her fists in his shirt and slammed him into a nearby table. "I ought to wring your worthless neck." She felt several hands pulling at her from behind, as she continued to slam his head onto the scarred wood. "Take it back, you son of a bitch!"

Hubert almost smiled as his sister proceeded to take her anger out on him. "Please," he called weakly, "get her off of me." He continued to lie back passively on the table as several men finally managed to pull her away. *Perfect.*

Lex continued to try and wrestle away from the strong hands holding her. "Let me go, dammit." She stopped her struggle when a slender man in uniform blocked her vision. "Shit."

"What's going on, Lex?" Charlie looked into her shadowed eyes, and then down at her bleeding knuckles.

"Nothing," she mumbled, unable to meet his gaze.

Hubert stood up and wiped at his bleeding face. "That's not true. She attacked me." He looked around the bar. "Anyone in here can tell you that. Right, Francine?"

Charlie looked at the blonde, who was biting her lip. "Well? What happened in here?"

"Lex and I were talking," Francine started, looking from one sibling to the other, "and he came over and started mouthing off at her." The incredulous look on Hubert's face almost made her laugh. "He got right up in poor Lex's face, and started talking about their father. She was just pushing him away, and he must have hit his face on the table."

"That's a complete lie, you little slut!" the big man yelled. "She attacked me, unprovoked. Ask anyone here."

"Is that true, Bob?" the sheriff asked the bartender. "Did you see what happened?"

Although Hubert was a good customer of the bar, Bob shook his head. *I never did like that asshole.* "I'm sorry, Sheriff. I was busy serving my other customers. I didn't see a thing." He caught the wink from Francine, and smiled inwardly. *I know I don't have a chance with her, but I can't help myself.*

"You're not supposed to be within one hundred yards of your sister," the lawman reminded Hubert.

"Don't blame me, I was here first. There's not a law against that, is there?" Hubert whined.

Deciding to let the matter drop, Charlie turned his attention back to Lex. "Maybe I should just take you home."

"Or maybe you should let me take her home," a voice from the end of the bar offered. Amanda limped by Francine and stood next to her lover. "I think we need to talk."

Lex nodded. "I guess we do." She forced herself to look into the sheriff's eyes. "I'm sorry about the trouble, Uncle Charlie." Lex turned around to face the bartender. "Bob, if you'll just send me a bill, I'll gladly pay for any damages." She allowed Amanda to take her by the arm and lead her from the bar.

"I'm sorry about your father, Lex," Francine whispered in her ear as she walked by. "You take care of yourself, you hear?" She kissed the tall woman on the cheek and then sat back down on her barstool. "C'mon, Bob, pour me another. I've got some catching up to do."

"I'll see your ass in court, little sister," Hubert yelled after the women. He turned around to glare at the other people in the bar. "What the hell are y'all looking at? Assholes." His hands found his drink on another table, and he sat back down to finish it. *Damn. Nothing's going my way today.*

Chapter 5

The small house was dark and quiet as Amanda pulled Lex's truck into the driveway. Only a couple of blocks from her grandparents' house, the two-bedroom rental was nice, but she still missed the ranch. Lex had approved a design similar to the old house with only a few modifications, and construction on the new ranch house was moving along well. Amanda sighed as she turned off the ignition, and looked over at her sullen partner. "Lex?"

"Hmm?" The rancher's eyes had been closed, but she opened them and looked around at Amanda's entreaty. "Oh, sorry." She quickly unfolded her long limbs from the vehicle and walked around to help her lover out.

Once inside, Amanda dropped the keys on the table in the hallway and led Lex into the adjoining living room. "Do you want to talk about it?" she asked, sitting down next to her friend on the colorful sofa.

"Um, I'm not sure where to start." Lex began to pick at a loose thread on the floral print.

"How about the beginning?" Amanda grasped Lex's hand and pulled it close to her. "It's okay, love. Just take your time."

"Hubert was right. I probably killed Dad."

A small hand touched her chin and forced Lex to look into Amanda's eyes. "No. The cancer killed him, honey." She pulled the dark head down onto her lap. "Why don't you get comfortable." Amanda began to gently stroke her lover's head.

The exhausted woman closed her eyes and allowed the gentle touch to soothe her. "You remember when I packed up after getting Dad out of the hospital?"

"Mm-hmm."

"Well, once we got started, I realized how weak he had become. I should have kept him closer to town, or at least near a main road. He had no business being out there in his condition."

Amanda's hands stilled for a moment, then continued their ministrations. "You were honoring his last wishes, Lex. Nothing you could have done would have helped him." She leaned down and softly kissed the dark head. "Did you get to talk to him much?"

Lex wiped her face with the palms of her hands. "Some. But he was so worn out once we made camp. He slept the rest of that day, and I was afraid he wouldn't wake up the next morning." A muffled sob broke from her chest. "Dad woke up early that morning and couldn't even get out of his bedroll. I watched him sleep some more until late that afternoon. He woke up again just long enough to tell me that he loved me." She felt herself being pulled up into Amanda's arms and held tightly. "He left me again, damn him!" Lex wrapped her arms around Amanda and buried her face in her lover's chest.

"Shh. It's okay, love. I've got you." Amanda rocked them both back and forth, crooning words of comfort and stroking the strong back. "I've got you."

Amanda pulled the blanket over Lex's slumbering form, then quietly left the living room. She went to their bedroom at the other end of the small home and picked up the telephone.

"Hello?"

"Martha? This is Amanda." Her voice quavered slightly as she pictured the kindly face of the older woman. "I found Lex and brought her home."

"What's wrong, honey? Is she all right?"

She shook her head, then realized that Martha couldn't see her. "No. Yes. Oh, damn. Physically she's fine, I suppose. But—"

"Do you want me to come over? I can be there in about half an hour." Martha was unable to keep the worry out of her voice.

"I don't know," Amanda choked, as tears fell from her eyes. "She's feeling a lot of guilt about her father's death, Martha. I'm not sure how to handle it."

"Where is Lexie now? Is she there with you?"

"No. She's in the living room, asleep on the sofa." Amanda

fell back on the bed, her eyes searching the ceiling for answers. "You were right. She was at that little bar down on Third Avenue. When I got there, Charlie had just broken up a fight between her and Hubert."

"I was afraid of that. That boy always did pick on her when she was down. He didn't hurt her, did he?" Martha's voice warned that there would be consequences to pay if he had.

The unusual vehemence in the older woman's tone caused Amanda to chuckle slightly. "Uh, no. Her knuckles are a bit raw, but I don't think he touched her." A shuffling sound at the doorway caused Amanda to look up. *Oops. Busted.* She covered the mouthpiece with her hand. "Hi, honey. Can I get you anything?"

Lex shook her head. "Nah. I thought I heard voices, so I just wanted to make sure you were okay." She turned to give her friend some privacy.

"Hold on," Amanda whispered, waving her hand. "Come here."

The tired woman shook her head, but walked over to the bed and sat down. She studied Amanda's face for a long moment, then looked down at the navy blue bedspread. *Damn. She looks worn out. I've been so caught up in my own troubles, I haven't been paying attention to what's been going on with her.*

Amanda watched the emotions flicker across Lex's face, then remembered that Martha was waiting patiently on the other end of the line. "Can I call you back?"

"Lexie must be with you," Martha guessed. "If you need me, just call. I'll keep the line free, okay?"

"Thank you, I sure will. Bye." Amanda hung up the phone and exhaled heavily.

"Are you all right?" Lex asked quietly. She reached over and brushed the hair out of Amanda's face with one hand, smiling slightly as she leaned into her touch. "I'm sorry about earlier."

"Don't you dare apologize, Lexington Marie." Amanda reached up with both hands and captured Lex's fingertips. "You've been through an awful lot lately, and I'm very glad that you felt comfortable enough to confide in me." When Lex lowered her face, Amanda took one hand and gently forced the tired eyes to meet hers. "After all the times you've been strong for me, how could I do any less for you?"

Silent tears began to fall from Lex's face. "I don't know what I did to deserve you, but I hope to God I never stop doing it." She sniffled and leaned forward, lightly kissing Amanda on the lips. "I love you."

"I love you too." Amanda reached up and tangled her hands in Lex's hair, pulling the rancher down with her as she leaned back onto the bed.

Lex felt her heart speed up as she gently draped her body across her lover's. *God...what she can do to me with just one kiss.* She felt sure hands tug at her tee shirt, pulling it free from her jeans. Warm fingers began to trace over her back, and she gasped as Amanda unclasped her bra with one hand. "Where did you learn to do that?" A sudden hunger replaced the sadness in her heart as Lex felt the overwhelming need to reaffirm the love they shared.

"You'd be surprised at the things I know." Amanda lifted the tee shirt over her partner's head. She tossed the garment to the floor, then found herself quickly divested of her shirt as well. Soft lips began to blaze a trail down her throat as Amanda vaguely wondered when she'd lost control of the situation. Feeling the button on her jeans released, she decided that she didn't care.

"So," Lex asked much later, "who were you talking to on the phone, earlier?" She was leaning back against the headboard of the bed, Amanda's equally naked body sprawled comfortably across her chest.

"Martha. I promised I'd call her after I found you."

Lex's mouth turned upwards into a wry smile. "I was going to ask how you found me so quickly. I'm sorry about running out like that." She ran her fingers through Amanda's hair, mesmerized by how the soft strands felt against her skin. "I just felt like the walls were closing in on me."

"You don't have to apologize, love. I just wish you weren't hurting so badly."

"That's still no excuse for my running off like a kid. You deserve better than that." The rancher's fingertips traced the contours of Amanda's face. "I was afraid," she whispered.

Amanda sat up. "What were you afraid of?"

Suppressing the urge to race from the room, Lex dropped her gaze to the sheet that had tangled around their bodies. *No. You're going to talk this through with her if it kills you, Lexington. Quit being such a damned coward.* "When I heard you two talking about my dad, it brought back a lot of memories. I had to leave before I did something stupid."

"Memories?" Amanda brushed her hand lightly across Lex's arm.

"Yeah." Feeling the calming touch, Lex closed her eyes. "All my life, I've had to listen to folks talk about how he wasn't much of a father." She reopened her eyes and sadly met her lover's gaze. "I've defended him for as long as I can remember."

Tears of compassion filled Amanda's eyes. "Oh, honey. Martha was just concerned about you. I don't think she meant anything by it."

"That's not it. Don't you see?" Lex took a deep breath to try and calm herself. "I wasn't mad at her, or you." She ran her fingers through her hair. "It was me that I was so upset with," she whispered sadly. "I felt the same way she did."

"Lex," Amanda placed her fingertips under the older woman's chin, forcing Lex to look up at her, "you have every right to be upset."

"No." Lex angrily wiped at her eyes. "I don't. He wasn't even going to tell me he was sick, until I forced it out of him." Sitting up and tangling her hands in the sheet, she looked longingly at the doorway. "I had no right at all. He came back to say goodbye, and I practically forced him to stay."

Amanda shook her head. "You're his daughter, Lex. Of all people, you have the right to be upset." She ran one hand down the taut back. "Quit being so hard on yourself, love. Maybe deep down inside, he wanted you to find out—he just didn't know how to tell you."

Swallowing hard, the upset woman tried to hold back the tears. "Right before he died," Lex murmured, "Dad told me that he loved me, and was proud of me." Her voice broke and she covered her eyes with one hand. "Why did it take him dying for him to say that?"

The ringing phone saved Amanda from trying to answer the difficult question. She watched as Lex wiped the emotions from her face and picked up the handset.

"Hello? Oh, um, hi." Lex cleared her throat and looked at her partner. "Thanks, Michael. I really appreciate that. Would you like to talk to your daughter?" She gave Amanda a half smile and handed the phone to her.

"Amanda, sweetheart," Michael's gentle voice filled her ear, "how's Lex holding up? I'm sorry I missed you two at the cemetery."

She smiled to herself. Lex and her father had become very good friends recently. He was teaching the rancher what he knew about business, and she had agreed to give him riding lessons as soon as the weather began to cooperate. Much to Amanda's amusement, the two of them would spend hours talking about all sorts of things. *Amazing what a few months can do.* "Hi, Daddy." Amanda watched as Lex quietly picked up her clothes and dressed. "I'm sorry we missed you, too."

Lex tilted her head towards the door, and then with a small wave she left the room.

"—do for you right now?"

"Hmm?" Amanda's attention was on the empty doorway. "I'm sorry, Daddy. What were you saying?"

Michael chuckled. "I asked if there was anything I could do for you, or Lex. I know she's got to be taking this pretty rough."

Remembering the look on her lover's face, Amanda sighed. "Rough doesn't even begin to cover it, I'm afraid. She's got a lot of unresolved issues, and I think that helping him leave the hospital put a lot of guilt on her shoulders."

"Would you like me to talk to her? Maybe I can give her a father's perspective. I think I can appreciate where Rawson was coming from." Michael had only recently mended his own fragile relationship with his youngest daughter. He could understand all too well the feelings that Rawson Walters had when he realized that he was dying. *To face death knowing that your children may hate you for the rest of your life; no wonder he came back when he did. I don't think I could have handled that. I'm lucky that Amanda was so forgiving.*

Amanda heard the emotion in her father's voice. *I didn't think about how her father felt, only about what it was doing to Lex. Maybe I've been going about this the wrong way.* "Would you mind? I think that Lex is going out to the ranch in the morning. Maybe you could talk to her out there."

"Consider it done, sweetheart. Is there anything else I can do? I know you're both too tired to cook; can I bring anything over?"

"Are you offering to cook for us, Daddy?" Amanda stifled a giggle at the thought of her father in the kitchen.

He laughed along with her. "Uh, no. But I can pick up something and bring it over, you know. I'm quite adept with the takeout menu from the Peking Palace."

Nodding to herself, Amanda knew her father was right. "I'm sure you are. But no, we don't need anything. Gramma told me that the Ladies Auxiliary took over the kitchen earlier, so it's probably loaded. I haven't been in there yet to see just how much they left."

"That's right, I'd forgotten all about that," Michael admitted. "Well then, I guess I'll leave you to their tender mercies," he teased. "But if either of you need anything, please call. I'd like to be here for you both, if you'll let me."

"I know, Daddy. Thanks. Just see what you can do for Lex tomorrow. Maybe talking to you will help her."

"You've got it, honey. Now, why don't you get some rest? I'll talk to you again tomorrow."

Amanda smiled. "Yes, Daddy. I will." Her voice cracked with emotion. "I love you."

"I love you too, sweetheart. Goodnight."

As she hung up the phone, Amanda marveled at how well her life had turned out in the past seven months. *I'm in love with a wonderful woman, have the relationship I've always wanted with my father, and have a job I enjoy. What more could I possibly ask for?* She smiled and climbed out of bed, grabbing her clothes that had been strewn about the floor. "Think I'll go see what's in the kitchen," she murmured to herself, dressing quickly. "And see what I can coax a certain tall, dark, good-looking rancher into having for dinner."

Chapter 6

"No, no, no. You've got to make sure the labels face the front. That's what makes this job so important." The teenager used his index finger to push his glasses back on the bridge of his nose. He proudly pointed at his nametag. "I'm a stocking supervisor now, Uncle Rick. If you work really hard and apply yourself, you could be one, too."

The big man put his hands on his hips and glared down at the gangly youth. "Look, Kenny, I appreciate you putting in a good word for me to get this job, but this is only temporary." Rick Thompson had been out of work since his firing from Sunflower Realty months earlier. His nephew had finally talked him into coming to work at the Super Mart, Somerville's largest grocery store. Since he had no prior experience, Rick had been placed as a stock boy under the seventeen-year-old's tutelage. "I'm just waiting to hear back from a couple of places."

"Uh-huh. Right. Mom told me to get you this job. She said you had to be tired of living in our garage." The boy crossed his arms over his chest and shook his head. "Just because we're family, don't be expecting me to cut you any slack. I'm up for an assistant manager position as soon as I turn eighteen." Walking away, Kenny tossed one final comment over his shoulder. "Make sure this entire aisle is fronted properly before you clock out, Uncle Rick. I'd hate to have to put a written reprimand in your file your first week on the job."

"Smart-mouthed little pissant," Rick growled. He turned his attention back to the shelves, angrily straightening the boxes. *If he weren't my sister's kid, I'd smack him into next week.*

"Excuse me," an elderly voice interrupted his thoughts. "Can you tell me where the artichoke hearts are? I can't seem to find them anywhere." The small gray-haired woman peered at him over her wire-frame glasses. "I don't think I've seen you in here before. You're kind of old for a stock boy, aren't you?"

Rick frowned. "You're kinda old to be walking around without a keeper, aren't you?" Under his breath he mumbled, "Senile old broad."

She raised herself up to her full five feet. "Well! I never." Spinning her cart around, the woman beat a hasty retreat down the aisle.

"That's probably your problem, granny!" Rick yelled after her. Remembering where he was, he looked around cautiously. "Obnoxious old bat," he grumbled. "But I can't afford to lose this job yet." As he watched the woman leave, he noticed a familiar face passing by the end of the aisle. "Shit. That's just who I need to run into here. I'll never live it down." Rick turned around and continued to neaten the items on the shelf in front of him. *Maybe they won't notice me.*

"Well, what do you think?" The builder stood by patiently as the tall woman opened and closed every cabinet. "I don't know why you wanted those built so low, Ms. Walters. You don't seem to have any problem reaching them."

Lex looked over her shoulder at the man and raised one eyebrow. "Although I really don't see where it's any of your business, my fiancée isn't as tall as I am." She bent her knees slightly as she reached for one of the doors again. "This seems about right."

Embarrassed by her chastening comment, he agreed quietly. "Yes, ma'am. We followed your specifications exactly." He walked over to where she was standing and tapped the sink with his index finger. "I put in the shallow sink like you asked, although I could have just as easily given you the deeper one."

"And how would a person of smaller stature reach the bottom of the sink, Mr. Wells? Or did you even think about that?" Lex leaned back against the countertop and crossed her arms over her chest. "I really don't like having my instructions questioned. Do I need to find another builder?"

"No, of course not! I was just trying to—"

She held up a hand in warning. "You were just trying to tell me what I wanted. I'm not some stupid female, Wells. Don't try to treat me like one." Lex pushed away from the counter and walked out of the kitchen.

He shook his head. "No, you're not a stupid woman. Just a rude one," the builder mumbled quietly. "I'm glad this job is almost done."

After taking the stairs two at a time, Lex crossed through the master bedroom and stood at the entrance to the bath. "That's not what I ordered," she stated flatly from her position in the doorway. She was leaning against the doorjamb, her arms crossed over her chest.

The heavyset man turned his head to see who had spoken. He was bolting down the porcelain fixture with one hand, while the other reached for a pack of cigarettes that was lying in his toolbox. He cleared his throat and winked at her. "Don't you worry your pretty little head, sweetheart. I know what I'm doing." He sat back and placed a cigarette in his mouth.

Already angry from the confrontation in the kitchen, Lex stomped over to where he was sitting. Seeing the cans of chemical adhesive, she grabbed the man by his shirtfront and yanked him to his knees. "Obviously, you don't." She grabbed the cigarette and tossed it to the floor. "Don't you dare light one of those things in this house. Especially around all this flammable material. I won't have another house burn to the ground, just because of your stupidity!"

"Now wait just a damned minute, lady. You can't talk to me like that." He roughly brushed her hands away and stood up. "Who in the hell do you think you are, anyway?"

Lex stepped back, trying to control herself. "Your former employer, asshole. Pack it up and get out," she ground out through clenched teeth. "And take that tiny excuse for a toilet with you." She turned around and stormed from the room. *I'm surrounded by incompetent jackasses. It's like I've stepped into Bubbaland.*

"Ms. Walters," a feminine voice called from the guest bedroom at the end of the hall, "may I have a moment of your time?"

With a heavy sigh, the rancher followed the voice and stood in the doorway. "Yes, Mrs. Compton?"

A short, heavyset woman stood in the middle of the room, a friendly smile on her face. She was about the same age as Martha and was, in fact, good friends with the housekeeper. Her husband had passed away several years before, and she seemed content to run her business and leave the dating to her daughter, who was a couple of years younger than Lex. "I'm really sorry to bother you, Lexington, but I heard your voice and needed your opinion on something." She grabbed the taller woman by the arm and led her further into the room. She waved a couple of scraps of paper under Lex's nose. "I have these two different borders for the wallpaper, and I'm torn as to which would look better in here."

"And you're asking me?" Lex asked incredulously. "You've got to be kidding, right?" She gestured at herself. "Do I look like I'd know which of these, um, thingies would look better?"

Lois Compton laughed. "Give yourself more credit than that, dear. I know you have opinions. And even if you don't choose to use it, I'm sure you have great fashion sense." She took both scraps over to the nearest wall and held one of them up. "This one is a bit more masculine, but I think it would look nice in here—depending on how you're going to furnish it, of course." She replaced it with the other piece of paper and sighed. "I'm rather fond of this one, although it may be a bit flowery for your tastes."

"Um." Lex blinked several times. "We're gonna furnish this room with oak; it'll be used primarily as my grandfather's room, I think," she stammered. "I don't think he'd appreciate the second one, much." She tipped her hat and smiled nervously. "If you'll excuse me, ma'am, I've got, um, stock to tend to." Lex practically raced from the room, leaving the confused decorator behind.

"I wonder what's wrong with her?" she mused. "You'd think decorating made her nervous or something."

Escaping to the outside of the house, Lex studied the men who were putting the vinyl siding on the top floor. She and Amanda had agreed on having the new house bricked, but it still needed a wood-look on some of the smaller portions. The wood for the wraparound porch had already been treated with a fire-retardant chemical, and the entire house had been given an extensive fire alarm system. Lex wasn't going to take any chances with Amanda's safety. *Especially with her mother still alive. I don't trust that woman one bit.*

Elizabeth Cauble was still in a high-security mental facility in Austin, but Lex was afraid that it was only a matter of time before she was released. The psychotic woman had set fire to the ranch house, thinking that if she did, Amanda wouldn't have any place to live and would go back to California with her. She had been considered too unstable to stand trial for her actions, and was instead placed in the State's care.

"Penny for your thoughts."

She turned around at the familiar voice. "Michael. I didn't expect to see you out here."

He smiled and looked at the house. "It's looking good. When do you expect to be finished?"

"The decorator is hanging wallpaper right now. I should be able to start bringing in the furniture early next week." Lex placed her hands in the back pockets of her faded jeans and leaned back slightly. "If you're looking for Amanda, she isn't here."

"Actually, I came out to see how you were doing. I missed you at the cemetery yesterday." Michael walked over and touched her arm. "I'm really sorry about your father, Lex."

Why won't everyone just leave me the hell alone? "Thanks. But if you'll excuse me, I've got a lot of stuff to do." Pushing by him, Lex started around the side of the house. Footsteps behind her caused Lex to stop and turn. "I appreciate you coming all the way out here, Michael, but go on back to town. I'm just fine." She spun around and stomped to the barn.

He shook his head and sighed. "That went better than I expected."

Michael watched as the distraught rancher walked away. *I wish there was something I could do to take that sad look off her face.* He shook his head and turned his attention back to the ranch house. "That's really coming along well."

"Isn't it, though?" a cheerful voice agreed. The woman standing on the front porch brushed her hands down the denim apron she was wearing. "I'm sorry. I don't believe we've met. My name's Lois Compton." She stepped down and met him in front of the house. Holding out her hand, Lois smiled brightly. "You'll have to forgive my appearance—I'm just finishing up the wallpaper in the bedrooms."

Meeting the woman halfway, Michael shook her hand. "It's a pleasure to meet you, Ms. Compton. I'm Michael Cauble."

Understanding dawned on her lovely features. "Of course—you're Amanda's father, right? And please, call me Lois."

"That's me." It was a new feeling, being associated as his daughter's father, instead of the other way around. But Michael found, to his delight, that he enjoyed it. "Should I be worried that you've heard of me, Lois?"

"Oh, no. Amanda's had nothing but wonderful things to say about you, Mr. Cauble. Your daughter is very fond of you."

He smiled happily. "I'm a very lucky man—and call me Michael."

Nodding, she pointed to the front door. "Okay, Michael. Are you very busy at the moment?"

"Um, no. Is there something I can help you with?"

"As a matter of fact, there is. I need a man." Seeing the color drain from his face, she blushed. "Oh, dear. I've definitely put my foot in my mouth, haven't I?" She grabbed his arm and began to pull him across the porch. "I'm trying to decide on the paper for the guestroom, and I would really appreciate a man's view of things. Poor Lexington ran out of here like her tail end was on fire when I asked for her opinion."

Michael laughed. "I can understand why. From what I know about Lex, she's not much for decorating." He allowed the decorator to lead him through the house. "So, tell me how you got into the interior decorating business," he said as they started up the stairs.

"I don't believe it," she whispered with a smile on her face. Her eyes took in the sight before her and sparkled with glee. Nudging her companion's shoulder, she pointed down the aisle. "Take a look at that, honey."

With a heavy sigh, the man followed his wife's line of sight. His interest was suddenly piqued when he saw the man she was referring to. "Hey, isn't that—"

She nodded. "Rick Thompson." Wanda Skimmerly chuckled at her good fortune. "Let's go say hello." She turned the shopping cart around and headed for the unsuspecting man.

Hearing a cart stop behind him, Rick was almost afraid to turn around. *Please, let it be another old biddy asking for directions.* Before he could work up the courage to face the unknown shopper, he heard a familiar voice that caused a deep flush to spread over his face. *Aw, shit.*

"Rick Thompson. As I live and breathe! I never thought I'd see you in here," Wanda gushed, her delight at finding her former manager evident in her tone. "As a matter of fact, ever since you, um, left the real estate office, I haven't seen you around anywhere."

He turned around and nodded at the couple. "Wanda, Dirk. It is a small world, isn't it?" Rick brushed his hands down the bright red apron he was wearing. "I'm helping out my nephew for a bit. They were running shorthanded, and I just couldn't tell the boy no."

Wanda smiled knowingly. She'd heard the rumors around town. Rick hadn't been able to get a job anywhere, not even working cleanup at the meat packing plant. "That's really wonderful of you, Rick. What else are you doing with yourself these days?" She couldn't resist tweaking her old boss just a bit. *I can't wait to tell the girls in the office about this. Maybe we could sell tickets.*

The big man ran a nervous hand through his thinning hair. "I've, uh, got a couple of things lined up. But I postponed them until I could bail Kenny out of this bind."

"I see." Wanda was about to continue her interrogation, but her husband grabbed her arm and began to lead her away.

"Nice seeing you again, Rick," he said, pushing the still-babbling woman down the aisle. "Take care."

"I wasn't finished," she complained loudly.

Dirk nodded his head. "Oh, yes you were, dear." He pushed her and the cart to the checkout line. "C'mon, leave the poor man alone."

Wanda positioned the heavily laden cart at the end of the line and turned to look at her husband. "Poor man? Do you have any idea the h-e-double hockey sticks he put poor Amanda Cauble through? Not to mention some of the other women in the office. Why, I could tell you stories..."

He sighed and rolled his eyes. "I'm sure you could, dear." Dirk resigned himself to an evening of hearing all about the goings on at Sunflower Realty. Again.

Amanda locked the front door to the real estate office, thankful that the day was finally over. Since Lex had left early that morning to spend the day at the ranch, she decided that she might as well go back to work, too. The paperwork stacked on her desk took up most of her day. She looked at her watch as she walked to where her car was parked. *Maybe Lex will be at the house when I get home.* Remembering their discussion from the morning, Amanda sighed. *I hope she's okay.*

"What are you doing up so early?" Amanda groggily asked her partner, who was slipping a crisp denim shirt over her broad shoulders.

Lex spun around, surprised. "Um, I thought I'd go out to the ranch and get some work done." She buttoned up the shirt and quickly tucked it into her faded jeans. "Why don't you go back to sleep? It's still early."

Amanda sat up in bed and rubbed her face. She glanced at the clock and her eyes widened. "I know that you want to go out today, but it's five-thirty in the morning. What on earth is there to do out there this time of day?"

Her partner ducked her head, avoiding Amanda's steady gaze. "I've been neglecting the ranch for too long. There's more than enough to do until the workers arrive." Lex grabbed her boots and sat on the edge of the bed. She pulled the comfortable footwear on with ease, and turned to face Amanda. "I need to do this, sweetheart," Lex murmured quietly. "Please understand. I've got to get my life back to normal. I can't just sit around this house all day, feeling sorry for myself."

Amanda reached out and caressed the tired face across from her. "I do understand, love. Do you want me to come with you?"

The rancher shook her head. "No, you'd just be bored. I'm going to do a fence check after the sun gets up, so there's no sense in you wasting your day." Lex leaned over and kissed Amanda tenderly. "I love you."

"I love you, too," Amanda returned. "How long will you be?"

Lex stood up. "Probably until dark. I really do have a lot of things to do out there."

Amanda climbed out of bed and wrapped her arms around Lex. "Try to stay out of trouble, okay?"

"I always try," Lex promised as she kissed the head under her chin.

"That's what I'm afraid of," Amanda whispered as the tall figure left the dark bedroom.

Amanda was about to pull out of the parking lot when another car blocked her path. An image of their truck being forced off the road and into the accident that had injured both her and Lex flashed through her mind. "What the..." Not recognizing the vehicle, she felt her heart speed up. Shielding her eyes against the setting sun, the nervous young woman could only make out the outline of the person that was walking up to her car. When the large hand beat against her side window, she screamed.

"Damned no-good, rotten, worthless piece of shit-eating sorry excuse for a jack!" Lex kicked the offending device. Her truck was parked on the side of the deserted road, the right front tire flat. She leaned into the vehicle and pulled out the owner's manual. "How the hell do they expect you to raise a three-quarter ton truck with a friggin' aluminum jack?" Wiping her dirty hands on her jeans, she flipped through the book. "Shit!" She tossed the book back into the truck and slammed the door, hard. Breathing heavily, Lex looked down the dark road. "I'm gonna get me a piece of those stupid-assed builders, leaving nails all over the damned place."

She had spent the majority of her day at the ranch house, demanding corrections from several different subcontractors. Remembering her argument with the man who was installing the plumbing in the master bedroom, Lex felt her anger rise again. *Stupid asshole.*

The sun had just set and had taken any warmth from the day with it. Lex shivered and rubbed her hands over her arms. She had worked up a sweat just before she had left the ranch, and now the damp shirt clung to her clammy skin. Not for the first time this evening, Lex wished for her cellular phone, which was comfortably resting in her coat—the same coat that was hanging up in the entry closet of the rented house. "Of all the stupid, dumbass things to do, forgetting my phone has got to be on the top of the friggin' list!" Kicking at the pebbles alongside the road, she went back to the jack, which was lying in the dirt beside the flat tire. "Guess I'll keep trying. It's gotta work sometime."

Half an hour and several skinned knuckles later, Lex finally finished changing the flat tire. Tired and dirty, she tried to open the passenger door. It was locked. "Shit." Leaning her forehead against the window, she could see the keys dangling from the ignition. "Perfect. What else could possibly go wrong?"

An ominous drumbeat of thunder rumbling overhead provided her answer.

The shadow standing outside of Amanda's car reached for the handle of the door. She lunged to lock the door but missed, cursing her luck as it swung open slowly. "Whatever it is you want, just..." She began to slide quickly to the other side of the car to get away from her unknown attacker.

"Amanda? Honey, what's the matter?" Michael knelt down and reached out to his daughter, whose face had gone pale. "Are you okay?"

"Daddy?" Amanda rushed towards him, wrapping her arms around his neck and almost knocking her father to the ground. "You. You. Oh, God!" She buried her face against his neck and held on tightly.

Concerned, Michael held his daughter, rubbing her back with soothing motions of his hand. "I thought you knew it was me. I didn't mean to frighten you."

She leaned back and wiped the tears from her face. "I'm sorry, Daddy. I just didn't recognize the car, and because of where the sun was I couldn't see you clearly." She looked behind him as the sun slowly disappeared. "What are you doing here?"

"Can't a man just come to see his daughter without having an ulterior motive?" Michael pointed his thumb over his shoulder. "Seriously, I wanted to show you my new car."

"I knew I didn't recognize it," she mumbled, allowing him to help her to her feet. "What kind is it?"

Michael grinned as he led his daughter to the beige vehicle. "Well, it's not completely new, but it's new to me. I figured Dad would want his Suburban back any time now." His father allowed Michael to borrow the vehicle whenever he needed, but the photographer wanted to become more self-sufficient. He opened the driver's door and motioned for her to sit inside. "It's a ninety-seven Buick LeSabre, one owner, and only has twelve thousand miles."

"It's really nice." Amanda put her hands on the steering wheel and leaned back into the plush seat. "Kinda big, though, isn't it?"

"I needed something to haul all my camera equipment around in, and a friend of your grandma's wanted someone to take it off her hands. So I got a nice car out of the deal, and the payments are within my budget." Michael leaned inside and pointed at the passenger seat. "See? It looks brand new, doesn't it?"

Smiling at her father's enthusiasm, Amanda nodded. "It certainly does. When do I get a ride in it?"

"Scoot over, kiddo. I'll take you for a spin right now."

They had ridden for several minutes when Amanda remembered the favor she had asked of her father. "Daddy? Did you get a chance to talk to Lex today?"

"I tried," Michael admitted sadly. "That woman's got a lot of hurt going on inside."

"What do you mean? Is she all right?" Amanda asked. She turned her body so that she could watch her father as he drove. "What happened?"

Rounding the corner back to the real estate office, Michael pulled into the parking lot next to the light blue Mustang. He shut off the engine and unbuckled his seatbelt, sliding around to face the worried woman beside him. "I caught her as she was coming out of the house this afternoon, and tried to talk to her. She really wasn't in a very talkative mood, I'm afraid."

Amanda closed her eyes, almost feeling her lover's pain. "No, she probably wouldn't be. I'm sorry, Daddy. I shouldn't have asked you to try and talk to her."

"You have nothing to be sorry about, honey." Michael reached over and grasped one of her hands. "And if you think I'm giving up after one measly attempt, you're sadly mistaken." His eyes sparkled with emotion. "I owe that young woman quite a lot. If it wasn't for her, I probably wouldn't be here right now."

"I'm glad you can think of it that way. If she hadn't sold all of her stock in your company, you probably wouldn't be broke, either."

"I'm richer now than I ever was, Amanda. I have the love of my children and the respect of my parents, and I'm finally doing what I've always wanted to do." Michael leaned forward until they were inches apart. "And I'm driving a really nice car, too."

She laughed in spite of her worry over her partner. "You're crazy." Hearing the rumble of thunder, Amanda looked up at the sky. "I hope she's already home by now. I'd hate to think of Lex driving in a thunderstorm." Her protective instincts had grown since their accident on New Year's Eve.

"She's a big girl, honey." Michael patted his daughter's leg. "But I guess I'll let you go home and find out."

"Thanks, Daddy," Amanda leaned over and hugged the smiling man. "Are you going over to Gramma's for dinner tonight?" She knew that her father took a lot of his meals at his parents' house. Amanda personally thought that he was making up for all the years they had spent apart. Seeing Michael blush, she laughed. "What?"

He suddenly found the steering wheel fascinating. "Um, no. I've got a..." His last word was unintelligible.

"You've got a what?"

"A date," he mumbled, embarrassed.

"Really?" Amanda practically squealed, wrapping her arms around him tighter. "That's so cool." She leaned back and looked into his eyes. "Is it someone I know?"

"She's your interior decorator."

Smiling, she crossed her arms over her chest and nodded. "Have you known her long?"

"I, um, just met her," Michael stammered. *Why do I suddenly feel like the kid here, and she the parent?*

"Today?" Amanda laughed, enjoying her father's discomfort.

Still embarrassed, Michael nodded. "Yes. After Lex had walked away, I was admiring how well the construction on the ranch house was going, when this woman stepped out onto the front porch."

Stepping out of the car, Amanda smiled. "That's great. She's a really sweet lady, and I hope you have a nice time, Daddy. Let me know how it goes, all right?" She leaned back inside and kissed his cheek. "I love you."

Swallowing the lump in his throat, Michael waved. "I love you too, Amanda." He watched as she climbed into the Mustang and returned his wave. *I'm the luckiest man in the world.*

Chapter
7

After a short argument with herself, Lex decided to walk back to the ranch. She had thought about just breaking a window to get into the truck, but hated the thought of what the rain would do to the interior. *And it's not that far back to the ranch.* She knew that she could depend on Martha and Charlie to be at home at this time of the evening. The woman she loved like a mother always had an extra set of keys to the ranches' vehicles, just in case of an emergency. As far as Lex was concerned, tonight was definitely an emergency. Although the couple would probably tease her endlessly about her situation, it would still be better than having to walk all the way into town. She had only gone a few yards when the rain started to fall.

"Dammit." Lex started jogging along the road, her boots clomping loudly on the pavement. She had traveled for almost half an hour before she finally crossed the old wooden covered bridge that led to her ranch. Once in the relatively dry structure, Lex considered staying inside until the worst of the rain passed. Another cold chill chased down her back, making her decision for her. Tugging her soggy black hat down further over her eyes, the drenched woman took off again at a quick jog.

The cold wind cut through her soaked shirt and jeans, which caused Lex to quicken her pace until she was running full speed down the muddy, dark road. Deciding to think about more pleasant things, she let her mind wander back to last month, when Charlie and Martha made a surprise addition to their family.

Lex pulled the Jeep up to the bunkhouse with a tired sigh. She had spent the better part of the day shuffling back and forth between the courthouse and the juvenile detention center, filing papers and making certain that everything was in order for the evening. "Well, here goes nothing," she mumbled, hoping that the young man would be happy at the end of the night.

The door to the bunkhouse opened before Lex had a chance to knock. Lester's worried face greeted her. "Miz Lex? What in tarnation are you doing here this time of day? Is something wrong?" He knew better than anyone else did how ill her father was. Rawson stayed at the bunkhouse with the rest of the hands, doing what he could to help; but the bunkhouse cook realized that it was only a matter of time before the cancer took his life.

Lex raised a hand to forestall his questions. "Everything's fine, Lester. I came here to see Ronnie." She gestured inside. "Can I come in? Or do you guys have a bunch of women in here that you don't want me to know about?"

The blush covered the parts of his face that his beard didn't. "Ah, um..." Lester stepped aside and motioned for his boss to enter. "Doggone it. I swear that mouth of yours is gonna get you into trouble one of these days," he grumbled, closing the door behind her.

"You're starting to sound like Martha." Lex laughed and patted him on the back.

Several of the men were sitting at a long table, the teenage boy between them. Upon hearing the rancher's voice, all heads turned to greet her. Several waved, as others murmured their hellos.

"Hey, boss. Whatcha doing down here?" The ranch foreman stood up and took Lex's hand. "You're looking a bit on the ragged side, Lex," he whispered, so that only she could hear him. "Is everything okay?"

"Things are just fine, Roy. Thanks for asking." Lex smiled at the group of men. "I came to get Ronnie, if you boys can spare him."

He grinned. "Spare him? How about sparing us? We've been attempting to help him with a paper he's trying to write for history class."

Ronnie closed his books and jumped up from the table. "Thanks for the help, guys," he told the group, "but I think I'll ask Martha, just in case." He spent many of his afternoons in the housekeeper's kitchen, while she helped him with his studies. Martha had quickly become the mother he never had, and Ronnie was flourishing under her gentle guidance. The young man stood proudly in front of Lex, his eyes shining with admiration. "Hi. Did you need me for something, Lex? I can always work on my paper later. It's not due for another week yet."

"As a matter of fact, I do. Would you mind coming over to Martha's house with me? I need a bit of help moving some furniture around, and I think she's been baking your favorite cookies."

The teen puffed up with pride. "I'd be glad to, Lex. Maybe afterwards, she'll help me with my homework."

"I'm sure she will," Lex laughed, as she put an arm around Ronnie's shoulders and led him to the waiting Jeep.

When the vehicle pulled up to the small house, Ronnie turned to Lex with a concerned look on his face. "It's awfully dark. Do you think anyone's home?"

Lex bit back a chuckle as she climbed out of the Jeep. "I think so. She's probably in the kitchen. Why don't you go on in? I've got to get something out of the back of the Jeep." She was hard-pressed to keep the smile off her face as the teen reached to open the front door.

The lights came on in the living room. A huge banner stretched across the room, proclaiming Welcome To Our Family, Ronnie. *"Surprise!" everyone cheered, much to the young man's amazement.*

Despite the downpour and her soggy clothing, Lex smiled as she thought of the look on Ronnie's face when he learned that he had been adopted into the family. With renewed effort, she jogged up the hill. *Almost there.*

"It's after seven o'clock. Where on earth could she be?" Amanda looked out the front window for the third time in as many minutes. "It's not like her to be this late without even calling." She allowed the curtain to close as she turned away and reached for the nearby phone. Hitting number one on the speed dial, Amanda waited patiently for someone to answer.

"Hello?"

"Martha? This is Amanda."

"Well hello, honey. It's so nice to hear from you. To what do I owe this pleasure?" Martha sounded extremely happy to hear Amanda's voice.

"Um, have you seen Lex today?" Amanda asked, hoping against hope that her lover had decided to stay there for dinner and just forgot to call. "She's not home yet, and I'm a little worried." *More like extremely worried.*

Martha was quiet for a long moment. "I saw her truck up by the main house for most of the day, but I could have sworn that she left over an hour ago. Did you try to call her on the cell phone?"

Mentally slapping herself, Amanda groaned. "Duh. I didn't even think about that. Could you hold on for a second, while I—"

"Sure. You go ahead. I'll be right here."

After hitting the "flash" button on the cordless phone, Amanda quickly hit the speed dial number for Lex's cell phone. After a moment, she heard a faint rendition of *Bolero* from the front entryway closet. Rolling her eyes, Amanda walked over and opened the door, seeing the new black duster hanging in the corner. She reached into the pocket and pulled out the phone, shaking her head. Another tap on the "flash" button, and she closed the closet door. "Martha? She left her phone in her coat pocket again."

The housekeeper laughed. "It's nice to know some things haven't changed. She could have had car trouble. Do you want me to send Charlie out to check the roads, just in case?"

"Would you mind?" Amanda asked, breathing a sigh of relief. "I hate to bother him like that, but ever since the accident, I'm a little paranoid."

"Hush, now. There's nothing to be worried about." Martha covered the mouthpiece on her phone and walked into the next room. "Honey, would you mind taking a drive? Lexie isn't home yet, and Amanda's worried."

The sheriff stood up and stretched. "Of course not, sweetheart. Let me put my boots on, and I'll head out." He walked over and kissed his wife gently on the lips. "Be back before you know it."

Martha watched him leave and a happy smile formed on her lips. The voice on the other end of the phone reminded her about the situation at hand. "Oh, I'm sorry, dear. What were you saying?"

"Tell Charlie that I'll bake him that chocolate cake he's so fond of, for doing this."

"I'll do that, sweetie." The housekeeper peeked out the front window as the sheriff's car drove off into the darkness. She shivered as a gust of cold air rattled the pane, and huge drops of water began to fall from the sky. "Ooh, it's getting nasty out there."

Charlie squinted at the windshield, trying to see through the driving rain. The old police cruiser he was driving slid slightly on the muddy road, making him slow down even more. He cursed the weather as the windshield wipers beat frantically. "Lexington Marie Walters, you'd better be in one piece when I catch up with you," he grumbled.

The road from the house was quickly becoming a churning quagmire, the torrential rain washing large bits of it away. Thinking about the young woman possibly out in this mess, he slowly pressed down on the accelerator. As the car started for the final hill, his headlights caught a tall figure rushing directly at him, and he hit the brakes to keep from hitting it. "Damn." He turned the steering wheel hard, which caused his car to begin sliding directly towards the form.

"What the hell?" When he saw the figure slip off the road and tumble down the sharp incline, Charlie jumped from the vehicle before it completely stopped. "Aw, damn. Lex?" He stood at the edge, looking down the muddy slope.

Lex raised her head slightly and shook it. "Shit." She was lying face down at the bottom of the incline, her body draped none-so-gently against a large tree. Reaching to wipe the water and mud from her eyes, she glanced up and saw a figure standing at the top of the slope.

Slowly climbing to her feet, Lex tried to wipe off the worst of the mud. The red clay-like substance was ground into her clothes, and she had a feeling that it had seeped through to various parts of her body. "Ugh. Amanda's gonna kill me," she muttered, glad for once that the heavy rain continued to pelt her body. She started up the steep hill, then slipped and fell down. With her mouth full of mud, Lex stood up again and spat. "Damn."

"Lex? Is that you?" Charlie called from his position at the top of the incline.

Great. What else could possibly go wrong? Lex froze. Remembering what had happened the last time that she said those words, she cringed. "Uncle Charlie?" she yelled, pulling off her drenched hat and using it to shield her eyes, straining to see the figure above her. With a heavy sigh, she crammed the black felt back onto her head and attempted to climb the hill again.

The sheriff studied the lanky form with a chuckle. *Looks like she's* okay, *although it's gonna take hours to get her clean.* "What are you doing out in this storm?" he asked, giving her a supporting hand and pulling the bedraggled woman up beside him.

"Jogging," she grumbled, looking down at her mud-covered frame. "What are you doing out here?"

"Looking for you," he snickered. "Do you expect me to let your filthy body in my car?" Charlie reached over and flicked a blob of mud off her shoulder.

Lex glared at him. "If you want, I'll walk the rest of the way back." She couldn't suppress a shiver, as another blast of wind almost knocked her from her feet. "Get in the car, before you catch pneumonia. Martha will have both our hides."

He reached over and pulled her to him. "Not without you, honey. C'mon. I'll give you a ride to the house, and you can tell me why you're out in this weather."

Hanging up the phone, Martha shook her head. "I swear that girl has trouble tattooed across her forehead." She looked outside at the raging storm. "I'd better call Amanda and let her know." She had just finished talking to her husband, who had called her and told her about his run in with Lex. After dialing the phone, Martha waited patiently until Amanda answered.

"Hello?"

"Amanda, honey," she started, but was quickly interrupted.

"Did he find her? Is she okay? What happened?" Amanda's questions were rapid-fire, before she realized how she had sounded. "Oh God, I'm sorry, Martha. I didn't mean..."

The housekeeper chuckled. "That's okay, sweetie. Lexie's just fine. She just had a bit of trouble with the truck, and was on her way back here when Charlie found her."

"Trouble with the truck? What kind of trouble? She didn't wreck it, did she?"

"No, no, no." Martha smiled as the sheriff's car pulled up in front of the house. "She's okay, really. If you can wait for just a minute, you can ask her yourself. They just got here."

Charlie opened the front door and took off his hat, shaking it off before coming inside. "Hi, sweetheart. Look what I found," he joked, gesturing behind him.

Martha's eyes widened at the mud-covered figure beside him. "Oh, my Lord." The hand that held the phone slowly dropped to her side, her conversation forgotten for the moment.

"Hi, Mada. Hope you don't mind if I don't come in," Lex smiled ruefully. "Most of it washed off, believe it or not."

"What's going on? Martha? Hello?" The distraught voice could be heard across the room. "Are you still there?"

Walking over and taking the phone out of his wife's hand, Charlie put it to his ear. "Amanda? I'm sorry about that. I just got back to the house, and Martha's a bit, um, shocked."

"Charlie? Could you please tell me what on earth is going on? I'm losing my mind here." When the sheriff began to laugh, she stomped her foot. "It's not funny. What happened to Lex? Do I have to drive out there myself to find out?"

Still laughing, Charlie wordlessly handed the cordless phone to the woman still standing on the front porch. She had been resisting Martha's attempts to pull her filthy body into the house, and refused to come inside. Lex gladly accepted the phone, but gently slapped Martha's hands away.

"Charlie?"

"No, sweetheart, it's me. I'm sorry if I worried you."

Amanda calmed immediately. "Thank God. I was going to send out another search party." She took a moment to take control of her emotions before speaking again. "What happened?"

Lex gratefully accepted a large towel from Charlie, while still not allowing the housekeeper to drag her in off the porch. "I had a flat tire, and then locked my keys in the truck. I was coming back to Martha's to pick up the spare key when Charlie found me." *Not a lie, just a slight omission of the truth.* "I'm pretty muddy, but as soon as I can get a ride back to the truck, I'll be on my way home, okay?"

"Okay. I'll have you a nice warm bath ready when you get home," Amanda promised. "And then you can tell me about your day, all right?" After her discussion with her father earlier, Amanda knew that Lex was going to need some TLC, and she was more than happy to supply just that.

"Um, okay." The shivering woman smiled gratefully at Martha, who had given up trying to get her charge into the warm house and had wrapped a thick blanket around her shoulders. "I'll be home soon, sweetheart. I love you."

"I love you, too. Be careful." Amanda hung up the phone, anxious to get things ready for her lover.

Martha pulled the blanket tight around Lex's shoulders. "I ought to take a spoon to your backside, young lady," she threatened. "Going around without a proper coat."

"Mada, please," Lex handed the older woman the phone. "It was a nice day when it started out—just quickly went downhill from there."

"You could at least come in and get cleaned up. I can't even tell where the mud ends and your skin begins." Martha looked at the mud-covered hands that held the blanket closed. "How on earth did you get all that red mud all over you, anyway?"

Charlie walked up beside his wife and wrapped an arm around her. "That's my fault, I believe." He handed Lex a set of keys with an awkward smile. "She was running down the road, and I almost hit her. Poor girl slipped right off the road and down the side of the embankment."

Lex shook her head. "It's not your fault, Uncle Charlie. I shouldn't have been running down the center of the road like that. I know that hill is dangerous." She accepted the keys happily. "Do you think I could talk you into a ride back to my truck? I'll gladly clean out your car for you tomorrow." Even though she grinned, the smile didn't quite reach her eyes.

Martha noticed the haunted look in Lex's face, but didn't comment. Deciding to give up trying to keep her there, she reached over and wiped a spot clean on Lex's filthy cheek. "You be careful going home, Lexie." She rose up onto her toes to kiss the troubled face. "I'd like for you two to come over for dinner tomorrow night, all right?"

"Yes, ma'am," Lex agreed, glad for the reprieve. She hated arguing with Martha, but wanted to go home even more. *I have got mud in places that I shouldn't.* "We'll be here."

"You just see that you are, young lady," Martha huffed, fiddling with the blanket around Lex's shoulders. She almost lost her composure when the younger woman kissed the top of her head.

"I love you, Mada," Lex whispered. She quickly turned and rushed from the porch, before the housekeeper could see the tears in her eyes.

Amanda stared out of the front window, waiting for her lover to come home. *Where is she?* She'd assembled the various bath items that she'd wanted to pamper Lex with, and had the rancher's favorite terry cloth robe warming in the dryer. She'd drawn the bath about the time that she thought Lex's truck would pull into the driveway. The water was now cold, as was the cup of tea that she'd prepared to give to her lover the moment Lex came through the doorway.

While she'd been waiting, Amanda's thoughts had been filled with the contrast between her life and Lex's. *I'm so lucky. Even when I didn't have my parents' support, I still had Jeannie. I had my grandparents. I knew they loved me. I knew Daddy loved me, even when he first disapproved of Lex. Now I have him back, too.*

But, if it weren't for Martha, Charlie, and Lester, Lex wouldn't have had any family at all. Her mother died, her father emotionally abandoned her, one brother died, and the other hates her very existence. Then she finally got her father back, and he died, too. I bet she's scared that everyone who loves her will leave her somehow.

She saved me from that flood when my car went into that storm-ravaged creek. I thought Lex was the strongest woman I'd ever met when she did that. She took me home, cared for me, and fell in love with me. I thought she was so strong, so tough. But then, she's had to be. Look at what life has thrown at her. And she's taken every bit of it and refused to let it break her. Lex is tough on the outside—but she's so wounded inside. She has this wall of invincibility that she projects, but behind that wall is a woman, just like any other, who wants to be loved and accepted unconditionally. She has the most precious heart I've ever known. Look at the way she takes personal responsibility for everyone else's happiness. I don't think Charlie and Martha would have ever gotten married if it hadn't been for Lex.

My love doesn't allow too many people to get close to her, either. I can understand why. But she's let me in. She's made herself a new family with all of us—me, Martha, Charlie, Ronnie and Lester. Amanda smiled. *And her grandfather. Thank God he's back in her life. That's the first time any one of her relatives has come back to her and stayed.*

It's funny. The people that were related to Lex by blood abandoned her in one way or another during her life. But the people who've become her family are all related by the love they share for her. It's like we've got this unspoken conspiracy going to love and support her any way we can, drawing on one another for help in protecting her. Martha used to be the one to take the lead in this conspiracy. Now it's me. She trusts me to look after Lex. I won't let her down. I won't let Lex down.

Amanda placed the cup of tea down on a nearby table. She resumed her vigil at the front window and sighed. *Where is she?*

His mind on other things, Hubert didn't even hear the back door to his office open. He was looking over an old copy of his father's will, hoping for his own sake that the man hadn't changed anything before he died. "Lex won't be in complete control of the ranch anymore. She'll have to share it with me," he chuckled gleefully. "And I know with the right amount of pressure, I could either get my sister to sell her shares to me, or buy me out. I'll win either way." Hearing a throat being cleared behind him, Hubert turned around and jumped up. "What the fuck are you doing here?"

"Are you surprised to see me?" The tall form was leaning casually against the doorframe.

Hubert glared at the intruder. "Not really. What do you want?"

"Maybe I just wanted to visit," the low voice commented, as the figure stepped closer. "You're working late."

"Yeah, well. Some of us don't get things handed to them on a silver platter," Hubert grumbled, pushing the intruder back with his hand. "Get the hell out of my office. I'm a busy man." Surprise registered on his face when a fist connected with his nose. "Aah!" he cried, falling back against the desk, covering his face with his hands. "What did you do that for?"

The angry intruder grabbed him by the front of his shirt, pulling the whining man to his feet. "I've had it with you, asshole." Another punch, this time aimed at Hubert's midsection, caused the man to fall to his knees. "You've crossed me for the last time."

"Wait," Hubert grunted, his arms wrapped around his stomach. "Have you lost your fucking mind?" A well-placed kick, and he heard as well as felt his ribs give way. He groaned and rolled over onto his back, looking up into the eyes above him. "Fuck you," he coughed, unable to take a deep breath.

Hubert saw a dark boot come towards his face, blacking out as it connected. He never felt the other blows land, as the tall figure's rage continued to be slaked on his unconscious body.

Lex stepped wearily through the front door of the house and leaned up against the door after she closed it. *God, I ache all over.* She had bent down to take off her boots when a gentle voice startled her.

"Oh, Lex," Amanda cried, standing across from the muddied figure. "You look awful." Although the majority of the mud had been washed away, Lex's skin and clothes still bore a reddish hue. "C'mon, love. I've got the bath waiting." She had drained the cold water, and waited until she heard the truck pull into the driveway before refilling the tub.

"Thanks. Sorry it took me so long to get home. I, um, wanted to stop by the car wash first and use a high-pressure hose to rinse my clothes off a bit more." Lex allowed herself to be gently guided into the bathroom. She smiled slightly as nimble fingers began to unbutton her shirt. "I can get that, Amanda. You'll just get dirty."

Amanda continued to work the wet shirt from her lover's body. "I don't care." She touched the chilled skin and looked up into Lex's eyes. "You're like a block of ice," she commented worriedly.

"Yeah. That rain's pretty cold." Lex eased out of her jeans, her stiffened muscles protesting the motion. "Damn." She removed the rest of her clothes and tried to blink away the fatigue that was settling in on her body.

"What's wrong?" Amanda guided Lex to the tub and helped in, then sat down on the edge.

"Nothing. I'm just a bit sore." Lex sunk down lower in the water, allowing the fragrant bubbles to cover her. "Ooh, this feels great."

Amanda reached over and brushed the damp hair away from Lex's eyes. "Why don't you soak for a while, then I'll scrub your back, okay?" She watched as the blue eyes closed. "I'll be back in a little while, love," Amanda murmured, leaning over and kissing the troubled brow. She stood up and left the bathroom, closing the door quietly behind her.

Seeing the office light on, Doris Weatherby shook her head. *He always forgets to turn off the lights, and then complains to me when the electric bill comes in.* She pulled her vacuum cleaner inside with her, backing into the small office. Hearing a pained groan behind her, the cleaning woman spun around and gasped. "Dear Lord." She dropped the supplies that were in her hand and rushed over to the bleeding man, who was lying partially hidden behind the desk. "Mr. Walters? My goodness, what happened to you?" Afraid to touch him, she reached for his phone to call for help.

"Sheriff's Department, how may I help you?"

"This is Doris Weatherby. I clean the offices down on Fourth Street," the older woman gasped, unable to look at the still form on the floor. "I just found Mr. Walters in his office, and it looks like someone tried to beat him to death." *Not like he probably didn't deserve it, the snake. I can't remember how many of his checks to me have bounced.*

"Hold on, Mrs. Weatherby. Let me get an ambulance moving." The dispatcher put the call on hold while she dialed the ambulance service.

Doris heard Hubert moan again, and she knelt down to see what he was trying to say. "Just stay still, Mr. Walters. Help is on the way."

"Hurts," he choked out, blood seeping from his mouth. One eye cracked open slightly, hampered by the congealed blood on his face. "What—"

"Shh. You're gonna be fine," Doris whispered. She wasn't too sure, though. He looked like someone had worked him over with a vengeance. *What if whoever did this is still here?* She looked around fearfully. The office looked as it normally did, and nothing seemed to be missing. *No, it looks like he's been here for a little while.* The voice on the phone caught her attention. "What was that?"

"I said, that I've got a deputy and an ambulance on the way, ma'am. Try not to touch anything, okay?"

The sight of flashing lights through the front windows caused Doris to stand up. "They're here," she told the dispatcher, then hung up the phone. Walking to the front of the office, she watched as a short deputy stepped out of his car.

"Ma'am," he nodded to the woman as he walked into the office. "I'm Deputy Thomas. Could you please wait here while I check out the scene?" He was new to the Sheriff's Department, having been transferred from a nearby county only last week. *Finally—a little bit of action in this podunk town. God, I miss my old job.* He had been "volunteered" by his boss for an exchange program between the two departments. Each county had wanted to see how the other one handled different situations, so they agreed to swap officers for a short period of time.

The ambulance arrived, and the technicians jumped out and pulled the gurney through the door quickly. Looking at Doris, they nodded their thanks as she pointed to the back of the office.

Deputy Thomas was leaning over the injured man, his notebook open. "Mr. Walters, do you know who did this to you?" He was almost sickened by the man's appearance. *No one deserves to be beaten like this. I hope he can give me a good description of the assailant.*

"God," Hubert groaned, barely able to understand what the deputy was asking of him. When his pain-fogged mind made the connection, he almost smiled. *Oh, yeah. This is gonna be good.* "Don'd led her hurd be anybore," he gasped, his words barely intelligible.

"I won't, sir. I promise you'll be safe." The deputy leaned down so that he could hear the softly spoken words. "If you'll tell me the monster that did this to you, I'll toss them into jail."

Hubert choked on the blood in his mouth. "By sisder. Lex Walders," he breathed, then closed his eyes.

The emergency technicians shoved the deputy aside. "You've gotten what you need, Deputy," one of them said. "Now let us do our job and get him to the hospital." They eased the unconscious man onto the stretcher and wheeled him from the room.

"His sister?" The shocked deputy shook his head. "Guess I'd better see if I can find her."

Chapter 8

"Dispatch, this is Unit Four." Deputy Thomas sat in his car and watched as the ambulance pulled away.

The radio crackled. "Unit Four, go ahead."

He pulled out his notebook and glanced at his barely legible handwriting. "I need a ten-twenty on a Lex Walters, ASAP." The silence from the radio was deafening. "Did you copy, Dispatch?"

Carla, the dispatcher on call, scratched her head. "Uh, yeah. Hold on a minute, will you?" The Sheriff's Department didn't usually use the ten codes, so she had to scramble to find her copy. Pulling the wrinkled and stained paper out of the desk drawer, she followed the numbers down the page until she reached twenty. *He needs a location on Lex? What on earth is going on out there?* "Um, Unit Four. Did you say Lex Walters? I can always call her at home and let her know about her brother."

"Negative, Dispatch. I need to make contact with the subject, over." He shook his head at the casual use of the radio. *I've ended up in freakin' Mayberry. These bumpkins are thirty years behind.* "Do you have a," he paused and sighed. "Do you have an address for her?"

"Of course. Everyone knows where she's staying right now. It's fourteen thirty-three Sycamore Street. Are you sure you don't want me to call her?" Carla didn't know what was going on, but she knew for certain that she needed to call the sheriff. *He's not going to like what Deputy Butthead is doing, that's for sure.*

Ted Thomas rolled his eyes. "Negative, Dispatch. I'm en route, and will advise. Unit Four, out." He closed his notebook and pointed the car in the direction of Sycamore Street. *So, she has friends in the department, huh? Well, they're not going to help her this time. I can't wait to see what kind of woman she is, considering how awful her brother looked. Poor guy.*

Already in her boxer shorts and tee shirt, Lex was lying back on the bed when Amanda stepped into the room. The recumbent rancher looked up at her lover, who was carrying a handful of medical supplies.

Amanda sat down on the edge of the bed and pulled one of Lex's hands into her lap. "What did you do to your knuckles, love? They look absolutely horrible." The left knuckles were raw and still oozing a bit of blood, and were already beginning to bruise. Amanda covered the cuts with antiseptic and wrapped a bit of gauze around the hand.

"Kept slamming them into the ground while I was trying to change the tire on the truck. I feel like a complete idiot." Lex smiled as Amanda finished bandaging her hand and then placed a gentle kiss above the dressing. "Thanks."

"Any time." Amanda reached up and brushed the dark hair away from Lex's face. "You look completely worn out, honey. Why don't you stay here while I go and fix you something to eat?"

"You don't have to do that. I'm really not that hungry, anyway." Lex leaned her head back against the pillows and closed her eyes. "Do you mind if I just go to sleep?"

Amanda left a kiss on Lex's forehead. "Not at all. Get some rest, and I'll join you in a few minutes, okay? I need to call Martha and let her know that you made it home all right." She waited a moment for an answer, then realized that Lex was already asleep. *Rest well, my love.* Amanda was about to lean over to place another kiss on her lover's brow when she heard a knock at the front door. *Who could that be?*

The knocking continued, and Amanda hurried down the hallway. She flung open the door to see a sheriff's deputy standing on the front steps. *Maybe Charlie sent someone to be sure that Lex got home okay.* "Can I help you?"

Deputy Thomas allowed his hand to drift casually to his holstered gun. The woman who had answered the door was small, but he knew from experience that looks could be deceiving. "Lex Walters?" he asked, politely.

"Um, no. I'm her partner, Amanda Cauble. Is there something we can do for you?" A small kernel of fear began to spread through her stomach. "What's wrong?"

He stepped forward and removed his hat. "Ma'am, I must speak with Ms. Walters. Is she at home?"

"Yes, but she's resting right now. Are you sure I can't help you?"

"I'm afraid not, ma'am. May I come in?" At the young woman's nod, he stepped across the threshold and into the entrance hall. "Where is she?"

"In the bedroom," Amanda answered, pointing down the hallway. "But, as I said before, she's resting." She watched as the deputy walked down the hall carefully. "Hey, wait just a minute."

Turning around, he held up one hand. "Please stand right there against the wall, ma'am. I don't want to have to restrain you." The deputy reached down and unclipped his gun, but left it holstered. He stood in the doorway of the bedroom and looked inside. "Lex Walters? I need to ask you a few questions," he directed to the woman lying on the bed.

"Hmm?" Lex rolled over and wrapped her arms around Amanda's pillow, breathing deeply. Strong hands grabbed her arm and flipped her onto her stomach, causing her to wake up with an unwelcome jolt. "What the hell?"

The nervous lawman had jumped on the bed when she moved, and proceeded to place his knee in the small of her back. He grabbed her wrists and cuffed her hands behind her. "Ms. Walters, I'm placing you under arrest for assault."

"What the hell are you talking about?" Lex yelled, grimacing as his knee found her kidney. "Who the hell are you?" She twisted slightly to look over her shoulder. "I don't know you."

"No, you don't. But you've been named by the victim as the assailant in an assault, and I'm taking you in." He roughly jerked Lex to her feet, only then realizing how she was dressed. *Too bad. I'm taking you in just the way you are, lady.*

Amanda stood in the doorway, an outraged look on her face. "Stop it! Have you lost your mind?" She started into the bedroom, and he reached for his gun.

"Ma'am, I'm going to have to ask you to stay where you are," he ordered. "Don't make me do something we'll both regret." The deputy grabbed Lex by one arm and pulled her to the door. "Let's go, Walters."

Lex struggled slightly, but the look on her lover's face caused her to stop. "You want to at least tell me who I supposedly assaulted?" she asked, as he led her through the house.

He stopped at the front door and turned to look at the person he held in custody. *Damn, she's a big woman. I could see her doing that kind of damage to someone. I'm just lucky she was sleeping when I showed up. That could have gotten nasty.* "Like you don't know."

"Wait. It's still raining out there. Can I at least put her coat on her?" Amanda asked, meeting Lex's gaze. The blue eyes showed confusion, so she knew this man was dead wrong in his assumptions. "Don't worry, love. We'll get to the bottom of this," Amanda assured her lover in a quiet voice.

"Make it quick," the deputy countered. "I want to get down to the office before my shift ends." He watched as Amanda grabbed a heavy black coat from the closet. "Hold on, ma'am. I need to check the pockets." Pushing Lex up against the wall so that he could keep one eye on her, he quickly searched the pockets of the duster. Deputy Thomas pulled out a small cell phone and handed it to Amanda. "I don't think she'll be needing this."

Amanda accepted the phone. "Thanks," she muttered. She looked over at Lex and frowned. "Can't she at least put on some clothes?"

"No time for that, ma'am. If you want to bring a change of clothes to the lockup, we'll give them to her after she's been processed." He draped the coat over Lex's shoulders and turned her to face the door. "Let's go."

"Who said I assaulted them?" Lex demanded to know as her bare feet splashed through the mud on the way to the waiting patrol car.

Standing on the front porch with tears in her eyes, Amanda watched as the deputy none-too-gently forced her lover into the back seat of his car. She heard Lex's question, and gasped in shock at the lawman's answer.

"Your brother, Ms. Walters. He was able to identify you before they took him to the hospital."

After watching the patrol car leave the drive, Amanda rushed into the house and grabbed the phone. She hit the familiar speed dial and waited impatiently for an answer.

"Hello?"

"Martha, thank God. Is Charlie there?"

The housekeeper looked over at her husband, who was polishing his boots. "Yes, he is. Did Lexie make it home okay?" The strangled sob on the other end of the line caused her to panic. "Amanda? What's wrong?" Her phone beeped as another call started to come through. "Hold on, there's another call." She didn't want to quit talking to the obviously distraught young woman, but being the wife of the sheriff, she couldn't ignore an incoming call. "Hello?"

"Mrs. Bristol? This is Carla in Dispatch. I need to speak to the sheriff."

Oh, Lord. What's happened now? Martha turned to her husband. "Charlie, I have the dispatcher on the phone—and Amanda's on the other line, mighty upset." She handed the phone to him and waited patiently to find out what was going on.

"This is Sheriff Bristol." He listened for a moment, and then closed his eyes. "Damn. Has he already gone to the house? That's just great. You tell him that I'm on my way, and she'd better not have a damned scratch on her, you got that? Thanks for calling, Carla." Charlie looked at his wife and shook his head. He hit the button on the phone. "Amanda? I know, honey, calm down. We're on our way into town, right now. No. I'm going to drop Martha off at your house so that she can keep you company until I get this sorted out." *I'm gonna kill that boy.* He sighed, and handed the phone back to Martha. "She wants to talk to you. Our temporary transfer arrested Lex a few minutes ago."

"What?" Martha grabbed the phone. "Amanda, honey. We'll be there in a few minutes, okay? Don't you worry, Charlie will take care of everything." She looked at her husband. "Right?"

He shook his head. "I don't know. Once she's been arrested, I have to let them process her. And unless the charges are dropped, she'll have to stay in jail until the judge sets her bail."

"This is ridiculous. Why did that idiot arrest her?" she whispered, covering the mouthpiece of the phone with one hand.

"Hubert was beaten up in his office this evening, apparently pretty badly," Charlie answered, pulling on his boots.

Martha shook her head. "So? The man's a weasel; it's about time someone put him in his place." She couldn't bring herself to feel sorry for the man who had tormented Lex for so long. "What does that have to do with Lexie?"

The sheriff clipped his holster to his belt and slipped on his coat. "Before he lost consciousness, Hubert named Lex as his assailant." He grabbed Martha's coat. "C'mon, sweetheart. Let's go get this taken care of."

The small voice on the other end of the phone continued to cry. "She's," Amanda bit back a sob. "She's not even wearing shoes, Mada. He dragged her out of here in her shorts and tee shirt. What are we going to do?"

"Amanda? You just try and stay calm, and we'll be there before you know it, all right?" Martha hung up the phone and shook her head. "That poor girl, she's so worried." She accepted her husband's help with her coat and allowed him to escort her out of the house. "Did you know that sorry excuse for a deputy took Lexie out in her pajamas? She wasn't even wearing shoes."

Charlie opened the passenger door and helped her into the car. "The little turd came over from another county, and he thinks he's working in some big-time department. I'll have a little chat with him when I see him."

Lex felt a simmering anger, and her cheeks burned with embarrassment as the deputy shoved her through the Sheriff's Department. She stumbled and would have fallen except for the uniformed woman that stepped in front of her.

"Lexington? What on earth is going on here?" the woman asked, glaring over Lex's shoulder at the deputy. She had gone to school with the rancher, but now was one of the women deputies in charge of the jail.

"I wish I knew, Daylene. This guy practically dragged me out of bed and arrested me. He tells me that Hubert's been beaten up." Lex felt a hard shove between her shoulder blades as she was pushed into the jailer again. She turned her head and glared at the man. "Watch it, asshole," she growled, barely being restrained by the woman officer.

The deputy pulled up his belt and pushed her again. "Shut up, lady. I saw what you did to your brother—you don't deserve any kindness." He pulled Lex's coat from her shoulders and folded it over his arm. "You want to process her? I've got a load of paperwork to finish up. I'll just take her personal effects and log themin."

Daylene watched as the arrogant deputy left the room. "I'm sorry, Lex, but I'm going to have to take your picture and fingerprint you. If you give me your word you won't make a fuss, I'll take those stupid handcuffs off of you."

"I swear to you, Day, I'm not gonna cause you any trouble." Lex closed her eyes as the woman stepped behind her and unlocked the metal cuffs. "Thanks. I think those damned things were cutting off my circulation." She rubbed her hands over her wrists, trying to ease the pain.

"What happened to you there?" The jailer pointed to the bandage on Lex's left hand.

Lex looked down at the floor, embarrassed. "I got a flat tire on the way home tonight, and kept slamming my hand against the pavement because of the stupid jack." She looked at the bandage, then back at the other woman with a concerned look on her face. "Hey..."

"Don't say another word, Lex. Please," the jailer pleaded. "Let's just get you finished up, and I'll put you in the sheriff's office for the time being." She looked at the lack of clothing on her friend. "Unless you want to be put in the jail dressed like that?"

"Um, no. Thanks, Day. I really appreciate all that you've done to help." Lex submitted to the humiliation meekly, hoping that Amanda was faring better.

Charlie stomped into the building, an ugly frown marring his handsome features. He stopped at the booking desk and looked around. "Where is she? You didn't put her in the lockup, did you?"

"No, sir. Deputy Thomas asked me to take care of things, so after I followed the booking procedures, I placed her in your office." Daylene shook her head in disgust. "He didn't even have the decency to let her dress. Poor Lex is barefoot and half-naked."

The sheriff patted her on the shoulder. "Thank you, Daylene. I'm glad you were here to take care of her."

"I've known Lex most of my life, Sheriff. And I can tell you, she was just as confused and upset about this whole mess as any of us were."

"I know. Thanks again." Charlie hurried to his office and opened the door. Lex was sitting in his visitor's chair with her arms wrapped about her body. Half-dressed and shivering as she was, she looked almost as miserable as when he had picked her up on the road—soaking wet and covered with mud from head to toe. Eyeing the bandaged hand, he gave his head a little shake. "Lex."

She stood up and studied his face carefully as he entered the room. Lex tracked his gaze and shrugged as she raised her injured hand. "Stupid truck jack," she said in explanation.

"You should have told Martha and let her clean that up at the house. You know if we'd seen that you were hurt, you wouldn't have had as easy a time getting away."

Lex smiled at that—he was concerned over a few skinned knuckles when there was a lot bigger trouble facing her. "Well, actually, between the mud and the cold rain, I didn't notice how bad it was myself until I washed up. Even if I had, though, I wouldn't have bothered you two with it. I really wanted to get home to Amanda." She took in a deep breath, then considered her surroundings and grimaced. "But then, that plan didn't work out so well, did it?"

Charlie patted her shoulder sympathetically. "We'll get this all straightened out, I promise."

"Is someone staying with Amanda? I'd hate for her to be alone at a time like this."

Charlie pulled her into his arms. "Martha's with her. They're probably on their way up here now."

"Thanks, Uncle Charlie," Lex murmured into his shirt. "God, what a bitch of a day it's been."

"I know the feeling, girl. Unfortunately, I'm going to have to put you in a cell for tonight; but I'm going to wait until you get some decent clothes on, okay?"

Lex nodded. "I understand. I don't want you to get into any trouble."

"I don't care about me, but if it comes to light that you received special privileges, it could hurt your case."

"My case? Do they actually have a case against me, Uncle Charlie?"

The sheriff walked over to his desk and sat down. "I don't know. But I guarantee you that I'll double-check everything." He looked at the young woman who was like a daughter to him. "I hate to ask you this, but—"

"I didn't do it. I don't know what Hubert's up to, but I swear to you, I didn't go anywhere near him tonight." Lex began to pace back and forth around the office. "Either he didn't see who did it, or he did, and figured this was the perfect opportunity to get back at me." A knock at the door stopped her pacing.

"Come in," Charlie smiled when the door opened and

Amanda and Martha stepped into the room.

"Lex!" Amanda dropped the sack she was carrying and raced into her lover's waiting arms. "Are you okay?" She buried her face in the soft tee shirt that Lex was wearing.

Lex rubbed Amanda's back and kissed the top of her head. "I'm fine. Confused and pissed off, but fine."

Amanda pulled back slightly so that she could look at her lover's face. She reached up with one hand and caressed Lex's cheek. "You look tired, love." She turned her head to make eye contact with the sheriff. "What happens now, Charlie?"

"I'm afraid she'll have to stay in the lockup overnight." He was grateful that his wife had walked over and placed her arm about his waist, which gave him the strength to continue. Addressing Lex, he added, "The prosecutor will have to study the charges and see if there's enough evidence to hold you. Then we'll meet with the judge, and have him set your bail."

Martha shook her head. "This is the most ridiculous load of bull puckey that I've ever heard. Has someone talked to Hubert? Maybe the deputy misunderstood him."

"I doubt that," Lex growled. "Hubert will use any opportunity he can to screw with my life. I wouldn't be surprised if he paid someone to beat him up, just so he could blame me." She didn't realize how tired she was until Amanda led her to a chair and gently pushed her into it. "Thanks." Lex smiled, which widened when Amanda dropped onto her lap.

The knock on the door caused the people gathered in the room to fall silent. A gray-haired woman stepped into the room and placed a manila folder on Charlie's desk. "I'm sorry to bother you, Sheriff, but I thought you might want a copy of Deputy Thomas's report." On her way out, she patted Lex on the shoulder and winked. "Hang in there, hon. It'll all work out."

Charlie had been watching Lex try to hide the chills that were causing her to tremble. "Sarah? Could you please escort Lex to the ladies room so that she can get dressed? I'd hate for her to sue the county for letting her catch pneumonia."

Amanda stood up regretfully. "Go ahead, honey. We'll be waiting for you when you get back." She walked Lex to the door and picked up the large paper bag she had dropped. "Here. Boots, socks, jeans, and your favorite flannel shirt."

"Thanks." Lex leaned down and kissed Amanda. "Be back in a flash." She smiled at the uniformed woman standing in the door.

"Think we should bring back coffee for everyone, Sarah?" She continued to talk to the older woman as they walked out into the outer office. "How's your husband doing?"

Closing the door, Amanda turned around and leveled her gaze at Charlie. "Okay. Now it's just us in here now. What are the charges, and how soon can I take her home?"

He closed the folder on his desk. "Sit down, Amanda." After she had taken a seat next to Martha, Charlie shook his head. "I'll give Thomas one thing—he fills out a very thorough report. He even called the hospital to get a rundown on Hubert's condition." *This is not going to be easy. I can't find any mistakes here.*

"So? Lex didn't do anything; it doesn't matter," Amanda said confidently. "This is all just a big misunderstanding, right?"

"I hope so, Amanda." Charlie looked back down at the report. "But we'd better get her a lawyer. This isn't something that's going to be cleared up overnight, I'm afraid."

Martha jumped to her feet. "This is ridiculous. Lexie always owns up to her mistakes. If she says she didn't do it, then she didn't do it." She put her hands on her hips and glared down at the paperwork in front of her husband. "I don't give a rat's hind end what that idiot says—I'm going to get to the bottom of this." She spun around and rushed from the room, slamming the door behind her.

Charlie grinned slightly and shook his head. "She's taking this a lot better than I thought she would." He looked up at Amanda. "As soon as Lex gets back in here, I can give you a couple of minutes alone; but then I'm afraid I'll have to lock her up for the evening."

"I know, Charlie. I just appreciate what you've done for her so far. This has got to be terrible for you, too." Amanda stood up, walked around his desk, and gave the lawman a hug. "We'll get through it."

"Already found someone else, huh?" Lex teased from the doorway. Looking around the room, she asked, "Where's Martha?"

Amanda gave Charlie one last squeeze and stepped away. "She needed some air, I think." *Or maybe she's gone to see how much damage a wooden spoon can do to the backside of a deputy.*

"Actually, I was just going to look for her." Charlie had followed Amanda from behind the desk and stopped at the door. "I'll give you girls a couple of minutes alone." He patted Lex on the back and left the room.

Lex pulled Amanda into her arms and held her close. "Been one of those days, hasn't it?"

"You can say that again," Amanda half-giggled, half-sniffled. "Charlie said I'd better get you a lawyer. Do you think it's going to come down to that?"

"I hope not. But, it might be best to call Melvin Taft, anyway. His number is in my wallet." The last time she had seen the young attorney, he had excitedly given her his newly printed business card. Not thinking, Lex had placed it in her wallet. *Good thing I did, since my address book is nothing but ashes now.* At the thought of spending the night away from Amanda, she swallowed the lump in the throat. *God, I don't know if I can do this.*

Feeling the body pressed up against hers stiffen, Amanda looked up into Lex's face and saw the rigid set of her jaw. "Lex? Hey, look at me."

As she dropped her gaze, Lex was caught up in Amanda's shining eyes. "Hmm?"

"I know you're upset, and scared." Seeing the look of consternation crossing Lex's features, she shook her head. "I'm scared, too. But we're going to get through this. You and me together—there's nothing we can't do." She buried her face in her lover's shirt, prolonging the contact for as long as possible before they would have to be separated.

Chapter 9

Extreme pain was the first thing that registered as he returned to consciousness. Hubert opened the one eye that wasn't swollen shut and looked about. *Hospital?* When he took a deep breath to speak, the pain almost caused him to pass out again.

"I see you're awake," a gentle voice observed quietly. "Let me go get the doctor." The nurse hurried from the room before he could move.

Moments later, an older man stepped into the room, a serious look on his face. "Mr. Walters, good. I'm glad to see you're back with us." When the injured man opened his mouth to speak, the doctor waved his hand. "No, no. You need to be quiet, young man. Your injuries aren't life-threatening, but they will be painful for a while."

A knock on the door caused the doctor to turn away as Deputy Thomas stepped into the room. "Doctor, I heard that Mr. Walters was awake. Is there any way I can have a word with him?"

"Only for a moment, Deputy. Then I'm afraid I'll have to ask you to leave."

"Thank you." The deputy walked over and leaned over the bed. The cuts that had bled so badly were now stitched closed, yet the injured man still looked terrible. "I'll make this as brief as possible, Mr. Walters. If you could just nod or shake your head, I need to ask you a few questions."

Hubert nodded.

"Okay. When I first saw you in your office, you told me that your sister did this to you. Is that correct?" At the man's nod and smile, he looked down at his notes with a pleased look on his face.

"Good. You have nothing to worry about, she's already been taken into custody." *I don't blame him; I'd smile too, if they caught the person that just beat the hell out of me.* He didn't realize that Hubert had smiled *before* he told him that Lex had been arrested. "Are you willing to file charges, sir?" Another emphatic nod. "Excellent. I'm going to let you get some rest. If there's anything else I can do for you, give me a call. I'll leave my card on this table." Deputy Thomas left the room, whistling a tune to himself.

Painful as it was, Hubert smiled again. *I wish I could have seen the look on her face when they arrested her.* He looked up as the doctor stepped back into the room.

"While you're awake, I thought I'd go over your injuries. We'll have to keep you here for a couple of days, to make sure there's no internal damage. Believe me, Mr. Walters, it looks and feels a lot worse than it actually is." He pulled out the chart and studied it for a moment. "You have two broken ribs, a concussion, numerous minor cuts on your face that required stitches, and I'm afraid you're missing several teeth. On the bright side, your jaw is only bruised, and we've already set your broken nose." The doctor closed the chart and smiled. "Due to the stitches in your mouth, it will be difficult for you to form words. As soon as the swelling has gone down, you should be able to speak. Until then, I'll leave a notepad with you so that you can communicate. Do you want me to contact anyone for you?"

Hubert shook his head.

"All right. Just give the nurse a buzz if you need anything. I'll be back to check on you in the morning." He smiled again and left the room.

Lex eyed the small room with trepidation. "No bars?" Butterflies the size of tanks were flying around in her stomach, and her weak attempt at humor did nothing to alleviate her fear.

"Nope. We remodeled a couple of years ago, and now have these lovely semi-private rooms, instead." The matron unlocked the heavy door and opened it. "We're not real full at the busiest of times so at least you'll be by yourself." Feeling sorry for Lex, she patted her on the back. She had known this young woman since she was a toddler. "Don't worry—it's really not that bad. You can sit back and enjoy a little peace and quiet for a while."

"Right." Lex stepped into the small room and looked around. She was holding a folded blanket against her chest and was suddenly overwhelmed with the feeling of the walls closing in on her. *Damn. I don't think I can handle this.* She swallowed hard as the door closed and locked. The square window in the center of the door insured her little privacy, but at least it gave her something to look through.

She dropped the blanket onto the steel cot that protruded out from one wall. Sitting on the chilled surface, Lex took a deep breath and tried to calm her pounding heart. *I can do this. It's only until morning, then I'm out of here.* She stood up again and began to pace the small room. *Okay, Hubert tells them it was me that beat him up. I wish. Jackass.* Shaking her head at the negative thoughts, she started pacing again. *That's not gonna help, Lexington. Think. I don't have an alibi, since I went to the stupid car wash to clean up. There's got to be some way to prove it wasn't me.*

Lex stopped in her tracks. "Wait a minute. If I supposedly beat him so badly, then my clothes would have blood on them." She hurried over to the door and looked out the window. *I've got to get in touch with Amanda, and hope like crazy that she hasn't already put them in to wash.* She began to beat on the door. "Hey. I need to talk to the sheriff," she yelled, trying to catch someone's attention. "Hello? Can anybody hear me?"

One o'clock in the morning. Amanda and Martha had come back to the rental house after Lex had been taken away, and both women were trying to figure out some way to expose Hubert's lies. Amanda was sitting at the dining room table writing notes on a yellow pad, while Martha cleaned and baked. Angrily tossing her pen down, Amanda jumped up from the table. "This is ridiculous." As her chair fell to the floor behind her, she covered her face with her hands and burst into tears.

"Oh, honey." Martha dropped her spoon into the mixing bowl and rushed to the other side of the room. She pulled the younger woman into her arms and began to rock her back and forth gently. "Hush, child. Everything's going to be just fine, you'll see." She held Amanda as she cried, whispering words of comfort and rubbing her back.

Finally getting her emotions under control, Amanda sniffled

one last time and pulled away from the portly woman. "Thanks, Martha. I guess I needed that." She ran one hand through her hair and sighed. "Maybe I just need to be busy. I think I'll gather up our laundry." Before she could leave the room, the telephone rang. She raced for the phone and picked it up before it could ring again. "Hello?"

"Miss Cauble? This is Melvin Taft. You left an urgent message for me?" He had just returned home from a late dinner with friends, and was glad he'd remembered to check his answering machine before going to bed.

Amanda smiled and mouthed to Martha, "Lawyer." Then she directed her attention to the telephone. "Thank you for calling back so quickly, Mr. Taft."

He chuckled. "Please, call me Mel. Mr. Taft is my grandfather. Your message said something about Lex needing my help?"

"I'm afraid so. Her brother was found beaten in his office this evening, and he told the deputy that Lex did it."

"Damn." He paused a moment for the information to sink in. "They arrested her?"

Allowing Martha to lead her to a chair, Amanda sat down. "Um, yes. The deputy is a transfer from another county, and he rushed over here to the house and took her away. He didn't even let her get dressed, just took her out in her bare feet and pajamas," she cried, upset again at the cruel treatment of her lover.

"Okay. Now don't get mad for me asking this, but did she do it?" He had to know, so that he could figure out his defense strategy.

"Of course not!" Realizing that she was yelling, Amanda lowered her voice. "I'm sorry, Mr., um, Mel. It's been a really long evening."

Melvin sighed. "That's okay, Miss Cauble. I know you've been under a lot of stress today. Does she have an alibi for the time in question?"

"Please call me Amanda. And no, she had been at the ranch supervising the construction, and was on the way home. Of course, then she had a flat tire, and then locked her keys in the truck, and then—"

"Hold on. I'm going to have to write all this down." He paused for a moment, and then cleared his throat. "I know it's really late, but would you mind if I came over? I think this would be easier face to face."

Amanda covered the mouthpiece on the phone and looked at Martha. "He wants to come over to discuss Lex's case." At the housekeeper's energetic nod; she smiled. "That would be great, Mel. I think Martha's even baked up something sweet, and we've got a fresh pot of coffee on."

"All right, then. That settles it. Martha's about the best cook around. If you'll just give me your address, I'll be over in a few minutes."

After giving the lawyer meticulous directions to the house, Amanda hung up the phone and looked at Martha. "He said he'll be here in ten minutes," she shared with Martha. "Do you think I have time to start up some laundry? I know that the clothes Lex had on earlier probably need a good soak to get all the mud out of them. I may as well get them started."

"Calm down in there," the jailer yelled, slamming his metal baton against Lex's cell door. "You're disturbing everyone else with all that noise. Now go lie down and get some sleep."

Angered at the man's attitude, Lex continued to pound her hands against the thick glass. "Go get the sheriff," she yelled, her voice becoming hoarse with overuse. "It's an emergency."

He walked up to the window and glared at the excited woman. "I don't give a good goddamn what your problem is. Don't make me come in there and put restraints on you."

Another jailer walked into the hallway. "What's going on here, Dave?" He looked at the woman in the window. "Lex? What the hell is she doing in there?"

"You know this lunatic?" Dave asked. "She keeps screaming about needing to see the sheriff."

With a heavy sigh, the second man shook his head. "I'd listen to her if I were you, Dave. Her mother's married to the sheriff."

Shit. I knew I should have called in sick tonight. "Really? Do you think she's in here by mistake?" he asked. *Thank God I didn't restrain her; I'd have probably lost my job.*

"I dunno. Open up, and we'll see what she wants." The late arrival stood back as Dave unlocked the door. "Hi, Lex. What on earth are you doing in here?"

Lex stood inside the cell, afraid to come out after the way the other jailer had spoken to her. "Long story, Dan. Is there some way I can see Charlie? Or at least get a message to him?"

Dan smiled. "Why don't I take you upstairs to see him? I know he's still in his office." *And seeing her in here, explains why.* "C'mon. I don't have to chain you, do I?"

"No. I'll behave," Lex whispered, her voice almost gone. "Thanks, Dan. I owe you one."

He waved off her appreciation. "Don't mention it." He motioned for her to walk in front of him as they left the row of cells. "Just don't take off running. I could never catch you." Dan rubbed his slight beer belly and laughed. Leading Lex to an upstairs interrogation room, he opened the door. "I can't let you back into the offices, but if you'll wait in here, I'll go get the sheriff for you."

Lex looked around the small room. One table and a couple of folding chairs were all that could fit inside. *It's even smaller than that damned cell.* "Um, okay. Guess I don't have much choice, huh?"

"'Fraid not." He waited until she was seated. "I'm going to have to lock you in, but we'll be back in a flash." With that, Dan closed the door and hurried off to find Charlie.

"Wonderful. I traded one box for another." The rancher stood up and paced around the room. Seeing the large mirrored glass on one wall, she smiled slightly. "Just like on TV," she murmured, touching the glass with her index finger.

Moments later, the door opened and a very tired looking sheriff walked in. "What's going on, Lex? Dan said you were raising a ruckus downstairs." He sat in one of the chairs and motioned for her to join him at the table. "I know it's no picnic, but you have to—"

"Uncle Charlie, wait. I just wanted you to get the clothes that I wore today from Amanda. If Hubert was beaten as badly as that deputy led me to believe, then whoever did it—"

"Would have his blood on them," Charlie finished for her. "Damn, I must be getting old. Why didn't I think of that?" He jumped up from the table so quickly that his chair fell over. "Wait right here, I'm going to go make a quick phone call."

She watched him rush from the room. "Like I can go anywhere," Lex mumbled, as she crossed her arms on the table in front of her and lay her head down upon them.

Amanda was carrying a large hamper full of laundry to the

garage when the phone rang. "Could you get that, Martha? I want to get these filthy clothes soaking, before they dry completely."

Martha heard Amanda's request and picked up the phone in the kitchen. "Hello? Charlie? Is everything okay?"

"Hi, sweetheart. Look, I don't have a lot of time, but could you have Amanda take the clothes that Lex wore today and set them aside? It's important."

The housekeeper frowned. "Well, sure. Does Lexie need more clothes? We can bring—" Understanding of the situation dawned on her. "The clothes, of course! Oh, no. Hold on a minute, hon." Martha dropped the phone and raced through the house. "Amanda! Don't wash those clothes." She reached the garage just as the younger woman was about to pile the muddy clothes into the washing machine. "Wait!"

"Aah!" Amanda screamed and fell back away from the machine onto her rear end. "Good grief, Martha, you scared me half to death. What's wrong with you?"

"I'm sorry, sweetie," Martha apologized, offering her hand to the woman on the floor. "Charlie needs the clothes that Lexie was wearing this evening."

Amanda stood up and rubbed her backside. "Ow." She picked up the discarded hamper and pulled the still damp jeans and shirt from inside. "They're nasty, but he's welcome to them." Amanda piled the messy garments next to the washing machine and glared at the older woman. "You scared the crap out of me, hollering like that."

Martha chuckled. "I know, and I really am sorry. But Charlie's hoping that the lack of blood on Lexie's clothes will prove she didn't thrash that no-good brother of hers." Her eyes widened. "Oh, poop. Charlie's still on the phone." Martha charged from the garage, with Amanda's giggles following behind her.

"I had no idea she could move that fast." Amanda dropped the hamper and followed her friend back to the kitchen.

Dreams of expensive cars and beautiful women floated through his subconscious as Hubert lay resting in the semi-private hospital room. The other bed was empty, so no one noticed as a tall figure slipped into the room and pulled the privacy curtain around the occupied bed. A hand around his throat woke the resting man, who was groggy from all the drugs in his system.

"Shh," the man standing over the bed whispered. "Damn, Walters, you look like someone kicked your ass." He smiled, proud of his handiwork.

The partially open eye looked around wildly. "What—," Hubert rasped, barely able to speak.

"The only reason I didn't kill your sorry ass earlier was because you owe me money," the man informed him. "We tried to help you out, running your sister off the road New Year's Eve. You keep promising to pay us, or I would have put you in here sooner. We ruined our boss's truck, too. You were supposed to pay for all the repairs, remember?"

"Didn'd pollow dhrough," Hubert wheezed. "She's sdill alibe."

"You stupid asshole. You never told us to kill her, just mess her up a bit." He leaned down to get in Hubert's face. "I may look stupid, and talk stupid," he thumped the end of the swollen nose in front of him to make his point, getting a perverse thrill out of the moan of pain from the bedridden man, "but I ain't stupid, Walters. You'd best be figuring out how to pay me, or this," he indicated the bed, "is gonna look like a paper cut."

Hubert blinked the tears of pain from his eye. "I don'd habe id." Seeing the man's face darken with fury, he stammered, "B...b...bud, I can ged id. I jusd need your helb."

The man leaned back and laughed. "You've got to be shitting me, boy. Do I look like someone who wants to help you?"

"W-waid. The wanch is word a vordune."

"So? I've seen where you live, Walters. You ain't got the ranch." The large man began to crack his knuckles as he paced around the room. "What are you trying to say?"

Finally—the idiot's gonna listen. Jeez. Inhaling a painful breath, Hubert groaned. "I'm dryin' do say, dad ib anydin' were do habben do my sisder, I'd be de sole heir do de wanch. And—"

"And if you were the sole heir, you'd have all the money." The man slapped at a covered foot, ignoring the hiss of pain from the man on the bed. "So, what do you have in mind?"

Morning couldn't come soon enough for Lex. After she had been escorted back to her cell, she spent the remainder of the night pacing the small room and fighting off a case of chills. *Wonderful, probably got a damned cold to top it off. What else could possibly go wrong?* When she heard the key in the lock, she spun around to see Dan standing in the doorway.

"Good morning, Lex. Your lawyer is here, and he's waiting with the county prosecutor for you." He noticed she was standing with the blanket draped over her shoulders. "Are you all right?"

The tall woman nodded. "Yeah." She tried to clear her throat, but her voice was a mere whisper. "Don't you guys ever turn on the heat in this place?" Lex tightened her grip on the blanket as she walked through the door. "I felt like a side of beef in there last night."

"I'll check it out, but no one else has complained." Dan motioned for her to go in front of him as they reached the stairs. "C'mon. I'll buy you a cup of coffee to warm you up."

"Thanks." Lex took the lead, and was finally standing in front of one of the interrogation rooms. "I hope this one's bigger than the last one," she muttered, stifling a cough. She straightened her shoulders and pulled the blanket away, handing it to the deputy.

"Don't worry, it is." He opened the door for her to enter. "Why don't you go on in, and I'll go get you that coffee."

The room was almost twice the size of the other one, and was already occupied by Melvin Taft, the sheriff, and an unfamiliar woman not much older than Lex. Charlie stood up and smiled. "Lex, come on over here and sit down." He pulled out the chair next to him for her to sit down. "This is assistant county prosecutor Vicky Evans. She'll be asking you some questions." He looked at Mel. "That is okay by you, isn't it?"

"Of course, Sheriff." Melvin looked at his client. "Lex? Are you okay?"

"Yeah," Lex whispered. "Just a little tired." She glanced over at the other woman in the room. "Don't take this wrong, but where's Mr. Campbell?"

"He sent me to work on this case, because he was afraid of a conflict of interest," the woman informed her. She had short brown hair and glasses, and appeared to have an attitude. "Robert told me of the situation, and I agreed to drive in this morning." She opened up a folder and looked down at the paperwork. "Ms. Walters, do you have any witnesses to your whereabouts last evening, between nine and ten o'clock?"

"I don't think so. I was on my way home from Charlie's house and stopped at the car wash on Sunset to rinse some mud off my clothes." At the woman's frown, Lex agreed to herself that the excuse sounded lame to her, too. She stifled a sneeze, then gratefully accepted a handkerchief from Charlie.

Ms. Evans made a few notes, then looked up at Lex. "I've read your statement, Ms. Walters, but would you care to tell me again why your left hand is bandaged?"

With a heavy sigh, Lex looked down at the hand and shook her head. "Have you ever had a flat tire, Miss Evans?" she asked, looking back up at the other woman. "On the way home last night, one of my front tires went flat. I had to use the tire iron and jack that came with the truck. I don't think it would have worked right on an import, much less the truck that I drive." She picked at the bandage for a moment, lost in her thoughts. "Anyway, the tire iron kept slipping while I was trying to remove the tire. I must have slammed my knuckles down on the pavement half a dozen times, at least." Lex quietly blew her nose, giving Charlie an apologetic shrug.

The prosecutor looked over at the sheriff. "If, as according to your statement, she was at your house after changing the tire, why didn't you notice the injury to her hand?"

Charlie shook his head. "She was covered from head to toe in red mud, Ms. Evans. I was lucky to be able to identify Lex, much less see any injuries."

"I see." Deciding to change the subject, the prosecutor leaned forward and pulled her glasses down to look Lex in the eyes. "You don't get along with your brother very well, do you, Ms. Walters? I've read several reports of fisticuffs between the two of you, some of them from this year. What kind of provocation did it take for you to beat him so severely that it'll take months to heal?"

Melvin slapped the table. "Hold on. You have no proof that Lex did this—just the word of a man, that in your own words, she's had trouble with in the past." He glared at Ms. Evans. "A man who is awaiting trial for his part in the wreck that injured my client earlier this year. This is all obviously a ruse by Hubert to throw suspicion away from himself. I wouldn't be surprised if he paid someone to work him over."

"Perhaps. But it still doesn't explain why your client decided that she needed to clean up at a car wash." She turned to look at Lex. "Was it because you had your brother's blood on you? Were you afraid that someone would notice, and possibly question your appearance?"

Lex's eyes widened. "No!" She coughed and shook her head. "Listen, lady, I don't care much for Hubert. I'll admit that." She waved off Mel's hand, which had grasped her forearm in warning. "Hell, anyone in this town that knows us could tell you that." She leaned over the table, so that she could be heard. "But, if I had beaten him, I'd have admitted to it." A wry smile crept onto her face. "And he'd be a lot worse off, believe me."

"Aw, Lex," Mel sighed, rubbing his forehead with one hand. This was not going as well as he had hoped. *Don't give her any more ammunition, my friend. Please.* "Don't volunteer anything. Just answer the questions that she asks, will you?"

Charlie had sat by quietly, proud of the way Lex was handling herself. He saw her shiver and shook his head. *Got another cold playing in the rain yesterday, didn't you? Amanda's going to have a fit, for sure.* He looked up as someone knocked on the door. "Come in."

Dan stepped into the room with a cardboard box and the same blanket from earlier draped over one arm. "Sorry it took so long, Sheriff. Thought I'd bring everyone some fresh coffee. Got some cinnamon rolls in here, too." He pointedly ignored the prosecutor, placing the first cup in front of Lex. "This ought to warm you up. And you forgot this," he added, laying the blanket over Lex's shoulders.

"Thanks, Dan," she whispered, taking a cautious sip. "Mmm, this tastes like Martha's."

He passed the box around the room. "It should. She made it, and the rolls, too." The sheriff had brought the thermos of coffee and container of rolls in early that morning, and had asked his secretary to bring them in once they got settled. Dan had met her in the hall and taken the load from her. With a quick wave, the deputy left the room and closed the door.

The prosecuting attorney looked around the room. *Does everyone know everybody else in this damned town? Getting a conviction may be harder than I thought.* "All right. Let's get back to the business at hand. You claim that you were at the car wash, trying to get mud off of you? Just how much mud are we talking about here?"

Lex blushed. "A lot," she mumbled, then sneezed. "Sorry about that. Um, you can ask Charlie—my clothes were solid with that damned red mud." She looked up at the sheriff, who was trying to control his laughter. "Go ahead and laugh. I probably looked ridiculous."

"I'm afraid you did." Charlie glanced over at the prosecutor, who was frowning. "I can vouch for the state of her clothing, Ms. Evans. As a matter of fact, I brought them in this morning and checked them in as evidence."

"That probably won't be necessary, Sheriff, but I'll take it under advisement." The last thing she wanted were some smelly old clothes under her nose.

Charlie opened his own folder and pulled out several instant snapshots. "Here's the office where the assault took place. As you can see, there are no muddy footprints anywhere on the floor, and no other signs of outside debris."

"So? This only shows that she was able to clean herself up before the crime. I don't see—" A large clear plastic bag that Charlie tossed up onto the table cut Ms. Evans comments short. "What is that?"

"Her boots," he said, pushing the bag across the table. "They were sitting next to the front door of her home, still damp from last night. And before you say anything else, I plan on having a doctor examine Lex's hand, to corroborate her story."

Damn. This means the only true evidence I have is the word of her brother. No wonder Robert gave me this stupid case. Conflict of interest, my ass. He just didn't want a no-win case. The assistant prosecutor stood up. "In light of the information that I've received here this morning, I'm going to suggest to the court that we do not pursue this matter any further at this time." She closed her folder and crammed it into a leather briefcase. "Ms. Walters, I'd be more careful, if I were you. You might not get off as easily next time." Vicky Evans picked up her briefcase and left the room before anyone could say a word.

"She's got a bug up her ass this morning, doesn't she?" Lex asked Mel, who just shook his head then dropped it onto the table. "What?"

Charlie stood up as well. "C'mon, honey. Let's get you home so that you can get some rest. You look horrible."

Lex allowed the older man to help her to her feet. "Gee, thanks, Uncle Charlie." She coughed slightly and shook her head. "Not one word, you got that?" Holding her hand out to Melvin, she smiled. "Thanks for being here, Mel. I knew I was in good hands."

"You're welcome, Lex. Just try to stay out of trouble for a little while, okay? I'm supposed to go fishing next weekend with my granddad." He shook her hand and followed the pair out of the small room.

Amanda checked her watch again. "We should have heard something by now." She reached over and took a large sip of coffee.

"Not necessarily," Martha disagreed, looking at the set of cards in her hand. "When there's lawyers involved, something that should take minutes, takes hours. I'm sure they have to see who wins the whizzing contest."

Amanda almost spewed coffee through her nose. "Ugh. Don't say things like that when I'm trying to drink. I have this awful mental picture in my head, thank you very much." She had gotten used to hearing colorful phrases from the housekeeper, but sometimes Martha still surprised her. "You did mean whizzing, as in—"

"Peeing, pissing, or as I've heard you say, tinkling," Lex quietly teased from the doorway. "Why are you two on that subject?" She wasn't prepared for the armful of woman that rushed into her, but laughed as they both landed against the wall. "Miss me?"

Amanda wrapped her arms around her lover tightly. "I guess you could say that," she mumbled, burying her face against Lex's neck. She leaned back and looked up into the shadowed eyes. "You're hot."

"Nice of you to say so." She flinched as her side was slapped. "Ow."

"Smart aleck." Amanda reached up with one hand and touched Lex's cheek. "You're running a fever. Too much playing in the rain and mud yesterday?"

"Probably," Lex agreed with a small cough.

"How did it go? Are you—"

"Home to stay. The county prosecutor, or should I say the assistant county prosecutor, admitted they didn't have enough evidence to hold me in jail, let alone charge me." Lex leaned down and stuck her nose in Amanda's hair. "God, I missed you."

Martha cleared her throat from where she stood by the kitchen table. "You two can moon over each other later," she scolded. "Lexie, get yourself over here and sit down. I made biscuits and gravy this morning, and you need a decent meal."

Regretfully releasing the hold she had on Amanda, Lex walked across the kitchen and wrapped her arms around the cook. "I love you too, Mada." She kissed the older woman on the cheek and swatted her on the rear before sitting down at the table. "Okay, I'm here. You gonna stand there glaring at me all morning, or feed me?"

"Ooh, you brat. I bet I can find a wooden spoon around here, somewhere," the housekeeper threatened, but smiled broadly as she began to assemble a plate.

Amanda sat down next to her lover, twining their fingers together. She frowned when a plate laden with food was set in front of her as well. "Martha, I don't—"

"Don't you dare argue with me, Amanda Lorraine. You barely touched your food today, and you're too scrawny as it is." Martha looked up and winked at the grinning man in the doorway. "C'mon in, handsome. There's more than enough to go around."

Charlie laughed and sat down at the table across from the two women. "I've learned to never argue with that woman. She wins every time."

Martha dropped a plate of steaming food in front of the sheriff. "You've got that right. Now hush up and eat." She sat down next to her husband, reaching under the table and squeezing his leg. "Thanks for taking care of our girl," she whispered.

"I told you I would," he answered. "And I always will."

After breakfast, Charlie excused himself to go back to the office. "I'd like to stay and visit with you ladies this morning, but I want to get a deputy over to the hospital and see if we can't get Hubert to recant his earlier statement." He kissed his wife and was almost to the door before he turned around. "I'll be by later to take you home. Think you can keep these two out of trouble until I get back?"

"I certainly intend to try." Martha waved to Charlie as he left the house. "Lexie, you go take a nice hot bath and climb into bed." As Lex opened her mouth to argue, she shook a finger at her. "Don't be giving me any lip, young lady. Git!"

Lex sighed, but stood up from the table and pushed her chair in. "Yes, ma'am." She looked over at Amanda, who was trying to hold back her laughter. "What's so funny?" Lex reached down and tickled Amanda's ribs. "That'll teach you to laugh at me," she grumbled, slowly walking from the room. Turning around at the doorway, Lex asked, "Amanda? Are you going to work today, or could I interest you in a nice warm bed?"

"Work?" Amanda slapped herself on the forehead. "Darn it, I forgot all about work." She waved Lex away. "Go on, I'll call the office and tell them I won't be in today, then I'll come in and scrub your back for you." *Oh, yeah. Snuggling instead of thumbing through boring old paperwork all day. No contest.* Suddenly her eyes widened and her face paled. *Work...my grandmother. She doesn't know what happened.* "Oh, no."

Martha put a hand on her shoulder and looked into her eyes. "What's the matter?"

"My grandparents are going to kill me," Amanda grimaced, covering her eyes with one hand. "I never called them last night."

"Don't worry, dear. I'm sure they'll understand. It was pretty late when we got back to the house."

Amanda sighed. "I don't think that's going to be a good enough excuse, but it's worth a shot." She rose and picked up the kitchen phone. Hitting the speed dial for the familiar number, she closed her eyes. *Please don't be home...please don't be home...please...*

"Hello?" Anna Leigh answered the phone.

Darn. "Hi, Gramma, it's me."

Martha laughed as she left the room. "Good luck," she mouthed, as she went to check on Lex.

"Mandy, dear. What a surprise. I just got off the phone with Wanda—she was worried about you."

"Um, yeah. Sorry about that. I'll call her as soon as I finish talking to you." Amanda walked over to the kitchen window to look outside, enjoying the way the sun glistened off the dew in the backyard grass. "I didn't get any sleep last night, so I'm not going in to work today."

Anna Leigh chuckled. "Do I want to know why you didn't get any sleep last night, dearest?"

"Gramma," Amanda blustered, fanning her heated face with her other hand. "It's nothing like that. Lex got arrested last night, and I was so worried about her I couldn't sleep."

"Arrested? Good heavens, whatever for?" The older woman gasped. "Is she all right? Have they let you see her? Let me get in touch with our lawyer, he'll know what to do."

Amanda almost laughed at her grandmother's outpouring. "Wait. It's okay, Gramma, she's home now. It was just a very long night."

"Why didn't you call us, Mandy? I would have been more than happy to come over and keep you company." The tone in Anna's Leigh's voice told of the hurt she felt at being left out. "You know you can depend on us, don't you?"

"Oh, Gramma. It's not that at all. But by the time I got back to the house, it was terribly late, and there really wasn't much for you to do. Martha drove in with Charlie, and she stayed here with me." Amanda didn't know whether this last bit of information would hurt or help her case. "I'm sorry. I should have called you sooner."

"No, no. I was just worried about you, dear. As long as you had someone there with you, that's all that matters. Is Lexington all right? She must have been terrified."

"She's okay. As a matter of fact, Martha sent her to take a bath, and then I'm going to get her into bed." Realizing what she had said, Amanda blushed again. "I mean, um—"

Laughing, Anna Leigh wanted to crawl through the phone and hug her granddaughter. "You are just too precious, Mandy." She decided to give Amanda a break and change the subject. "Why don't the two of you come over for dinner tonight? We'd love to have you, and I know Travis would enjoy seeing you both. I swear, he and your grandfather are worse than two little boys when they're together. Maybe if you're here, they'll behave. They seem to get into all sorts of things when I'm not watching them."

Amanda laughed at that thought. "I'll just bet they do. Let me check with Lex, and I'll call you back later to let you know for sure. I don't think we have any plans."

"You do that, dearest. Now go on and take care of Lexington. Hopefully we'll see you tonight."

"I sure will, Gramma. I love you."

"I love you too, Mandy. Get some rest."

As she hung up the phone, Amanda looked around the small kitchen. Martha had completely cleaned up the breakfast dishes and put everything away without her realizing it. *I really wish I knew how she did that. I never actually see her do it, but it always gets done. Must be some sort of magic.* Shaking her head, she turned off the light as she left the room.

Chapter 10

Light footsteps stopping by his bed caused Hubert to jerk awake suddenly. Fear of another visit from his "friend" made his eyes snap open, or at least as wide as they could, considering his injuries. He blinked several times until the person standing next to him came into clear view. *Just great. Can't a guy get a break around here?*

"Hello, Hubert. I've got a few questions for you," Charlie remarked conversationally. He couldn't help but notice the younger man's nervousness, and he smiled as he pulled up a chair. The sheriff had changed his mind and decided to speak to Lex's brother personally, hoping that he could somehow catch Hubert in his lies. *Besides, I want to make sure this is done right. He's not going to get away with anything else, if I can help it.* "The doctor tells me that you're having a bit of trouble talking, but I need to go over the statement that you gave the deputy yesterday. We'd like to determine if this was a random act, or if someone is after you. I promise to get you the protection you need if someone is threatening you."

Shit. She must have had an alibi. Well, there goes that idea. I'll just have to figure out something else. Hubert slowly raised the bed until he could reach the notepad on the table. He scribbled something down and turned the tablet so that the sheriff could see it. "I don't remember much about yesterday," the hastily scrawled words read.

Charlie nodded. "That's understandable, Hubert, but we'd really like to see whoever did this to you caught." *And given a medal,* he added silently. "Did you get a good look at whoever hurt you? The deputy last night put in his report that you mentioned Lex being present—which would have been hard for her to manage, since she was at my house last evening." It wasn't completely a lie, and Charlie wanted to eliminate any opportunity the injured man might seize upon to implicate his sister again.

With a pained grunt, Hubert took the notepad and began to write. He spent several minutes trying to compose his answer, making it appear that he was having trouble writing. In fact, he was thinking furiously about how to recant his earlier statement. "Big guy came in the back door of my office, I think looking for money," he lied. "Don't remember much after that. It all happened too fast."

"Okay. But that doesn't explain why you told the deputy at the scene that Lex beat you up." Charlie looked over his notes and then glared at Hubert. "You said, and I quote, 'Please don't let her hurt me anymore.' I'd say that your sister has a good case against you for defamation of character."

"No," Hubert groaned, raising one hand to stop the sheriff's tirade. His whole face hurt, but he knew that he'd have better luck getting his point across verbally. Since the stitches in his mouth were somewhat dry, the injured man had trouble speaking. "I was combused. He didn't umnersdand me. He's wying." Hubert reached for a nearby glass of water and wrestled with the straw, sucking painfully to moisten his mouth.

As he struggled to keep the smirk off of his face, Sheriff Bristol folded his notepad and placed it back into his shirt pocket. "All right, then. Would you be able to identify the man who did this to you if we were to bring him in? We've got a few leads right now that we're trying to follow up." He really had no idea who had beaten Hubert, but Charlie wanted to see how the younger man took the news.

Almost choking on the water, Hubert set the glass down and gently wiped his mouth. "Uh-uh." He reached for the notepad, deciding that writing was much less painful than talking. "It was dark, and he came in from behind. I have no idea who it could be." His hands began to shake when he considered what might happen if Bobby got caught. *He'd sell me out, for sure. I can't let that happen.*

Charlie stood up and patted Hubert on the leg. "It's okay, son. We'll get to the bottom of this." He had noticed the look of fear on the injured man's face, and even though there was no love lost between the two, he felt a pang of sympathy. "Don't you worry. I know we've never gotten along, but I won't let anything else happen to you, all right?" He met the nurse at the door and handed her his business card. "Could you have someone contact me if Mr. Walters has any other visitors? I can be reached at the bottom number twenty-four hours a day."

"Certainly, Sheriff. I'll let the other nurses know," she agreed, slipping the paper into her pocket. As she pulled the rolling table away from the bed, the young nurse smiled at her patient. "Well, now, Mr. Walters, let's see about taking your temperature." When he opened his mouth, she shook her head. "No, dear. With all the damage in there, we'll have to take it the old fashioned way." She snapped her rubber gloves, then flipped open the sheet. "Turn over."

Blinking to clear her eyes, Amanda looked around the room to get her bearings. Due to the dark curtains that she had closed earlier, she was unable to tell if it was daytime or evening. A quick glance showed her that the small digital alarm clock read two-thirty. Lex had both arms wrapped around her waist, and her head was pillowed on Amanda's chest. She reached down and lovingly brushed the hair away from Lex's face, shaking her head when she felt the heat emanating from the flushed skin. *Caught another cold, didn't you? I don't know what I'm going to do with you.* Realizing that Lex would need some aspirin when she awoke, Amanda started trying to extricate herself.

"No," Lex mumbled, tightening her grip, still deeply asleep. "Don't leave me. Please."

Oh, Lex. Amanda wrapped her arms around the shaking shoulders and began to gently rock back and forth. "Shh. It's all right. I'm here." She leaned down and placed tender kisses on the fevered brow beneath her. "You're okay, love. I'm here."

Lex struggled for a few more moments before she jerked awake. "Amanda?" Her normally clear eyes were glazed, and the dark circles beneath them attested to her illness. She shivered slightly and pulled back from her lover's embrace. "What happened?"

Amanda brushed the damp hair away from Lex's face. "You were having a bad dream."

"It seemed so real," Lex whispered. She rubbed her face with one hand, trying to fight down the feeling of total helplessness that pervaded her dreams.

"Do you want to talk about it?"

Shaking her head abruptly, Lex climbed out of bed. "No, I don't really remember it that well, anyway." She peeked through the curtains and almost gasped as the bright afternoon sunlight assaulted her sensitive eyes. "I can't believe I slept so long. I've still got a lot of things to do out at the ranch."

"I don't think so." Amanda jumped out of bed. "You're sick, and you're going to get right back into that bed and rest." She placed one hand on Lex's arm and was surprised when it was shaken off.

"I can't." Lex pulled away, the fear of her dreams still fresh in her mind. "I've gotta—"

Amanda stepped forward again and gently wrapped her arms around her lover's body. "Shh. I'm not going to let you go, Lex." Her quiet resolve was just what her lover needed, and Amanda felt the strong arms embrace her tightly. She slowly led them over to the bed and pushed Lex back against the mattress.

With a shake of her head, Lex tried to lift herself off the bed. "I don't want to go back to sleep," she argued, her voice shaking slightly. When an insistent hand crept under her tee shirt and began to lightly stroke her belly, Lex felt her eyes close involuntarily. "Got stuff to do," she mumbled.

Whatever the dream was about, it certainly scared her. Amanda continued her gentle ministrations until her lover's chest rose and fell in a steady rhythm. After she was certain that Lex was sound asleep, Amanda stopped her stroking. Hearing a rustling in the next room, she eased out of bed. Seeing a light on, she stumbled to the kitchen.

Martha was scraping something from a plastic container into the garbage, muttering under her breath. When she heard a noise in the doorway, she turned around with a concerned look on her face. "What are you doing up? I didn't wake you with all my puttering around in here, did I?"

Amanda shook her head and ambled over to the half-full coffeepot. She yawned as she poured herself a mug and sat down at the table. "No, Lex is running a bit of a fever, and I wanted to get her something for it. I saw the light on in here, and thought I'd make sure that I hadn't left it on by mistake. After I got up, I heard you in here and thought I'd see what you were doing."

Amanda frowned slightly when she noticed the empty container in the housekeeper's hand. "What exactly are you doing? I wouldn't think that the stuff that was brought over after the funeral had gone bad yet."

"True. But after being with you girls for so long, I kinda know what you like." Martha wrinkled her short nose as if she had smelled something terrible. "And I thought I'd spare you from Mrs. Webster's spaghetti with tuna fish. I swear, that woman has a heart the size of Texas, but she makes up some of the most god-awful stuff I've ever heard of."

"Spaghetti with...eeeew." Amanda shook her head. "That's almost as bad as that dish that was loaded with onions. I honestly couldn't tell what everything was." She propped her feet up on the chair across from her and sighed. "Maybe I've just become spoiled. Between my grandpa and you, I've never had it so good."

"Really?" Martha sat down at the table, intrigued. "I figured that you were used to good food. After you got back from California, Lexie mentioned to me that she'd never seen such a huge kitchen. Must have had some really good meals growing up, didn't you?"

Amanda shook her head. "Not really. I mean, we always had cooks." She looked down into her coffee mug, somewhat embarrassed. "Chefs, really. But taste wasn't important, as far as my mother was concerned. It was all about appearance."

Martha patted the younger woman on the arm. "I'm truly sorry to hear that, honey." Deciding that the subject was upsetting Amanda, the housekeeper leaned back in her chair. "Speaking of kitchens, have you seen the new one at the ranch? Lexie won't let me see it yet. The brat keeps telling me it's a surprise."

"No. She won't let me see the house yet, either. I'm almost afraid of what I'll see, to tell you the truth. Does the outside look much different?"

Martha shook her head. "Not so's I can tell. Although she did finally get rid of that awful stucco—the stuff never looked clean. I kinda like the new brick. It's a multicolored red, and looks like one of those expensive houses that you see in magazines."

"Really? I can't wait to see it. We've already got the furniture picked out, just waiting until the inside is finished so it can be delivered. I think that was the hardest part for Lex. She was so upset that the bed her dad had commissioned for her mother was lost in the fire."

"I know. Most everything else was replaceable except for her mother's piano and her father's guns. Thankfully we'd stored a lot of Ms. Victoria's things over at my place, and a lot of the pictures are there. Did you get the new furniture locally, or did you order it off the computer? I swear, I don't understand how folks can shop without actually looking at something."

Amanda chuckled at the disgusted look on Martha's face. "Don't worry. Lex is almost as bad as you are when it comes to things like that. We went down to McCormick's and picked everything out personally, although we did get the appliances at David Wade's store. Now that was a fight."

"Why was it a fight? He and Lexie have been really good friends for years."

"Because he wanted to give us a discount, and Lex wouldn't hear of it. You know, that's one stubborn woman you raised."

Martha waved her hands in front of her. "Oh, no. Don't be blaming her upbringing. She was born stubborn." She watched as Amanda stifled a yawn. "As much as I'm enjoying your company, you need to get yourself back to bed." Martha stood up and pulled Amanda up with her. "Go on. I'll wake you both when dinner's ready. You've got a lot of sleep to catch up on."

Knowing it was useless to argue, Amanda nodded. "Yes, ma'am." She was almost through the door when she turned around. "Dinner? Oh, no."

"What's wrong?"

"I told my Gramma earlier that we'd have dinner with them tonight, but I don't think Lex will be up to it."

Martha made a shooing motion with her hands. "Don't you worry about a thing. I'll give her a call and let her know. Now off to bed with you."

"Thanks, Mada." Amanda rushed over and hugged the heavyset woman, placing a quick kiss on her cheek. "You're the best." She hurried from the room before Martha could say a word.

"I swear, that girl gets more and more like Lexie every day," Martha murmured with a smile. She waited for a moment until she knew she was alone, then grabbed the nearby phone.

"Hello?"

"Anna Leigh? This is Martha. How's everything going?"

"Just wonderful, dear. How are our girls doing? I'll admit I've been a bit concerned that I haven't heard from Mandy much today."

Martha chuckled. "They've been sleeping since this morning. I think the past couple of days finally caught up with them. Lexie got a cold from all that playing around in the rain and mud, so she'll probably sleep until supper time."

"I'm sorry to hear that, Martha. Is there anything we can do for her?" Anna treated the rancher as another granddaughter, and hated to know that Lex was ill or hurting.

"No, I don't think so. But I think the girls are going to stay in tonight, if that's okay with you. Amanda told me that they were supposed to come over to your place this evening for dinner, and I told her I'd give you a call." Martha leaned back against the counter and smiled. "I got that information you've been wanting," she whispered conspiratorially.

"That sounds so cloak-and-dagger, doesn't it? Well? Don't keep me in suspense."

Martha looked around as if she were afraid of being overheard. "McCormick's. But you didn't hear it from me."

"Your secret's safe with me, Martha. Thank you for finding that out for us. You tell the girls to get some rest, and we'll see them another time."

"I sure will. Goodbye." Martha hung up the phone and looked around the kitchen. "I just hope Lexie takes it in the spirit in which it is being given."

The knock on the door caused him to lift his gaze from the paperwork in front of him. Rubbing his eyes, the sheriff had to control the anger brewing in his stomach. "Come in."

"You wanted to see me?" Deputy Thomas swaggered into the room and sat down in one of the visitor's chairs. "I hope this won't take long. I've got a bit more footwork to do on that assault case from yesterday." He leaned back in his seat and stretched his legs out in front of the desk. "I want to canvass the neighborhood and see if I can get anyone to admit seeing that woman's vehicle in the area at the time the assault occurred."

Charlie slowly closed the folder in front of him, silently counting to ten. After a moment, he looked up at the deputy and cleared his throat. "Shouldn't you have done that before you jumped to conclusions and made an arrest?"

Thomas shook his head. "Nah. I had the word of the victim; this is just a formality."

"You arrogant little pup!" Charlie jumped to his feet and slammed his hands down on his desk. "Good police work consists of more than the word of one person, and you put an innocent person in jail because you were too damned sure of yourself to follow through." He stormed around the desk until he was towering over the deputy, who had sat up taller in the chair. "You didn't even bother to check for an alibi before dragging a half-dressed woman out in the rain. You, and our department, could be in for one hell of a lawsuit."

"Give me a break—she had a bloody bandage on her knuckles, and her own brother implicated her in the crime. I followed the proper procedures. How do we know she didn't do it?" Deputy Thomas had only met the sheriff briefly when he was first transferred. He'd had no idea the man could get this out of control.

Clenching his fists to keep from grabbing the seated man, Charlie took a deep breath and stepped back. "Because she was at my house at the time in question." He sat back on the corner of the desk and crossed his arms over his chest. *What do you have to say about that, you little shit?*

"Your house? What was she doing at your house?"

"I'm married to her mother," the sheriff replied softly. "And I don't take kindly to wet-behind-the-ears whelps like you harassing the young woman I consider to be my daughter."

Oh, shit. I shoulda known that everybody in this fucking town was related one way or another. Deciding to take the offensive, Thomas stood up. "Then how do you explain that her own brother incriminated her in the brutal assault that sent him to the hospital?" He pulled out his notepad and flipped through the pages. "I asked him point blank who did that to him, and he answered, 'My sister—Lex Walters.' What was I supposed to think?"

Although he was typically an easy-going man, Charlie Bristol had heard enough. He moved away from the desk and stood directly in front of the smaller man, their noses almost touching. "That's just it, boy. You didn't think. You didn't follow procedure. Had you followed procedure and called for a backup before you went to Lex's house, you would have been told the circumstances between the two of them. You wouldn't have arrested her, and we wouldn't be having this conversation." Wanting to slam the young deputy down on the floor and pound some sense into him, the sheriff stepped back and stood at the window behind his desk. He looked outside at the sun glinting off the chrome of his police cruiser and sighed. "I won't have a loose cannon in my department, Deputy Thomas. Pack up your gear and go back to where you came from. I don't want to see you in my county again."

"Now just a damned minute." Thomas advanced on the sheriff. "You can't—"

Charlie spun around and shoved his finger into the surprised man's chest. "I just did, boy. Either walk out on your own, or I'll have someone escort you." He jabbed hard. "Your choice."

The deputy looked as if he was about to fight back, but backed down. *Obnoxious old fart. We'll just see about this.* He stepped away and started for the door. Turning back, Thomas pointed at the sheriff. "You haven't heard the last of this, Sheriff Bristol. When my superior hears—"

"I've known Walter Simpson longer than you've been alive, son. Don't be threatening me with him. I'd advise you to go back to your own department and study up on procedures, because next time you might not be so lucky." He shook his head as the door slammed behind the departing deputy. *Don't screw with me or my family, boy. You'll lose every time.*

Anna Leigh knocked on the heavy wood door before opening it and stepping inside. She closed the door behind her and stood for a moment, trying to let her eyes adjust to the dark interior after being out in the bright sunlight. "Jacob? Are you in here?" She passed through another doorway into a large room filled with furniture in different stages of construction.

"We're over here, love." Jacob rose from where he had been kneeling and met his wife halfway. "I'd give you a hug, but I'm covered in varnish," he told her as he pulled off his rubber gloves.

Travis stood up also, dusting off the knees of his heavy jeans. "It's good to see you, Anna Leigh. What brings you out to the shop?"

She allowed her husband to lead her over to the piece they had been working on. "Oh, my. This is incredible." Smiling at Travis, she patted him on the arm. "I can't believe he has you out in this dusty old place with him, but it looks like you two work well together."

"I think so. Travis is a natural at this, honey. And if it wasn't for his help, we'd never get this done in time." Travis walked over and pulled a tarp off of another piece of furniture. "Well? What do you think?"

Narrowing her eyes in concentration, Anna Leigh studied the piece carefully. She walked all the way around it, running her hands along the top and sides. After a moment, she bent down and looked at the front, which bore detailed engraving. Touching the carved letters, Anna Leigh turned around and smiled at the waiting men. "This has to be the best work you've ever done, Jacob. I don't think I've ever seen such amazing detail before." Her eyes clouded with tears. "It's absolutely beautiful."

"So, you think it'll be a hit?" Jacob asked, standing next to his wife. He smiled as she turned and wrapped her arms around him, not caring about the varnish that was splattered over his clothes.

"It's perfect." Anna Leigh melted into his embrace as she felt his lips touch her head. "I took care of the other arrangements a few minutes ago. The truck will stop by here on their way and pick everything up."

"I should have had you on my board of directors—you certainly know how to get things done quickly."

"I don't know if that would have been such a good idea, my friend."

"Oh? Why not?"

"Because," Jacob stepped closer to his friend and whispered loudly, ignoring the look his wife was giving him, "you'd have lost control within the first month. She's ruthless."

"Why, you little—" Anna Leigh charged after her laughing husband, who took off at a run. "Wait until I get my hands on you, Jacob Wilson Cauble!"

Martha looked in on the scene before her with a happy sigh. *They look so darned cute together, all snuggled up like that. But neither one of them has had anything to eat since early this morning, so I had better get them up.* She crossed the room and sat down lightly on the bed, reaching up with one hand and gently brushing the dark hair away from the slumbering woman's face.

Lex was curled up facing the doorway with Amanda tucked snugly behind her, one arm draped possessively across her waist. She smiled in her sleep at the housekeeper's touch, obviously dreaming.

"Lexie, it's time to wake up." Martha stroked the flushed cheek softly. "C'mon. Let me see those baby blues."

"Mmm." Lex stretched and leaned into the touch, the cool hand feeling good against her fevered skin. She turned her face and kissed the palm, waking up when she heard the familiar snicker. "Mada?" *Oh, God. I can't believe I did that.* She blinked several times and propped her head up on one hand. "What time is it?"

Ruffling the dark hair, Martha laughed. "It's almost six in the evening, hon. I think you need to get up and get something in your tummy before it rebels."

"Six? I've slept that long?"

"Yep. I'd have let you sleep even longer, but you're nothing but skin and bones right now. You can't afford to miss any more meals."

"C'mon, Mada. I'm not gonna blow away anytime soon," Lex argued. A tickle on her belly caused her to chuckle. "Looks like someone's playing possum." She rolled over slightly and grinned at her lover. "Ready for dinner?"

Amanda wriggled her eyebrows suggestively. "Oh, yeah." When she realized that Martha was sitting on the bed, she blushed and buried her head in the pillow. "Uh, I mean...oh, darn."

Martha laughed and stood up. "I think I'll give you girls a chance to get awake. Don't be too long, or your dinner will get cold." She quickly excused herself and left the room, much to Amanda's relief.

"I can't believe I said that." Amanda pulled the sheets over her face in embarrassment. "She probably thinks I'm some sort of sex maniac or something," she mumbled from beneath the covers.

Lex laughed, then rolled over and began to search for a way to reach her lover. "C'mon out of there, you little deviant," she teased, pulling ineffectually at the top of the covers.

"No." Amanda crawled lower, tightening her grip on the sheet over her head.

"If it makes you feel any better," Lex offered as she climbed off the bed, "I kissed her hand, 'cause I thought it was you." She pulled the sheets away from the bottom of the bed and peeked under the covers. "Peek-a-boo."

Amanda glowered at the woman who continued to crawl up her body. "Stop it." She squirmed as long fingers found their way under her shirt. "Lex, I'm warning you."

"Mm-hmm." Lex continued to place kisses along Amanda's smooth skin.

"You two quit playing around and get in here," Martha yelled from the kitchen. "Don't make me come back in there and get you."

"Busted." Amanda ruffled her fingers through Lex's hair, then dropped a quick kiss on pouting lips and squirmed away. "C'mon, Slim. I really don't want her catching us in here like this again." She flipped the covers off the bed and scooted away quickly.

Lex shook her head as Amanda grabbed a robe and raced from the room. "Brat."

When she finally stepped into the kitchen, Lex was pleasantly surprised to see Charlie sitting at the table. "Hi, Uncle Charlie. It's good to see you." She bent down and placed a kiss on his cheek before sitting across from him and next to Amanda.

"Hello there. I was just telling everyone what a nice visit I had with your brother today." He smiled broadly at Martha, who shook her head.

"If the man's still on the loose, then it couldn't have been too good. He should be put in jail for the trouble he's caused Lexie." Martha placed a large platter on the table.

Lex looked down at her plate. As much as she disliked the man, he was her brother. "How did he look, Charlie? I heard he got beaten pretty badly."

Charlie shrugged his shoulders. "He's got a bunch of tiny little cuts all over his face, and his eyes are black and puffy from the broken nose. But I think the worst of the damage is his mouth."

"That's not a surprise," Lex muttered.

Amanda poked her partner in the ribs. "Be nice." She looked up at Charlie, hoping he'd continue. "What's wrong with his mouth?"

"He's missing several of his teeth, and the swelling is horrible. I never thought I'd say this, but I almost felt sorry for him."

Lex's fork stopped on the way to her mouth. "He's that badly hurt?"

"I don't think it's that serious, but it certainly looks painful. The doctor I spoke to before I left said that they were going to release him day after tomorrow. He's in for a long haul with an orthodontic surgeon, I'll bet." Charlie accepted a generous helping of roast from Martha. "Thanks, sweetheart."

"Day after tomorrow?" Lex met Martha's curious glance. "Maybe I should go over and see him tomorrow, and see if he needs anything."

"You'll do no such thing!" The housekeeper slapped her hand on the table in disgust. "You're fighting off a cold, Lexie. He's not worth the aggravation."

"He's family, Martha. And—"

"No, Lexie. He's got some of the same blood running though him, that's true; but family wouldn't act the way he does. And some of the things he did to you when you were growing up, I can never forgive him for." Martha reached across the table and took one of Lex's hands in hers. "Don't believe for a moment that he's ever gonna change. You'll just end up getting hurt."

Lex looked down at her plate, her appetite gone. "But if I don't try, I'm no better than he is." She felt Martha squeeze her fingers in compassion. "I can't stop hoping that one day, either sooner or later, he'll come around and be the brother I need him to be."

"Maybe," Martha conceded. "But I just don't want you to open yourself up to being hurt by him, honey."

"Thanks. But I know what an ass he is—you don't have to worry about me." Lex smiled at Martha and released her hand. "Dinner smells great. You're gonna spoil us, you know."

"I'm glad she has a houseful to cook for again. Since Ronnie's out of town on that school trip, I'm the only one benefiting from her cooking." Charlie leaned back and rubbed his stomach. "She keeps it up, and I'm gonna have to buy bigger britches."

Amanda eyed the slim man. "I think you have a ways to go before that happens, Charlie." She winked at her lover. "But I know what you mean. I bet I gained ten pounds the first month I lived out at the ranch."

"Yeah, right." Lex leaned over and pinched her in the ribs. "I don't think so, kiddo."

Giggling, Amanda slapped Lex's hand away. "Stop that." She was secretly relieved that the all-day nap seemed to have perked up her partner. "Quit picking on me and eat your dinner."

"Yes, ma'am." Lex winked at the older couple and started eating. "She's worse than Martha, sometimes," she whispered across the table to Charlie. A light slap on her leg caused Lex to chuckle, and concentrate on her food.

"Teach you to mess with me," Amanda shared a knowing smile with Martha.

Chapter 11

Lex shifted the basket of flowers to her right hand nervously. She paused before knocking on the door, unsure of why she was there. *What in the hell was I thinking? I shouldn't have come here. All this is going to accomplish is starting another fight.* She was about to turn away when the door opened and a middle-aged nurse smiled at her.

"Oh. I didn't realize that Mr. Walters had a visitor. I'm afraid I just gave him something for pain, but you're welcome to come in for a minute and see him."

"Uh, sure." Lex smiled at the smaller woman and followed her into the room. *So much for running like a chicken with its tail feathers on fire.* "Thanks."

"No problem, dear. If you need anything, just give me a buzz." The nurse waved as she left the room.

Hubert's head was turned away from Lex, so she couldn't see if he was even awake. *I could just leave the flowers and sneak out of the room.* She stepped closer to set the basket on the nearby table.

When Hubert heard feet shuffling by his bed, he spun his head around fearfully. With his eyes still swollen, it took a moment for him to realize who was in his room. "Whu—"

"Hello, Hubert. Thought I'd drop by and see how you're doing." Lex placed the flowers on the table and put her hands in her pockets. "How are you feeling?"

"Whu do you care?" he mumbled painfully. "Did you cobe here do gload?"

"No. Like it or not, we're family. And no matter what's been between us in the past, I still care about what happens to you." Lex stepped closer and studied his face, frowning sympathetically. "Is there anything I can get for you?"

"Puck you! You dink you so buch bedder dan me."

"No, I never—"

He pointed a finger at Lex, who had backed up a step. "Idn't id bad enoup you killed our podder? Do you habe do come in here and lord id ober me, doo?"

Even though she was used to his attitude, Lex still felt the stab of each vicious word. "I didn't." Lex tripped over a chair as she tried to back away from his hatred. "You know that's not what happened, Hubert. He asked me—"

"Bitch! You killed him. Just so you could ged your hands on de wanch."

Lex picked herself up off the floor and shook her head. "No. It was what he wanted. Dad didn't want to die in the hospital, Hubert. If you'd come to see him when he was here, he would have told you that."

Hubert wrinkled his face as if he were trying to spit. "Bulldid! I was doo budy working. He neber wiked me anyway." Reaching for the glass of water on the table, he noisily sucked through the straw. After draining the glass, Hubert glared at his sister. "You couldn't waid for him to die, so you killed him."

"That's not true," Lex argued, as she fought to keep the tears from falling. "He was very sick, and the doctors told us it was only a matter of time. At least he died happy." She ducked as her brother threw the empty glass across the room, almost hitting her in the head.

"Ged oud," he yelled.

The nurse from earlier almost ran into the room. "What on earth is going on in here?" She stared at Lex, waiting for an answer.

"I was just leaving." Lex stepped around the nurse and slipped on the broken glass, falling to one knee. "Damn." She quickly got up and raced from the room, leaving the concerned nurse behind.

Amanda took a deep breath before opening the door. *I don't know why I have to do this. I'm sure my leg will get better on its own.* She straightened her shoulders and stepped into the small office, smiling at the woman who greeted her.

"Hello there. Please sign in, and fill out this paperwork. Things are a bit slow this morning, so someone will be with you shortly." The receptionist, who wasn't much older than Amanda, handed her a clipboard and went back to staring at her computer screen.

"Okay. Thanks." Taking a seat near the door, Amanda set her briefcase and purse down on the chair next to her, and read over the form. *Jeez. Sometimes I wish I just carried extra copies of my life story around—would certainly make filling this stuff out a lot easier.*

She had just finished the last question when another door opened and a perky blonde woman wearing multi-colored surgical scrubs looked around the room. "Amanda Cauble?"

"That's me." After gathering up her belongings, Amanda dropped the clipboard on the receptionist's desk and followed the woman. *I bet she was a cheerleader in school. Uck. Save me from perky people.*

"All righty, if you'll just step into room number two, the therapist will be with you in a couple of minutes, okay?"

Amanda followed her instructions. "Okey dokey," she mimicked the woman's overly cheerful demeanor. When the door closed, she sat down on a chair. "God, I hope Lex is having a better day than I am." Dr. Anderson had checked her leg earlier, and sent Amanda directly to this office. He was concerned that the injury had left her right leg weak, and wanted to take every precaution to see that it healed properly.

Moments later, a light knock on the door signaled the arrival of the therapist. When the door opened, a tall, well-built man stepped into the room. He had dark hair and eyes and appeared to be in his mid-thirties. After glancing at her file, he looked up and met Amanda's gaze. He held out a hand as he introduced himself. "Well, hello there. I'm Peter Chatwick, and it appears that I'll be your physical therapist for the next few weeks."

She shook his hand and smiled. "Hi. I'm Amanda Cauble. I don't know why Dr. Anderson was so insistent that I come here, to tell you the truth. My leg doesn't give me that much trouble." Shaking her head she added, "I'm afraid this is just a waste of your time."

"Amanda. I can call you Amanda, can't I?" At the young woman's nod, he continued. "From the notes that Dr. Anderson faxed over, he's concerned that you've lost too much strength and flexibility in your leg. If it's not rehabbed, it could cause you serious problems down the road." Peter motioned to the long table against one wall. "Would you mind sitting up there, and I'll just have a look."

Glad that she had worn sweat pants to the doctor's office, Amanda easily sat up on the paper-covered cushioned table. She gasped as he slid up the leg of her sweats, his cool hands gently grasping her calf.

"Sorry about that. We keep it so cool in the offices that I have terminally cold hands." Peter turned her leg in several different motions, watching Amanda's face for any sign of discomfort. "Let's just run a few little tests and see what we come up with, all right?" He found himself charmed by the young woman's open manner. "I promise to be gentle."

Half an hour later, Amanda slowly limped from the physical therapist's office. She was upset that she would have to spend three days a week for the next several weeks in therapy to strengthen her slow healing leg. *I can't believe this.* Although he had not made any overtly indecent overtures, she felt vaguely uncomfortable with the way the good-looking therapist acted around her. *He didn't exactly flirt, but I don't like the way he looked at me.* She climbed into her car and decided to stop by her grandmother's on the way to the office. *I need to change clothes before I go to work, anyway.*

Twinkling blue eyes studied the woman sitting on the bench. "Well, well. Who do we have here?" The tall woman stood directly in front of the seat and crossed her arms over her chest. "You look like you're waiting for someone."

"I am, you big goofball." Barbara scooted over so that there was room enough for two on the outdoor bench. She had been sitting in the town square for almost ten minutes, waiting for her friend to show up. "I hope you brought something decent for lunch; I'm starved."

"Now it comes out. You only hang around me for my food gathering skills." Janna sat down and rummaged through a large paper bag.

"Depends on what you brought," the smaller woman teased. They had been seeing each other since New Year's Eve, when

Janna had defended Barbara from Hubert's attack at the Ladies Auxiliary dance. "It better not be another greasy hamburger. Thanks to you, I've gained five pounds in the last couple of months."

Janna laughed as she pulled a wrapped bundle from the bag. "You're safe this time. It's a submarine sandwich from the deli on the corner." She took the other package and set the crumpled bag on the bench beside her. "And for your information, you're still too skinny. So I wouldn't worry about it if I were you."

They ate their lunch in companionable silence, both enjoying the crisp spring day. A large dark-green truck rumbled by, coming to a stop on the other side of the square from where they were sitting. It parked underneath a group of shade trees, but the driver made no attempt to leave the cab. Barbara had finished her sandwich and studied the vehicle carefully. "Isn't that Lex's new truck?" she asked her friend. "I wonder what she's doing just sitting there."

"You know, I think you're right. Maybe she just needed a quiet place to rest for a bit. Things have been pretty rough for her lately." Janna strained to see the driver's side of the truck. "The windows are too darkly tinted to see inside. Maybe I should go over and see if she's okay." Noticing a garbage can on the other side of the street, she stood and gathered up their trash. "I'll be right back."

Barbara watched the tall figure walk purposefully across the street, a soft smile on her face. They had frequently exchanged kisses, and she didn't know how much longer she could keep from pushing their relationship to the next level. *She is just so wonderful. I never thought I'd feel this way about someone, especially in this town.* Janna had been almost shy in their courtship, which only endeared her to the bank teller even more.

Tossing the handful of trash into the nearby garbage can, Janna cut a quick glance at the side window of the truck. The driver's head was against the steering wheel, her face hidden between her arms. Torn between worry and the knowledge that her friend might want to be alone, Janna looked across the street to where Barbara was sitting. She held up her hands and shrugged her shoulders, and sighed when her friend made a shooing motion with her hands. *Great. Hope she is good with puzzles, 'cause if I bother Lex and she wants to be left alone, she could tear me apart.* Gathering her courage, Janna tapped lightly on the window.

Of all the stupid, idiotic things to do, Lexington, that had to be top of the list. You know the sorry bastard will never change. Why do you subject yourself to him over and over? A light knock on the window broke into Lex's mental self-chastising. Struggling to control the tears that coursed down her face, she refused to look up. *Maybe if I ignore them, they'll just go away.* A heavier, more insistent knock erased that possibility. *Shit.* "Go 'way."

Janna heard the entreaty, but her concern outweighed her good sense. "Lex? Are you okay?"

"Leave me the hell alone," Lex yelled, not caring who was at the window. "Just," her voice broke, "go away, please."

Janna reached over and opened the door, ignoring the half-sobbed plea. "I'm sorry. I can't do that, Lex. We're friends, and friends don't let friends hurt." She leaned down to look at the rancher's face. "Are you injured?"

Lex sniffled and wiped her eyes with the palms of her hands. "No. Just stupid." She pulled a tissue from the box of facial tissue in the truck's console and blew her nose.

"You could be called a lot of things, my friend, but stupid isn't one of them." Janna reached over and put her hand on Lex's shoulder. "Is there something I can do? Maybe go kick someone's ass for you?"

A mirthless laugh escapted Lex's lips. "Uh, no. Somebody beat you to it." She turned her head and looked up into Janna's concerned face. "You haven't seen Hubert lately, have you?" *Lord knows she could do that kind of damage to him, not that I'd blame her any.*

"No. Should I have?" Janna's face reddened in anger. "Did he do something to you?"

"No, not really. He's in the hospital, and I made the mistake of going to see him."

"Hospital? What happened to him?"

"Someone kicked his ass," Lex responded drolly. "Real good, too."

"Good!" Realizing how that sounded, Janna squeezed her friend's shoulder. "Sorry. I know he's your brother, but—"

"But he's a huge pain in the ass. I know." Lex took a deep breath and wiped her eyes again. "Sorry I yelled at you, Janna."

"No problem, my friend. Barbara and I were just about to run over to the diner for chocolate shakes. You wanna come?" Although it wasn't exactly true, Janna hated to see Lex sit around by herself when she was in this state. "C'mon, you can help me convince Barbara that she's not fat."

Lex stepped out of the truck and closed the door. "You having that problem, too? Amanda swears that Martha's cooking has made her put on pounds." She felt Janna's reassuring arm around her shoulders and leaned into the embrace. *It's good to have friends.*

Barbara watched as the two women walked across the street, Janna's arm around Lex. Although they were close to the same height, the difference in their appearance was virtually night and day. Lex had the dark good looks, with her almost black hair, while Janna's light blonde hair was short and her eyes several shades lighter than the rancher's. *I bet they have no idea how good they look.* She studied both forms appreciatively, then frowned.

"What's up?" Janna asked, seeing the frown on her girlfriend's face.

"Lex, what happened to your leg? You're bleeding." Barbara pointed to the torn knee on Lex's faded jeans, then stood in concern. "Are you okay?"

Both women stopped, and Janna dropped to her knees to check out the injury. "Damn, Lex. This looks nasty." She looked back up at her friend. "What did you do?"

"I dunno." Lex allowed the two women to guide her to the bench as she puzzled over the origin of the gash. "Oh. I must have cut it when I fell. No big deal." She looked down at the ripped denim. "It doesn't hurt."

"When did you fall?" Barbara asked as she dabbed around the injury with a paper napkin she had saved from her lunch. "You really should get this checked out. It looks like there's something in your knee."

Lex tore the jeans more so that she could get a better look. "Shit. I must have landed on a piece of glass." She started to pull out the small bloody small wedge of glass, but her hand was captured by Barbara's.

"Hold on. You could cut your fingers on that."

"It'll feel better if I just get the glass out." Lex didn't feel like seeking medical attention for such a minor injury. "Would you mind?"

Barbara folded up another paper napkin and wrapped it around the embedded shard. "Okay, don't move." Biting her lip, she tugged gently until the piece of glass pulled free. "Good Lord, Lex. How were you able to walk with that in there?" She held up the offending glass and studied it. The bloody chunk was nearly an inch wide, and about half that size long.

"I honestly didn't feel it," Lex mumbled. She looked up as Janna raced across the town square, ducking into a nearby shop. "Don't tell me she can't handle the sight of blood."

Barbara followed her gaze. "I don't know. She seemed okay." Moments later, Janna rushed back across the street with a paper bag in her hand.

"Sorry about that, but I thought we might need some supplies." She dropped down beside Barbara and pulled a few things from her bag. "Eeww. That looks painful."

"Hush." Barbara thumped her on the shoulder and took the items away from her. "Good job, honey. This will work perfectly." She flipped her light brown hair over one shoulder to keep it out of her way.

Lex propped one arm on her good leg, and dropped her chin into her open palm. "You're not gonna give me stitches, are you?"

"No, silly. I don't think it's that bad. Just needs to be cleaned up and bandaged."

"Good. 'Cause I don't like needles."

Janna looked up at the rancher, trying to decide if she was teasing or not. *The woman walks around with glass embedded in her leg, but is afraid of a needle? Jeez.* When Lex flinched, Janna felt responsible for her pain. "I'm sorry. They didn't have any of the no-sting ointment. Just the stuff that burns like hell."

"That's all right. I figure I'll live." Lex continued to watch Barbara work, fascinated by the woman's steady hands. "You do this often? Sure seem good at it."

Barbara looked up. "Not really. Although I do some volunteer work at the hospital, I never do anything like this." She kept the small gash closed with a couple of butterfly bandages, then covered it up with a gauze pad and tape. "There. That should take care of it. But you might want to let a doctor check it out and make sure that there's no more glass under your skin."

Lex shook her head. "No need. I think you got it." She stood up and gingerly put weight on the injured leg. "You've got a really nice touch, Barbara. It doesn't even hurt. Thanks."

"You're welcome, although I'm afraid your jeans are ruined." Barbara stood up and handed the supplies to Janna, who put them back in her bag.

"Nah. I'll just bribe Martha, and she'll patch them up, good as new. She's used to it by now." Lex looked at the two women and smiled. "How about I buy the chocolate shakes, for taking such good care of me?"

Barbara peered over at Janna, who suddenly looked extremely guilty. *Chocolate shakes, huh?* She linked her arm with Lex's and laughed. "Sounds good to me."

Janna watched as the two women headed for the diner, arm in arm. "Oh, sure. Run off with my woman, why don't you." Smiling at their laughter, she jogged to catch up with them.

"Calm down, Grandpa. It's really not that bad." Amanda had told her grandparents and Travis about her visit to the physical therapist, and was now exercising a little damage control. "It's probably just me."

"I don't think so, Mandy. You're an excellent judge of character, and if this man somehow makes you feel uncomfortable, then it certainly is not you." Anna Leigh reached over and patted her husband's hand, trying to calm him.

"Harumph. I still want to go over to that office and horsewhip him," Jacob grumbled. His ordinarily gentle nature fell by the wayside when anything threatened his family. He looked over at Travis, who was trying to keep a grin off his face. "Well? What if it was your granddaughter this happened to?"

Travis's smile widened. "As far as I'm concerned, it is my granddaughter." He winked at Amanda. "But I also know that she's more than capable of taking care of herself, so I'm not too terribly worried just yet."

"Thanks, Grandpa Travis. Honestly, he's been nothing but professional. It's just a feeling I got—like I'm dessert or something."

If his wife hadn't been holding on to his hand, Jacob would have jumped from the loveseat where he and Anna Leigh were sitting. "That tears it. I'm going down there and give that man a good thumping."

Upset with herself for causing such distress, Amanda got up from her chair and dropped to her knees at her grandfather's feet. "Please, Grandpa." She took his hands in hers and squeezed them gently. "I really appreciate how you feel, but I promise you that if he does anything that I'm not comfortable with, I'll let you have what's left of him."

"I guess I'll just have to accept that, won't I, Peanut?" He smiled down into her worried face. "I know you're perfectly capable of taking care of yourself, but I can't help feeling highly protective of you." Jacob released her hand to cradle Amanda's face. "You'll always be my little girl, no matter how old or how capable you become."

"And you'll always be the number one man in my heart." Even though she loved her new relationship with her father, Amanda would always treasure the role her grandfather played in her life. He was the father figure she'd needed, always available to provide love and guidance as she grew up.

Anna Leigh was about to say something when the phone rang. "I'll get that," she said, as she rose and crossed over to the table where the phone lay. "Hello?" She listened for a moment and turned to face the others. "It's for you, Travis."

"Thank you." He stood up and accepted the phone. "This is Travis Edwards, what can I do for you? You did? Well, it's about damned time. You've had months to— No. Bring the information over here. Yes, now." He hung up the phone in disgust. Seeing the others looking at him curiously, Travis blushed. "Sorry about that, everyone."

"You have nothing to apologize for, Travis," Anna Leigh assured him. "I take it we're about to have a visitor? We can always make ourselves scarce if you need privacy."

"No, that won't be necessary." Crossing to help Amanda to her feet, he grasped her hands and looked into her eyes. "Honey, after the accident, I hired a private investigator to try and find out who nearly killed you two girls." He saw her eyes widen in surprise. "Unfortunately, whoever did it covered their tracks very well, and it's taken the detective this long to find anything."

Shocked, Amanda allowed him to help her to a nearby chair. "Are you telling me that you know who ran us off the road?"

"Not exactly. But he did say that he thinks he may have found the truck. I'm hoping that once I give the information to the sheriff, it will be easier for him to pick up their trail."

Jacob shook his head. "That's incredible, Travis. Why didn't you tell anyone that you had hired a private investigator? We would have been more than happy to help with the expense."

"It really wasn't necessary, my friend. I've accumulated quite a tidy nest egg in the past few years, and I have no real bills to pay." Travis shook a finger at the other man in mock anger. "Especially since a certain couple won't let me pay rent while I'm staying with them."

"Please, you're family, Travis. I could no more ask you for rent than I could Mandy over there," Anna Leigh scoffed. "You certainly make up for it, sneaking around and paying for the groceries and utilities when we're not looking."

The distinguished man had the sense to blush. "Um." He ran a hand through his thick silver hair and looked at Amanda.

"Don't look at me to save you, handsome. You got yourself into this one," Amanda teased, glad for the change of subject. The accident had happened over three months before, yet the pain and fear she had felt was still fresh in her mind.

"I need to call Charlie and see if he has time to come over. I'd like for him to be here when the man gives us what he has." Deciding a retreat was in order before Anna Leigh realized just how much money he had been contributing to the household, Travis hastily left the room.

When the three women entered the diner, they found out that the machine that blended the milkshakes was broken. Not wanting Lex to head out on her own, Janna suggested that they go around the corner to Dooley's, one of the local bars. She had already decided to take the rest of the day off to watch over her highly emotional friend. As they stepped into the dark pub, Janna rubbed her hands together gleefully. "How about we play a little pool? I really don't feel like going back to the office today."

"Uh, okay. But I warn you, I truly suck at pool." Lex walked over to the bar and then turned back to her friends. "What would y'all like?"

"I'll have a glass of iced tea." Barbara poked Janna in the ribs. "Some of us have to go back to work today."

"Not my fault, darlin'. You could always accept my offer and have a really nice boss, you know."

"Right. And like I told you, darlin'," Barbara stressed the word sweetly, "I've worked at the bank for almost six years. I really enjoy it there."

Afraid she was about to get into more trouble than she could handle, Janna looked over at Lex. "Why don't you and I work on a pitcher of beer? Might as well enjoy playing hooky, don't you agree?"

"Sure. I'll get the first round." Lex headed for the bar.

"That's not fair." Barbara linked arms with Janna and sighed. "I can only stay for about fifteen minutes, then I've got to run."

"Works for me. Fifteen minutes with you is much better than a second without you," Janna whispered into her ear, nibbling lightly on the lobe.

Lex walked over to where they were standing, placing a tray laden with the drinks on the closest table. "The bartender told me that since it's so slow, we can have the table for free today." She chuckled a bit. "I think he was trying to be a bit more friendly with me than he should be, but what the hell."

Janna wrapped an arm around her friend's shoulder. "Should Amanda be jealous?"

"I don't think so, smartass." Lex handed her the tray of balls. "Since you're so frisky, you can rack 'em."

"Gee, thanks." Janna began to set up the colorful array on the table.

Barbara studied Lex carefully. Although the rancher was friendly enough to them, she could tell that something was still bothering her. Reaching across the table and touching the other woman's hand, she asked, "How are you doing, Lex? Is there anything that I can do for you?"

Considering the question seriously for a long moment, Lex finally shook her head. "I don't think so, Barbara. But thanks." She checked her watch, then realized that Amanda wouldn't be home from the office for several hours. *Might as well enjoy the company, I guess.* She took a long swallow of beer, relaxing a bit when it hit her empty stomach.

Chapter 12

The nervous man gently shook the bouquet of flowers he was holding, killing time while he waited for someone to answer the door. He looked down at his khaki slacks and berated himself. *Maybe I shouldn't have brought flowers. What if she's allergic? I should have gotten roses instead of the wildflower mix. Maybe I should have worn a tie. She'll probably think I'm not taking it seriously. What if—* His internal argument was halted in mid-question when the door opened and a lovely, slightly overweight woman wearing dark jeans and a pale green cotton blouse smiled brightly at him.

Lois opened the door wider and stepped back. "Michael. Please come in." Her shoulder-length brown hair bounced slightly as she led him into the living room of the modest home. "Why don't you have a seat. Would you like something to drink?"

He started to sit down, but remembered what he was holding and thrust the bouquet in front of his body. "Um, these are for you." Michael watched as Lois took the bouquet from him and inhaled deeply of their scent.

She smiled happily, her dark eyes twinkling. "Thank you. What a thoughtful thing for you to do. I haven't been given flowers in years." Still in shock, Lois directed him to the sofa. "Oh, my. I can't get over it. Flowers! Let me just go put these in water. I'll be right back." Rushing from the room, she continued to rave about his thoughtfulness. "I just love wildflowers, they're so colorful."

Michael chuckled as he sat down. *Well, I guess that worked out okay. And she's dressed pretty casually, too. Now I don't feel so bad. I've never seen someone get so excited over such a little thing.* When she came back into the room, he stood up. "I'm glad you liked them. To tell you the truth, I wasn't sure if you would."

The decorator laughed and sat down, Michael reurned to his seat beside her. "Not like flowers? Goodness." She patted Michael on the knee. "They really are lovely, thank you. Do you have any preferences for what you'd like to do tonight?"

"Ah, not really. I'm still learning my way around. I'm afraid that Somerville has changed quite a bit from when I grew up here." *When was the last time a woman asked me what I wanted to do? Now I begin to see what I've been missing for so many years.* Michael turned so that he could focus more on Lois. "I was hoping you had a few good ideas."

"Do you like to dance? There's a quiet little bar off the town square that has a pretty good deejay after six."

Nodding his agreement, Michael stood up. "That sounds like fun. Although I hope you are wearing steel-toed shoes. I haven't danced in I don't know how long."

Lois stood up also, her bright smile infectious. "Me either. So I guess we'll just have to wing it, don't you agree?" She led him to the door, but turned back before exiting. "Don't think me too forward, but I'd like to buy you dinner tonight." When Michael opened his mouth to argue, she held up one hand. "Please? Consider it a payment for helping me decide on which wallpaper to hang in the guestrooms. It would have taken me hours to finally get Lexington to decide, if I could have kept her there with me at all."

"Well, since you put it that way, I don't see how I can refuse." Michael stepped outside with her and waited as Lois locked the door. "But only if you let me at least buy the drinks."

"It's a deal," Lois agreed, sighing happily as he opened the car door for her. *Handsome, comes from a wonderful family, and a gentleman to boot. The woman that let him get away should be locked up.* She had no way of knowing just how accurate her assessment was.

Amanda stepped out of the living room with a concerned look on her face. The young woman had spent the last half-hour trying to track down her errant partner, with no luck. She had decided to take the rest of the day off from work so that she could sit in on the meeting with the private investigator, and wanted to let Lex know where she was. Amanda was so lost in her thoughts that she almost knocked down her grandmother in the front entryway. "Oh! I'm sorry, Gramma. I didn't see you there."

"That's quite all right, dear. You look troubled, is something the matter?" Anna Leigh put an arm around Amanda's waist and guided her to the kitchen. "Sit down and tell me what's bothering you."

"I'm worried about Lex. She's not at home, and according to Martha, she hasn't even been out to the ranch today. I've called around, but no one's seen her." Amanda glanced up at the clock on the wall. "It's almost six o'clock. Where on earth could she be?"

Sitting down next to her granddaughter, Anna Leigh placed her hand on Amanda's arm. "Did she give you any idea what she was going to do today?"

"No, not really. I guess I just assumed that she'd spend time on the construction of the house while I went to work." She looked down at the tablecloth. "I kinda forgot to mention to Lex that I had a doctor's appointment today. She's going to be furious with me when she finds out."

"Mandy, you can't keep something like that from Lexington. She loves you, and deserves to know these things."

"I know. But I was afraid that if she knew, she'd want to come with me. And you know how antsy she gets at the doctor's office. I just didn't want her to suffer through that because of me."

Travis walked into the kitchen and spotted the women at the table. "Hello, ladies." He saw the look on Amanda's face and sat down on the other side of her. "What's the matter? Were you able to reach Lexie and ask her to come over for dinner?"

"No. She doesn't answer her cell phone, and I can't seem to find her anywhere. She's not at home, and she hasn't been at the ranch today, either. I don't know what to think."

"Maybe she had some errands to run here in town. Did she say anything to you this morning?" He exchanged glances with Anna Leigh, who shrugged her shoulders. "You girls didn't have a spat or anything, did you?"

"No, of course not." Although, now that she thought about it, maybe she had said something that had upset her lover before they had gone their separate ways. Amanda thought back to the early morning, when they were both getting ready for the day. Actually, Amanda sat in her bathrobe and enjoyed the view as Lex got ready.

Lex was being overly quiet, her demeanor suggesting that her mind was somewhere else. Her partially clad form stomped back and forth from the bedroom to the bathroom several times, a scowl marring her beautiful face. "Amanda, have you seen my hairbrush? It's not on the bathroom counter or on the dresser."

"The black-handled one?" Amanda was stretched out on the bed, leaning back against the headboard. Not wanting Lex to know about her doctor's appointment, she decided not to get dressed until her lover was out of the house. Wearing sweats would be a dead giveaway that I'm not going to work, that's for sure. *As she took another sip of her coffee, Amanda couldn't help but notice that something was bothering her friend.*

"Yes."

"The one that's in your hand?"

Lex stared at the offending item as if it had appeared by magic. "Uh, yeah. Thanks." She stepped back into the bathroom, muttering under her breath.

Hoping to change the subject and cheer up the obviously distracted woman, Amanda tried another tack. "So," she asked loudly so as to be heard, "what are your plans for today?" When she didn't get an answer, she tried again. "Honey? Did you hear me?" There was only silence from the other room. Concerned, Amanda climbed off the bed and walked over to stand in the bathroom doorway. "Lex?"

"I heard you. I just didn't think that I had to account for every second of every day." Lex threw the brush onto the counter, then ran one hand down her face. "I'm sorry, Amanda. I didn't mean to jump all over you." She turned away, ashamed of her outburst. "I don't know what's wrong with me lately."

"Honey," Amanda stepped into the small room and carefully placed her hand on the bare back. Lex was wearing her jeans but hadn't put on a shirt, content to run around in just a beige satin bra. "It's okay, really. I know you didn't mean anything by it."

Turning back to face Amanda, Lex fought to keep her composure. "No, it's not okay. I would rather cut off my arm than intentionally hurt you. It's just that I've got such a short fuse right now, and I don't know how to get past this."

With one hand, Amanda took Lex's arm and pulled her out of the bathroom and led her to the bed. She pushed her lover down gently and sat beside her. "We'll get past it, together." She ran her hand down the muscular arm until their fingers entwined. "You've had a lot of things on your mind lately. Would it help to talk about it?"

"I dunno." Lex looked down at their linked hands. "I feel like I'm about all talked out."

Amanda released her and wrapped her arm around the strong shoulders. "Okay, no talking for now. But I want you to know that I'm here for you, and we can talk about this any time you're ready." She leaned over until her head was under Lex's chin, and she kissed the bare skin. "Do me a favor?"

Still feeling the effects of the gentle kiss to her throat, Lex blinked. "Uh, sure." She tilted her head downward and sniffed the flowery bouquet of Amanda's shampoo. "Mmm. What?"

"Take it easy today? I'd feel a whole lot better knowing that you weren't trying to overdo it. Especially since you're just getting better from that cold." She was very thankful that Lex seemed to suffer no lasting effects from the illness she had picked up while spending the night in lockup.

"I'm fine, Amanda. And I've got a lot of things that need to be done. I can't just—" Lex paused, thinking about her partner's request. "Okay."

"Really? Just like that?"

"Yeah. Just like that." Lex leaned down and covered Amanda's lips with her own.

"Amanda? Are you all right?" Travis's concerned voice broke through her thoughts.

"Huh?" *Lex gave up way too easily this morning. I should have gotten her to stay home longer and then tried to get her to open up about what was bothering her.* "Oh, yes. I'm sorry about that."

"What's going on in that cute little head of yours, Mandy? Is there something we can do to help you?" Anna Leigh had a pretty good idea what, or whom, her granddaughter's mind was on, but wanted to make sure that the young woman knew that her family was there if she needed them.

"Not at the moment, Gramma. But as soon as I know something, I'll let you know." Amanda stood up and left the room, determined to find Lex and have a long talk with her.

Janna rose awkwardly from the table, placing one hand on the back of the chair to keep her balance. "I'll be back in a minute. You wanna order another one?" she asked, pointing to the empty pitcher. They had been at the small bar all afternoon, alternating between playing pool and polishing off containers of beer. "I gotta—" She pointed with her thumb over her shoulder at the restrooms.

"Sure. I'll take care of it." Lex grinned as her friend slowly made her way to the back of the room. They had matched each other glass for glass, and the rancher was hard-pressed to remember just how many pitchers of beer they had consumed. She waved at the waitress, who had come on duty in the last hour.

The young blonde weaved her way through the tall tables, balancing her tray on one ample hip. She was about Amanda's age and height, but was easily forty or so pounds heavier. "Hiya, hon. You gals need another round?"

"Yep." Lex pulled a ten-dollar bill from her wallet and tossed it on the tray. "Keep the change."

"Ooh. I sure will." She hurried away, intent on keeping a good customer happy.

Lex rubbed her face as she tried to sort out her feelings. *Jeez, Lexington, getting drunk isn't gonna help matters any.* But no matter how hard she tried, she just couldn't summon up the desire to stop. *I'll worry about it later. One afternoon out isn't gonna hurt me.* Before she could dwell too deeply on these thoughts, Janna returned to the table.

"Didya get another one?" Janna climbed into her chair with a bit of difficulty. "Someone must have changed chairs on me. This one seems taller."

"No. You're just a bit drunker, that's all." Lex looked up at the waitress who placed a ten-dollar bill back on the table. "What's that for?"

"I'm sorry, hon. But the bartender is afraid you two have had enough."

Lex stood unsteadily. "That's bullshit. He can't do that."

"Hang on. Let me go talk to him, okay?" Janna knew that her friend had a short fuse, and silently cursed herself for allowing their drinking to go so far. "I'll be back in a minute." She stood up and slowly staggered towards the bar.

"Stupid jerk, trying to tell us what we can do. Who the hell does he think he is, anyway?" Lex dropped back to her chair, trying to muster a glare to send in the direction of the bartender. "Jackass." She didn't notice when someone walked over to her table and sat down, until he began to speak.

"Hey there." The young man that slid into Janna's chair pulled out a cigarette and lit it, studying Lex as if she were dessert. "Don't think I've seen you in here before, babe."

Michael opened the door for Lois, squinting as his eyes adjusted to the hazy atmosphere of the bar. "I had no idea this place was here," he commented loudly, trying to be heard over the thumping beat of a dance tune.

"I've been here several times. It's fun, and I don't have to worry about being bothered if I want to be left alone," Lois explained, squeezing through the jumble of chairs to find a table near the bar. When her date pulled out her chair for her, the decorator smiled. "Thank you, Michael. I'd forgotten what it was like to be around a gentleman."

"You're welcome, Lois." He leaned closer to her so that he could whisper in her ear. "My father would tan my hide if I wasn't. A gentleman, that is."

She laughed and lightly slapped him on the shoulder. "God, I love a man with a sense of humor!"

Michael smiled back in pleasure. "Would you like for me to get you a drink?"

Lois checked her watch. "It's a bit late, but I'd love a rum and coke."

"Great! I'll be right back." He tapped the table once and stepped through the crowd.

Having been disappointed in the dating scene before, Lois was enjoying the evening thoroughly. *There's got to be a catch—no man can be this perfect.* She heard a bit of yelling at the back of the club, but directed her attention to the bar. *He's just so darned sweet.*

"What did you call me?" Lex sputtered, glaring across the table at the kid. The music had continued to get louder, so she thought she had misunderstood him. "I know you didn't say what I thought you did."

He held out his hands. "Don't get your panties in a bunch, sweet thing. I just noticed you and your friend from across the room, and thought you could use some company."

"What?" Lex knocked over the empty pitcher when she jumped to her feet. "Get lost, kid. I don't feel like messing with you."

"C'mon, sugar. You look kinda down. I figure that you just need the right man to help you forget all your troubles." He twisted in his chair and looked behind him, giving his friends who were standing at the bar a thumbs up. "Let's go outside where we can have a bit more...privacy."

Lex stormed around the table and grabbed the front of his shirt, pulling the arrogant young man to his feet. "Get the fuck out of my sight, before I embarrass you in front of your buddies."

He tried to fight off her grip. "What are you, a lesbian or something?"

"That's exactly what I am, Boy Scout. Now back off before I get mad." Lex shoved him backwards, causing him to knock over another table.

"Hey," two burly men barely got out of the way before their table collapsed, "watch it!"

The enraged woman was about to yell something back to them when another man stepped in front of her. "Get out of my way, buddy, or you're next." Squinting in the dim light, she recognized him as Amanda's father. *Shit.*

"Lex, hold on." Michael had seen the commotion from the bar and hurried over, worried about his daughter's partner. He reached over and touched her arm, which she easily batted away.

"Go 'way, Michael. This has nothing to do with you." She looked around for the man who had bothered her, but he seemed to have disappeared in the smoky room. "Damn."

Janna stepped up next to Michael and looked at her friend. "You okay, Lex?" She had unsuccessfully tried to get another pitcher of beer from the bartender, and was now trying to figure out how to break the news to the obviously pissed-off woman.

"I'm fine." Lex glared at the man in front of her. "Go back to where you came from. Everything's just fine here."

"No." Michael studied Lex carefully. *She's drunk.* He looked at Janna, who was leaning unsteadily against the table. *And her friend's in worse shape. I need to get them both home before something else happens to them.* He was about to say something else when he was roughly shoved aside.

"Get out of my way, old man. This bitch owes my friend an apology." A large man practically threw Michael to the floor, which caused Lex's eyes to narrow.

Lex leaned down and helped Michael to his feet, then turned and glared at the intruder. "I think you're the one who needs to apologize, asshole. That's my future father-in-law you just knocked down."

The burly man looked around the room. He was several inches taller than Lex and easily outweighed her by fifty pounds. "Where's your boyfriend, then?"

"My *girlfriend* is probably at home by now, wondering where I am." Lex started to shove by him, but was stopped when his hand grabbed her shoulder.

"Girlfriend? You're a dyke?"

Lex couldn't help it, she laughed. "Yeah. Probably because of guys like you." She shook off his hand and started to leave.

"You bitch!" The large man spun her back around and punched Lex in the face. "People like you ought to—" Whatever helpful suggestion he was about to make was cut short when her foot met his groin. Falling to the floor, he gasped in pain.

"Asshole." Lex sniffled and wiped at her face, surprised when she felt blood on her hand. *Shit. Amanda's gonna kill me.* Looking around, she realized that Michael had disappeared. *Great. Now I've pissed off her dad, too.* She looked over at Janna, who had held off the man's two friends without much trouble. "You about ready to get out of here? I need to get home."

Janna pulled a few napkins off another table and handed them to her friend. "Yeah. I think we'd better call a cab, though. Neither one of us is in any shape to drive."

"You're probably right." Lex held the napkins under her nose, trying to stem the flow of blood. "Jackass got in a lucky shot."

When he realized that Lex was all right, Michael had hurried across the room to where he had left Lois. "I'm sorry I was gone for so long."

"That's all right, Michael. Was that Lexington over there?"

"I'm afraid so. She and her friend are a bit drunk. Would you mind very much if I took them home?" Although he was having a good time with Lois, Michael's first concern was getting Lex home safely.

"Of course not. As a matter of fact, let me help you. I can follow you in your car, so you can drive hers. That way you don't have to get a ride back." Lois gathered up her purse and stood. "I think they're trying to leave. We'd better hurry."

Just returning the phone to the cradle, Amanda was startled when it immediately rang again. "Hello?"

"Hi, honey. I was just looking for you." Michael breathed a sigh of relief. "I was hoping you'd be over there."

"What's up, Daddy?"

He paused for a moment, trying to gather his thoughts. "Um, I had to bring Lex home. Why don't you come to your house, and we can discuss it further when you get here."

Concerned, Amanda stood up. "*Had* to bring her home? My God, what happened? Is Lex all right?" Her panicked voice alerted Anna Leigh, who hurried into the room.

"Calm down, Amanda. I think she'll be just fine. I found her and Janna at Dooley's. They just had a little too much beer." Michael looked over at Lex, who was sprawled out on the sofa with her head tilted back, dozing. Her nose had finally quit bleeding, but she sported a nice bruise above her lip, which bore a small split from the man's knuckles.

"You *think* she's going to be okay? That's it. I'm on my way right now. Thanks for calling, Daddy." Amanda hung up the phone before Michael could say another word. She looked up at her grandmother. "Dad found Lex and brought her home."

"Found her? Where was she?" Anna Leigh followed her granddaughter out of the room, watching as Amanda gathered up her things to leave. "What's going on, Mandy?"

Stopping at the front door, Amanda turned around. "She was in the bar off of the town square, drinking beer with Janna. I don't know exactly what's up with her, Gramma, but something's got to be wrong if she had to be driven home. I'll call you when I find out, okay?"

Anna Leigh nodded, pulling Amanda close for a hug. "Please do. And if you need me to do anything for you, just let me know. I love you, Mandy."

"I love you too, Gramma. Thanks." She raced down the front steps as fast as her healing leg would allow, in a hurry to get home.

Michael had filled a plastic bag with ice and forced Lex to put it on her face. After the initial argument, she had quietly surrendered to his firm request and was now sitting on the sofa with her head resting on the back cushions, her eyes closed. He had driven the huge truck to the house, while Lois had volunteered to use his car to take Janna home. She promised to come and pick him up when she was through, although it would take her quite a while to get back. He knew that Janna lived out of town with her grandfather on the property neighboring Lex's ranch, and realized he had a long wait ahead of him. The sound of a car door slamming caused him to smile. *She made good time.*

The front door opened and Amanda raced into the house. "Daddy?" She saw her partner's still form sitting on the sofa, but was blocked from going over to her when Michael stepped in front of her.

"Shh." He reached over and touched his daughter's arm. "I just got her settled down a few minutes ago. Let's go into the kitchen to talk."

"Okay." Allowing him to lead her, Amanda held her tongue until they were in the other room. "What happened? Was that blood on her shirt?"

Sitting down, Michael released a heavy breath. "Yes. She got into a little altercation at the bar this evening." He waited until Amanda sat down beside him before continuing. "Lex was there with her friend, Janna, and it looked like they had been there for most of the day. Some guy came over and started something, and when she didn't agree with him, he popped her in the nose. It looks a lot worse than it is, believe me."

"She got into a bar fight?"

"It really wasn't her fault. I was there and saw the whole thing."

Amanda shook her head, confused. "You were there?" She braced her elbows on the table and buried her face in her hands. "Lord. It just keeps getting better and better, doesn't it?" Now that she knew that her lover was all right, the fear she had felt initially had turned into a weary resignation.

"Amanda, please. She probably wouldn't have even done anything, if that guy hadn't shoved me. I feel a bit responsible."

"What?" Amanda's head popped up and she looked at her father incredulously. "Who shoved you?"

Oops. Now I've done it. "Um, well, Lois and I had gone in for a drink, and I saw Lex arguing with some guy. Since I didn't want her to get into any trouble, I went over to see if I could help. Well, this guy had friends, and one of them shoved me so that he could get up into Lex's face." He chuckled. "He was huge, but she never batted an eye—told him he owed me an apology."

The blonde nodded. "That sounds like her, all right. Then what?"

"Uh, let me think a minute. Oh, yeah. He called her a," Michael flushed, "a dyke, and she said that it was because of men like him. That pissed him off, and he punched her in the face. Gave her a nosebleed and busted her lip, nothing serious."

"Okay, that explains the blood on her shirt. What happened next?" Now that she realized that Lex was not seriously hurt, Amanda was curious about the rest of the evening. "Did she fight back?"

He nodded enthusiastically. "Oh, you bet. Brought him to his knees with one swift kick. I went back over to where Lois was, and we decided to give Lex and Janna a ride home."

"Lois. That's right. You had a date tonight. How did that go, anyway?" Amanda smiled at her father's sudden embarrassment.

"She's a really sweet woman. As a matter of fact, she should be here soon with my car."

Amanda smiled. "I'm happy to hear that. I'm sorry your evening was ruined, though. I'm going to have to have a little talk with Lex."

Michael touched her arm. "Not on my account, please. We had a great evening. Something like this just reinforced what I thought about Lois—she's got a beautiful heart. I can't wait to get to know her better."

"I'm really glad, Daddy. So, tell me more about your date tonight." Amanda leaned forward and smiled as her father blushed again. *He's like a teenager with his first crush. That's so sweet.* "C'mon, let's hear it."

Amanda closed the front door with an exhausted sigh. "She's really sweet, but I'm glad they're gone. I'm pooped." She glanced over at the sofa, where her partner was still stretched out, her face covered with the towel that Michael had wrapped around the bag of ice. Lex hadn't moved all evening, and Amanda was beginning to think that she had passed out from too much alcohol. *I'll get her to bed in a minute. I need to call Gramma before it gets to be too late.* She decided to go into the bedroom to make the call, so as not to disturb Lex.

She dialed her grandparents' number and waited for someone to pick up. All the while, Amanda's mind raced with thoughts of her troubled lover. She'd known Lex long enough to understand how deeply she could be affected by the disappointments and losses in her life, yet how incapable her partner was of dealing with the deep emotions that she felt.

"Gramma? I'm fine. Yes, Lex is fine. She's resting in the living room." Amanda let out a deep breath while she listened to her grandmother express her concern for the two women.

"Really, Gramma. I know you love Lex too, and I understand how worried you are for the both of us, but—" She could hear the distress in the older woman's voice. Amanda knew that her grandmother had come to love Lex as if she were her own grandchild, but she also knew that Anna Leigh was even more concerned about the possible toll that her lover's troubles were taking on her.

"No, wait. Please listen to me. I know you worry that this is too much for me. But so does Lex. That's the point, don't you see?"

Lex pulled the towel-wrapped bag from her face. She could hear Amanda's voice coming from the bedroom, and she quietly got up and approached the partially opened door. She was still half afraid to come face to face with the woman she loved more than life—afraid of what Amanda must be thinking of her. She was startled by her lover's words and couldn't help but continue to eavesdrop.

"Think about how you and Grandpa felt when you were estranged from Daddy. Lex just got her grandfather back. She has only one living member of her immediate family, and he loathes her very existence. She's also lost her home—we've lost our home," Amanda corrected. "One more thing: even though Rawson died the way he wanted, I can tell that Lex is eaten up with guilt over the circumstances. And, although I know it's wrong to feel this way, I can't help but be angry with him for choosing to die in the manner he did. She spent her whole life feeling like she failed her father somehow. For years he left Lex to wonder what she did that made her so unlovable to him. Then he did this. This time he left her wondering if she could have done more, should have done more, or if anything she did do contributed to him leaving her again."

A tear tracked its way down Lex's cheek as the truth of Amanda's words pierced her heart. *Hubert was right. I killed him. Dad would probably still be alive if I had left him in the hospital.*

"She's hurting, Gramma. Lex is in so much pain, and she doesn't know what to do. Can you imagine how worried she is? How scared she has to be?" Amanda listened for a moment as Anna Leigh compassionately agreed with her assessment.

Amanda had been pacing as she talked with her grandmother. "I'd bet even money that she is worried about me leaving her, too." The heaviness in her heart caused Amanda to drop wearily onto Lex's side of the bed. As she laid her head down and breathed in the scent of her lover's hair that lingered on the pillow, she continued. "All I want to do is wrap my love around Lex like a protective cocoon so that nothing can touch her anymore. But I can't do that. No matter how much I love her, I can't take away the pain in her heart."

Lex moved closer to the door. Peeking in, she saw Amanda lying on the bed, clutching the telephone receiver in one hand and her pillow in the other, tears streaming down her face.

"Gramma, Lex is afraid that there will be one final thing that will be too much for me, and then I'll leave her, too. She knows that I love her, that I need her. Still, there's a part of her that is so afraid that something will happen, and I'll abandon her like everyone else has. She's in such a dark place right now, and she can't find her way out."

Lex slid down the wall she had been leaning on and collapsed in a tearful heap. Every word that Amanda had spoken was true. That was how she felt. That was what scared her—that the one woman that had so completely taken ownership of her heart would blame her for everything and leave. *I couldn't take that.* She buried her face in her arms and silently wept.

"Yes, I've tried to reassure her. But words alone aren't enough. Lex has to see that I'm here to stay. I'll always be here. And hopefully, she'll find her way back to me. All I can do is to be here for her and let my love light the way back."

Hearing enough, Lex raised her head and then crawled to her feet. She opened the bedroom door and stood there, silently.

Amanda gazed into eyes that were full of sadness and regret. "I need to go, Gramma. Lex needs me." Hanging up the phone, she sat up and held out her arms to her lover.

Lex crossed the room to climb onto the bed and snuggled into the Amanda's embrace. "It hurts. I hurt."

"I know, baby. I know." Amanda continued to hold and caress Lex, whispering words of love, comfort, and forever into her ear until, finally, they both drifted off to sleep.

Anna Leigh hung up the phone and went in search of her husband. Following her conversation with Amanda, her concern for her granddaughter was warring with her love for Lexington. Both women held deep places in her heart, but her first priority was to the young woman that she had practically raised as her own. She knew about the rough time that Lex had gone through when she was younger. As a matter of fact, the entire town knew about the rancher's partial breakdown several years before. The woman that Lex had taken into her home had unceremoniously dumped her, breaking her young heart. *The drinking, the fighting; I don't want Mandy to see her like that. But I'm afraid that's exactly where she's heading.*

Travis stood at the top of the stairs, watching as an obviously upset Anna Leigh went into the office. *I wonder what's going on? I hope the girls are okay.* He hurried down the stairway, but paused outside of the room. *It's probably none of my business.*

"Hello, beautiful," Jacob greeted, then caught the look on his wife's face. "What's the matter, love? Has something happened?" He rose from his seat at the desk and met her in the middle of the room. When she wordlessly wrapped her arms around him, his heart began to pound. "Anna Leigh? What's wrong?"

She buried her face in his shirt, allowing the aftershave that Jacob wore to calm her frazzled nerves. "I'm so worried about Mandy."

"Why? Was that her on the phone? What's going on?"

"You remember when she didn't know where Lexington was? Well, Michael called here and told Mandy that he had found Lexington in a bar and brought her home." Anna Leigh didn't resist when Jacob led her to the nearby loveseat and sat down, pulling her onto his lap.

Jacob rubbed her back gently, trying to calm the woman he loved. "Okay, so Michael took Lex home." He paused for a moment as he realized the implications. "Oh, no. Do you think—"

Anna Leigh nodded. "That's what I'm afraid of. What if she goes on another binge, like she did a few years ago? That would just about kill Mandy."

"A binge? What the hell are you talking about?" Travis had heard enough of the conversation from his position in the hallway to upset him. "Are you saying that Lexie is in trouble?" He entered the room and sat across from his friends. "I'm sorry to have been eavesdropping on your conversation, but I saw Anna Leigh rush in here and I was worried about her."

"That's quite all right, Travis." Anna Leigh turned slightly so that she could look him directly in the eyes. "I forgot that you missed that part of Lexington's life, I'm sorry."

"What exactly are you talking about? What part of her life?"

The Caubles exchanged glances; it was Jacob who spoke. "My dear friend, let's go into the living room where we can all be more comfortable. We have a bit of history to share with you, and I'm afraid it's not very pleasant." Jacob helped his wife stand and motioned for Travis to lead the way. "But maybe it will help you realize why we're not just concerned for Lex, but for how all of this could affect Amanda, as well."

Travis wiped at the tears in his eyes. *Dear Lord, poor Lexie has been through a lot. I can understand their concern now.* He leaned forward and covered his face with one hand, trying to sort his feelings. *Lainey, my love—how could we not have been here for her through all of this? I wonder why Lester never mentioned this to us in his letters?*

The story that Jacob shared was a sad one: Shortly after their younger brother Louis had been killed in a boating accident, Hubert returned from a Las Vegas vacation with a new girlfriend. She had quickly attached herself to a very vulnerable Lex, raising eyebrows in the small community. Not long after, the woman unceremoniously dumped the young rancher, and Lex seemingly went off the deep end. Her drinking and brawling kept the gossips busy for over a month, until she finally cleaned up her act.

So many years I missed. Travis's heart ached for the loneliness and pain his granddaughter had gone through. A light touch on his shoulder caused the grieving man to raise his head.

Anna Leigh hated to see their friend in so much anguish. "Travis, I'm sorry that we had to be the bearers of such awful news. But we wanted you to know why you overheard us saying the things we did. We love Lexington as if she were our own, you know."

"I know. And I appreciate you helping me to understand more about my granddaughter. It just tears me up inside, knowing that she went through all of that alone."

Jacob stood and crossed the room to stand beside his wife. "She wasn't completely alone, Travis. I think Martha did a fine job with Lex; look how well she turned out." He put an arm around Anna Leigh's shoulder. "She's a fine young woman, my friend. You should be proud."

"I am, believe me. I just wish we had been there to support her when she needed us. And now you think that Lexie is so disturbed that she is reverting back to her old ways? I just don't see it, myself."

"We don't actually think that way, Travis. We're just very concerned. She's been under an inordinate amount of stress lately, and did have to be driven home from bars in two separate instances in the past few days." Anna Leigh crossed over to sit on one arm of Travis's chair. "All that we're saying is that we want to help Lexington any way we can, and Amanda, too."

Travis found it hard to believe that Lex would get that out of control so quickly. "I know she's upset and hurting right now, but I just refuse to believe that she'd throw away everything she's worked so hard for just because things are a little rough for her. The Lexie I know is much stronger than that. You've talked to Amanda. What does she say about all of this?"

"Mandy insists that everything is okay. But I'm afraid that her love for Lexington is blinding her to the seriousness of the situation." Anna Leigh looked at her watch and stood up. "I don't normally like to pry into other people's business, but I think we need to help the girls through this rough time. Maybe if we sleep on it, we could figure out some way to help them."

Realizing how late it had gotten to be, Travis stood up as well. "Perhaps. Thank you both for what you've told me this evening. I know it wasn't easy for you."

"My dear Travis," Anna Leigh put her arm around the shaken man, "try to get some rest. It will all look better in the morning." She allowed him to pull away slowly, and stared after him as he left the room in silence.

Jacob wrapped his arms gently around her waist. "Poor man.

It's got to be rough to hear those sorts of things about your only granddaughter."

Anna Leigh nestled into the comforting embrace. "He's hurting, love. But I'd rather he heard it from us than from the busybodies in this town. That would have destroyed him for sure." She grabbed one of his hands and began to lead her husband from the room. "We had better get some rest, too. I have a feeling it's going to be a long week."

Chapter 13

Morning came, and Lex woke to the realization that large amounts of alcohol coupled with heavy doses of tears added up to one gigantic headache. She slowly cracked open her aching eyes and peered around the room. During the night she had completely wrapped herself around her lover, and it took her several moments to disentangle their bodies and slip from the bed. Amanda stirred, but quickly nestled into Lex's pillow and stilled.

Lex staggered to the bathroom and quietly closed the door. After relieving herself, she stood at the sink and washed her hands. Looking into the mirror, the face that stared back at her was that of a stranger. Her eyes were bloodshot, and the dark circles beneath them only highlighted her gaunt appearance. A dark bruise shadowed her upper lip, and Lex hissed as she gingerly touched the now-closed split below the discoloration. *Beautiful, Lexington. It's a wonder Amanda didn't kick you out of the house. What the hell were you thinking? Just how many times will she forgive you for acting like a complete ass?* The fear of losing the person she loved more than anything caused tears to well up in her eyes. She dropped to her knees on the tile floor and wrapped her arms around her body, her breath coming out in strangled sobs. *Oh, God. I'm losing it. I can't—*

Amanda woke up when she realized that she was alone in bed. Glancing over at the digital clock, she sat up, looked around for her partner, and saw the light leaking out from under the bathroom door. Climbing out of bed, she tiptoed quietly to the door, listening to see if Lex was okay. When she heard what sounded like crying, Amanda pushed open the door and felt her heart break.

The rancher was huddled up in one corner with knees drawn up and her arms wrapped around them. Her face was buried in her arms, and her entire body shook with silent sobs. She never heard the door open, but glanced up when she felt Amanda's presence. Lex sniffled a few times and wiped at her eyes, as if to hide what she was feeling. She struggled to stand up, and was helped to her feet by her lover. "Thanks," she rasped, her throat raw from the crying jag. "Wha...what are you doing up? It's still early."

"I missed you," Amanda whispered gently, fearing that one wrong word from her would cause her vulnerable partner to bolt. She reached for a washcloth and dampened it, turning Lex to her and then wiping at her face. "This looks like it hurts," she commented, dabbing lightly at the split lip.

"Not really. But my head feels like it's about to explode." *And the pain in my heart is almost more than I can bear.* Lex could see the exhaustion that Amanda wore like a blanket, and knew that she was to blame. *I've hurt her by the way I've acted. But I swear, I don't know what to do to make it up to her. Maybe she'd be better off without having to always worry about me.* The thought of leaving Amanda, even for her own good, caused Lex to close her eyes. *I don't think I can handle much more right now.* She gripped the edge of the counter to keep from falling.

Amanda saw her lover waver slightly. "That's it. Back to bed for you." She took Lex's arm and pulled her to the bedroom.

Following silently, Lex prayed to herself that once they were in bed, Amanda wouldn't want to talk. *I really don't think I can tell her what she wants to hear right now. Something is broken inside of me, and I don't know how to fix it.* Shakily, she lay down on the bed, closing her eyes so that she couldn't see Amanda's face. *I've disappointed her. I know that. She deserves so much better than that.* When she was covered up with the comforter, Lex forced a smile to her face. "Thanks."

"Anytime, love." Amanda sat down on the edge of the bed and reached over to stroke the exhausted woman's face. "Do you need to talk?"

Lex shook her head and fought back the panic and tears. "No. I...I can't, Amanda. Please." She took a shuddering breath. "I know we should, but I just can't. Not right now."

"Shh." Amanda continued to gently touch Lex's face, trying to reassure her lover that she understood. "Just rest, baby. Everything's going to be okay. I promise you that." She leaned down to place a soft kiss on Lex's lips. After waiting until her lover fell asleep, Amanda stood up and left the bedroom, afraid that if she stayed she'd fall back to sleep herself. *And I need to call Gramma and see how they're doing this morning.*

With the breakfast dishes cleared away, Jacob was on his way out of the kitchen when the telephone rang. He waved off Anna Leigh, who was still sitting at the table with Travis. "Hello? Peanut, we were just thinking about you. No, everything's okay here. How's Lex?"

Travis watched as his friend's smile slowly faded. *I think I just may take a little drive. I want to see for myself how my granddaughter is feeling.* He stood up and walked over to the doorway, looking back at the two people who had become family to him. *As much as I love Jacob and Anna Leigh, I can't just sit here and wait to find out second hand what's going on.*

"Good. She needs the rest. Is there anything we can do for either of you?" Jacob felt his wife move to stand next to him, and he shook his head at her questioning glance. "All right, then. Give her our love when she wakes up, okay? And if you need anything at all, just give us a call. We love you, sweetheart. Take care of yourself, too." He hung up the phone and looked up, just as Travis left the room. "I wonder where he's going?"

Anna Leigh followed his gaze to the empty doorway. "I think he just needs a bit of time alone." Hearing the front door close, she shook her head. "Or maybe not. I believe our friend is on his way over to see the girls. I just hope Lexington is up for a visitor."

The sound of a car door slamming jarred Amanda from her trance-like state. The sun had only been up for a short while, yet the concerned woman was too keyed up to go back to bed. She had been sitting on the living room sofa wracking her brain for some way to help her lover, but kept coming up empty. She knew from past experience that Lex would balk at any attempts to help her cope with the problems she was having. Lex was a proud woman, and thanks to the example her father had set her, she felt that showing any kind of emotion was a weakness. Amanda stood up as a quiet knock came from the front door. *I wonder who that could be at this time of the day?*

Amanda opened the door to the distressed face of Lex's grandfather. "Grandpa Travis? What are you doing here?" Remembering her manners, she pulled the door open wider. "I'm sorry. Please come in and have a seat."

"Thank you, Amanda." Travis walked into the living room and sat down on the comfortable sofa, patting the empty space beside him. "Join me?"

"Sure." Amanda sat down next to him and turned so that she could see his face. "Lex is resting right now, but—"

He raised his hand to stop her. "That's quite all right. I'd really like to talk to you, if you have a few minutes."

"Okay. Is there something I can help you with?" She tucked one leg underneath her and tried to smile.

"Relax, sweetheart. I'm just concerned about a few things that I heard last night. Your grandparents are very worried about you and Lex. They're afraid she's reverting back to her old ways of coping with problems."

"What?" Amanda sat up straight and her eyes narrowed. "What exactly did they tell you?"

Travis reached over and touched her arm, relieved when Amanda took the opportunity and captured his hand in hers. "They explained to me what happened when that woman left her a few years ago." His eyes clouded with unshed tears. "I just wish that we had known about it. Melanie and I would have been here for her in a heartbeat."

"I'm sure that she realizes that. But why, after all these years, did they tell you about that time of her life?"

"I think that Jacob and Anna Leigh are afraid that Lexie is going down that same path again. They're worried that she's following the same pattern, especially since your father had to bring her home from a bar last night. To tell you the truth, I'm a little concerned about the same thing, myself. But I wanted to check with you and Lexie before jumping to any conclusions."

Amanda's normally kind eyes hardened. "I wish that they would have done the same thing before upsetting you."

"Hold on, Amanda. It's not like that at all." Travis tried to make her see the situation from the other side. "They both love Lexie as if she were their own grandchild. I can't really blame them for wanting to protect and take care of both of you."

"We're both adults, Travis."

Hearing the "Grandpa" missing from Amanda, he nodded in understanding. "Yes, you are. But you have to see it from their perspective, honey. They knew of Lexie's past history, and when your father had to bring her home—"

"Dad brought her home because she and Janna both had too much to drink, and at least had the good sense not to drive themselves. They had been playing pool, and simply didn't realize how much beer they had gone through. It's nothing like before, honest."

Travis smiled in relief. "I believe you, honey." The smile became a wry chuckle. "I imagine she'll have one heck of a hangover this morning, though. She's not used to drinking—at least not anymore."

"She's already been up this morning, and you're right. But I'm hoping that more sleep will help." She scooted a bit closer to the older man and lowered her voice. "She's hurting, Grandpa Travis. All that mess with her father, and now with Hubert, is tearing her apart. I don't know what to do for her. Maybe if we were able to get away from everything for a few days, it would help. I just don't know."

Travis nodded, and pulled her into his arms. "Don't you worry about a thing, Amanda. I'll help you any way I can. We'll get her through this." He finally allowed his tears to fall as he embraced the younger woman, feeling her tears dampen his shirt. *Help us, Lainey. We need you,* he implored the spirit of his departed wife. *Lexie needs you.*

After the long talk with Amanda, Travis drove around town, trying to think of something he could do to help. Seeing the sheriff's cruiser parked out in front of the diner, he pulled his new silver Volvo into a parking space nearby.

Charlie sat at the last stool by the counter. He always dropped into the diner around ten in the morning for coffee to show an official presence and keep the riff-raff away. Although Somerville was a small town, it still had some of the same problems as larger cities. Charlie was determined to keep the crime to a minimum, and the rest of his department shared his persistence. When the front door opened, he glanced up then set his mug down. "Travis. What brings you out at this time of day?"

"Thinking, mostly." Travis sat on the stool beside Charlie.

"Do you have a minute?" he asked a bit more quietly. "It's about Lexie."

"For you, I always have a minute. What's the problem?"

Travis looked around to make certain no one was trying to listen in on their conversation. *The last thing the girls need is everyone in town knowing their business.* Satisfied that they were being left alone, he shook his head. "I'm not real sure how to say this without sounding like I'm trying to poke my nose in someone else's business, but I was wondering if you had any ideas on where we could send Lex and Amanda for a few days to get them away from everything." He leaned closer and whispered under his breath, "Lexie's not doing too well. I think that she needs some quiet time to regroup."

"I was afraid of that. She hasn't been herself since Rawson came back. Martha's wanted to move the girls out to our place so she could keep a closer eye them, but I don't think that's the answer." Charlie leaned back and looked around the diner. "It would have to be someplace close, because you know we'd never get Lex to take a real vacation while the ranch house is being rebuilt." His eyes sparkled with an idea. "Let me check into something, and I'll give you a call later today. I think I may have a solution."

"Excellent." Travis stood up and patted his friend on the back. "I owe you one, Charlie."

"You don't owe me anything, Travis." Charlie stood up and shook the taller man's hand. "We're family." As he watched Travis leave, the sheriff couldn't help but wonder how he was going to explain things to his wife. *If she finds out that Lex isn't one hundred percent, she'll race over there and drive both girls crazy.*

Amanda sat at her desk, staring down at the same sheet of paper for what seemed like the tenth time. Rubbing her eyes, she pushed the paper away and looked out the window of her office, unable to concentrate on anything except thoughts of her lover. Lex had stubbornly refused to spend the day at home, citing several deliveries scheduled at the ranch house that she needed to be present for. Although Amanda couldn't fault her reasoning, a stronger part of her wanted to keep the emotionally fragile woman tucked into bed for the entire day. She was so focused on her personal concerns that her buzzing phone startled her. "Yes?"

"I'm sorry to bother you, Amanda. But there's someone here to see you."

"Thank you, Wanda. Ask them to come on in." She pushed her chair back and stood up to greet her visitor. When the door opened, her carefully neutral expression turned into a large smile. "Daddy?" Racing around the desk, Amanda wrapped her arms around the grinning man's neck and hugged him. "What are you doing here?"

After he had returned his daughter's hug, Michael stepped back and pulled a folded piece of paper out of his coat pocket. "I thought I'd see if you would like to celebrate with me." He handed the page of parchment to her.

"What..." Amanda wrinkled her brow as she opened the paper and began to read. Scanning the print quickly, she looked up in confusion. "Your divorce is final? I thought you'd be stuck fighting for years."

"Normally, I probably would have. But with the charges filed against Elizabeth and the fact that she's serving time in a criminal mental hospital, the proceedings got put on the fast track. So," he held his hands out to his sides, "you're looking at a free man."

"That's great, Daddy." Her enthusiasm was forced, but Amanda tried to smile brightly. "I know you've been waiting a long time for this."

Michael studied his daughter's face carefully. "What's wrong, sweetheart?"

"I don't know." Amanda sat in one of the two chairs in front of her desk, waiting until her father took the other one. "I know she did some awful things, and goodness knows she wasn't much of a mother to me growing up, but I guess it's just a little hard to accept that the two of you won't be together anymore." Seeing Michael open his mouth to say something, Amanda raised one hand to silence him. "No, wait. You deserve to be happy. We both know that Mother can't give you that. I guess it's just a bit of the child in me, wanting my family to stay together. Although now that I think about it, we never really were a family together, were we?"

Reaching across the space between them, Michael grasped his daughter's hand. "I don't suppose we were." He ached for the years that he'd wasted, ignoring everything in his drive for money and power. *Now I finally have what's important.* "You had a pretty rotten childhood, didn't you, Amanda?" To his surprise, she laughed.

"Not at all, Daddy. I have so many happy memories, it would take years to tell them all."

"I guess Mom and Dad did all right by you, huh?" Although he was relieved, the former executive felt regret at the thought that he probably hadn't contributed to his children's happiness.

Amanda nodded. "Gramma and Grandpa were wonderful. Would you like to hear one of my favorite memories?"

Not trusting himself to speak, Michael could only nod.

"I guess I was about four, or maybe five. I'm not sure why, but you had just bought this really nice briefcase, and were sitting at your desk cleaning the old one out."

"You came into my office, carrying a coloring book and crayons," Michael remembered, smiling. "Clomping around in a pair of your mother's Italian shoes and one of her best silk blouses."

She laughed again. "Boy, was she mad about that. But I wanted to look good enough to go to work with you, and my teddy bear jammies weren't quite it." Amanda smiled wistfully. "When I kept dropping my 'work,' you pulled me up into your lap and put everything into your old briefcase."

"I was just going to toss that old thing out anyway. But it seemed to make you happy. I figured it would end up in the bottom of a toy box within a week and then get thrown away."

"Not exactly. I kept it a bit longer than that."

"Really?"

Amanda took a deep breath, releasing it as a sad smile crossed her face. "It was ruined when my car was washed into the creek last September." Laughing at herself, she wiped away a tear that had fallen down her cheek. Unable to look her father in the eye, she fixed her gaze on a picture of her and Lex that was sitting on the bookshelf behind her desk. "Lex must have thought I was crazy, crying over an old beat up satchel like that. She spent days trying to clean it up and fix it, but it was beyond repair."

"I had no idea," Michael whispered. "I really blew it, didn't I?" he said, referring to his inattention throughout the years. "It's a wonder you're even speaking to me."

Turning her head, Amanda watched in disbelief as tears began to well in her father's eyes. "Oh, Daddy." She slipped out of her chair to kneel next to him. "I love you." She sniffled as he brought their linked hands up and kissed her knuckles. "We're together now, that's the important thing."

"Thank you, sweetheart. You have no idea how much your love and forgiveness mean to me." Michael pulled her up and wrapped his arms around his youngest daughter. "I love you too, Amanda. And I swear that I will spend the rest of my life trying to make it up to you."

"You already have," she whispered, burying her face in his shirt.

Lex walked through the entire house, checking every detail until she was satisfied with the end result. She had spoken to McCormick's delivery manager earlier, and told them to start bringing out the household furniture first thing in the morning. *I can't wait to move back into our own home.* She was so preoccupied with her thoughts that she almost ran into one of the contractors in the hallway. "Oh, sorry."

He glared at her, still smarting from their last meeting. *Talk to me like I'm some sort of idiot, will you?* "We just finished the installation of the new intercom system. I thought you might want to check it out." Not waiting for an answer, the angry man stomped off to the office.

"Wonder what bug he's got up his ass?" Lex murmured, shrugging and following behind. Once in the office, she walked over to where the main intercom box was built into the wall. "Where are the other ones?"

"One in the kitchen, one in each bedroom, and we placed one in the horse barn, per your instructions."

"What about Martha's house? She should have one, as well." Lex pressed one of the buttons and frowned. "Isn't this hooked up, yet?"

"I just finished wiring it, and haven't had the time to flip the breaker switch. It'll work. And as for the servants quarters, we didn't put one there because you didn't tell me to."

Lex spun around and grabbed the contractor by the front of his shirt. "She's not a servant. You need to walk your lazy ass over there and ask Martha what she wants. If she needs an intercom, then by God you'll wire her house for a fucking intercom, you got me?" She shoved him away and stormed from the room.

"Hateful bitch." The contractor smiled as he remembered Lex's bruised face. "Maybe she needs another fat lip." He gathered up his tools, intent on leaving the house before he went after the owner with a hammer. *She can just get someone else to wire the housekeeper's house. I'm sure as hell not gonna do it.*

Halfway to the barn, Lex noticed the rear door of Martha's Explorer open, with no one in sight. Still fuming, she changed her course and was almost to the vehicle when the housekeeper came out of the small home and beat her to the truck.

"Hello, Lexie. I didn't know you were here." Martha stepped up to the tall woman and then gasped. "Good Lord, child! What on earth happened to your poor face?" She reached up and tenderly stroked the strong jaw, noticing Lex's upset. "What's the matter?"

"I'm fine, Martha. Just had another argument with the damned contractor. I swear that man couldn't pour piss out of a boot if the directions were printed on the heel." She ran her hand through her hair in an effort to calm down.

Martha stifled a laugh, fearing that it would not be well received at this moment. "Come on into the house. I've got an apple cobbler that just came out of the oven this morning, and you can have first dibs before Charlie gets home." She grabbed the last grocery bag from the back of the vehicle and closed the door. With her free hand, Martha pulled her frustrated charge into the house. "And while you're here, you can tell me who punched you in the face. I need to know who I'm gonna take a spatula to." Her threat got the desired effect, as Lex laughed and allowed herself to be escorted into the neat home like a small child.

Chapter 14

"If you'll just have a seat, we'll get started as soon as the other party arrives." The middle-aged lawyer directed Lex and Amanda to a pair of leather chairs across the desk from him. He lowered his corpulent frame into an expensively upholstered office chair and picked up his glasses from the desk.

Amanda turned and looked at her partner. Lex had come home from Martha's the night before quieter than usual. This morning she seemed to be just going through the motions, and Amanda was afraid the older woman was close to the breaking point. Before they left the house, they had received a phone call from Melvin Taft, Lex's lawyer. He told them that another judge had rescinded the restraining order against Hubert, and that it looked as if he would be the same one hearing the case two weeks hence. The rancher was livid, but Amanda was able to calm her down enough to get them here for the reading of the will. She was about to reach over and say something, when the door opened and a tall man slowly entered.

"Dook me vorever do vind dis blace," he grumbled. His mouth was still swollen, and he was having trouble speaking due to his missing front teeth.

Lex stood up and grinned. "Glad to see you could make it, brother." She stepped behind Amanda's chair. "Here, take my chair. You look like you could use it." Even in the mood she was in, it took all her considerable control not to laugh at the pathetic man.

Hubert's face was still covered with mottled bruises, and the dark smudges under his eyes attested to the broken nose he had received. His stitches had been removed the day before, but the tiny red lines on his face still appeared painful. "Puck you," he growled, dropping painfully into the chair.

"Heh. Are you inviting me to a hockey game, Hube?" Lex was immediately swatted on the arm by Amanda, who also gave her a warning glance. *Ruin all my fun. Maybe I can buy him some soup later.* She chuckled at the thought. *His birthday is next week—I could always send him an embroidered bib.*

The lawyer cleared his throat. "Ahem, yes. Now that we're all here, let's get started. I'm sure you all have better things to do."

"Thank you for your time, Mr. Benton. We do appreciate you holding off on this until we could all be here," Lex told him, placing her hands on Amanda's shoulders.

"No problem, young lady." The attorney opened up a file folder and began to flip through the papers. "I have all of Rawson's legal papers here, but I don't suppose we need to go through all of them, do we?"

Hubert shifted in his chair. "Can we ged on wid id? I'be god a dendisd 'boindmend."

The lawyer bit back a grin and nodded. "Of course." He looked down at the open folder and took a deep breath. "This is the last Will and Testament of one Rawson Lee Walters, which was updated a few days preceding his death."

"Whad? Days?" Hubert leaned forward angrily. "You'be god do be kidding!"

"Shut up, Hubert. Let the man do his job, and you can whine afterwards." Lex stepped around Amanda's chair and towered over her brother. "Don't make me toss you out of here."

Amanda reached out and pulled her lover back. "Honey, please." Waiting until Lex complied, she smiled at the attorney. "We're sorry, Mr. Benton. Please continue."

"Thank you, dear." He frowned at the papers in front of him. "Now, where was I? Oh, yes. Here we are. As I was saying, the will was updated shortly before Mr. Walters's passing. It states that all his belongings, including his saddle and, um, other tack, go to his daughter, Lexington Walters." He looked up at Lex. "He also states that his entire savings, which I show here consisted of two-hundred and forty-three dollars and seventy-nine cents, go to you as well, dear."

"Whad aboud duh wanch?" Hubert asked, looking somewhat

smug. *Here it comes, finally. So nice of my sister to rebuild the house for me.*

Mr. Belton shook his head. "What about it, Mr. Walters? According to these other papers, your father signed it over to your sister years ago. She's had complete ownership for quite some time."

"Buh-shid! Dad wanch ids mine! He pwobised id do me before he lefd." He stood up and pointed at Lex. "She wad only in charge dil he came back."

"I'm sorry, but all the papers are in order–your sister is the rightful and sole owner of the Rocking W Ranch. It was legally granted to her when she turned twenty-five." The attorney reached into his desk drawer and pulled out a crisp one-dollar bill. "I'm afraid all that was left for you was this." He tried to hand the money to the angry man, but it was shoved back into his face.

"Puck!" Hubert kicked his chair over and stormed from the office.

Lex shook her head. "I'm sorry, Mr. Benton. My brother has always been short on manners." She reached across the desk and shook the man's hand. "Thank you again for your time." She turned to pull Amanda to her feet, but was stopped by the attorney.

"You have nothing to apologize for, Ms. Walters. Lexington," the older man was holding a sealed envelope in one hand, "when I met with your father before his passing, he gave me this. I was to give it to you when we were alone." Benton smiled at Amanda. "But I don't think he'd mind the company we're in now."

"Thank you." Lex folded the envelope and slipped it into the pocket of her shirt. She swallowed hard and took a deep breath to get her emotions back under control. "Let me know if there's any fees that my father might have forgotten about." She reached down and righted the chair that Hubert had knocked over in his tantrum. "C'mon, Amanda, let's go. We can have lunch and then go to the ranch to wait for the delivery people."

Frantically searching the parking lot, Hubert almost cried in relief when he saw the vehicle he was so desperately seeking. He parked near the front entrance of the building and rushed inside, hoping to find the man he was looking for. On the third aisle he searched, he found his target stocking the shelves with feminine products. "Hey."

Jeez, now what? Rick turned around and saw a tall man walking quickly towards him. *Who the hell? Hubert?* "What the hell happened to you, guy? Your little sister finally kick your ass?"

"Shud ub." Hubert grabbed Rick by the front of his apron. "Sdubid sdock boy."

Rick shoved Hubert's hands away from his body. "Back off, asshole. You really shouldn't be calling anyone names, considering the way you sound." Looking around to make certain no one had seen them, he crossed his arms over his chest and leaned back against the shelf. "I'm sure you didn't come in here to show off your makeover, Hubert. What do you want?"

"I need do see dat guy, duh one you send do me, member?" The tall man was perspiring heavily. "I godda dalk do him. Duh number I 'ad for 'imb is disconnecded."

"Shut up, you idiot." Rick surged forward and seized the other man's arm. "C'mon. Let's go out back where we can talk." He led Hubert through the store and out through the back dock doors, then glanced around to make certain they were alone. "Okay. Why do you need to contact Bobby? I told you to just pay him off and leave him the hell alone. The guy's a psycho."

"I vigured he was juzdt a 'ired idiod—didn't know he was such a duff guy." Hubert rubbed at his injured ribs. "'e was gonna dake care of a broblem vor me. But dere's been a change in blans."

"Jeez. You treated Bobby like hired help, and he beat the shit out of you?" Realizing why the thug would beat Hubert, Rick shook his head at the other man's stupidity. "You stiffed him, didn't you?"

"Id's nod like dad," Hubert whined. "He didn'd vinish duh job."

"You stupid fucker. He'll probably come after me next!" Rick ran his hands through his hair and began to pace. "I'm the one who sent you to him. He's gonna blame me."

"I need do zee him," Hubert almost begged. "Before he duz zomeding, and wandz more money."

"What would he be trying to do?"

"Um."

The ex-realtor grabbed Hubert's shirt and pulled him close. "What?"

Hubert pushed him away. "Idz nod my vauld," he grumbled. "I wad zuppozd do ged duh wanch."

"Ah, shit. You sent him after your sister? You stupid asshole." Rick put his hands in his pockets and began to pace again. "Lemme think. Because if he does something, and you don't have the money to pay him, he's gonna come after me."

Amanda studied the silent profile beside her as Lex pulled the truck out of the attorney's parking lot. She tried to think of a gentle way to ease into the question that she wanted to ask. "You didn't seem too surprised by the reading."

"I wasn't."

Okay. That worked well. Let's go for three words, this time. "Um, can I ask you something?"

The rancher turned her head and looked at Amanda with a slight smile on her face. "Anything." She looked back at the road, waiting to see what the question would be.

"When he said that your father had signed the ranch over to you years ago, did you know about that? I thought that you had only signed an agreement to manage the ranch until he returned." *Yeah, the agreement with the stupid little cohabitation clause in it that almost lost you the ranch last year. I wish we had known then that it was no longer valid. It sure would have saved Lex a lot of heartache.*

"I didn't learn of the other papers until recently," Lex admitted. "Mr. Benton called me the other day and said that he had found a safe deposit box in my father's name at the bank. There was a notarized document in there that deeded the entire ranch over to me on my twenty-fifth birthday, as long as the ranch was prosperous." *Wish I had known about it sooner—it would have certainly gotten Hubert off my back a long time ago.* "I'm sorry I didn't tell you about it, but it was the day of the funeral. I had forgotten all about it until he mentioned it this morning."

Amanda reached over and squeezed Lex's forearm. "There's nothing to apologize for, love. You don't have to tell me every little thing that goes on in your life—you're allowed to have privacy, you know."

There was a slight chuckle from the woman driving. "That's not true."

"What? Of course it is. I don't—"

"Shh." Lex put her finger to her lips and shook her head, keeping her eyes on the road in front of her. She looked in her rear-view mirror and flipped on her right turn signal then pulled the truck into a nearby parking lot. Once the vehicle had stopped, Lex unbuckled her seat belt and turned to face Amanda. "You are the most important person in my life, Amanda. I have no secrets from you." Lex looked down at their hands, which were suddenly clasped together. She looked back up into her lover's eyes. "Even with everything that's happened, this has been the best eight months of my life. I never thought..." Her voice broke. Tears tracked silently down Lex's cheeks and she bowed her head.

Taking one hand from Lex's grasp, Amanda used her fingers to force Lex to look into her eyes. "I wouldn't change a thing since I've met you. Well, maybe having my mother locked up sooner, so we'd still have a house."

"The house isn't that important," Lex argued. "Everything in it can be replaced."

"But you grew up in that house. I feel so bad about that."

Lex shook her head. "Don't. I really don't have that many special memories of the place—at least until you came along." She captured the hand that stroked her cheek. "I would have never made it through all of this without you. Every time that I felt like giving up, I could look into your eyes and find the strength to go on." Lex leaned closer and framed Amanda's face with her hands. "Thank you, my love—for being my anchor." She covered Amanda's lips with her own for a long, sweet moment. Feeling fingers tangle in her hair, Lex deepened the kiss.

They pulled apart a few moments later, breathing heavily. Foreheads touching, both women were loath to break the contact. "Wow." Amanda could still feel the tingles racing through her body. "If that's a thank you, remind me to keep doing things for you," she gasped, smiling at the answering chuckle.

"Oh, yeah. Wait 'til later, then I'll really show you my gratitude." When Amanda quickly pulled away, she frowned. "What?"

"What are we waiting for? Let's go," Amanda ordered, fastening her seat belt and running her fingers through her hair.

Laughing, Lex shook her head. "Your wish is my command, milady." She buckled up and started the truck.

After they had driven a few minutes, Amanda pointed to a parking lot. "Do you mind pulling in there? I just remembered that we need a couple of things."

"Sure. Is it something we absolutely need? I thought you were in a hurry to get home and have," Lex winked, "lunch." She remembered the envelope in her pocket, but decided that it could wait until later, maybe even the next day. *I'm not going to let anything ruin the rest of the day for us.*

"I am. But I also know how you get if you don't get your morning coffee, Slim. And I have this urge for whipped cream and strawberries. But, if you'd rather wait—"

"Uh, no. We're definitely stopping." Lex parked the truck and quickly jumped from the vehicle. She raced around and opened the passenger door, practically dragging Amanda out. "Well? C'mon, Blondie. We've still got a hot date for lunch."

Amanda laughed as she allowed her lover to lead her into the supermarket. "Slow down, honey. Not all of us have long legs."

They walked through the store hand in hand, stopped periodically by people they knew. After fending off the well-intentioned condolences of yet another person, the rancher shook her head. "Maybe I should have stayed in the truck." When her partner stopped to stare down the aisle of feminine products, Lex frowned. "I thought your period wasn't due for another week or so. Do you need—"

"Oh, my God. I can't believe it."

Alarmed, Lex quickly put her hands on Amanda's shoulders. "What's the matter? Are you all right?"

Not hearing her lover's question, Amanda pointed down the aisle and began to giggle. "This is just too good."

At the end of the aisle, a large man dressed in faded jeans and the signature red apron of the supermarket was placing boxes of feminine hygiene products on the shelf. Only his profile was visible, but Lex would have recognized him anywhere. "Ooh." She brushed by Amanda and proceeded quietly down the aisle. "Looks like you've finally found your true calling," Lex directed to the man.

Shit. Like this day wasn't bad enough. I hope they didn't see Hubert leaving. Rick didn't even bother to turn around. "Piss off, Kentucky."

"Is that any way to talk to a customer?" she asked, reaching around him and grabbing a box. "You had this upside down," Lex commented, righting the box of douche. "The big print goes on the top."

Rick spun around and jabbed his finger in her chest. "Back off, bitch, or I won't be held responsible for what happens."

"Rick, what a surprise." Amanda gently eased between the

two antagonists. "I didn't realize you were working here." She backed up a few steps, casually pushing Lex away from him.

"Uh, yeah. My nephew works here, and asked if I'd give them a hand until I decide which job offer to accept." He crossed his arms over his chest and glared over Amanda's shoulder. "You should keep your dog on a leash, sweet thing. No telling who she might bite."

Lex could feel her control slipping, and wanted nothing more than to pound the obnoxious man into the tile floor. Only Amanda's hand on her chest kept her from following through on her urge. Lex tried to reach him, but Amanda held her back. That didn't keep her from cautioning him. "Shut your damned mouth."

He smirked at the rancher's temper, which only infuriated the woman more. "What's the matter, Kentucky? Killing your old man not enough for you? You gotta go after innocent people now?" Hoping to goad Lex into doing something stupid, he was surprised at the reaction he got...from Amanda.

The usually calm Amanda turned around and poked him in the chest with one finger, her eyes blazing. "You listen to me, you pathetic excuse for a man. I kicked your rear end once, and I'll gladly do it again, if you don't shut up." Amanda continued to poke him, forcing Rick against the shelves. "So," Poke. "back," Poke. "off," Poke. "or," Poke. "else!"

"Get out of here," he growled, although it came out more like a whimper. "I don't have time to mess with the two of you." Rick turned his back and began to stock the shelves again, his hands shaking.

Amanda turned and grinned at her partner, who just shook her head. "What?" She linked her arm through Lex's and led the way to the coffee aisle.

Charlie opened the door and ushered his guests into the house. "It's good to see all of you. Come on in." Once everyone was comfortably seated in the living room, he helped Martha bring in a tray with coffee and cookies. "Sorry about the short notice, folks."

"That's quite all right, Charlie. We wanted to be out here when the furniture arrives, anyway. But you just sounded so mysterious on the phone. What exactly is this all about?" Anna Leigh accepted a steaming mug of coffee from the sheriff. "Thank you."

Martha helped to pass out the coffee, and then placed the plates of cookies on several small tables within easy reach. "Charlie told me that Travis was worried about the girls, especially Lexie. And to tell you the truth, I am too. I agree that the best thing for them would to get away from everything for a few days. But, it would have to be close by, because neither one of them would leave their commitments here for very long."

"You're right," Travis agreed. "I was hoping that someone might have an idea, because frankly, I'm stumped." He looked over at Martha, who had a self-satisfied smirk on her face. "What?"

"Does Amanda like to fish?" she asked Jacob and Anna Leigh.

Jacob turned a questioning glance at his wife, who shrugged. "I'm not sure. She's never mentioned it." He looked at the housekeeper. "Why?"

"Well, a friend of mine in town owns a little cabin on the lake. She had actually offered the use of it to Charlie and me after we were married, but we went on that wonderful cruise instead." Martha winked at the other couple. "It was a tough choice, cruise or drive out to the lake—but I think we made the right decision. Anyway, Betty said she never uses the place since her husband died a few years ago. It's rather secluded, off one of the coves. I called her last night, and she said that the girls were more than welcome to it."

Travis rubbed his hands together happily. "That's great. Do we need to get out there first and do some cleaning up? Is it stocked with provisions? Is there—" He stopped when Martha held up her hand.

"Hold on there, Travis. I've already got folks volunteering, if we decide to do this."

Everyone in the room laughed, breaking the tense atmosphere. "This is a wonderful idea, Martha. But how on earth are we going to get Lexington to agree to it? It's not going to be easy."

The housekeeper laughed. "My girl's stubborn, that's for sure. But, there is one weakness she has, and I'm not above exploiting it to take care of her."

"Amanda!" Five voices called out at once. The room erupted into laughter once again.

"What?" Amanda turned away from the window, her eyes slightly unfocused.

"I've called your name a couple of times. Is anything wrong?" Lex reached across the seat and touched her lover's arm. "You seem a bit preoccupied." They had finished a nice quiet lunch at the house and were now driving out to the ranch.

"Not preoccupied, exactly. Just," Amanda raised her other hand and then dropped it back onto her lap, "I don't know. Guess I'm still trying to reconcile to the idea that my parents are no longer married."

Ah. She finally talks about it. Good. Lex squeezed the arm her hand was resting on while she turned the truck off the main pavement and onto their private road. "How's your dad taking the whole thing?"

"He's thrilled. I really can't blame him, but it's a weird feeling. I always thought that they were meant to be together, like us." Amanda shook her head. "Well, nothing like us. But I never really thought about one without thinking of the other, you know?"

"I know," Lex commiserated. She was unsure of what tack to take to help Amanda express what she was feeling, and was secretly happy when her friend continued to talk.

"Now that I think about it, I don't think I ever saw them touch each other." Amanda looked down at her arm, where Lex's hand was gently stroking the skin. She smiled and raised her hand to grasp her lover's. "How can a person survive without touching, without love? I don't know how my father did it for all those years."

"I'm not sure, but I think he may have just shut out his emotions. He sure seemed to be all business when we went out to get your stuff last year." *Of course, living with the Ice Bitch would screw anybody up. I can't believe that old broad gave birth to someone as sweet as Amanda.*

Amanda squeezed Lex's hand. "I know. And it's not that I don't understand, it's just a bit difficult to wrap my mind around right now. I'll be fine." She gasped as they pulled up to the house. "Wow. It looks great."

"Yeah. I had them keep the design basically the same, just added brick to the bottom floor. We should be able to move back in this next week, if you want." Lex stopped the truck and turned to face Amanda. "I know it's been easier for you, staying in town, and—" Her mouth was covered by Amanda's hand.

"Hush. This is our home, Lex. I'd move back in this instant if we could." She opened her door. "You ready to give me a quick tour before the furniture arrives? I'd like to see the inside with only the two of us."

Lex smiled, then hurried out of the truck and helped her lover from the vehicle. "I thought about putting all the furniture in first, but I wanted you to tell them where everything goes." She led Amanda up the steps, but stopped when they were at the front door. "Hold on."

"What?" Amanda almost squealed when she was picked up and cradled like a baby. "Lex, you nut. Put me down!" She struggled half-heartedly, then gave up and wrapped her arms around her ride's neck. "You are so sweet."

"Nah." Lex gently kicked open the door and carried Amanda across the threshold, setting her back on her feet when they were inside. "Just didn't want you to trip and sue me."

Amanda slapped Lex on the arm. "You are such a brat. Good thing I love you so much." She wrapped one arm around her lover's waist. "Well? You going to show off this place, or what? I'd like to see what all the paint samples and wallpaper swatches we picked out look like." She had been surprised when Lex had left the decorating ideas up to her and Martha. The rancher had hired Mrs. Compton to handle all the work, and had steadfastly refused to become involved in choosing any of the interior colors or patterns. She had told the woman to speak to Amanda or the housekeeper about it all, and to not bother asking her for any input.

"Sure. Want to start upstairs?" Lex grabbed Amanda's hand and began to lead her up the staircase. "It's gonna be weird," she commented halfway up, tapping one step with her booted foot, "not having this board squeak." Shaking her head, she laughed. "I wonder what Grandpa's room looks like. Mrs. Compton had two different patterns picked out; I hope she didn't go with the frufruey one."

Fru-fruey? Oh, boy. I forgot to tell her which room was which. I'm toast. "Think he'll mind daffodils?" Amanda asked as they walked to the end of the hall. "Maybe we can use it as an excuse to get him into the large guest room."

"Good luck. He kept saying he's happier in the back of the house." Lex opened the door to the rear guestroom and peeked cautiously around it. "Oh, good. We're safe." She stepped into the room and held out her arms. "Well, what do you think?"

The room was larger than before and had light ash paneling covering the lower half of the walls. The upper half was covered with cream-colored wallpaper that held a very faint geometrical design. There were two other doors, and Lex walked over and opened one. "Thought he should have a private bathroom. Think we'll be able to get him out of your grandparents' house?" She closed the bathroom door and looked into the walk-in closet. *Nice.*

"I'm not sure. He and Grandpa seem to have become best buddies. But maybe if we promise to bring him back to play, he'll go for it." Amanda was eyeing the room, already deciding where the furniture would go. "Shall we go check out the rest of the house?"

"Sure. But let me warn you, the mud room is no more." Lex started to leave the room, when she was stopped by a hand grabbing her belt. "Hey."

Amanda turned Lex around to look her in the eyes. "What do you mean, the mud room is no more? What happened to it?"

"It really wasn't that necessary, since the wraparound porch goes all the way around the house now. Why?" Lex could see that her friend was upset at the revelation, and couldn't understand the reason behind it.

"I have fond memories of that room. It was the first place I got a good look at you," Amanda admitted sheepishly.

"Ah," Lex laughed, taking Amanda's hand and pulling her down the hallway. "Well, it makes a much better dining room. But, if you're real nice, we can make some memories in there, too."

Chapter 15

After a short discussion with the driver of the delivery truck, Lex found herself on the front porch of the ranch house, waiting patiently while the men unloaded the truck. The first piece of furniture was a long oak dresser, which was partially covered with a quilted blanket to protect it during the trip. The rancher eyed the piece suspiciously and tapped one of the men on the shoulder. "Hold up there. We didn't order anything shaped like that." *Not that I'd mind. I think I like the size of this one better than the one we had to settle for. It's at least a foot longer.*

Trying to hide his grin, the first man nodded at his partner and they gently set the piece down. He reached into his back pocket and unfolded a piece of paper. "This was signed by a Ms. Cauble."

"Are you sure?" Lex questioned. At his nod, she sighed. "Can you hold on for a second? Let me go get *Ms. Cauble* so we can see about straightening this out." She jogged into the house and looked around. *Where did she run off to?* "Amanda? Could you come here? We've got a slight problem."

A blonde head peeked out from around the kitchen doorway. She was smiling, but looked guilty. "Um, okay." Amanda disappeared back into the kitchen for a moment and then stepped into the hallway. "What's up?" When she saw her partner begin to walk toward her, she hurried to meet Lex halfway.

"The delivery guys are trying to bring in furniture different from what we picked out. They say their orders were signed by Ms. Cauble."

"Really? Imagine that." Amanda tried to keep the patently

guilty look off her face. "Why don't we go out there and see what this is all about?" she asked, a little too loudly.

Lex looked at her friend quizzically, but shrugged and followed behind her. "Okay." She was so intent on the problem at hand, she didn't hear the footsteps tapping lightly at their heels.

Amanda smiled at the two men waiting patiently for them. "Hi. I'm sorry about the confusion. Would it be too much trouble to uncover this so that we can take a look at it before you have to haul it up the stairs?"

"No, not at all," one man agreed. He untied the rope that held the quilt over the dresser and pulled the fabric away.

The heavy oak not only bore intricately carved designs, but the two doors that flanked the six wide drawers showed an elegant "L" and "A" twined together. "Th...that's our initials," Lex stammered.

Laughter from behind the two women caused Lex to spin around. Standing just inside the doorway, Jacob and Anna Leigh were both smiling broadly. Beside them, a proud Travis grinned also. "Lexington, your powers of deduction never cease to amaze me," Anna Leigh stepped forward and patted the speechless woman on the back.

"How did—" Lex reached over and touched the furniture gently. "It's beautiful," she murmured. Raising her head, she looked back at Jacob. "You did this?"

"Well, Travis and I did. We thought that—" Jacob's explanation was cut short by an armful of rancher.

Lex pulled the surprised man into a firm hug. "Thanks, Grandpa Jake. This means more to me than you'll ever know," she choked out. She released him after a long moment, then pulled her grandfather into her embrace. "I didn't know you did carpentry, Grandpa."

Travis enthusiastically returned her hug. "Let's just say I've developed a great respect for the folks that do." He turned and looked at Amanda, who had just finished hugging her grandparents. "What do you think of it, sweetheart?"

"I think it's incredibly thoughtful, as well as beautiful." She watched as the men picked up the dresser and began to take it into the house. "Let me just show them which room it goes into, and I'll be right back." Amanda placed a quick kiss on Travis's cheek before chasing after the deliverymen.

The sun was fighting a losing battle with the darkness as the furniture truck lumbered slowly away from the ranch house. Lex stood on the west edge of the wraparound porch, enjoying the familiar sights and smells, while the others could be heard laughing in the den. She took a deep breath and closed her eyes. *Home.* Soft footfalls behind her caused her to smile to herself. *I was wondering how long it would take her. She always seems to know.*

"Beautiful," Amanda murmured reverently, as the sun at last escaped behind the hills in the distance. The oranges and reds of the skyline turned purple and gray as the crickets began their song. She stepped up beside her lover and covered the strong hand that was braced against the top rail of the porch.

Lex turned to face the woman beside her. "You certainly are," she agreed with a smile. "Thought you'd be inside with everyone, enjoying the champagne that Grandpa brought."

Amanda shook her head. "I like the company out here even better." She sighed happily as she was enveloped in Lex's arms. "Oh, yeah. This is nice." Amanda felt something crinkle against her cheek and leaned back to look up into her lover's face. "What's this?" she asked, poking lightly on Lex's breast pocket.

"If you don't know by now, we must not be doing something right." Lex pulled back far enough to reach into her shirt pocket and pull out a folded envelope. "I'd forgotten all about this." Seeing her father's familiar handwriting on the outside, she swallowed the lump that had suddenly formed in her throat. "Guess I might as well see what it's all about, huh?"

"You don't have to do this right now, Lex. Maybe tomorrow, after you've had some rest." Amanda wasn't certain what was in the sealed letter, but she worried about the effect it would have on the emotionally fragile woman. "Why not come back in the house with everyone? You can hear Gramma tell embarrassing stories about me."

"Actually, I was gonna go down to the barn and check the horses. Save me a place inside? It won't take me that long."

Amanda nodded. "Sure." She reached up and caressed Lex's cheek. "Are you sure you don't want me to come with you?"

"Nah. Go back inside and enjoy yourself. I'll be back in a few minutes." Lex leaned down and placed a tender kiss on Amanda's lips. "See you in a bit." She winked and then vaulted over the railing onto the dirt below.

It wasn't long before Lex stepped into the quiet barn and

closed the door behind her. She grabbed a brush from the wall and walked over to Thunder's stall. "Hey there, fella. I've missed you." The horse nickered softly and nuzzled her chest, causing the rancher to chuckle. "Yeah, yeah, I know. You've missed me, too."

She spent the next fifteen minutes brushing the dark stallion until his coat shone. After putting the brush away, Lex sat down on a nearby bale of hay and pulled the folded envelope out of her shirt pocket. "Guess I've put this off long enough." With a shaky hand, she tore the top open and pulled out several sheets of stationery. The expensive letterhead bore the name of the attorney, and Lex realized that her father must have borrowed it from Mr. Benton right before she took him out of the hospital.

Lexington,

Well, since you're reading this, I imagine I'm dead. Hope I didn't trouble you too much, and that we had some good times together before I went. Here I am, lying in this damned hospital bed, staring at four walls and almost wishing the good Lord would take me soon. I ain't afraid to die, girl, but I hate thinking that my last days will be spent inside, when all my life I've lived in the open spaces.

It's probably God's joke on me, since I wasn't much for praying, or even going to church. That was more your momma's style. She was a wonderful woman, and Lord help me, you got lucky and grew up like her. Not just in looks, either. You've made me proud, Lexington. I reckon I've never actually told you that, but it's always been true. Not many could have done what you've done, girl. That's why I gave the ranch to you. I know you love it as much as I do—probably even more.

When I found out I was dying, part of me wanted to just hide somewhere and fade away. But, I've never took the easy way out, and I didn't see any sense in starting now. I wasn't much of a father to you, and I know you have every right to hate me for that. I was just going to drop by and see you one last time, and then leave before I got too sick to travel. You've turned into a fine woman, Lexington. I'm glad I got to know you again before it was my time to go.

When you drop by to see me this afternoon, I'm gonna ask you to do something, and part of me hopes you say no. I don't want to die in this hospital bed—I want to be out under the stars when I close my eyes for the last time. I know it's going to be a lot harder on you than it is me, and for that I'm dearly sorry. I wish things could have turned out differently, my daughter. I wish that your dear momma hadn't left us so soon, and that you hadn't had to outlive most of your family. That ain't right. I'm sorry I kept you away from your grandparents—I had no right to do that. I was just so damned scared that if you found out about them, you'd leave me. If I had to do it all over again, I'd probably do the same thing. It ain't right, but I can't help it. You're my kid, and I love you. I always have, girl—just been real rotten about letting you know.

If you do agree to get me out of here, thank you. It's hard for a man like me to ask a favor from anyone, especially from someone I've wronged so. I can't make it up to you, but I hope this note gives you some peace. Knowing you, I reckon my leaving you again is tearing you up inside. Don't let it, Lexington. I spent most of my life bitter and angry for your momma leaving me. Look where it got me—a traveling rodeo bum who never saw his kids grow up. That little gal that you hooked up with is a prize. Never thought I'd say this, but I'm glad you two are together. Hang on to her, girl. She looks at you like your momma looked at me. That's just about the best feeling in the world.

You'll be here in a few hours. I guess I'll try and get some rest, so that I'll be fresh to visit with you. If you only know one thing about me, Lexington, know this. I love you, and I've always been proud to call you my kid. Now put this paper away, and go give that gal of yours a hug from me.

Love,

Your Dad

Lex carefully folded the pages and slipped them back into the heavy envelope. She wiped at her eyes and looked at the ceiling. "I love you too, Dad." Emotionally drained, Lex fell back against the hay and closed her eyes. *I never thought I'd say this, but he's right. I need to focus more on what I've got, instead of what I've lost.* She was so consumed by her thoughts, she never heard the barn door open, or a figure slip stealthily inside. "Guess I'd better get back up to the house and give Amanda that hug."

"That's one of the best ideas you've had all day." Amanda sat down next to the prone woman and reached over to brush the hair away from Lex's eyes. "Are you okay? It's been a while, and I was beginning to worry about you."

"Yeah, I'm doing good. Just finished reading the note that my father left me." Lex handed the envelope to her. "Go ahead, he mentions you in it." As she watched Amanda read the letter, Lex had time to get her emotions under control. *Don't you worry, Dad, I'm gonna take real good care of her for the rest of our lives. Maybe even longer than that.*

Amanda finished the letter and looked up at her partner. "That was beautiful, Lex. I think he's finally at peace now." She took a long moment to examine Lex's face. *I think you are too, love.* She sent a silent word of thanks to the deceased man. *Thank you, Rawson. I know it wasn't easy, but I'm forever thankful for your insight.*

"I think he is, too. I have a feeling he and my mother are smiling down on us right now." Lex sat up and leaned forward. "Let's give them something worth looking at." She pulled Amanda down next to her and kissed her lovingly, feeling her world stabilize for the first time in months.

Anna Leigh shifted the comforter over slightly. "I think that's about even." She had volunteered to help Martha put the new sheets on the bed, in case Lex and Amanda wanted to spend the night in the house. "Are you sure they'll like it?"

"They'd better, since Amanda is the one who picked it out. She left the bedding over at my house to surprise Lexie with, and I took the liberty of washing everything so it would be ready." Martha fluffed the pillow on her side of the bed and stepped back, eyeing their handiwork critically. "I think this looks perfect, don't you?"

"It sure does," Jacob agreed from his position by the door. "I'm mighty tempted to drive back into town and bring all their belongings back tonight." He was met halfway across the room by his wife, who happily snuggled into his arms. "Speaking of the girls, has anyone seen them lately?"

Martha followed the couple out of the room and closed the door behind them. She noticed Travis standing at the other end of the hallway staring into another room. "I think Lexie went down to the barn, and Amanda followed her." Inclining her head to the solitary figure, she gently pushed the couple in the opposite direction. "Why don't you two see what that husband of mine is up to? The last time I saw him he was puttering around in the kitchen."

"Ah. Good idea. We'll see you downstairs, Martha." Jacob winked and led his wife down the stairs, whispering in her ear.

Travis heard the light footsteps come up behind him, but he couldn't take his eyes off the large bedroom. "Did you know they were going to do this?" The room had a definitely masculine feel, and somehow after the furniture had been brought in, one lone picture had been placed on the nightstand beside the bed. Tears sprang to his eyes as he recognized one of the last pictures taken with his wife and granddaughter.

"I did. I had taken all of the old pictures from the storage room, and was going to put them in albums in chronological order. So when the house burned, everything was all safe and sound on my coffee table." She placed an arm around his waist and pulled Travis into the room. "I have the old box of your letters that Lester had kept, and that picture was inside. I had a couple of copies made, and when I gave Lexie hers, she asked if I would sneak another one up and put it in your room here."

"That's really sweet, Martha. Thank you." He sat down on the bed and picked up the picture. "I remember this trip to the zoo. Lexie was so full of questions that day." Travis looked up into the concerned woman's face. "But, I'm not sure whether or not I'm coming back out here to live."

Martha dropped down next to the emotional man. "Why on earth not?"

He patted her leg gently. "They don't need an old man underfoot out here. Their lives are just beginning, and I'd hate to be in the way. Besides, I've still got a house in Dallas I need to get back to. I only stayed around because of Rawson's illness and because I thought Lexie might need me. Since everything is under control around here, I should be going home."

"Have you talked to Lexie about this? I don't think she's gonna be too happy about that."

Travis stood up and crossed the room to look through the window into the inky darkness. "They need their privacy, not some old man mucking up the works all the time."

This is so not like him. I wonder what's going on inside that thick skull of his? "Travis." Martha waited until he turned around and looked at her. "You've gotten to know both the girls really well, haven't you?" She stood up and started for the door. "Think about this, will you? Have you ever known either one of them to do, or say, anything that they don't mean? Look at this room very closely, my friend. If they didn't want you to stay here, I doubt it would have looked like this." She smiled and walked out of the room, leaving Travis to his own thoughts.

Damn, but that woman is sneaky. Travis wiped a tear from his eye and sat back down on the bed, picking up the picture and studying it closely. *What do you think, Lainey? Am I being a foolish old man?* He closed his eyes and imagined his wife's face. *You're right, as usual, my love. We have no idea how long we're on this earth. I should make the most of it.*

Downstairs, the rest of the group was in the kitchen sitting around the new table and drinking a carafe of coffee that Charlie and Jacob had brought from the sheriff's house.

"So tell me again why they can't move back in right now," Anna Leigh asked. "The house is finished, isn't it?"

"It sure is. But it has to pass inspection first, and that could take weeks." The look on his face revealed exactly what Charlie thought of that notion. "Stupid politicians." He was referring to the County Commissioner's Office, where the inspector was based. Lex had upset the commissioner on more than one occasion when she sided against him on different projects concerning the Historical Committee, and the man had never forgotten it.

"Politics, huh?" Travis had followed Martha downstairs, and stood smiling in the doorway. He winked at the housekeeper, who took his brightened demeanor as a good sign. "You know, I've spent the majority of my life handling politicians," he admitted, taking a seat next to Anna Leigh. "Most of them don't have a lot of sense, but with the right words, you can make them think that something is their idea."

Jacob was encouraged by the gleam in his friend's eye. "What do you have in mind, Travis?" *I'm going to miss him at the house, but I think living with the girls is better for him.*

"Let's just say, by the time the girls get back from their trip, they'll be able to live here."

Hearing the back door close, mouths closed as well and all eyes turned to the doorway.

"What are y'all up to?" Lex asked, seeing the guilty looks. She frowned slightly until Martha stood up and walked over to her, grinning. "What?"

The housekeeper pulled several strands of hay out of Lex's hair, then smiled broadly and did the same with Amanda standing next to her. "You two look like you've been having fun."

"Mada!" Lex blushed and lowered her eyes. "I can't believe you said that," she whispered. A giggle from beside her caused the rancher's head to turn. "Not you, too."

Amanda patted her friend on the stomach. "It's not that bad, Lex." She grimaced and reached under her shirt, removing more hay. "That sure itches, though."

The entire assemblage broke out into laughter, causing both young women to grin. "You girls are adorable." Martha grabbed both women by the arm and pulled them over to the table. "Come sit down, girls. We have a proposition for you."

Uh-oh. I should have known not to let the bunch of them get together. I'm about halfway afraid of what they've come up with. Lex exchanged worried looks with Amanda as they were each pushed gently into a chair. "Should we be nervous?"

"Of course not, sweetheart. We've just got a little present for the two of you." Jacob looked at his wife, who in turn looked at Martha. "Well?"

"Sure, sure. Look at me to pull your fat out of the fire." Martha sat back down in her chair and looked at the two younger women. "Before you say a word, Lexie, I want you to hear everything I have to say, all right? No interruptions."

Lex nodded. "Yes, ma'am." *Now I'm really getting worried. What on earth are they up to?*

Martha felt Charlie squeeze her hand and turned her head slightly to smile at her husband. "We all know what a rough time you girls have had lately, and have been trying to come up with a remedy." When Lex opened her mouth to speak, Martha held up a warning hand. "Hush, child. I'm not through." She looked at Amanda, who covered her own mouth to hide her smile. "You girls need a few days away from everything. No phones, no nosy relatives, and no noise."

"She's right. A few days of peace and quiet will do you both some good. And forgive your nosy relatives," Anna Leigh winked at Martha, "but I think we've found just the right place."

Lex looked back and forth among the older people. "Can I say something now?"

"As long as it's not no, of course you can," Martha allowed generously.

"I think it's very nice of all of you to think about us like this," Lex began, trying to convey her thanks to everyone with a look, "but I don't think it's really necessary." A foot connected with her leg under the table. "Ow." She glared at Amanda, who had an innocent look on her face. "What did you do that for?"

Amanda smiled sweetly. "Can I talk to you in private for a minute, honey?" She stood up and held out a hand to Lex, who took it cautiously.

"Um, sure." Lex stood up and looked around the table. "Be back in a minute, folks." She meekly allowed herself to be escorted from the kitchen. A moment later, Lex found herself in the den. "What's up?"

Amanda pushed Lex down onto the soft leather sofa and sat down on her lap. "They've got a point, you know." She wrapped her arms around her lover's neck and looked deeply into her eyes. "A few days' vacation wouldn't hurt either one of us."

"I've got too much to do, Amanda. It's a nice thought, but completely unnecessary." Lex studied Amanda's face for a moment, noticing the shadows that lurked underneath her eyes. *Maybe unnecessary for me, but what about her?* Lex reached up and caressed the face before her. "You really want this, don't you?"

"I think we both need it, love. Would it be so bad to be somewhere quiet with me for a few days?" *I'd better call and cancel my physical therapy sessions for a while—thank goodness. Maybe I'll feel better about them after a few days with Lex.*

"No, of course not. Okay. If you want to go, let's do it."

"Really? Just like that?" Amanda asked.

"Yep. I can think of a lot of things worse than you and me alone together." Lex leaned forward and kissed the tip of Amanda's nose. "Shall we go back to the kitchen and give them the good news? I think we've left them in suspense long enough."

"I suppose." Regretfully, Amanda stood up to help Lex to her feet and followed her out of the den.

"...just kidnap them and drag her out there, kicking and screaming," Travis offered. He saw a movement at the kitchen doorway and looked up. "Oh, hi. We were just talking about you."

"Sounds like it," Lex drawled, directing her lover to a chair. She stood behind Amanda and shook her head. "I really can't believe you people."

Martha jumped to her feet. "Now you wait just a doggoned minute, Lexie. There's no call to be like that."

Lex laughed. "Gotcha." She backed away as Martha stepped around the table. "Now, Mada. Don't do anything rash." She held her hands out in front of her and backed away slowly. "It was just a joke."

"Don't you be sassin' me, young lady. You're not too old to take a spoon to, you know." Martha backed Lex up against the wall and pointed a finger in her face. "Just remember one thing, child—"

Eyes wide, Lex nodded slowly. "Whatever you say, Mada." She jumped as the housekeeper's arms wrapped around her shoulders and pulled her close. "What?"

"You're my little girl, Lexie. Ain't nobody, or nothing gonna change that," Martha whispered in her ear. "And don't you forget it." She smiled as she felt Lex's long arms wrap around her and squeeze.

"Never," Lex swore quietly. "You're the best mother I could have ever asked for. I love you."

Martha pulled back slightly and looked up into Lex's face. "I love you too, sweetheart." She reached up and brushed the hair away from the expressive eyes. "It's getting late, though. Why don't you girls go upstairs to bed, and we'll tell you more about your little vacation tomorrow? Come over to the house for breakfast."

"Yes, ma'am." Lex blinked when she realized what the other woman had said. "Upstairs?"

"That's right. We got the bedroom all fixed up for you. Now get yourself upstairs and get some rest. No one has to know you stayed here tonight."

Charlie stood up. "Give me your keys, and I'll move the truck around to the back. That way you won't be disturbed." He winked as Lex tossed the keys. "Good girl."

"I'm going to go back on into town," Travis said as he stood up from the table. "I've got a few things to do in the morning." He shared a secret smile with Jacob and Anna Leigh before walking around the table and embracing Amanda. "You two get some rest, and I'll talk with you again tomorrow, okay?"

Amanda nodded. "Okay, Grandpa Travis. Thanks again for everything," she whispered in his ear.

Travis kissed the top of her head and met Lex at the kitchen doorway. He pulled her into his arms and squeezed her tightly. "I'll see you again in the morning. Try and get some rest."

"I will, Grandpa. Love you." Lex kissed his cheek and then buried her face in his shirt. "I can't wait until we're all out here together again."

"Me either, kiddo. I love you, too." He squeezed her again and then left the room.

The sound of chairs being pushed caused Lex to look up and see Anna Leigh and Jacob embrace Amanda. The older woman whispered something which caused Amanda to blush. Anna Leigh laughed and patted her granddaughter on the cheek, before heading over to wrap an arm around Lex.

"Lexington, we'd love for you two to come over for dinner tomorrow night, if you're not too busy. As a matter of fact, we'd love to have everyone over. It would be a perfect time to go over your trip."

"Sure, if it's okay with Amanda." A nod from her lover was the only answer she needed. "We'd love to, Gramma."

Jacob clapped his hands together. "Excellent. I've got some steaks that are just begging to be grilled. Tomorrow evening will be perfect." He kissed his granddaughter on the head. "See you tomorrow, Peanut. You take care of Lex, you hear?"

"I sure will, Grandpa. Thank you again for the beautiful furniture. It's perfect." She hugged the older man tight.

Anna Leigh laughed. "I swear, this is a longer goodbye than

some old movie. Jacob, let's leave these girls alone." She whispered a few parting words to Martha and then left the room, her husband and the housekeeper trailing behind.

"Wow." Amanda stood in the kitchen, empty now except for her and Lex. "That was something, wasn't it?"

"It sure was." Lex took Amanda by the hand and led her up the staircase, stopping at the top and looking back down on the now-darkened hallway. "We're home, Amanda."

"We certainly are." Amanda followed Lex into their bedroom and shut the door behind her.

Chapter 16

"Tell me again why we're doing this?" Lex asked as the truck hit yet another deep rut in the road. It had been two days since Martha had told them about their little vacation, and she was trying to keep the vehicle on the right track. "Are you sure this is the right road?"

Amanda braced one hand against the dash to balance herself. "According to the map that Mrs. Charlton drew, yes, it is." She looked at the white knuckles on the hands gripping the steering wheel. "And we're doing this because our family thought it would be restful." She almost screamed as the truck tipped precariously to the left. "Is this a road, or a creek bed?"

"Restful. Right. If we live to see the damned cabin, I'll be impressed." She was thankful her window was rolled down, or else she would have slammed her head against it when the vehicle lurched. "Damn."

After a few more minutes of wrestling with the steering wheel, the road leveled out and they came upon a secluded cabin nestled in the trees. Amanda squinted through the windshield as the truck pulled up to the left of the cabin. "It looks really nice. Someone has been taking good care of the place."

"Sure looks like it," Lex agreed, turning off the truck. "She told Martha they didn't use it any more, right?"

"That's what she said." Amanda climbed out of the vehicle and grabbed her bag from the back seat. "C'mon, we might as well go check it out."

The rancher grabbed her duffel bag and hurried around the truck. "Wait up. I've got the key." She climbed the steps and looked around, enjoying the quiet around them. "As soon as we get our things inside, let's go out back and check out the lake. We're supposed to be in a private cove." Lex had brought her fishing tackle and several poles, hoping to get Amanda interested in one of her favorite pastimes. She unlocked the door and pushed it open. "Ladies first."

Amanda backhanded her across the stomach and shook her head. "You are such a brat, sometimes." She flipped on the light switch and looked around. The living area was quite large, and very well furnished. Amanda ran her finger across the wooden back of the western-style sofa. *Not a speck of dust. That's strange.* She dropped her bag on the floor and peeked through another doorway. The bedroom held only a king-sized oak bed, a matching dresser, and two side tables.

"See anything interesting?" Lex asked quietly in Amanda's ear.

"Ack!" Startled, Amanda jumped forward. She spun around and pointed a finger at the laughing woman. "Don't do that."

Lex was laughing so hard that she had to brace herself against the doorframe with one hand to keep from falling. "You should have seen your face. Priceless."

"I'll get you back for that, Slim." Amanda stepped past Lex and sat down on the sofa. "This doesn't seem too bad."

"No, it all looks pretty nice," Lex admitted. She walked over and glanced in the other doorway. "Kitchen's a decent size, too." She turned around and watched as Amanda bounced up and down a few times where she was sitting. "What are you doing?"

"Just making sure that there are no loose springs. I'd hate for you to be too uncomfortable out here tonight."

"That's nice. As long as it's comfortable, I think—What?"

The raised eyebrows and look of dismay sent Amanda into a fit of giggles. "Teach you to pick on me, tough stuff." She stood up and wrapped her arms around Lex. "This is kinda nice, isn't it? Just you and me, all alone with no phones and no interruptions."

"You've got that right," Lex agreed. "Wanna take a walk around? We can look for the best fishing place while we're at it." Her eyes sparkled with excitement as she thought about fishing.

"Sure." She hadn't seen Lex so excited in a long time. "I've known you for a while now, but I never knew that you enjoyed fishing so much. You never mentioned it before."

Lex pulled her friend through the kitchen and out the back

door. "No cause to, really. It's been too cold until recently, and besides, I've been a little preoccupied with much more important things. I'm just glad you're not averse to the idea. I'd hate to have to choose between my two loves."

Amanda poked Lex in the ribs. "You are just begging for it, you know." They stood on the back porch of the cabin and looked out over the lake. The cabin backed up to a large cove, and the surrounding trees gave it a very secluded feel. There was a small wooden dock and an aluminum rowboat turned upside down nearby. "Whoa. This is really a beautiful spot," Amanda exclaimed.

"Yeah, it sure is." Lex bubbled with excitement as she dragged Amanda down the steps. "C'mon. Let's check out the boat." She rushed down near the water's edge and flipped the small craft over. "Looks like it'll do just fine."

"If you say so, Lex." Amanda felt a sudden chill down her spine, and turned to look back into the woods. *That was creepy; it almost felt like someone was watching us.* She scanned the area but couldn't see anything out of the ordinary. *Probably just my imagination.*

Damn it, just pick up the phone! The sweating man paced around his bedroom, only slowing down to kick dirty clothes out of his way. After too many rings, the ringing sound in his ear went to a fast busy signal. "Shit." He tossed the cordless phone and ignored it as it crashed against the wall. "Where the hell could he be?"

A loud thump outside his window caused Rick to spin around and scream. "Aah! God, please don't hurt me," he pleaded to the empty room. It took him several deep breaths to calm down. With a trembling hand, the ex-realtor pushed the curtains out of his way and checked outside. On his windowsill, a large squirrel stared back at him. "What the hell are you looking at?" he yelled, slapping the glass hard.

The furry rodent's tail twitched and it cocked its head to one side, studying the man in the window. It continued to stare for another long moment, then jumped down and bounded away.

"Stupid little shit," Rick grumbled as he closed the curtains. As he looked down at the pieces of the phone lying at his feet, he quickly remembered his other problem. *Shit. What if Bobby decides to come after me? He could be on his way over here right now.*

Rick began to gather clothes from the floor and toss them onto the bed. Even though he had only moved into the apartment a few days before, the entire place already looked as if it hadn't been cleaned for years. He reached under the bed and pulled out a large duffel bag, recoiling momentarily when several cockroaches scurried out of it and into his sheets. "Gotta get out of here. That son of a bitch is just crazy enough to hunt me down because of the stupid shit that Hubert's pulled."

Hearing the phone ring, he looked over at the empty base. "Dammit." Rick hurried into the other room and picked up the corded phone hanging on the wall between the living room and the kitchen. "Yeah?"

"If you think I'm actually going to climb into that thing, you're sadly mistaken, Slim." Amanda stood on the shoreline with her arms crossed over her chest. "How do you know we won't sink?" Earlier they had gone inside to unload their supplies and change into their shorts, and the slight breeze coming off the lake made her shiver.

Lex had the small aluminum craft tied up to the dock and was standing in the center of the boat. "C'mon, Amanda. It'll be fun." Lex's normally tanned legs had paled over the winter, but the muscles still flexed impressively as she stood on one foot, then the other.

"What part of drowning sounds fun to you, Lex? No way."

"It doesn't even have a motor, just paddles. We'll stay in the cove, I promise." Lex's smile faded slightly. "Please?"

Don't give me that face, Lex. No...not the lip, too. Crap. "All right. But just for a little while, okay? You promised me we could take a short hike through the woods."

"Sure. Just for a few minutes, I guarantee it." Lex grinned widely and held out her hand to assist Amanda into the craft, then directed her to a spot in the front of the boat. She waited until her lover was seated before untying the rope from the dock. Seeing her hands grasp the edges tightly, Lex leaned forward and kissed Amanda lightly on the lips. "Trust me, sweetheart. I won't let anything happen to you, I promise."

Amanda returned her smile. "I do trust you. It's just that I've never been too fond of the water." She loosened her death grip on the sides of the boat and looked around. "This isn't too bad."

"Told you." Lex used one of the wooden paddles to push the boat away from the dock. After they had floated silently away from the shore for several minutes, she put the oar away and closed her eyes. "Hear that?"

"I don't hear anything."

"Exactly. Isn't it great?"

"It sure is, love." Seeing the happiness on her lover's face was priceless. Amanda decided that she'd take as many boat rides as it took to keep that look there.

They were too far away from the shore to see the dark figure just inside the tree line, watching them intently.

"I'be been looking all ober vor you. Where da hell habe you been?"

Rick pulled the phone receiver away from his ear and glared at it. "None of your damned business, asswipe. How did you get this number?"

"I called your sister's house, and the snotty kid dat answered gabe it to be." Hubert's speech was better than it had been, but despite the dentist's handiwork, he was still having trouble articulating.

I'm gonna kill that worthless nephew of mine one of these days. "What do you want? I'm a busy man."

"Yeah, right. What's de matter, Ricky? You get in a new shibment of tampons to stock?" The accountant laughed at his own joke. "I'm tired of your bullshit, Rick. Were you able to reach Bobby? I haben't been able to vind him, either."

"No, not yet. I'm sure he's just real busy right now. I've got a message in for him to call me, so I'm sure I'll hear from him any time now." Rick looked around his living room, trying to decide what items to take if he had to leave in a hurry. "Now leave me alone—I need to get to work."

"Don't hang me out to dry, Rick. Iv he comes avter me again, I'll be sure and send him your way—you don't want dat, do you?" When his comments were met by only silence, Hubert panicked. "C'mon, buddy. I know we haben't always seen eye to eye, but I'be been pretty good to you, haben't I?"

"Good to me? What the hell are you talking about? Where the fuck were you when I lost my job? I didn't see you offering to help me then." Rick chuckled humorlessly. "If I were you, buddy, I'd find me a nice, heavy rock to crawl under and stay there." He slammed the phone down and ran his hands through his hair. "Stupid prick."

"Rick? You dere?" Hubert heard the dial tone and smashed the receiver back onto the base of the phone. "Shit." He looked around the kitchen where he was sitting and thought about what his old "friend" had told him. "I'm a dead man." His lawyer had called earlier to tell him that the county prosecutor had offered him a deal: testify against the men who drove the truck, and he would serve less than a year in the county jail.

The only catch was, Hubert only knew of Bobby. The other men were still nameless, faceless people who had almost killed his sister. *Lex. To hedge my bet, maybe I should warn her about Bobby. If they trace him back to me...* He frowned at his thoughts. *Fuck it. Let my perfect little sister worry about him. She'll probably meet up with Bobby soon enough.*

As promised, Lex brought the boat back to shore after a short trip around the cove. After a leisurely walk through the nearby woods, she and Amanda were reclining in front of a large hollow log, each holding a fishing pole. Lex had her legs stretched out in front of her and a baseball cap low over her eyes. "Remind me to give Martha a big hug and a kiss when we get back. This is a perfect way to spend the afternoon."

"You've got that right. Tell me again why we haven't done this sooner?"

"Blatant stupidity and pure bull-headedness on my part." Lex felt her pole jerk slightly, so she sat up and pushed her cap back to look out on the water. "I've got a bite." She jumped to her feet when the pole began to bend sharply. "Whoa."

Amanda jumped to her feet as well, dropping her pole in her excitement. "It looks like a monster, Lex. Don't lose it!" She enjoyed watching the muscles in her lover's arms bunch and strain as Lex struggled with the pole and fought with whatever was on the other end of the line. "I know what we're having for dinner," Amanda chortled happily.

"We'll see about that," Lex growled, as she continued to wrestle with her catch. After a few more minutes, her prize could be seen as it was dragged out of the water. "Hope you're hungry."

"Eww. That's nasty. But it *is* one heck of a catch."

At the end of Lex's line hung a large, dark, smelly...tire. It was too small to belong to an automobile, and more than likely came from a boat trailer. She set down her pole and walked to the water's edge to haul in her catch. Raising it with one hand, she put the other hand on her hip and grinned. "Should I pose for my picture with it?"

Amanda wrinkled her nose. "Yuck. What are you going to do with it?"

"I dunno. Guess I'll toss it in the back of the truck and dispose of it when we get back to town." Lex threw it further up onto the shore and then leaned over in the water to wash off her hands. She felt someone grab her hips and looked back over her shoulder. "Don't you even think about it."

"What's it worth to you?" Amanda knew that she could easily toss her partner into the lake and make a run for it.

Both women were so caught up in their playing that they didn't notice the dark figure walking out of the trees, a shotgun trained on them. "You two need to step away from the water, slowly," the quiet voice demanded.

Lex looked past Amanda and saw a slightly overweight young woman standing several yards away. The woman had short dark hair and was dressed in jeans and a navy blue tee shirt. She was wearing dark sunglasses and appeared to be close to the same age as they were. Lex straightened to her full height and stepped casually in front of her lover. "Why don't you put that thing down before it accidentally goes off?"

"Shut up." The stranger pulled the gun up closer under her cheek. "Don't make me use this on you." Waving the barrel, she pointed to the cabin. "C'mon. Let's go inside."

"I don't think so." Lex replied. She held out her hands in front of her to show she was unarmed. "Why don't you tell us what's going on?"

The woman pulled the gun away from her shoulder, but kept it pointed at the pair by the water. "You're trespassing. I'd be completely within my rights to shoot you where you stand."

Lex started forward, but was pulled back by the hands tangled in her shirt. "Trespassing? I don't think so." She studied the young woman in front of her for a moment and made a decision. Gently prying the hands off the back of her shirt, Lex began once again to walk towards the gun-wielding woman. "Now put down the gun, before someone gets hurt." She continued to move forward until the barrel of the gun was pressed against her chest.

With her heart in her throat, Amanda gasped as her lover slowly edged closer to the stranger. *Good Lord, she's lost her mind.* She looked on nervously as the two women faced each other in a standoff. "Lex!"

"Stay back, Amanda." She smiled gently at the young woman in front of her. "You don't want to hurt anyone, do you?" Seeing the indecision cross the woman's face, Lex reached up and wrapped her hand around the barrel of the shotgun. "C'mon. Let it go."

Amanda watched in relief as the weapon was released and confiscated by Lex. *I swear, I'm gonna kill her myself, one of these days.* Deciding that the danger was past, she slowly walked over to where the other two women were standing. "Um, is everything okay here?"

"Who are you people, and what are you doing at my parents' cabin?" The young woman's face still harbored an angry look. "You have no right to be here."

"Look, lady—" Lex was beginning to get angry herself.

"I'm sorry, did you say your parents' cabin?" Amanda asked, pulling on one of Lex's arms to bring her back a few steps. "Let's start over. Hi, my name's Amanda Cauble, and this is my fiancée, Lex Walters." She held out her hand.

The woman accepted her hand slowly. "Fiancée?" She looked from one woman to the other curiously. When she met the angry glare of the tall woman, she shrugged her shoulders. "Oh, sorry. I'm Sherry Charlton. My parents have owned this cabin since before I was born."

"Well, Ms. Charlton, your mother gave us permission to use the cabin for a few days. We didn't see any sign of anyone else here, so we assumed it was deserted." Lex had her empty hand on her hip, still upset at having had a gun pointed at her. "You shouldn't go pointing guns at folks until you know what's going on."

"Not my fault. You are the ones who just came in and took over. I live on the other side of the lake, and I always come over here to check on the place and make sure there's no trespassers." She gave Lex a dirty look of her own. "And besides, the shells to the gun are in my pocket. I wouldn't have shot you."

Lex broke open the gun and checked the chambers. *Shit. She's right.* "That still doesn't give you the right to scare us half to death." She tossed the gun back to its owner, who draped the weapon casually over her shoulder.

Even though Lex was at least five inches taller than she was, Sherry refused to back down. "Get over it, Stretch. Nobody was hurt." Her short dark hair blew gently around her face as she smiled at Amanda. "I really am sorry I scared you like that. How long do you plan on staying here?"

"Only for a couple of days." Amanda linked arms with Lex and smiled at the newcomer. "Why don't you come in for some coffee, Ms. Charlton? You can tell us about the lake."

"Only if you call me Sherry. Ms. Charlton makes me sound old." She looked up at Lex and held out her hand. "Truce?"

"Yeah, truce." Lex shook her hand. "Sorry I got so bent out of shape."

"No problem. Sorry I pointed a shotgun at you. It's just that no one's been out to the cabin since before my father died a few years ago, and I was a little concerned."

Amanda touched Sherry's arm. "I'm sorry. If you want us to leave—"

"Nah. 'Bout time this old place had some guests. There's a storage shed on the west side of the cabin—should still have a barbecue grill in it. How about I go get some steaks and cook dinner for you two to apologize?"

Lex shook her head as they climbed the steps to the cabin. "You don't have to do that." She held open the door for the other two women to enter, looking around the perimeter of the cabin before following them inside. *Now I'm gonna be looking over my shoulder for the next couple of days. I must be turning into a paranoid fool.*

"Thank you again for stopping by, Mr. Wise. I really do appreciate all your cooperation and hard work on this case." Charlie stood up and offered his hand to the man on the other side of his desk. "You haven't changed your mind about my offer, have you?"

The small, stocky man stood up and brushed off his khaki slacks. "I'm sorry, Sheriff. But I'm afraid the county couldn't begin to match my salary." He gathered up his briefcase from the floor and started for the door. "I'm just glad we were able to help. Mr. Edwards emphasized to me that we were to turn over any leads to your office."

"Travis is a good man, and a good friend. I know he was afraid of stepping on my toes by hiring you." Charlie opened the door. "But there's no way my office would have ever found that truck in Austin. We just don't have the manpower. Thanks again."

"Any time, Sheriff. Good luck." The private investigator left the office with a smile on his face. *Nice to be treated like a colleague by the local law, for a change.*

The sheriff closed the door and sat back down at his desk. *An auto repair shop in Austin. Who would have ever thought?* Someone had dropped it off less than a month ago, paying a cash deposit and leaving a phony name. The flyers the detective agency had sent out all over Texas and the neighboring states paid off, and luckily the shop owner had seen the reward offer before doing any work on the vehicle. From the description the man had given him over the phone, there were large traces of green paint still present on the sides and the front. After speaking to the owner of the body shop, Charlie sent two deputies down to Austin to bring the vehicle back to Somerville.

He looked at one of the pictures on his desk, which was a smaller version of the portrait Michael had given Lex and Amanda at Christmas. "Don't worry, girls. We'll catch these bastards soon. I promise."

"Hello, Rick. I've been looking for you," a deep voice drawled from behind the man stocking the store shelves.

Rick turned around slowly, dropping the box of cat box liners to the floor. With his heart pumping wildly, the skittish man almost fainted with relief when he saw the face of the store manager. "Mr. Michaels. You scared the hell out me."

The overweight man brushed his thumb and index finger over his greasy mustache. "Too bad, Thompson. Haven't you been listening to the overhead announcements? Some kid puked spaghetti all over aisle four, and they've been calling for a cleanup for the last ten minutes."

"So? I'm stocking the shelves. Get one of those damned kids that's always smoking in the men's room to clean it up."

"You don't seem to understand, 'stock boy.' That wasn't a request, it was an order." The manager gasped in surprise when the larger man grabbed his arms and shoved him against the shelves of cat litter. "What do you think you're doing? Let go of me."

"I am so sick and fucking tired of your attitude, Michaels. I used to make more in a week than you get paid for a month." Rick shoved the sweating man hard again and then released him.

The store manager brushed off his red vest and glared at Rick. "You must be so proud of how far you've come." Not waiting for an answer, he walked away, but turned back around when he reached the end of the aisle. "By the way, Thompson, you're fired. Turn in your apron to the courtesy booth and get out of my store."

Rick stared after the man, incredulous. *He can't—* "You can't fucking fire me, asshole," he yelled. "I quit!" Feeling somewhat vindicated, Rick Thompson tore off his apron and stomped through the store. He tossed the red fabric at the assistant manager as he left, pleased by the shocked look on his recently promoted nephew's face.

"Uncle Rick? What—"

"Fuck off, Kenny."

Once out in the parking lot, Rick sat in his car and contemplated his next move. "This is all that bitch Kentucky's fault. That smartass whore. I hope Bobby finds her and kicks her ass." He opened up the glove compartment and pulled out a small bottle of vodka. After a healthy swig, he laughed. "Boy, I'd like to be there to see that." Another few swallows, and he began to feel a buzz. "Maybe he'd take out that little blonde slut at the same time. Now that would be perfect." Rick sat in his car until he finished the bottle, then tossed it out the window. "Shit. Now I gotta go get some more." Struggling to slip the key into the ignition, the drunken man finally succeeded and drove off into the evening.

"I'm glad this day is over." Charlie gathered up a few files and tossing them into his briefcase. *I'll take these home and study them after dinner.* "Martha's gonna have my hide for sure if I don't get home soon."

The sheriff walked through the empty offices, stopping to turn off the lights and lock the doors behind him. He inhaled the sweet April air, glad to finally be outdoors. The crickets nesting in the shrubbery on either side of the sidewalk serenaded him, and the happily contented man whistled a nameless tune along with them. *It's great to be alive.*

"This is Sheriff Bristol, signing off," Charlie informed the dispatcher over the radio after he got settled in the police cruiser.

"Goodnight, Charlie. Give Martha my best," Carla answered. "And tell her I'm still waiting patiently for that chili recipe."

"I sure will, Carla. Good night." The sheriff buckled his seat belt and backed his car carefully out of the parking spot. "Damn. I need to go pick up some milk before I go home," he mumbled to himself. Turning the big car around on the deserted street, Charlie drove towards the nearby supermarket. *Think I'll pick up some flowers, too.*

A few blocks from the store, bright headlights blinded Charlie, making him lift one hand to shade his eyes. "That damned idiot has his high beams on." Moments later, he realized—too late—that the car was in his lane and barreling directly at him. And suddenly, the sounds of screeching tires and screaming metal filled the night air.

Chapter 17

"That was one of the best steaks I've had in ages." Lex leaned back in the chair and rubbed her stomach. "I won't be able to eat anything for a week."

Amanda took over the rubbing and laughed. "Yeah, right." She turned to look at their guest. "Believe me, Sherry, this woman can pack away enough food for three people and complain about being hungry two hours later." *Although this is the first time in weeks that I've seen her eat her food instead of pushing it around on the plate.*

"I'm just glad I haven't lost my touch with the grill," Sherry admitted. "I don't have much cause to cook out anymore."

Lex pulled Amanda into her lap and wrapped her arms around her waist. "Really? Do you live out here all by yourself?" After their rocky introduction, Lex found to her surprise that she really enjoyed Sherry's company. *I'd hate for her to be lonely. She seems like a nice kid.*

"Yep. Been out here for about four years now. Mom wanted me to live in this cabin, but it's too secluded for my tastes. That's why I bought a place on the other side of the lake. Lots of people out and about."

"I don't mean to pry, and you can just tell me to mind my own business, but what kind of work do you do?" Amanda wrapped one arm around her partner's neck and twisted so that she could see Sherry better. "It's kind of a long commute to town, isn't it?"

"It would be, if I had to. But I work from home, writing computer software." Sherry stood up and began to clear the table. "It's nice being my own boss." She looked back over her shoulder at the couple still seated. "I guess you know all about that, don't you, Lex?" While she had been grilling the steaks, Lex and Amanda had given her a brief rundown of their respective careers.

"Not anymore, my friend. I'm afraid this little thing sitting on top of me is the boss now." Lex grunted as her full belly was slapped. "Careful, boss. Don't want to stir up the beast, do you?"

Amanda giggled, but gently rubbed the spot she had just smacked. "Oh, no. Can't have the beast upset with me." She kissed Lex on the nose and stood up. "Hold on, Sherry. Let me help you with this stuff."

"Yeah, me too. I need to do something to work off this meal." Lex stood up and was reaching for an empty plate when a loud crash came from outside. She looked over at Sherry, who shrugged her shoulders. "Maybe I'd better check that out first." Lex grabbed a nearby flashlight then crossed to the front door and picked up the shotgun that rested by the doorway. "I'll be back in a minute."

Flashing lights and sirens disturbed the quiet night as several emergency vehicles rushed toward the accident scene. There was nothing left of the car but a crumpled heap—oil and water mixed with blood on the dark roadway, the accident's stench permeating the air.

The first deputy on the scene shook his head sadly as he watched the emergency crews finally pry the dead man from what was left of the car. "Damned drunk drivers. What a waste. I always hate these calls."

"Poor guy was probably dead on impact," one of the firemen added, noting the amount of damage the victim had suffered. "But I don't know. There's so much blood, he may have bled to death."

"Jeez." The deputy closed his eyes at the carnage, fighting the bile that threatened to disgorge from his throat. A strong hand on his shoulder caused him to yelp. He spun around, ready to yell at whoever had startled him. "Oh, hi."

The sheriff looked as if he had aged five years in as many hours. "Do we have an ID on the victim yet?" He was shaken up, but physically unscathed. Remembering the earlier events, he couldn't help but shiver.

As the bright headlights came closer and closer, Charlie

noticed that the car was on his side of the road. The tree-lined boulevard cut through a residential area, two lanes going each way with a grass divider between them. With nowhere to turn, he slammed on the brakes and cut the steering wheel hard to the right, causing the heavy police car to slide into a yard.

While he executed his defensive maneuvers, the other car tried to avoid his vehicle as well. It crashed over the median, narrowly missing several trees, and struck a nearby light pole.

The sheriff sat in his car for a long moment, shaking uncontrollably. His car had spun completely around in the soft grass, and as he raised his head and looked out the side window, his field of vision was filled with the large hedge that enclosed the entire front of the home he had almost run into. "God."

Charlie rubbed his hands over his face to pull himself together. Realizing that the other car had crashed nearby, he picked up his radio and called in the accident. Now, back in full sheriff mode, it still took him several minutes to climb out of the passenger side of his cruiser to check on the wrecked vehicle across the street.

Another deputy reached under the sheet and checked the dead man's pockets. "I've found a wallet." He stood up and gave it to Charlie, who studied the contents of it grimly. "That's what I thought. Richard Thompson. I thought I recognized him." *I didn't like the man, but smashing head-on into a power pole at that rate of speed is a horrible way to die.*

"You want me to notify the next of kin?" the deputy standing next to him asked. "I think his sister lives over on Grand Street."

"I'd really appreciate that, Todd. If you think you can handle things around here, I believe I'm going to go home and hug my wife."

"No problem, Sheriff." Todd waved over another deputy, who had just finished retrieving the sheriff's car from the torn-up yard. "Sam, you want to give the sheriff a ride home? I want to have his car checked out before he drives it." Ignoring the outraged look from his boss, Todd continued, "Have someone follow you out there, and leave your car, okay?"

The young man nodded. "You've got it, Todd."

"Now wait just a damned minute." Charlie grabbed Todd by the arm. "I don't need a babysitter."

"No, sir, you don't. But I'm not gonna be the one that tells your wife we let you drive yourself home after you were almost killed tonight." He put his hand over the sheriff's. "My insides are in one big knot, I can just imagine what yours are like." He felt a surge of protectiveness rush through him, and wanted to make certain Charlie was all right. There wasn't a man in the department that wouldn't walk through fire for Charlie. "C'mon, humor me. You know I'm partial to Martha's sweet rolls. She'll never let me near another one if I don't take care of you."

Charlie laughed. "You're right. Thanks, Todd. I'll see if she'll fix some up in the morning." He saw the younger deputy wave at him from across the road and slowly walked in that direction, thankful that he would soon be home and in Martha's loving arms.

Heavy clouds moved in after the sun set, obscuring the light from the half moon and stars. The only sounds coming from outside the cabin were the chirping of crickets and the lapping of the water against the shore. Lex slowly circled the perimeter of the cabin as she shook her head at her own carelessness. *Here I am—outside in the dark, on unfamiliar ground, and carrying an unloaded shotgun for protection. Not one of your brighter moves, Lexington.*

She continued to scour the grounds, looking for any hint of what might have caused the loud noise that brought her out of the cozy home. Unable to find anything, Lex was about to go back inside when she caught a movement out of the corner of one eye. *What was that?* A quick aim of the flashlight showed the slight movement of a sapling, and she grinned. *Gotcha.*

Lex leaned the weapon back against one shoulder and followed her beam of light into the dark woods. She could hear the break of a branch or twig somewhere in front of her, and decided to turn off the light in order to follow the intruder by sound alone.

Come on, where did you go? Lex had been trailing her unknown quarry for over twenty minutes, but had not been able to catch up to whoever or whatever was in front of her. Whatever it was, it didn't seem to be in any particular hurry, doubling back from time to time or changing direction at will. *Almost as if it were playing with me. Or luring me away from the cabin.* She stopped, turning on the flashlight and looking around. *Just where is the cabin?* A slow glance in every direction confirmed Lex's worst fear—she was lost. *Damn.*

The weary woman sat on the tattered sofa, a small toddler perched on one knee. She appeared much older than her thirty-five years, having struggled all her life only to end up living in the tiny house her parents had left her when they were killed in a plane crash. Angela Thompson realized long ago that she would never amount to much. The young woman had dropped out of high school when one of her older brother's friends got her pregnant. Just as she was getting her life back together, Angie became pregnant again. Four children and no husbands later, she was resigned to her fate of living off the state and raising her kids the best she could. "He's dead?" she asked the deputy across from her. "You're sure it's my brother?" The little girl on her lap started to fuss, and Angie absently handed the child a cookie to chew on.

"Yes, ma'am. I'm afraid so." Deputy Todd Steward hated this part of his job. But he would have hated to subject the sheriff to it even more. "Is there anyone you would like me to call to come sit with you?"

"No, I'm fine." She gave the young man a wan smile. "I know I shouldn't speak ill of the dead, but my brother Rick was a waste of skin. He was always getting calls all hours of the night, and never once apologized for disturbing the rest of us. He didn't mind eating our food, but didn't have the decency to bring groceries home, or offer to pay for what he ate. Deadbeat." She chuckled at her own play on words. "I guess he is now, anyway." The child squirmed, and she gently nudged her daughter off her knee. "I finally had enough and kicked him out of the house. Do you think he was dealing drugs or something?" Angie's tired eyes lit up at the prospect. "Maybe he left money behind in his apartment. Wouldn't it be mine now?"

Deputy Steward struggled to keep the surprise from showing on his face. *Drugs? Could that have been a contributing factor in the cause of the wreck?* "I'm not sure, Ms. Thompson. But do you have his address? I'd like to go by and check it out."

"Where on earth could she be?" Amanda cast another worried glance through the darkened window. She glanced back down at her watch and then turned around to look back at Sherry. "It's been over forty-five minutes. I think we need to go out and look for Lex."

Sherry shook her head. "I don't think so. Lex seems pretty

capable of taking care of herself. The last thing she needs is for us to be stumbling around in the dark making noise." She sat down at the table and gestured to the chair next to her. "C'mon, have a seat. If there is something out there, you really shouldn't be near the window, anyway." At Amanda's stricken expression, she mentally cursed herself. "What I meant was, I doubt that Lex would want you to spend all your time worrying, when she's probably just being extra sure nothing's there."

Hoping that her new friend was right, Amanda stepped away from the window. "Ten more minutes, then I'm going to go look for her. With or without your help." Unable to sit still, she paced across the hardwood floor. "I think there's another flashlight out in the truck."

"If it comes down to searching, I'll go." Sherry stood up. "I think there's an old lantern around here somewhere that we can use, too." She was about to go look for it when the back door opened, and a very angry woman stepped into the kitchen.

"Of all the ridiculous, idiotic, harebrained things I've had to do in my time, this has got to be on the top of the damned list." Lex stomped across the floor, tossing the flashlight onto the table. She ran her hands through her hair, causing leaves and small bits of debris to fall to the floor.

Amanda reached out to her partner, but pulled her hand back when she saw a wet, dark stain covering most of Lex's shirt. "What happened to you?"

Lex washed her hands and face, then turned and leaned against the counter. "What didn't happen would be easier to explain." She looked down at her drenched shirtfront. "I need to go take a shower."

"Not until you at least tell us a little bit about where you've been." Amanda stepped closer and wrinkled her nose. "You smell like the lake."

"I should; I washed up a bit in it before I came in the house." Lex tried to pull the cotton shirt away from her body. "Didn't help much, though."

Laughter from the woman on the other side of the room caused both heads to turn her way. "I'm sorry. But you must have run into Gus." Sherry started laughing again, wiping her eyes. "I'd forgotten all about him." She sat back down, trying to control her amusement.

Amanda looked from her partner to their friend. "Who's

Gus?"

"An orangutan, right?" Lex drawled in disgust. "One that likes to play hide and seek?"

"That he does. His family lives in a house not too far from here, although they only stay here during the summer. I didn't think about him because it's a bit too early in the year for them to be here."

Turning amused eyes up at her lover, Amanda tried to fight back her giggles. "You chased down a monkey?" She sniffed when she stood closer to Lex. "Just exactly what happened out there?"

"Um," the rancher backed away a step, "you don't want to get too close. I really do reek."

"And you reek because..."

Lex lowered her head in defeat. *I'm never gonna hear the end of this one, I bet.* "Have you ever tried to track something in the dark when the tracks kept disappearing?" She looked over at Sherry for help.

"He took to the trees, didn't he?" Understanding crossed the programmer's face. "Oh, no. You caught him over by the creek?" Like most of the year-round residents of the area, she knew that the orangutan had a certain area of the woods that he liked to hide in, and where he kept his stolen "booty"—bags of garbage that the weekend lake goers tended to leave behind. His owners would go out every few days and gather up the bags and dispose of them.

"Yeah," Lex murmured, looking down at the floor. "I didn't even know the little creep was that close, until he started bombing me with trash." She looked back up at Amanda and grinned sheepishly. "Scared the hell out of me. And on top of it all, I was hopelessly lost."

Amanda felt her mirth disappear at that quiet admission. *What would I have done? She was lost in the woods, chasing after an unknown entity, and was pelted with garbage from the trees? God, I would have been terrified.* She reached up and picked what appeared to be a piece of styrofoam from Lex's hair. "I'm just glad you're home, safe. He didn't hurt you, did he?"

"Nah." Lex closed her eyes for a moment when Amanda's hand started stroking her cheek. "I yelled at him, though." She opened her eyes and looked across the room at Sherry. "I think he laughed at me."

Sherry stood up. "Sounds like Gus, all right." She noticed that Lex was unarmed. "What happened to the shotgun?"

"I locked it in the truck before I went down to the lake to wash the garbage off of myself. Didn't want to lay it down in the mud."

"That's fine." Sherry decided it was time to leave. "As much fun as this evening was, I think it's time for me to head back to my place. Why don't you two stop by on your way back to town? You can drop off the gun then."

"Sounds like a great idea. I think I need to get the Great Hunter into the tub, anyway." Amanda flinched when she felt a poke on her ribs from behind. "Hey."

"I'll show you a great hunter, you brat." Lex leaned over Amanda's shoulder and kissed her on the neck. "Just you wait."

Sherry blushed. "Definitely time to go. Goodnight."

Jangling her keys, the frumpy landlady limped down the cluttered hallway. "Figures that sorry bastard would go and get hisself killed," she grumbled, the burning cigarette bouncing dangerously around her lips. "He owed me a week's worth of rent." She kicked an empty soda bottle out of the way and stopped in front of the last door. Turning to look at the young man in uniform behind her, she smirked. "You wouldn't be needing a place, would ya? I'd give you a discount, you being a man of the law and all."

"No, ma'am," Deputy Steward politely declined, fighting the urge to cough. "I stay with my mother." He looked around the decaying apartment building. *I had no idea we had dumps like this in Somerville. I may need to talk to the fire chief about this place; it can't be up to code.* "If you'll just let me in, I'll lock up and bring the keys back down to you." He hoped that he could get away from the chain-smoking woman before his lungs started to beg for mercy.

"I don't know if I can do that, hon. I have a duty to my residents to protect them. Just like you do." She pushed the old wooden door forward and stepped inside the room. Seeing the mess, she shook her head. "I told him no parties. Damned worthless man. Not a one of them worth the amount of crap it would take to cover 'em up." A look at the deputy and she winked. "Present company excluded, course."

Todd suppressed a shiver and hurried into the cluttered room. *Charlie's gonna owe me big time for this one.* Watching the older woman light another cigarette, he decided to take matters into his own hands. "Ma'am, I'm afraid I'm going to have to ask you to step out into the hallway, and not touch anything on your way out. I am conducting an official police investigation." *And my mom is going to hose me down in the front yard when I get home, since I reek of cigarette smoke.*

She took another look around the room and hacked a phlegmy cough. "All right. But I'm gonna be right out in the hall, just in case."

"Thank you." After pulling on a pair of rubber gloves, he took his notebook out of his pocket and began to take notes. *I'll just take a quick look around and get the hell out of this pigsty.* Todd looked over the living room first, careful not to disturb too much. Not finding anything of importance, the deputy brushed off the knees of his pants and moved to the kitchen.

There were several unopened envelopes strewn about the countertop, many of them marked "final notice." One had been flipped over and scrawled writing covered the back. "What do we have here?" On the upper half were the initial "H" and a phone number, which Todd quickly wrote down. Another phone number was listed under the name "Bobby." *Drug connections or friends? Guess I'll report this to the sheriff in the morning and check them both out tomorrow.*

Martha heard two cars pull up in the driveway, and looked through the front window to see who it could be. She watched in confusion as her husband climbed out of the passenger side of one of the police cars. *What on earth is going on?* Adding to her mystification, the young deputy driving the cruiser walked around and handed the keys to the sheriff, then patted him on the back and climbed into the other vehicle.

The front door opened a moment later, and a haggard Charlie walked in. He glanced around the room and spied his wife, and went quickly to meet her rush halfway. Wrapping his arms around her body, he leaned over and buried his face in her neck.

"Charlie? Honey, what's wrong?" Martha tightened her embrace and felt her husband shudder. Clearly upset, the normally talkative man hadn't spoken a word since he came into the house. "Charlie?"

He pulled back enough to look into his wife's worried eyes. "I'm sorry, sweetheart. Just been a rough evening." The shaken man allowed Martha to guide him over to the sofa. "Rick Thompson is dead."

In shock, Martha dropped down next to him. "Dead?" Her brain worked furiously to try and figure out why her husband would be in such a state over the death of the man. "Oh, no. They don't suspect—" She knew that Lex and Amanda had a history with the deceased.

"No, no. Nothing like that. He slammed his car into a light pole this evening. Apparently the man was drunk." Charlie shivered again, remembering with startling clarity the bright headlights as they'd rocketed toward him.

Martha felt the shiver and pulled Charlie close to her. "Shh. It's all right, sweetheart. Tell me what's wrong."

Feeling her love blanket him, Charlie calmed down enough to talk. "I was driving home, and remembered I needed to pick up a few things at the store. So, I turned to go down Alliance Boulevard. You know, the residential section?"

"Right. With the tree-lined median, just before the shopping center," Martha added. *Dear Lord, he must have seen it happen.* "Go on, honey."

"I hadn't gotten very far, when I noticed bright headlights up ahead. Took me a minute, but then I realized they were on my side of the street." He leaned back and looked into his wife's shocked face. "I didn't have anywhere to go, Martha. There were trees on one side, and houses on the other." Charlie raised one hand and cupped the side of her face tenderly. "All I could think about was what this was gonna do to you. I couldn't let that happen."

Hot tears began to stream, down Martha's face. "Sweet Lord! How did—" She felt his shaking fingers gently wipe the moisture away.

For the first time all evening, Charlie smiled. "I spun out in someone's yard, almost took out their front hedge." He shook his head. "I'm not sure what happened next, but Rick must have seen my car and tried to maneuver out of the way. He missed the trees in the median, but lost control and slammed full speed into one of the electric poles." Calmness suddenly descended on Charlie's soul as he realized that he was alive and in the arms of the woman he loved. "There's not one scratch on me or my car. But Todd wanted to have the cruiser checked out, just to be on the safe side. And he absolutely refused to let me drive myself home."

"I owe that boy some sweet rolls, I think," Martha decided,

pulling her husband back into her arms. "Tomorrow."

Amanda rolled over and felt cool sheets beside her. "Lex?" Not receiving an answer, she got up and padded through the living room on her way to the kitchen. It was early morning, and there was just enough sunlight coming in through the windows to make her squint as she looked around the small cabin. Entering the kitchen, Amanda saw her lover standing at the large bay windows that looked out onto the cove. "There you are. Is everything okay?"

"Everything's great," Lex answered as she turned around. The lines of stress had almost completely disappeared from around her face, and the dark circles that had been under her eyes for the past month were gone. Even the bruise above her lip had faded. "I figured that you would sleep longer." After Lex had gotten out of the tub the night before, they had gone to bed, then decided they weren't quite sleepy yet.

"My favorite pillow disappeared." Amanda stood in the doorway with a pouty look on her face. She reached up over her head and stretched slowly, the cool morning air causing chill bumps to rise all over her bare body. "Have you seen my pillow?"

Oh, boy. Lex blinked once and then a smouldering look appeared on her face. "I think I may have." She quickly crossed the room and lifted Amanda into her arms, holding her as if she were a baby. "Last time I saw it, your pillow was in the bedroom. Shall we go take a look?" A few short steps, and she was able to gently place her precious cargo on the bed. "Now," Lex murmured as she covered the squirming body with her own, "can you describe the missing pillow for me?"

Amanda reached up and tangled her fingers in Lex's hair. "Well, I guess you could call it a body pillow." Her other hand traced the smooth contours of her lover's face, stopping to brush her fingertip across the smiling lips. "A very good body pillow, in fact." She continued to trace a path down Lex's throat with the fingertip, stopping at the collar of the tee shirt Lex wore. "An overdressed body pillow," she whispered, tugging on the material.

"Really?" Lex pushed herself back to rest on her knees. She grasped the bottom of the gray tee shirt and began to slowly pull it up. "Does this help?" she asked as her nude body was exposed to view.

"Oh, yeah." Amanda extended her hands so that she could stroke the soft skin.

Lex felt cool fingers touch sensitive areas and shivered slightly. "Um...where were we?" she stammered. Her body was pulled back onto the woman beneath her.

"Right about here," Amanda muttered, her mouth suddenly taking over for her hands.

Lex moaned when she felt warm lips blaze a trail across her chest. Afraid that she would crush Amanda, she rolled onto her back and pulled her lover on top of her.

Eyes hooded with desire, Amanda looked down into Lex's face. She used her hands to gently caress the smooth skin beneath her, while her body slowly slid lower. Her fingertips roamed down Lex's chest and dragged across her stomach, both of which rose and fell erratically at her touch.

"Amanda." Lex tried to keep her eyes open, but the feelings coursing through her body were too strong. When she felt the teasing hand rake along the inside of her thigh, Lex's head slammed back against the pillows. "Oh, God." Her legs spread wider on their own accord at her lover's gentle nudge.

"That's right, love. Feel me loving you." Amanda continued to slide lower until she reached her goal. Taking a deep breath of the woman beneath her, she leaned downward and gave in to the need that drove her.

As he scanned the papers spread out across the desk, Deputy Todd Steward shook his head. "What would these two guys have to do with Rick Thompson? I didn't think any of them hung out in the same places." The report showed that the phone numbers belonged to Hubert Walters and Robert Sammons, two men who had absolutely nothing in common that the deputy could detect.

Hubert was an accountant, drove an expensive car, and played poker once a week with several of the town's city councilmen.

Robert Sammons was an unknown entity. He had lived in Somerville for just over a year, working as a supervisor for a heavy construction firm and keeping pretty much to himself. He had been arrested once for throwing a man through a plate-glass window in a bar fight, but other than that had not been in any trouble. For some reason the other man had refused to press charges, and he was let off with a fine—which he had paid.

"Why would Thompson have this guy's phone number? He worked in a grocery store, for God's sake." Deputy Steward had sent a couple of men over to Sammons's apartment to question the man, but was told by his landlord that he hadn't been home for a couple of days. He himself was going to talk to Hubert, deciding to go to the man's house after he talked to the sheriff. Todd picked up the phone and dialed Charlie's home phone number. After several rings, the sheriff answered.

"Sheriff Bristol speaking."

Todd breathed a sigh of relief. Charlie sounded like his usual self, and Todd concluded that his demeanor had a lot to do with his wife. "Good morning, Sheriff. I don't mean to bother you so early, but I wanted to update you on the investigation from last night."

Charlie sat back down and took a sip of his coffee. "Okay. What did you find out?"

"Thompson's sister claimed that he was a deadbeat, and she kicked him out of her house because he kept getting mysterious phone calls at all hours. So I went over to his apartment." Todd suppressed a shiver at the memory of the landlady. "It was a dump. We may need to contact the fire department about a surprise inspection. I don't think that anything there is up to code."

"Okay, I'll talk to the fire chief later. What else?"

The deputy cleared his throat. "After I sorted through all the debris in the apartment, I found an envelope by the telephone with a couple of phone numbers on it."

"Good. Did you run them?"

"Sure did. One number belonged to a guy name Robert Sammons. He works for Big Cat Construction, and has only lived in town for about a year. But the big surprise was the other number."

The sheriff almost sighed at the dramatic pause. *I swear, that boy has watched too many episodes of late night television.* "You gonna tell me sometime today?"

"Oh, sorry about that. The other number goes to Hubert's house." Todd waited for the information to sink in.

"Hubert? As in Hubert Walters?"

Hearing her husband's raised voice, Martha stepped out of the kitchen and joined him. *What's that man gone and done now, I wonder?* She sat on the arm of Charlie's chair and put one hand on his neck, rubbing gently.

"Damn. This just keeps getting better and better. Has anyone gone over to question Hubert? I'd like to know why Rick would have his phone number."

"Not yet, Sheriff. I thought I'd let you know what's going on, and then I was going to head over and talk to him myself."

Charlie leaned back into his wife's gentle touch and closed his eyes. "You do that, Todd. Take another deputy with you, though. I want this done by the book, you got that?"

"Got it. Will you be in the office later?" Todd hoped not, but he knew how the sheriff usually operated.

"Uh, no. My beautiful wife has convinced me to stay at home today. Just give me a call here later, okay?"

Gotta love a woman like that. "You got it, Sheriff. Give that wonderful wife of yours my best." He hung up the phone and grabbed his hat. *Might as well get this over with.*

The knocking on his front door woke Hubert from a sound sleep. "Go 'way," he yelled, rolling over and falling off the sofa. "Fuck." The knocking continued, and he stood up and rubbed at his aching eyes. He had fallen asleep in the living room while watching television; a half-empty bottle of bourbon sitting on the coffee table was his only companion. "Hold your horses, I'm coming." He jerked open the front door and his heart began to pound. Standing on the front porch were two deputies. "What the hell do you want?"

Deputy Steward stepped forward and tipped his hat. "Good morning, Mr. Walters. We'd like to have a moment of your time, if we could." He was determined to follow the procedures step by step, just in case Hubert had any illegal involvement with the deceased man.

"Why? What did my damned sister do this time?" Hubert struggled to zip up his wrinkled slacks. "She blaming me for something else?"

"No, sir. May we come in and discuss it with you?"

Hubert shook his head. "I don't think so. Just say what you came for, and leave." He held his shirt closed and glared at the two men. "Well?"

Todd pulled out his notebook and looked at it, even though he knew exactly what he wanted to say. *Let him sweat a little.* "Do you know a Richard Thompson?"

"Yeah, why? He in some sort of trouble?" Hubert crossed his arms over his chest and leaned against the doorframe.

"I suppose you could say that, Mr. Walters. He's dead." The deputy almost enjoyed the way the other man's face paled.

Shit, shit, shit. Bobby must have lost his mind. Hubert thought frantically. *That means he's gonna come after me, next. Shit.* "You've got to protect me," he pleaded. "It's not my fault."

Both deputies looked at the suddenly sweating man. "Protect you? From whom?" Todd asked, exchanging quick glances with the other deputy. "Why?"

"Bobby. He's crazy, I tell you. The man misunderstood me, and now look what's happened. I could be next."

"Mr. Walters, calm down. Why would this Bobby be after you? And why do you think he had anything to do with Mr. Thompson's death?" Todd nodded at the other deputy, who turned around and walked back to the cruiser.

Hubert stepped outside and grabbed Deputy Steward's arm. "Rick called him for me. I just wanted someone to scare my sister, you know? Kinda like a little joke? But the crazy son of a bitch took it too far. He almost killed her." He was sweating profusely, the expensive gray shirt now becoming stained with perspiration. "It wasn't my fault."

Gently pulling the frantic man's hands from his arm, Todd closed the front door of the house and began to lead Hubert to the car. "Whatever you say, Mr. Walters. Why don't you come with us, and we'll put you in protective custody?" He had just gotten what amounted to another confession from the terrified man, and didn't want to take a chance on Hubert calming down and realizing what he had said. "C'mon. We'll take good care of you."

"Don't let him hurt me," Hubert whimpered, as he quickly climbed into the back of the deputy's car. "Bobby's crazy!"

"You'll be safe with us, Mr. Walters," Todd assured him. "We'll put you somewhere he'll never be able to get to you." *In a jail cell, you sorry bastard.*

Chapter 18

Charlie's knuckles were white where he gripped the phone. "You what?" He looked back over his shoulder and gave his wife an apologetic look before wiping one hand over his face.

Deputy Steward had to pull the phone away from his ear in self-defense. He was sitting at his desk, and had called the sheriff to update him on the situation. "He practically begged me to, Sheriff. The man was a blubbering idiot. I told him we had to book him before we could put him in a cell. He was okay with that."

Hubert Walters was still whining for protection the last time that the deputy had seen him. He was terrified that Bobby Sammons had something to do with Rick's death, and feared that the big man was coming after him next. Even after being apprised of his rights, the accountant proceeded to tell the two deputies in the car with him how Bobby had tried to kill Lex. He admitted to knowing about the attempt after the fact, but continued to plead his innocence on the planning of the incident.

"You're telling me that you've booked Hubert Walters on the charge of conspiracy to commit murder, and he's not throwing a fit? And you got a second confession from him? This certainly changes things."

"I know. Do you want me to call the prosecutor? I'm sure he'll be interested in these latest developments."

"No, I'll do that. Have you had any luck in finding this Robert Sammons? I don't like the idea of him out there running loose." Charlie had put on his boots and was in the process of clipping on his gun belt. "I'm on my way in, Todd. Have every available man out looking for this guy."

I should have known he wouldn't stay home today. "You got it, Sheriff. Anything else?"

"Yes. Contact Hubert's lawyer, and have him meet me in my office. I'd like to question his client about all of this."

"Will do. See you in a bit." Todd quickly hung up his phone, wanting to call the lawyer so he could get back out on the streets.

Martha stood in the doorway, her arms crossed over her chest. "Did I hear you right? You're going to work today?" She knew her husband couldn't stay at home, but wanted to make sure he was up to the duty.

"I'm afraid so, sweetheart. That crazy Hubert has confessed again to having something to do with the girls' accident. He seems to think that the guy that ran Lex off the road also caused Rick's death, and now he's afraid he's next." Charlie walked over to where his wife was standing. "I want to go in and talk to Hubert. Maybe we can get enough out of him to catch this guy."

"I hope so, honey." Martha studied his face carefully. Charlie appeared to be fine this morning, with no ill effects from his near-death experience the night before. "Are you feeling up to driving in?"

"I feel fine. But I am concerned about that fellow who is running around loose. Why don't you come in with me, and we'll see if the Caubles and Travis want to join us for lunch?"

"Charlie Bristol, you're not trying to tell me that you think that crazy man will come out to the ranch, are you?" Her hands went to her hips in an angry gesture. "I've lived out here for over twenty-five years, and I've never been afraid. I'm not about to start now."

He reached out and ran one hand down Martha's arm to calm her. "Martha, please, humor me this one time, will you? If I didn't think that the girls were safe out at the lake, I'd send a man out to warn them, too. But the family is the only ones who know where they are, and I don't think any of us will be talking."

"I know you're concerned, Charlie. But surely this man knows you're looking for him now. He's probably already on his way out of the state, if he has any sense." Martha decided that being mad at her husband was pointless and snuggled up in his arms instead. *Much better.* "Lexie promised to take her cell phone. Should we give her a call, just in case?"

The sheriff thought quietly for a moment, enjoying the feel of the woman in his arms. *Should we? They're probably enjoying themselves right now. What good would it do to call and worry them unnecessarily?* "No. They'll be back tomorrow. There's no sense in bothering them before then." *I hope.*

The two women in question were enjoying a lazy day, having decided to forgo fishing and relax on a blanket near the water. Lex had her arms wrapped loosely around Amanda, who was propped up between her legs. A warm feeling of contentment surrounded them both. "Mmm." Amanda leaned back. "I never thought that just lying around in the sun would feel so good."

"Me either. I'm not going to want to leave tomorrow," Lex mumbled, her eyes hidden by her baseball cap. She tilted her head forward and rested her cheek against Amanda's head.

Amanda craned her neck and tried to see her partner's face. "You mean that? You're not all twitchy to get back to the ranch?"

"No, I'm not. This feels too good." Lex pushed the cap back slightly, so that she could see Amanda's face more clearly. "I know we've got a lot to do, like moving back to the house—but I can't seem to make myself worry too much about it."

"That's not a bad thing, you know."

"It is for me. I guess I've just gotten lazy in my old age."

Unable to help herself, Amanda laughed. "Yeah, right. You've got a long way to go before you convince me of that." She reached up and stroked the shadowed face. "Maybe we can come back sometime for a weekend."

Lex was quiet for a long moment, then smiled. "Maybe so." She had lain awake the previous night, thinking about how nice the cabin had been for a quick getaway. *I need to call Sherry and see if she thinks her mom would be open to an offer to buy this place.* "Do you like it here?"

"I love it," Amanda answered quickly. She smiled at the relaxed look on her lover's face. "And I especially love the effect it's had on you."

"Yeah?" Lex leaned into the loving touch and closed her eyes. "It has been nice, hasn't it?" She pulled Amanda close and nuzzled her neck. "It's not that far from town, but it's so quiet and peaceful here, it seems like we're a long ways away. I wonder if we've missed anything interesting."

The beige police cruiser pulled into the construction site and skidded to a stop in the loose gravel around the office trailer. Deputy Steward stepped out of the vehicle and looked around. Men hurried from place to place, no one looking up from their work to acknowledge the lawman's presence. Todd took a deep breath and climbed the rickety steps to the trailer. Once the door had closed behind him, two men with nervous looks on their faces stepped from the shadows nearby.

"Aw, jeez, Benny. You think he's here looking for us?" the smaller man asked his friend as they peered around the edge of the trailer. "I don't want to go to jail," he whined.

The heavier man punched his friend in the arm. "Shut up. He could be here for all sorts of reasons, you idiot." He pulled the other man further behind the office, where they could stand under an open window and listen to the conversation inside.

"I haven't seen Bobby Sammons for almost a week," the voice of the foreman complained. "He left a message on my answering machine about four days ago, saying he had some personal business to attend to. What do you need him for, anyway?"

"We have reasons to believe that he was involved in a hit-and-run on New Year's Eve. Are you missing any vehicles?"

"As a matter of fact, we are. Bobby borrowed one of our flatbeds for his personal use, and I haven't seen it around in months. Don't tell me that son of a bitch wrecked it."

Outside, Benny looked at the other man, whose eyes were wide with alarm. He grabbed a skinny arm and dragged his henchman away from the window. "Not one word, Rusty," he warned.

"Damn that Bobby! It was just supposed to be fun, he said. And now we're going to jail." Rusty jerked his arm free. "You know what happens to guys like me in jail, Benny? I'm gonna be *real* popular." He rushed over to where his lunchbox sat on a wooden table and gathered up what was left of his meal. "I don't want to be some big guy's girlfriend, Benny."

"Calm down, you ass! You're gonna draw attention to us." Benny poured out the remainder of the coffee from his thermos and picked up his jacket. "We're not going to jail, Rus. C'mon." He motioned for the other man to follow him to a beat up truck. "Let's get the hell out of here."

Rusty nodded and climbed in the other side of the truck, kicking several empty food containers out onto the ground. "Works for me. I never liked this damned job, anyway."

"I want to thank you for your time," Deputy Steward told the foreman, as the two men walked down the steps in front of the office. "If you happen to see or hear from Mr. Sammons, please give us a call."

The construction boss nodded. "I sure will, Deputy." He looked up as Benny's truck sped away from the site. "Now where are those two idiots off to?" Shaking his head he lamented, "It's downright impossible to find good help these days. I can't keep guys on the job."

Todd tipped his hat. "Well, thanks again, sir. Good luck." He climbed into his car and pulled away from the construction site, more convinced than ever that Robert Sammons was up to no good.

"Sheriff, I hope you have a good explanation for dragging me down here so damned early." Kirk Trumbull wasn't used to getting out of bed until after noon. He tried to pull his pants up over his protruding belly as he stomped into Charlie's office. Dropping his large frame into a nearby chair, the lawyer gasped in relief. "If your people don't quit bothering my client, I'll file a harassment suit against your entire department."

Charlie stood up. "Don't get too comfortable, counselor. I'd like to have a little chat with your client now that you're here." He walked over to the door and opened it. "Hubert confessed. Again. Maybe you should worry more about him and less about my department." The sheriff waved a hand in front of his body, indicating that the lawyer should precede him. "After you."

Before he opened the door to the interrogation room, Kirk turned around to address Charlie. "Would it be possible for me to have a word alone with him, first?"

"Sure. I'll just stand here at the window. Just give me a little wave when you're ready."

"Thanks." Kirk turned around and stepped into the small room. "Hubert? What the hell is going on?"

The big man jumped to his feet, his wrinkled shirt and slacks attesting to his preoccupation with other matters. Hubert was normally so concerned about his appearance that his expensive suits spent more time at the dry cleaners than in his closet. "It's about fucking time you got here, man. I need you to get hold of that prosecutor and accept the deal he offered."

"Deal? What deal was that, Hubert?" The overweight lawyer lowered himself into the chair across from where his client was standing. "Are you talking about the deal I had worked so hard on before you opened your big mouth?" He sighed heavily. "Sit down, dumbass. Let's see what I can salvage from this mess." Kirk turned slightly and waved at the mirror. "Might as well see what the sheriff has to say. But you," he waved a shaky finger in Hubert's direction, "keep your goddamned mouth shut unless I tell you otherwise, understand?"

Hubert sat back down and brushed a hand through his hair. "Yeah, whatever."

The sheriff entered the room, barely able to hide his amusement at the look on Hubert's face. He sat down at one end of the table and turned on a small tape recorder. After stating the date and identifying himself and the others in the room, Charlie looked over at his prisoner. "Hubert Walters, do you understand the rights that were read to you earlier today?"

"Yeah, yeah. Let's just get on with it." Ignoring the glare from his lawyer, Hubert leaned over and locked eyes with Charlie. "I want some guarantee that you'll protect me, old man."

"Protect you? From what?"

"Bobby." Now sweating profusely, the younger man grabbed the sheriff's arm. "That son of a bitch killed Rick, and I'm next. He thinks I owe him money."

Charlie none-too-gently disentangled the hand from his arm and leaned back in his chair. "Why would he think that?"

"You don't have to—" Kirk started, only to be interrupted.

"'Cause he's the one that almost killed Lex, that's why. Jesus, old man, think about it!" Hubert jumped to his feet again and patted his shirt pocket, realizing belatedly that he had quit smoking years before. "Okay, look. Rick introduced me to Bobby right around Christmas. We played poker a few times, and I guess I must have complained about my sister at some point." He glanced over at Charlie to make certain he was listening. When the sheriff nodded, he continued. "Anyway, Bobby musta got it in his head that I'd pay him to get rid of Lex."

As the lawyer lowered his head in dismay, Charlie sat up taller in his seat. "And how did he come to that conclusion, Hubert?"

"How the fuck should I know?" Hubert sat back down at the table and began to draw patterns on the desk with one fingertip. "I had no idea what he had done, until he came into my office and beat the shit out of me."

"This...Bobby is the one responsible for putting you in the hospital? Why didn't you tell us that earlier? You could have saved us all a bunch of trouble, son."

Hubert slapped the table. "Haven't you been listening, old man? That crazy bastard would have killed me for sure."

Charlie shook his head. "Why tell us all this now?"

"Because," Hubert enunciated slowly, "I'm afraid for my life. Since Bobby already took care of Rick—"

"Jack Daniels or one of his close personal friends took care of Mr. Thompson," the sheriff informed him. "The man was stinking drunk and drove into a telephone pole."

A frown covered Hubert's face as he looked from Kirk to Charlie. "What are you saying?"

"I'm saying," Charlie spoke slowly, much as Hubert had done a moment before, "that you jumped to conclusions and panicked." He stood up and patted the stricken man's shoulder. "Thanks for all the information, son. I'm sure your lawyer can fill you in on what to expect in prison." He fought the urge to chuckle as he picked up his tape recorder and left the room.

Frank Holden, county commissioner and the man in charge of building inspections, was up for reelection in the fall. It was the only reason he had agreed to meet the older man now seated in front of him—Travis Edwards had money, and he was sure that he could convince the old gentleman to part with some of it. "I appreciate your position, Mr. Edwards, but these things take time."

He leaned back in his chair and linked his hands over his expanding waistline. Travis smiled across the desk at the commissioner. *Pompous little pissant. We'll just see how your attitude changes.* He straightened his tie and leaned forward slightly in his seat. "You would think so, wouldn't you? Strangely enough, on my way in, I saw several men playing cards in your conference room. You're not trying to tell me that this is how your inspectors spend their days, are you?"

Damn. I told them to keep the door closed. "Are you insinuating something, Mr. Edwards?"

"Of course not, Commissioner. I would just like to make sure my granddaughter's house has been inspected before she comes back from her trip. That's not too much to ask, is it?" He leaned back and reached into his pocket. "While I'm here, I'd love to make a campaign contribution." Travis pulled out a checkbook and smiled. "How much is the going rate these days?"

Visions of dollar signs began to race through Frank's head. *Oh, yeah. I knew he was an intelligent man.* He quickly jumped to his feet. "Let me just go get one of the men out to the ranch house, Mr. Edwards. Then we can discuss my campaign funds."

Travis smirked as the man hurried from the room. *Sometimes these greedy idiots just make this stuff too easy.* He patted the hidden tape recorder in his pocket and shook his head. *I don't believe our friend will have to worry about getting reelected, but he may want to brush up his job-hunting skills.*

Lex tossed her duffel bag into the back seat of the truck, relaxed after another good night's sleep. She turned around and leaned back against the side of the vehicle, glancing at the cabin with a wistful smile on her face. *I'm going to miss this place. Maybe I can talk Mrs. Charlton into selling. Talk about a great wedding present.* Hearing the slamming of the front door, Lex watched as her lover slowly ambled to where she was standing. *Her leg must be bothering her. I'm going to have to send her back to Doc Anderson.* "Got everything?"

"I think so," Amanda reached up with her free hand and brushed the hair out of her eyes. "I don't think I want to leave, though. It's been so wonderfully peaceful."

"I know what you mean. I was just thinking the same thing." Lex took Amanda's bag and tossed it next to hers, closing the door. "But I guess we've played hooky long enough, huh?"

Amanda grasped the taller woman's arm. "Only if you feel like going back, honey. There's nothing that won't wait—you're much more important." Although the shadows were gone from beneath Lex's eyes, Amanda couldn't help but worry that it was still too soon for them to go back. "I'm sure our families can handle everything for a few more days, if we need them to."

"Nah. I'm ready to get home. But it has been really nice, just lazing around in the sun with you." Lex pulled Amanda into her arms and kissed the top of her head. "We will have to come back, though," she murmured, burying her face in Amanda's hair.

"Maybe take off for one weekend a month?"

"Sounds good to me, Slim," Amanda agreed, snuggling close. She stood quietly for a long moment, just enjoying the feel of the loving arms around her and the warm sun against her skin. The happy song of a nearby mockingbird was the only sound she heard, aside from the beating of Lex's heart under her ear.

Pulling away regretfully, Lex looked down into her lover's eyes. "We're not getting very far, are we?"

"Depends on what you mean. But I suppose we'd better head back, since we told my grandparents that we'd stop by their house for lunch."

"Oh, yeah. I forgot all about that." Lex released her hold on Amanda and opened the front passenger door to the truck. "C'mon. Maybe Grandpa Jake is whipping up some of his famous stir-fry."

After dropping the shotgun off at Sherry's, the two women settled in for the short trip back to Somerville. A few miles from the lake, heavy smoke could be seen just off the road. Concerned, Lex pulled the truck behind a couple of other vehicles parked on the shoulder of the two-lane highway. A harried older woman covered in soot rushed over to the vehicle and knocked on Amanda's window.

Amanda rolled her window down. "What's going on? Is there something we can do to help?"

"Brush fire," the woman gasped out. "My husband and three kids are trying to contain it a few hundred yards west of here. It's heading straight for a mobile home park."

Amanda traded a quick glance with her partner. *Here we go again.* She mentally sighed to herself and turned back to the other woman. "Have you contacted the fire department?"

"That's why I was coming back to my car," the stranger admitted. "We're not from around here, and my cell phone won't work in this area. I was just about to head into town when y'all drove up."

Already stepping from the truck, Lex pulled her hair back into a ponytail and grabbed her black Stetson from the back seat. "How'd you find out about the fire?"

The woman reached into the back pocket of her dirty jeans and dug out a grubby handkerchief, which she used to wipe her face. "We were building a new fence down the road a ways and saw the smoke. We haven't been here that long, to tell the truth."

"Amanda," Lex had walked around to the passenger side of the truck and opened the door, "would you mind driving into town and notifying the authorities? I'm gonna see if I can help these folks, okay?" She knew from prior experience that her cell phone wouldn't work in the area, and also thought that this would be a good way to keep her lover out of harm's way.

An irrational fear coursed through Amanda. She didn't want to leave Lex. "I can help."

Lex shook her head and leaned forward, raising her hands and cupping her lover's face. "Not with that leg still giving you trouble," she reminded gently. "But you can be more help if you'd get the fire department out here."

"I don't want to leave you."

"I understand, love, 'cause I really don't want you to leave. But someone needs to contact the authorities. And you really should let your grandparents know that we may be a bit late for lunch."

Amanda regretfully accepted the keys from Lex. "I'll go. But I won't like it." Not caring that they weren't alone, she wrapped her arms around her partner's neck and pulled her close. "I love you," she whispered, as she leaned up and placed a soft kiss on Lex's lips.

"I love you too," Lex returned, after they pulled apart. "Contact Charlie when you get into town, and tell him which direction the fire is heading. He may want to evacuate the trailer park."

"I will." Amanda swallowed hard and started around to the driver's side of the truck. "Be careful."

Lex grinned. "Aren't I always?" She stood for a moment and watched as Amanda drove away, then looked back at the other woman standing a few feet away. "Well? You have any more shovels handy?"

The woman shook her head to clear it and shrugged her shoulders. "Uh, yeah. C'mon. We'll grab a couple and head back to where my family is."

Travis pulled his car up behind the large truck and smiled. *Great, they're back. I can't wait to tell them about the house.* He had just returned from the ranch, where he had watched the inspector tag the residence for immediate occupancy. Feeling quite proud of himself, the retired oil tycoon practically jogged up the steps to the house and stepped inside. Hearing voices in the den, he quickened his step in anticipation.

"I'm not a child, Grandpa. I need to get back and see what I can do to help," Amanda pleaded.

Jacob looked up as his good friend stepped into the room. "Travis, thank goodness you're here. I could use some reinforcements about now." He patted his granddaughter on the knee and stood up. "Maybe you can help me convince Amanda that she'd be better off staying here with us."

"What's going on? Where's Lexie?"

"She's out near the lake helping fight a brush fire. I was on my way back to help, but Grandpa seems to think I'd just be in the way." Although her recently healed leg was aching, Amanda felt that her place was with her partner, not sitting in town waiting for news.

Both men sat down, one on each side of Amanda. Jacob put his hand on her leg and shook his head. "Honey, it's not that I'd think you'd be in the way—I'm just concerned about your welfare. When you came into the house, I could tell that your leg was still bothering you. How much help are you going to be out there if you're in pain?"

"He's right, you know. Have you ever been around a fire like that? It's strenuous work."

Amanda recognized the logic of Travis's words and knew when she'd been beaten. "No, I haven't." She wiped the tears of frustration from her face and sniffled. "But I can't just sit around here waiting, not knowing what's going on out there."

"You've done the important part, Peanut. I'm sure that with the fire department and all the volunteers, the blaze will be out in no time. I know how hard it was for you to leave Lex out there and come into town for help." Jacob wrapped his arm around his granddaughter's shoulders and pulled her close.

"I still don't like it. There's got to be something that I can do, or some way I can find out what's happening. The waiting around and not knowing is going to drive me crazy."

Travis patted her back and looked over at his friend. *There has to be a way to keep updated without actually being there.* A sudden idea popped into his head. "What about a radio?"

Jacob thought for a moment. "Of course. Why didn't I think of that?" He stood up, pulling Amanda up with him. "C'mon, sweetheart. We're going down the street to see a friend of mine."

"What? Who?" Amanda looked from one man to the other in confusion. She allowed herself to be escorted out of the room, but was at a loss to determine what her grandfather was up to.

Jabbing the blade of the shovel into the hard earth, Lex leaned on the handle of the tool and wiped her forehead against her shoulder. The heat from the fire that they had been battling for several hours was beginning to wear on her, and she silently cursed herself for her lack of stamina. She glanced to her right, where another woman was busy shoveling bits of dirt onto the slowly moving flames.

After she had watched Amanda drive off, Lex followed the older woman to the truck and gathered up several more tools. While they hurried back to where the woman's family was busy trying to contain the fire, she learned more about her new companion. Tammy Kirkpatrick was the mother of three adult children, ranging in ages from twenty-three to thirty-two. They all worked in the family business of fence and barn building. Her only daughter was twenty-five years old and, as she explained to Lex, was the most trying of the three.

"I swear, that girl will be the death of me some day. She's always got her head in the clouds, and can't seem to do a simple task without being led through it. Kathy's a dreamer, that's all there is to it." Mrs. Kirkpatrick handed Lex a shovel from the rear of the truck. "This is the first job we've been able to get her on in months. I don't know what I'm going to do with that girl."

Lex accepted the tool. "I can understand your concern. But maybe Kathy needs to find her own niche, and that might not be in the family business." She didn't expect the vehement response that erupted from the older woman.

"That's a load of bull puckey if I've ever heard it! I think the girl's just afraid of a little hard work. She needs to get her feet back on the ground and quit dawdling." The older woman's light-gray eyes looked up into the shadowed face above her. "I've been grooming her to take over for years. Lord knows her brothers ain't got enough sense to run the business like she could." She thumped Lex on the back and started back to the woods. "C'mon, hon. We'd best get to work."

Lex looked over at where the younger Kirkpatrick woman was busy throwing shovelfuls of dirt. *Doesn't look lazy to me. I just think she's just not interested in building fences for the rest of her life.* She had been given a brief introduction to Kathy, and could quickly tell that the young lady was no more suited for fence building than she herself would be at a desk job. *Seems like her mother has a bit in common with my old man—trying to make her kids into something they're not.* Shaking her head, Lex wiped the sweat from her brow again, and decided to circle around several yards away. She hoped to force the fire back into itself, which would cause it to burn out.

When she stepped over the small hill, Lex found out that several volunteers had the same idea as she. Three men were hacking down trees to make a firebreak, and one looked up and saw the rancher nearby. He waved one arm in greeting and then pointed her back into the trees. "We need more folks over there," he yelled.

"Okay," Lex returned, waving back and stepping into the denser brush. With a quick look around, she could see what the man had meant. There were no other people in this part of the woods, and the fire looked to be burning quickly beyond their control. "Damn. Guess I'd better get busy." She ducked in reflex as the top of a tree exploded, showering bits of ash and debris down around her.

Chapter 19

The threesome stood on a front porch, not unlike Jacob and Anna Leigh's. The door opened to show a wizened old man, who wasn't much taller than Amanda. Jacob took another step closer so that he could be seen more clearly. "I hope we're not disturbing you, Rob. This is my granddaughter Amanda, and my friend Travis. We were wondering if you had your scanner on."

Rob nodded as he opened the screen door and gestured for them to step inside. "Sure do. Been listening to them fight that fire out by the lake." He waved an arm at the furniture in the cluttered living room. "Have a seat."

Jacob gently guided his granddaughter in front of him. "Thanks. We've got family out there right now, and were hoping to listen in with you."

Amanda perched on one end of the sofa, sitting as close as she could to the radio that took up the center of the rickety coffee table. She could hear garbled static, and looked up at their host. "Have you heard any news?"

"Some." Rob dropped into a chair across from Amanda. "There's three different departments out there, as well as two volunteer agencies. They're afraid it's going to get out of hand, because of the wind."

Oh, no. "What about the people that are out there right now? Are they in any danger?"

"From what I've heard so far, there's already been injuries to a few of the firefighters. They're just hoping they can stop it before it gets to the populated areas."

"Injuries?" Her heart pounding in panic, Amanda looked at Jacob and Travis. "I've got to get out there."

Jacob, who had sat down next to her, grabbed Amanda by the arm. "No, honey. Stay here with us." He looked over at Travis, who had a worried expression on his face. "Lex is probably just fine, right?"

"Oh, right," Travis agreed, not looking too convinced. He glanced over at their host. "Did they mention any names of the people that had been injured?"

"Not—" Rob's answer was cut off by the radio.

"Dispatch, this is Unit Four. We need an ambulance immediately."

All four people stared at the device, waiting for more information.

"Ten-four, Sam. We've got one en route. How bad is it?" the dispatcher asked.

"Can't tell for sure at this time, Dispatch. The woman was trapped under a burning tree for a few minutes—she's still unconscious."

"Roger that. The ambulance is on the way, Sam. Dispatch out."

Amanda jumped to her feet. "I can't sit by and listen to this. That could be Lex!" She was almost to the door when a strong hand clamped down on her arm. Turning, Amanda looked up to see Travis's worried countenance. "I've got to go."

"No, sweetheart. If you want, we can go back to the house and wait, but I can't allow you to go running off half-cocked like this." Travis appeared to have aged in the past half-hour. His sad eyes looked out from a drawn and tired face. "You know Lexie wouldn't want you to place yourself in danger."

"I may know it, but that doesn't mean I have to like it." Amanda leaned into his arms for support.

Lex used her hat to brush the embers from her clothes. The heat from the fire was almost unbearable, and she took a moment to spare a glance a few yards away. Kathy Kirkpatrick had joined her a few minutes earlier, and was having problems of her own. The younger woman kept running her fingers through her blonde hair, fighting the bits of ash and fiery debris that continued to pelt the volunteers. After watching for a moment, Lex hurried over to check on Kathy. "You okay?" she yelled, to be heard over the noise of the fire.

"I think so," Kathy admitted, then screamed. "I think my hair's on fire—help me!" She frantically slapped at her head. "It burns!"

"Calm down!" Lex grabbed her and pulled her away from the blaze, waiting until they were well away from the fire before turning her attention to Kathy's hair. "Let me see."

Kathy leaned her head forward until her chin touched her chest. "God, it hurts." She placed her hands on Lex's hips to keep from digging at her own scalp.

"Looks like you've got a couple of nice little burns here." Lex took off her hat and placed it on Kathy's head. "Wear this. It should keep the burns fairly clean until you can get some medical attention."

"I can't take your hat. What about you?" Kathy lifted the brim of the hat back so she could see.

"I don't have burns on my head. I'll be fine. Do you want me to help you get back to the main road? I'm sure they have paramedics standing by who can treat you."

"No. I want to keep trying to get this damned thing under control. My mother would never let me hear the end of it if I stopped now." Kathy picked up her shovel from where she had dropped it and jogged back to the fire.

"Stubborn. But I can't really blame her." Lex picked up her tool and went back to work a few yards away from the determined woman.

The large man wiped the sweat from his forehead with the end of his shirt. *Sure got hot around here fast.* He continued to walk through the smoldering mess, doing his best to avoid the volunteers and firefighters. *Stupid wind. Damned fire was supposed to move to the lake, not away from it.* The idea had come to him the previous day, when he found out by accident where Lex was staying.

Bobby was picking up supplies at the hardware store when he overheard two women talking in the next aisle. "They're such nice young women, Ida. It makes me feel good to know that old cabin will actually be getting some use."

"I know what you mean, Betty. I don't know why you continue to keep that old place out at the lake if you're not going to use it."

"I can't seem to make myself let it go. It was our secret little hideaway from the world. But I'm glad that Martha called me. Poor Lexington. Her house burning down, and then having her father die."

Just as he was about to leave the aisle, Bobby stopped. Lexington, huh? Staying out at the lake? *He listened for a few more minutes, then decided to follow the women from the store.* All I need to do is find out her name, and then I can figure out which house at the lake is hers.

He carefully stepped behind the two women at the checkout counter, listening as they spoke to each other so he could recognize the voice of the woman he needed to learn more about. When the cashier thanked her by name, he almost laughed out loud. Mrs. Charlton, huh? Sometimes being in a small town comes in handy.

A few well-placed calls later, Bobby learned that the woman was a widow, and she owned a small cabin on the secluded side of Lake Somerville. He decided to take a nice quiet drive out to the lake to see if he could find the cabin, and the Walters woman. Lakes are dangerous places-no telling what kind of accident could happen to her out there.

Bobby continued to walk through the smoky brush. *I thought a fire would be a perfect idea. How was I supposed to know the damned wind would change directions? I shoulda parked my truck away from the fire. Now I'm going to have to find a ride back to the lake to pick it up.* Not wanting to walk very far, Bobby had parked his work truck just off the road from where he was planning on starting the fire. When the wind changed directions, it cut him off and forced him to run the other way to save himself.

Stepping into a smoke-filled clearing, he looked around and saw two slim figures fighting the fire. One was wearing a black western hat, which caused him to almost laugh out loud. *You've got to be kidding me.* After following Lex around to try and catch her alone, he was able to recognize her headwear easily. When she had disappeared, he was afraid she had left town to go into hiding. *I hope Hubert realizes just how much work I've gone through for him. The son of a bitch better pay me this time.* Bobby crept closer to the woman wearing the hat.

A few miles away, two men stood in a charred clearing. One was dressed as an officer of the law, the other in a heavy fireman's coat and hat. "Right there, Sheriff," the fire chief pointed to the lumpy remains of a melted gasoline container. "I figure it started here, then the wind caught it and blew it back in their face." He wiped a handkerchief across his face.

"Sounds about right. That means that whoever started this could still be out here, somewhere." Charlie looked around at the devastation that the fire had caused. "Why would someone want to start a fire out here? What possible purpose could it serve?"

"I don't know, Charlie. If it weren't for the melted gas can, I'd think it was a campsite that just got out of control—being this close to the lake and all. Why someone would want to start a fire this close to all those houses is beyond me."

The sheriff looked in the general direction he thought the lake was, but a small, blackened hill blocked his view. "Which side of the lake? Damn, I always get turned around out here."

The short, heavyset fireman laughed. "Now I know why you're a sheriff, and not a park ranger. But, to answer your question, we're on the east side—not as many houses, thankfully." He watched as Charlie paled.

"East?" The lawman closed his eyes. "It can't be," he mumbled. "How would he have found out?"

"Hey now. Maybe we should go back to our cars. You're not looking so good, my friend."

Charlie's eyes reopened, and a no-nonsense look came over his face. "You need me here for anything else? I've got some business to attend to." He turned on his heel and left without waiting for an answer.

Bobby edged up behind the hard-working figure, looking around until he was certain that the woman was alone. *I've been waiting a long time to do this.* He picked up a short tree limb and slammed it across the shoulders of the person in front of him.

The woman fell forward, stunned, the black hat falling off her head and exposing her blonde hair.

"Who the fuck are you?" Bobby yelled. He used a booted foot

to flip her over, and looked down at the unfamiliar face. The woman moaned and started to stir. "Shit."

A short distance away, Lex looked up from where she had been shoveling dirt. She glanced through the smoky haze around her. "Kathy?" She thought that she had heard someone yell, but with the crackling noise coming from the burning grass and trees, she couldn't be certain. "Now where did she go?" Deciding to go check on her new friend, Lex walked through the smoke to where she had last seen Kathy.

Still angry, Bobby kicked the black hat away from the barely conscious woman, who rolled over and blinked at him hazily. "Stupid broad. You shouldn't have been wearing that damned hat." He bent down and picked up the discarded shovel. "I ought to whack you a good one for that."

Lex stepped into the clearing and spotted an unfamiliar figure standing over a still body. "Hey!" She stopped in her tracks as the man turned around to face her. "What's going on?"

"You!" Bobby bellowed, charging Lex and wildly brandishing the tool. When he was close enough, he swung the shovel at her head.

She ducked and stepped back, falling backwards over the charred remains of a tree. "Are you crazy?" Lex yelled, barely raising her own shovel up to block another blow. She could feel the heat of the fire behind her, and looked around for a way to escape the deranged man in front of her.

Bobby looked down into the soot-covered face. "Why can't you just die like everyone else?" He pulled back the tool and stabbed it at Lex, who quickly rolled out of the way.

"What the hell are you talking about?" Lex could feel hot spots on her back, where she'd rolled over coals from the fire. "Have you lost your damn mind?" She swung her shovel like a baseball bat, enjoying the feel as the spade made connection with the side of the man's knee.

"You bitch!" Dropping his weapon as he fell, Bobby cradled his knee with both hands and rolled away from her. "I think you broke my fucking leg!"

Climbing to her feet, Lex stood over the whining man. "Serves you right, asshole." Realizing that she had seen him somewhere before, Lex was about to ask him who he was when she looked across the clearing to the fire. Only a few yards separated the blaze from the still form of her friend. She quickly covered the ground between them and dropped to her knees beside Kathy.

The groggy woman began to stir, and she blinked her eyes and tried to focus on the face above her. "No," she cried hoarsely, trying to push the person away from her.

"Shh...it's okay," Lex assured her in a soft voice. "It's just me."

"What happened?" Kathy gasped, struggling to sit up. She reached for her head and moaned in pain. "Oh, not a good idea."

Lex put one arm around the injured woman and helped her. "I think you got knocked out by a crazy guy. How are you feeling?"

Kathy looked up into her friend's concerned face. "Like I got knocked out by a crazy guy," she joked, then her eyes widened. "Lex!"

"I'll kill both of you!" Bobby had limped over to where Lex was kneeling, and stood over the two women as he raised the shovel over his head. Sweat mixed with the soot on his face and made the deranged man appear as if he were melting.

In an attempt to protect the injured woman in her arms, Lex covered Kathy with her own body as she braced herself for the blow.

"Hold it!" another voiced yelled from somewhere in front of the three. "Sheriff's department. Put down your weapon!"

"Fuck you!" Bobby yelled, as the dirt-covered blade began its arc towards Lex's head.

A single shot rang out, the sound echoing over the crackling and hissing of the nearby fire. The blunt side of the spade grazed Lex's shoulder as Bobby fell back away from them. A dark stain appeared in the center of his shirt, and he looked down in confusion before his eyes rolled up in his head as he hit the ground.

Charlie holstered his gun and raced to where the man had fallen. He dropped to his knees and placed one hand on Bobby's neck, closing his eyes momentarily when he didn't find a pulse. Shaking his head, he turned to look at the two women. "Lex? Are you okay?"

"Uncle Charlie?" Lex straightened up stiffly, turned around and saw the fallen man behind the sheriff. "Is he—"

"Dead," Charlie reached over and put an arm around her shoulder. "Are you two all right?"

"I think so." Lex leaned into his embrace. "You're going to

explain all of this to me, right?"

The sheriff half-laughed, half-cried. "I'll sure try to, sweetheart." He climbed to his feet, pulling her up with him. "C'mon. Let's get you two checked out. I'll have a deputy come out and clean up this mess."

"Sounds like a good idea to me," Lex agreed, helping a confused Kathy up as well. "What do you think?"

Kathy bent down to pick up the hat, then reached up so she could place it on Lex's head. "I think that next time you offer to give me your hat, I'll let you keep it." Exhausted, Kathy allowed herself to be supported between the other two and be led from the clearing.

Anna Leigh watched as her granddaughter paced across the living room. She had left the real estate office in Wanda's capable hands and hurried home at her husband's request. Jacob was at a loss as to how they were going to keep Amanda from driving back out to the fire, even though they had heard earlier on the radio that the blaze was finally under control. The young woman crossed the room and looked out through the windows, releasing a heavy sigh. "Mandy, dear. Please come over here and sit down for a few minutes. I'm getting tired just watching you."

"I'm sorry, Gramma." Amanda turned away from the window and walked over to the sofa to sit down. "I just hate not knowing anything."

"I understand, Mandy, but wearing a hole in the floor isn't going to help. "I'm sure that we'll hear from Lexington any time now."

"I hope so. I just have this feeling that something isn't right." The shrill ringing of the telephone caused Amanda to flinch and jump up, picking up the receiver before it could ring again. "Cauble residence, Amanda speaking."

"Amanda? This is Charlie."

"Charlie? Oh, God." The young woman faltered slightly, causing her grandmother to jump to her feet and hurry to her side. "Is this about Lex?"

"Don't panic. It's not bad, really. But—"

Feeling her legs go weak, Amanda leaned up against the wall. "Is she okay? Have you seen her?"

"Lex is going to be just fine, Amanda. We're at the hospital right now, and—"

"Hospital?" Amanda would have slid to the floor if not for her grandmother's steadying arm around her waist. "Why are you at the hospital? What happened?"

"It's just routine. Is there anyone there with you now?"

Amanda fought to catch her breath. "Why? What aren't you telling me, Charlie? What happened to Lex?" she asked tearfully. A gentle hand took the receiver away from her.

"Charlie? This is Anna Leigh."

"Thank goodness. I'm here at the hospital, Anna Leigh. I don't know if they're going to keep Lex overnight for observation, but I wanted to let you know what was going on. She's got a few minor burns on her back, and I think they're treating her for smoke inhalation. But believe me, she's going to be just fine."

"We're on our way, Charlie. Thank you for calling." Anna Leigh hung up the phone, then turned to look into her granddaughter's face. She's okay, Mandy. The hospital is just a precaution. We can—"

Travis and Jacob stood in the doorway, one with soapy hands and the other with a dishtowel, wiping a plate. "Who was that on the phone?" Jacob asked, accepting the dishtowel from Travis and wiping his hands with it.

Amanda wiped the tears from her face, taking strength in her family's presence. "It was Charlie. He said that Lex is at the hospital, but she's going to be all right."

"Well? What are we waiting for?" Travis set the plate on a nearby table. "Let's go see her."

Cool, efficient hands continued to daub ointment on the multiple, but minor burns. "You were very lucky. It appears that your shirt took the worst of the damage." The doctor placed gauze pads over the treated wounds to keep the medication from smearing or rubbing off.

"Yeah, right." Lex looked back over her shoulder at the composed man. "So, does that mean I can leave?"

"I don't think so, Ms. Walters. We're going to send you to X-ray for that bruise on your shoulder, and then keep you overnight to make sure your lungs stay clear. You inhaled quite a bit of smoke today." The doctor finished dressing the burns and pulled a thin sheet over her back. "Now just lie there and relax, and the orderly will be in shortly to take you upstairs." He patted her leg gently before leaving the room.

Lex put her head back down on the pillow. She was beginning to feel the effects of the shot the nurse had given her earlier for pain, and she struggled to keep her eyes open. "Stupid doctor." She heard the door open again, and turned her head to see who it was. The sturdy form of the housekeeper stood outlined in the doorway. "Martha?"

"That's right." Martha stepped into the room to stand beside the bed. She had been given a ride to the hospital by one of the sheriff's deputies, while Charlie followed the ambulance that brought Lex and Kathy in. Unable to keep her hands to herself, she gently stroked Lex's cheek. "How are you feeling, Lexie?"

"I'm fine, Mada." Lex blinked several times to clear her vision. "Just a bit groggy from the shot they gave me." She happily absorbed the attention for a few moments until her thoughts cleared. "Where's Amanda? Has anyone called her?" She tried to sit up, but was gently pushed back down by Martha.

"You just lie there and relax. Charlie called her, and her grandparents are bringing her over." Martha watched as her charge lost the battle with the tranquilizer and closed her eyes. "That's it, Lexie. Rest." She wrinkled her nose at the strong odor of smoke emanating from the sleeping woman. "It's gonna take days to get you clean, I'll bet," she murmured, a knowing smile on her face. "Some things just never change."

The door swung open and an emotional dynamo burst into the room. "Lex! Is she..." Amanda soon found herself next to Martha, both looking down with concern at Lex.

Martha put an arm around the younger woman. "Shh. She's going to be just fine. Before I got here, the doctor gave her a shot to help her rest."

"So she's all right?" Amanda reached down and brushed the hair away from Lex's peaceful face.

"Yes. I cornered a nurse out in the hall to find out what was going on before I came in. She's got a few minor burns on her back and a bruise on her shoulder. They want Lexie to stay overnight because of all the smoke, but it's just a precaution." Martha straightened the sheet, pulling it up around Lex's shoulders. "I swear, this kid can find more trouble."

"She sure can." Amanda's eyes met the sad ones across from her. "How did she get hurt, Martha? It's not like Lex to get careless around a fire."

The door opened again, and a burly man with a crew cut entered the room. "I'm sorry, folks. But I've got to get Ms. Walters upstairs to X-ray." He looked down at the paperwork in his hands. "She's assigned to room two-eleven, if you want to wait for her there. It shouldn't take too long." He placed the paperwork at the foot of the bed and unlocked the wheels. "I should have her back to her regular room in less than thirty minutes." With an apologetic smile, the young man wheeled the bed out of the room and down the hall.

"Well." Martha watched as he maneuvered the long bed through the doorway. "Let's go find that husband of mine. I'm sure he'll be glad to fill us in on any details."

Tammy Kirkpatrick sat next to her daughter's bed, holding the sleeping woman's hand. The family had returned to their vehicle after getting the fire under control and was met by a sheriff's deputy. He had been standing by their truck waiting for them to return, and told them of Kathy's injury. The deputy gave Tammy a ride to the hospital, while the rest of the family went home to get cleaned up. "My poor little girl," she whispered, brushing her hand down the slender arm that was exposed.

Kathy's eyes fluttered open and she focused on her mother's worried face. "Mama? What's wrong?"

The quiet question was Tammy's undoing. She leaned her head forward until it rested on the bed besides Kathy's arm, and began to cry.

"Mama, please don't cry. I'm fine." *Aside from a headache that would fell a moose.* Kathy reached down and stroked her mother's hair. "Where's that cantankerous woman I'm always fighting with?"

Tammy sniffled then raised her head. "Who are you calling cantankerous?" She looked up into her daughter's face and used one hand to caress Kathy's cheek. "I'm so sorry for all the fighting, honey."

Kathy squeezed her mother's hand. "Don't be. I'd kinda miss it if we didn't argue about everything. Keeps things interesting."

"Oh, baby." The older woman burst into tears again, burying her face in the blankets. She cried for a few moments and then raised her head again. "I've been thinking while I've been sitting here waiting for you to wake up." Tammy wiped at her face with her free hand. "And I've come to realize something."

"What's that, Mama?"

After standing up, the matriarch of the Kirkpatrick clan paced around the room. "All these years, I thought I knew what was best for you, and for the family. Your father allowed me free rein over you kids because he thought I knew what was best, too." Tammy peeked through the blinds to the darkness outside. She had been waiting in the hospital for several hours, and the sun had set while she was inside. "My stubborn pride wouldn't allow me to think that you never wanted what I did for you, Kath. And because of that, you could have been killed today."

"No, Mama. You can't blame yourself for that." Kathy sat up in the bed, grabbing the top of her head in pain. The topical antiseptic that the doctor had used for the burns on her head stuck to her fingers, and she grimaced at the gooey feeling. "It was a crazy man. It had nothing to do with you."

Tammy turned around. "But you would have never even been out there if I wasn't so damned insistent that you take over the family business." She walked back over to the bed and sat down on the edge, handing her daughter a tissue to clean her sticky fingers. "I don't think I can ever forgive myself for that, honey."

After wiping her hands free of the ointment, Kathy reached for her mother's hand. She studied the slightly gnarled fingers that had seen so much work in their lifetime. "There's nothing to forgive." She gazed at the small scars and age spots that were testimony to years of hard work in the sun. "I don't think I could ever do the work you do, Mama. It's just not in me." Kathy looked up into the tear-stained face. "But I never want to disappoint you, either."

"Then I guess you'll just have to do what makes you happy," Tammy told her, "because whatever you decide to do, I know I'll be proud." She leaned forward and kissed Kathy on the forehead.

The first things that registered with her upon awakening were that she was lying on her stomach, in the dark, and a tightness stretched across her back. Lex used her hands to push herself up and slowly rolled over, almost crying out when she put her full weight on the small burns. Her shoulder was aching as well, but she was more concerned for the small form curled up in a nearby chair. A thin shaft of light from the outside streetlights peeked through the blinds and splayed across the young woman's sleeping countenance. While Lex tried to decide on whether or not to wake her, Amanda's eyes opened and sleepily tracked to her face.

"Hey." Amanda stood up and stretched, then took the single step needed to stand beside the bed. "How are you feeling?" she asked, reaching down and running her fingertips over her lover's cheek.

"Not too bad," Lex croaked. She smiled her gratitude when Amanda poured her a glass of water and brought the straw to her lips. After taking several sips, she cleared her throat. "Thanks."

Amanda took the empty glass and set it down on the bedside table. "You're welcome, love." She felt a warm hand grasp hers and looked down to meet Lex's concerned gaze. "What's wrong? Are you in pain?"

"No, I'm fine." Lex pulled her lover closer until Amanda had no choice but to sit on the edge of the bed. "What time is it? How long have I been out?"

"You've been asleep for a few hours. The sedative that the doctor gave you was pretty strong."

Lex scooted over slowly to give Amanda more room. "And you've been here all this time? Why didn't you go and get some rest?" Even in the dim light, she saw the answering shrug, as Amanda refused to look her in the eyes. "Sweetheart, look at me, please." Lex squeezed the hand she was holding. When exhausted eyes looked into hers, Lex felt her heart ache. She tugged on Amanda's hand. "C'mere."

Amanda collapsed into the waiting arms and buried her face in her partner's neck. She allowed the tears she had been holding at bay to fall as Lex stroked her back and pulled her into a deeper embrace, murmuring soft words of love to her.

Chapter 20

Robert Campbell had spent the better part of the morning in a meeting with Sheriff Bristol and Judge Packer. The three men had come to the conclusion that justice would be better served by trying to work out a plea bargain with Hubert Walters, since the only concrete connection between the conspiring parties was now in the morgue. He decided that a little acting was in order, so that Hubert's lawyer wouldn't realize they didn't have much of a case for conspiracy to commit murder. The county prosecutor glared at the two men across the table from him. "Let me go on the record as saying, if it were up to me, you'd go to trial."

Kirk Trumbull nodded, the relief showing clearly on his face. He had been up all night trying to figure out how to keep from going to trial. He rarely made court appearances, except when he'd sat with Hubert in his attempt to try and take the ranch away from Lex. "So you've said, several times. What kind of deal are we talking about here? Time served? Or maybe probation?"

"You've got to be kidding me. We've got your client's confession. Not once, but twice." Robert looked over at Hubert, whose several days' growth of beard was liberally peppered with gray, unlike the completely black hair on his head. "With the charges brought against you, Mr. Walters, you could be looking at some serious time in the state penitentiary."

"That's bullshit! It was all Bobby's doing. All you have to do is catch him." Hubert looked from the prosecutor to his lawyer. "Help me out here, Kirk."

"Actually, we've already caught Robert Sammons, but he's not talking." *Dead men tell no tales,* he thought wryly. "You're going to take the fall all by yourself."

Hubert jumped up and pointed at the smirking man. "Fuck that! There's no way I'm taking the blame for what that psycho has done." He grabbed his attorney's arm and pulled, hard. "You need to fix this! Why the hell do I pay you?"

"Calm down, Hubert." The sweating lawyer pried his client's fingers away from his arm. "Sit down and shut up."

Looking as if he were going to argue, the agitated man grudgingly resumed his seat and glared across the table.

"If you can't control your client, Mr. Trumbull, you can wait and discuss all of this with the judge." Robert waited until both men were silent. "As I was saying, we'd like to save the taxpayers some time and money. So, I'm prepared to offer you a deal—four years in the state penitentiary, with a chance for parole in two."

The prisoner lept to his feet again. "You've got to be out of your fucking mind! Four goddamned years? No way in Hell."

Robert gathered up the papers that were in front of him. "Fine. Go to trial, and when you're found guilty of attempted murder, enjoy spending at least fifteen to twenty years behind bars." He stood up and placed the papers in his briefcase.

"Wait!"

The prosecutor looked at Kirk, who had stood up as well. "Yes?"

"Give me a couple of minutes with my client, Mr. Campbell. Please?"

"Certainly. I'll be outside waiting for you."

Once the door closed behind the prosecutor, Kirk leaned over his friend. "Now you listen to me, Hubert. We don't have a whole lot of options, here. You're going to go to prison—there's no doubt about that." When his client refused to look at him, Kirk grabbed his shoulder and squeezed. "Do you understand me, boy? When they find you guilty—"

Hubert impatiently shoved the hand off his shoulder. "How do you know they'll do that?"

"Because," the lawyer sat down so he could look Hubert in the eye, "they've got two confessions from you, you idiot. Make no mistake about it, you're going to prison. But it's up to you exactly how long you'll be there."

Defeated, the accountant lowered his head into his hands. "All right. Tell him we've got a deal."

Lex waited indulgently while Amanda opened the passenger door of the truck. She climbed into the cab gingerly, mindful of the small burns on her back. When Amanda slipped the seat belt around her and locked it, Lex couldn't help but chuckle. "Thanks, Amanda. But you don't have to—"

"Humor me, all right?" Amanda asked, gently closing the door and jogging around to the other side. Once she was buckled in, she turned to face her partner. "Are you sure you want to do this?"

"Yeah, I'm sure. It's something I really need to do." Lex leaned back carefully in the seat as the large vehicle rumbled to life. "But you don't have to stay. I'm sure I can get a ride home."

Amanda checked all the mirrors and pulled out of the hospital parking lot. "I don't think so. We're in this together, love. I'll be glad to go with you."

"Thanks." She closed her eyes and fought off the nagging pain of the burns. "It shouldn't take long, anyway."

Fifteen minutes later, Lex, Amanda, and the sheriff stood outside a small room. "Thanks for giving me this chance, Uncle Charlie." Lex looked over at Amanda, who was peering through a two-way glass and watching the inhabitant with some amusement. "What are you giggling at?"

"Sorry. It's just that he looks so different. I don't think I've ever seen him in bright orange." Amanda was getting a deep sense of satisfaction at seeing the man in the jail's normal attire.

"I'm glad you got here when you did, Lex. Otherwise, you would have had to drive to Huntsville. He's being transported out in the morning." Charlie grasped Lex's forearm. "Do you want me to go in with you?"

"No. I really need to do this by myself." Lex looked up into his concerned eyes. "But I don't mind if you want to stand out here and keep an eye on things." With a final look at both of them, Lex squared her shoulders and opened the heavy door, closing it quietly behind her.

Hubert looked up as the door opened. His face wore several days' growth of beard and his normally well-coifed hair sat plastered against his head. His reddened eyes glared into the similar pair that belonged to his sister. "Well, well. Come to gloat, little sister?"

Lex stood across the table from him, her hands gripping the back of the folding chair. "No, Hubert. I came to see if there was anything you needed me to do for you before you left." She studied his face for a long moment. "Maybe bring you some shampoo, or an electric razor?"

"Bitch!" He jumped to his feet, his chair clattering noisily to the floor. Hubert pointed an angry finger at her. "This is all your fault, you know. I bet our old man is rolling around in his grave, seeing what you've done to me."

"Don't you dare invoke our father's name with me, you pathetic excuse for a man." Lex placed both hands on the scarred wood and leaned across the table. "He asked for you every day he lay dying in that hospital, but you'd have nothing to do with him. So you have no right to speak of him now."

He reached for her shirt, but found his hands batted away almost effortlessly. "Fuck you! At least I didn't kill him!" Hubert leaned back against the wall and ran both hands through his greasy hair. "You disgust me."

Refusing to be baited, Lex straightened up. "Yeah, well, being considered disgusting by a prick like you really hurts," she retorted, turning and walking back to the door. She stopped and faced him one last time. "I hope you make lots of new friends in prison, big brother. Have fun." Lex stepped through the door and closed it, hearing a muffled yell through the wall as she exchanged looks with Charlie. "He's all yours, Uncle Charlie. Thanks." She held out her hand to Amanda, who wordlessly grabbed it and escorted her down the hallway.

The drive back to the ranch house was a quiet one, as Lex continued to mull over the conversation she'd had with Hubert. A part of her was hurt that, once again, her brother had disregarded her peace overtures. Another part was angry with herself that she had even tried. She continued to stare out the passenger window, torn by her warring emotions.

"Penny for your thoughts." A soft voice broke through her reverie as a hand squeezed her thigh.

Lex turned away from the window. "Doubt if they're worth that much. I was just thinking."

"About what?"

"My own stupidity, I suppose." When Amanda opened her mouth to argue, Lex waved her hand. "No, really. All my life, I've tried to live up to some twisted sense of family where Hubert is concerned. I guess it just took all this time to finally realize that he's never going to change." She dropped her left hand to cover Amanda's. "It just hurts, losing another part of my family."

"Lex, he may have been related to you by blood, but that bastard was never a part of your family." Amanda felt her temper flare at the incarcerated Hubert. "He doesn't deserve the right to be a Walters, Lex. You've given your family name more honor by your actions than he could ever hope to buy with his schemes—don't let that man take anything away from you. He's not worth wasting another thought over." She reluctantly removed her hand from the strong grip and used it to turn the truck on to the private road to the ranch.

"I know you're right, I guess I was just hoping for a miracle." Lex reached up and ran her fingers through Amanda's hair. "Thanks."

Driving over the old bridge brought a certain sense of déjà vu to Amanda, and she unconsciously tightened her grip on the steering wheel as she fought with the urge to close her eyes. She still got butterflies in her stomach each time she drove across the wooden structure.

"Amanda?" Lex felt her lover tense as the truck rumbled through the bridge. "What's wrong?"

"Nothing." Once they had crossed through to the other side, Amanda visibly relaxed. "Oh! I almost forgot. Martha wanted us to stop by her house, if you think you're up to it. She's probably whipped up a late lunch or something." She smiled as the ranch house came into view. The outside looked much nicer since it had been rebuilt, and the brick was a pleasant change from the dirty-looking stucco that it had replaced. Amanda glanced over at Lex, who was also studying the clean lines of their home with a faraway look on her face. The edges of her mouth were curved upward into a slight smile, and Amanda fell in love with Lex all over again. "Whatcha thinking about?"

"Hmm?" Lex turned and her smile widened. "You."

Amanda blushed as she parked the large truck behind the house. "Um..."

"You're cute when you blush." Deciding to take pity on her embarrassed friend, she unbuckled her seat belt and opened the door. "Let's go see what's on Martha's mind."

Amanda climbed out of the vehicle and followed Lex down the well-traveled stone path. "I have a pretty good idea."

Moments later, both women were greeted at the cottage door by Martha, who pulled them inside and wrapped her arms around them. "Goodness! I didn't expect you to come over the second you got home, girls." She stepped back and looked at Lex. "Honey, you look like you're about to fall down. Come sit down on the sofa."

"Mada, I'm fine," Lex argued, but allowed the older woman to guide her into the living room. She sat down and leaned back carefully as the burns on her back began to ache. *This is getting tiresome.* Her eyes closed against her will, the emotionally draining morning catching up to her.

Martha stood quietly for a moment and watched Lex drift off to sleep almost immediately. She felt a light touch on her arm and turned around to see Amanda gesture towards the kitchen. With a slight nod, she turned and followed her down the small hallway. After the door closed behind them, Martha wrapped her arms around the younger woman. "You look like you could use this," she whispered in Amanda's ear, hugging her tightly.

With a gasping sob, Amanda released all the stress and worry she'd held in for the past few days. She buried herself in the welcoming arms and allowed her emotions to let go.

"Shh, it's all right," Martha crooned gently, helping the distressed woman into a nearby chair.

"God, Mada," Amanda choked out a few moments later, "how do you handle it?" Taking a deep breath, she leaned back in the chair and wiped her face with one hand.

Martha pulled a clean handkerchief from her apron pocket and wiped the tear-stained face across from her. "I wish I could tell you it gets easier, but that kid of mine is definitely a handful. Trouble just seems to find her." She stood up and opened the refrigerator, pulling out a pitcher of tea and pouring two glasses. "You realize what's coming up next week, don't you?"

Amanda accepted the glass then took a sip of the cold beverage. "I'd almost forgotten, until we pulled up to the house a little while ago." The plans had been finalized almost a month before, prior to Lex's father being hospitalized. She played with the ring adorning her finger. "Do you think we should postpone it?"

"Changing your mind?" a voice asked from the doorway.

"Lexie, you should be resting," Martha took Lex by the arm and lead her to a chair. She brushed the unruly hair out of the tired woman's eyes. "Looks like it's about time for another haircut."

"Probably so, since I want to look my best next week." Lex looked over at Amanda uncertainly. "Do you still..."

"Of course! I just wasn't sure about the timing." Amanda looked at Martha, who gave her a brief nod.

"If you two will excuse me, I have a load of laundry to check on." She exited the room quietly to give them some privacy.

Lex watched her leave, a tiny smile appearing on her face. "Not very subtle, is she?" Her attention turned back to her lover, who was wiping away the condensation on her glass with one finger. "Amanda?"

Hearing her name, Amanda looked up. "Hmm?" Seeing the unasked question in Lex's eyes, she scooted over and sat next to her. "I'm sorry." Taking Lex's hand in hers, Amanda pulled it to her lips and kissed the knuckles. "I still very much want to marry you. I just didn't know if it was a good idea to have the ceremony this soon after your father passed away."

"I was kinda wondering the same thing," Lex admitted. "I haven't been the easiest person to live with lately. Thought that maybe you'd want to wait until things settled down some."

"You're kidding, right?" Amanda asked, reaching with her free hand and stroking her lover's cheek. "Lex, you've had a lot of things to work through, but you've done it. And you've been no harder to live with lately than usual." Tears filled the eyes across from her, slowly spilling down the tanned cheeks. Amanda wiped them away with her fingertips, then leaned forward and kissed the tracks left behind. "I love you, Lexington Walters. Will you marry me?"

Heaving a sigh of relief, Lex nodded. "It's a date," she whispered hoarsely. After clearing her throat, she leaned forward and kissed Amanda tenderly. "I love you, too."

The kitchen door opened and Martha breezed in, patting both women on the head as she passed by. "Glad that's settled. Why don't y'all stay for dinner, and we'll go over the details again." She didn't wait for an answer, reaching into the refrigerator and pulling out a package. "How does meatloaf sound?"

Lex looked at Amanda, who shrugged. "Sounds great. Thanks."

After dinner, Charlie followed Lex outside, at her request.

"What did you want to talk to me about, honey? Is something wrong?"

She sat down on the top step of the porch and patted the space beside her. "Wrong? No. Have a seat."

The sheriff scratched his head in confusion, but did as he was asked. He turned so that he could look directly into her face. "What's on your mind? Are you upset about your brother?"

"Not really," Lex snorted derisively. "I'd say the son of a bitch finally got what's coming to him." Leaning back on her hands, she smiled at him. "Um...you know that our ceremony is coming up next week, right?"

"Yep. Martha and Anna Leigh have been burning up the phone lines, making sure that everything is ready." Charlie reached over and touched the young woman's shoulder. "You're not going to postpone it, are you?" He knew that Lex had been deeply upset by her father's death. *Not that I'd blame her in the least. The poor kid's had a rough time of it lately.*

Lex shook her head. "No." She sat up and ran one hand through her hair. "After what's happened the past couple of days, I don't want to take one more minute with Amanda for granted. If everything were ready, I'd marry her tomorrow. Life's too short not to spend it with the person you love."

"That's good to hear, Lex. But it doesn't explain what—"

"Sorry," Lex interrupted. She grabbed his hands and held them still. "I guess you know that we have asked for a fairly traditional ceremony. Amanda's dad is going to walk her down the aisle, and Jeannie will stand beside her as her matron of honor."

"That's what I'd heard from Martha." Charlie wasn't sure where the conversation was going, but he tried to be as understanding as possible.

"And, well...I've asked my grandpa to walk with me." Suddenly Lex felt shy. "And since I'm not wearing a dress, I figured I'd go ahead and buck tradition even more." Lex waited until she was looking directly into Charlie's eyes. "Would you stand up with me, Uncle Charlie?"

He stared for a long moment, then blinked. "Me?" his voice squeaked. "With you?"

"During dinner tonight, when I heard how close you came to being killed by that asshole Rick, it made me realize just how important a part of my life you've become. My own father wasn't around much when I was growing up, but you always were. You're the best man I've ever known," she said in all seriousness. "I can't think of anyone I'd rather have."

Feeling a lump rise in his throat, Charlie didn't even try to hold back his tears. "I would be greatly honored, sweetheart." He found himself wrapped in a strong bear hug, and could feel Lex's tears dampen his shoulder.

"Thanks, Uncle Charlie," she whispered, hugging him as tightly as she could.

Even in the soft glow of the firelight, the small burns looked painful to Amanda's eyes, although the antibiotic cream she was spreading on didn't appear to be causing her partner any pain. After a long and playful shower together, she had offered to apply the medication. Lex was stretched out in the floor of the master bedroom, her eyes closed and her nude body relaxed. She had her head pillowed on her folded arms, and her breathing was slow and even. "There. I think that does it," Amanda whispered, running one fingertip down the smooth skin. When the body beneath hers flinched, she felt bad. "I'm sorry. Did that hurt you?"

"No," Lex sighed sleepily. "Cold hands." She reached back with one hand to stroke Amanda's thigh where the younger woman straddled her hips. "Your touch never hurts, love. Thanks for always taking such good care of me."

"You're welcome. I just wish I didn't get so much practice." Her hands continued to roam the muscled form. "That bruise is already beginning to fade," Amanda commented, lightly tracing around Lex's shoulder blade. "That was too close."

Lex rolled over slowly, sitting up and wrapping her arms around her lover's equally naked body. "Not really. The man was an incompetent idiot. He just got in a lucky blow." She mentally slapped herself when she felt Amanda tense. "I mean, he caught me off guard. I should have—"

"Shh. Let's not talk about that any more, okay?" Amanda kissed Lex on the chin and nestled her head into the nearest shoulder. "Would you do me a favor?"

"Sure. Name it."

"I've got an appointment at the physical therapist tomorrow. Would you come with me?" Part of her didn't want Lex to meet Peter Chatwick, but a louder voice inside of Amanda's head begged for her lover's presence at her next appointment. Something about the therapist still didn't feel right, and she wanted someone else to accompany her and set her mind at ease.

Lex kissed the head beneath her chin. "I'd love to." She felt the body in her arms relax, and wondered to herself what could cause such a reaction in the normally open Amanda. "Are you all right?"

"I am now." The only log left in the fireplace crumbled, sending out a momentarily flash of orange before settling down and fading out. Amanda looked up and could barely make out Lex's expression in the gloom. "Guess we should go to bed, huh? It is getting kinda late."

Lex grinned. "Oh, yeah. Bed is a very good idea." She allowed Amanda to stand, and took the offered hand that helped her up. "Thanks." A warm hand patted her bare bottom as she walked across the room. "Amanda..."

"What?"

"C'mere, you." Lex sat down on the bed and pulled Amanda into her lap, causing them both to laugh. Her roaming hands stopped trying to tickle the fair skin, and began a light caress instead.

Moaning quietly, Amanda fell back onto the bed, closing her eyes and enjoying the feeling of her lover's hands. Lex's touch gave rise to sensations that caused her to tremble. "Mmm..."

"Are you cold?" Lex asked, her warm breath tickling Amanda's ear. "I may need to warm you up." Her hands continued to stroke and tease, moans from her lover fueling her passion.

"God, Lex," Amanda breathed, her hands reaching up and tangling in the dark hair. Each kiss set her nerve endings on fire, and her hands couldn't stay still when moist lips blazed a trail down her chest.

With an evil chuckle, Lex slowed her descent and focused her attention on a small patch of skin beneath Amanda's ribs. She closed her eyes and enjoyed the taste and texture of her skin as a giggle escaped through Amanda's clenched lips.

"Not fair, Slim. You know I'm tickl—ooh." Her complaint was cut short and all thoughts disappeared when Lex continued on her course, laughing softly.

Chapter 21

Walking into the empty waiting room, Amanda signed in at the desk while Lex took a moment to look around. The pale blue wallpaper was textured, the pattern matching the chairs in the room exactly.

"Nice place." Lex finished her tour and sat down next to Amanda. "Not very busy, is it?"

"Doesn't look like it. I was the first person to sign in today, and it's already after ten."

A door on the other side of the office opened, and a smiling blonde woman peeped around it. "Amanda Cable?"

"Cauble," Lex corrected, standing up with her friend. "Mind if I come in with you?" she asked Amanda quietly. Lex wasn't sure why her partner was so uncomfortable coming to this office, but she was determined to get to the bottom of it, one way or another.

"Not a bit. I'd really appreciate the company." Amanda stepped through the doorway and followed the nurse down the hallway, with Lex right behind her.

After Amanda was ushered into one of the rooms, the nurse turned around and stopped Lex, closing the door before she could go inside. "I'm sorry, but you can't go in while Peter is working. He doesn't like an audience."

Warning bells went off in Lex's head. The empty waiting room, the two-faced nurse, and the therapist's need for "privacy" all made her feel extremely uncomfortable. "That's just too bad. Either you let me in, or I file a lawsuit. Your choice."

"Well, I don't think—"

A door opened and Amanda looked from one woman to another. She could see that her lover was dangerously close to doing physical harm to the nurse, so she reached out and took hold of Lex's arm. "There you are. I thought you had gotten lost."

Lex allowed herself to be pulled into the examination room, edging past the nurse and closing the door behind her. "Thanks, Amanda. I thought I'd never get away from her."

"No problem." Amanda looked around the room nervously, then sat down on the paper-covered table. She was relieved when her partner sat down in the chair next to the table and took her hand. *Stop it, Mandy. There's nothing to be nervous about. I'm sure it was just my imagination.*

Feeling the unusually clammy hand, Lex looked at her lover with concern. "Are you all right?" She rubbed the hand in hers until Amanda relaxed. "Do you need to leave?"

"No, I'm fine. Guess I'm just a bit nervous." When the door opened, Amanda unconsciously pulled her hand from Lex's and gripped the edge of the table tightly.

"Amanda! It's great to see you again." Peter reached out and squeezed her shoulder. "How's your leg feeling?" He pulled up a rolling stool and grabbed her leg, sliding the leg of the red sweatpants up past her knee. His hands began to knead the muscles lightly as they worked their way to the inside of her thigh. Suddenly he was pulled from behind roughly, almost falling from his stool as he hit the far wall. "What the..."

Lex stood over the confused man, her hands clenched at her sides. "Just what the hell do you think you were doing, slimeball? That was completely inappropriate!"

"And who are you?" Peter asked, standing up and looking down at the enraged woman. "I'm her physical therapist; it's my job to massage the healing tissue before we begin the exercises."

"Massage? Looks to me like you were copping a feel, you pervert," Lex yelled, refusing to back down from the much larger man. When he pushed her backwards, only Amanda's hand around her arm kept Lex from taking a swing at the therapist.

"Honey, wait."

Peter's smile turned into a nasty sneer. "Honey?" He wiped his hands on his shirt. "And you called me a pervert?" His eyes bulged as Lex gathered two handfuls of his shirt and shoved him into the wall.

"Watch your damned mouth, asshole. I ought to kick your ass

for touching her like that. She's a lady, not some piece of meat."

Amanda stepped in behind her lover and began to lightly rub her shoulders. "Lex, please. It's all right." As much as she wanted to see pieces of the therapist all over the room, she didn't want to have to bail Lex out of jail. "Come on, love. He's not worth it."

Closing her eyes for a moment, Lex took a deep breath. *I want to rip this son of a bitch apart.* Slowly releasing the hold she had on his clothes, she lowered her hands and stepped back. Lex never saw the fist until right before it made contact with her face. She stumbled back into Amanda, and they both tumbled to the floor.

"You fucking dyke!" Peter leaned down to pull Lex up and hit her again, but the foot that connected with his chest slammed him into the wall.

"Shut up," Amanda cautioned, climbing to her feet and pulling Lex up with her. She wiggled her right foot and smiled. "Looks like my leg is just fine, after all. Guess I won't be back." Without so much as a backwards glance, she pulled her partner out of the room.

The small hand gently probed the tender area, causing the woman to gasp and pull away. "Ouch," Lex complained as Anna Leigh placed the bag of ice on the bruise under her left eye.

"I'm sorry, Lexington, but the ice will make it feel better." Anna Leigh turned her head to look at her granddaughter, who was standing at the kitchen counter making several sandwiches. "Are you going to press charges, Mandy?"

"No. We discussed it on the way over here and decided to just let the entire matter drop. But I plan on calling Dr. Anderson and telling him what a slime Peter Chatwick is. That man is a disgrace to the medical profession." Finishing up, she put the fixings back in the refrigerator and carried the three plates to the table.

"I can't believe he had the nerve to try anything while Lexington was in the room. Not very bright, if you ask me."

"I don't think he saw me, Gramma. I was sitting in this little chair almost behind the examination table. Not to mention he was so focused on Amanda, I don't think he would have seen an elephant in the room." Lex accepted the plate she was offered, but continued to hold the bag of ice against her eye. "Stupid jerk sucker-punched me. I should have kicked his a—"

"Lex!"

"Well, I should have. He deserved it." She picked up half of her sandwich and took a tentative bite.

"Oh, Lexington. You are something else." Anna Leigh reached over and patted the irate woman on the arm. "I'm glad you were there to protect our Mandy's virtue."

Lex snorted, then groaned as the movement jarred her sore eye. "Protect her? You've got to be kidding me! She leveled that son of a..." A dirty look from the woman in question stopped her in mid-sentence. "Uh, I mean, she knocked him on his rear with one swift kick."

"Lex, please. It wasn't like that." Amanda tried to downplay her role. "I just pushed him away from you with my foot."

"Yeah, right. You pushed him so hard, he'll probably be nursing bruised ribs for a week." She laughed. "The bas...um, the bum deserved it." Ignoring the look of outrage on her friend's face, Lex continued to gingerly eat her sandwich, mindful of her own bruise.

Deciding a change of subject was in order, Amanda looked purposefully at her grandmother. "What time is Reverend Hampton supposed to be here? I probably need to go upstairs and get out of these sweats."

"In about half an hour or so. He was certainly thankful that you decided to meet him here, instead of making him drive all the way out to the ranch."

"I was really surprised when Martha told me he was interested in performing the ceremony, so I didn't think it would be fair to have him drive that far," Lex admitted, munching on a chip. "Thanks for letting us borrow your house."

"No thanks necessary, dear. This is as much your home as it is ours."

"Well, I still appreciate it." Lex removed the ice and blinked slowly. "Damn. I hope this stupid thing goes away before the ceremony."

"Oh, I dunno, love. I think it makes you look quite rakish," her lover teased.

"Gee, thanks. Don't you need to go change?"

"I suppose." Amanda stood up and kissed the top of Lex's head. "Try to stay out of trouble until I can get back downstairs, all right?"

Ignoring Anna Leigh's chuckle, Lex sighed. "Yes, dear." She covered her eye with the ice once again, a little harder than she meant to. "Ow."

Lex sat next to Amanda on the sofa, nervously picking at an imaginary spot on her jeans. They had been discussing everything but the ceremony for what seemed like forever to her, and she was quickly becoming bored. A sharp elbow in her side caused Lex to look up. Amanda frowned at her and nodded to their guest. "Huh?"

"Are we boring you, Lexington?" the reverend asked. "Perhaps we could find something more to your interest?"

"No, no. I'm sorry." Lex sat up straighter. "What were you saying?"

The cleric stood, threw back his head, and laughed. "You haven't changed a bit, my girl. I couldn't keep your attention in church, either." He winked at Amanda. "Lexington used to come to my church with her mother, God rest her soul. Poor Victoria always had her hands full with this one."

Amanda patted her lover on the thigh. "I know the feeling, Reverend. She's still a handful."

"Hey!" Lex tried to look insulted, but failed when her own smile broke through. "Look who's talking." She decided to change the subject, before he told too many stories about her. "You don't mind performing the ceremony away from the church, do you?"

"Not at all, dear. But may I ask why you won't consider the church? I'm sure it's large enough to accommodate your needs." He looked from Amanda to Lex, the latter finding something on the toe of her boot suddenly very fascinating. "Lexington?"

She looked up guiltily. "Um, well, it's mostly me, I'm afraid."

The minister's face frowned in concern. "What's the matter? Is there something that I could help you with?"

"It's just me, Reverend. The last time I was in church, aside from Martha's wedding, was when my mother died." Lex ran one hand through her hair nervously. "I don't feel comfortable there."

"Can I ask you a rather personal question, Lexington?" He leaned forward and placed one hand on the anxious woman's knee. At her nod, he continued, "Do you believe in God, or is that a part of the problem you have with the church?"

Lex contemplated the question seriously. "Probably not like you do," she finally answered. "I mean, I believe there is a higher power, but I don't feel the need to dress up and drive into town every Sunday to prove it. I've put up with enough hypocrites who are ruthless and nasty, and they seem to think that showing up in church on Sunday makes everything else that they do okay." She looked into his eyes. "Is it so wrong of me to feel that way, Reverend? Does that make me a bad person?"

He shook his head. "No, Lexington. It's not wrong at all. As long as you have a relationship with God, He doesn't care where you worship. And I understand your feelings completely. So," Reverend Hampton turned to Amanda to bring her back into the conversation, "I hear from your grandmother that you were considering an outdoor ceremony."

"That's right." Amanda took one of Lex's hands in her own. "We were going to have it out at the ranch, but Gramma suggested having it here in her back yard instead. What do you think?"

"Well, since it's just going to be a small family gathering, I say we go out back and take a look." He stood up and held out a hand to Amanda, who accepted his aid and stood up as well. "Lexington? Would you care to join us?"

"Sure. You two go on ahead, I'll be right behind you." After they had left, she leaned back against the sofa and closed her eyes. Feeling someone else in the room, Lex opened her eyes and saw a concerned Anna Leigh standing in the doorway. "Hi, Gramma. You just missed them."

Anna Leigh walked over to the sofa and sat down next to Lex. "No, I didn't, dearest. I saw Amanda showing Reverend Hampton the way to the back yard, and thought I'd come in and check on you." She reached over and brushed the hair out of the younger woman's eyes. "How are you feeling, Lexington? You look a bit tired."

"It's been a long week," Lex admitted. "And now with all this talk about the ceremony, I guess I'm just a bit out of sorts."

"Out of sorts? Are you having second thoughts?"

"No, nothing like that. I just never thought I'd be getting married. I'm not exactly the settling-down type, and living and working out on a ranch isn't usually the best way to meet people." Lex sat up and turned so that they were looking eye to eye. "Do you think Amanda will be happy, living the rest of her life out at the ranch?"

Seeing the worry in the face across from her, Anna Leigh reached down and clutched both of the rancher's hands. "Lexington, I think that if you were living in a cardboard box in your barn, Mandy would be happily sitting beside you. But, she adores the ranch, and I think you'd have a horrendous fight on your hands if you tried to move."

"You really think so?" Lex wanted to believe her. Still, there was a small knot of apprehension deep inside of her that feared losing the woman she loved. *Everyone else I've ever loved has left me, one way or another.* Much to her dismay, Lex felt tears well up in her eyes and slide down her cheeks.

"Oh, Lexington." Anna Leigh wrapped her arms gently around Lex and pulled her close. She continued to hold the weeping woman, rubbing the top of the strong shoulders in a comforting gesture. "Shh...it's all right. Let it go." Once Lex's sobs quieted down to sniffles, she felt her pull away.

Lex rubbed her wet face with her hands, embarrassed by her outburst. "I'm sorry. I don't know what's come over me lately." She bowed her head, unable to look the other woman in the eye.

Reaching behind the sofa, Anna Leigh grabbed a nearby box of tissue. She pulled several out and wiped Lex's face. "You have nothing to apologize for, Lexington. I believe that a good cry cleanses the soul."

"Well, mine should be nice and spotless, considering how much I've done this lately," Lex muttered. "I haven't cried this much in my entire life." Although she was still bothered by her outpouring of emotion, she felt strangely relieved, as if a large weight had been lifted from her shoulders. She accepted another tissue from Anna Leigh and quietly blew her nose.

"Perhaps it's because you feel so much more now," Anna Leigh offered wisely.

"You're probably right. Having Amanda in my life has certainly brought out my emotions."

Anna Leigh frowned. "Is that a bad thing, dear?"

"Not at all," Lex hurried to assure her. "Before I met Amanda, I wasn't living—just existing. Nothing held any interest for me except working on the ranch, and even that wasn't very fulfilling. She's made my life all the richer for being in it."

"Now that's one of the most honest statements of love I've ever heard," Reverend Hampton voiced from the doorway. "I'm sorry to interrupt, but we were growing concerned when Lexington didn't join us." He was standing behind Amanda, whose eyes were glistening with unshed tears.

Anna Leigh patted Lex on the leg and stood up. "I'm afraid

that was my fault, Reverend. Why don't we go into the kitchen for some refreshments, and you can tell me what you think of our plans for the wedding."

Needing to connect with Amanda, Lex stood up and met her in the center of the room. Arms wrapped around bodies as both women tried to meld into one another. "You heard all that, huh?" Lex asked, her voice muffled by Amanda's hair.

"Every word." Amanda words were hard to hear through Lex's shirt. She turned her head and rubbed her face against the soft cotton. "That was beautiful, love."

"Just the truth." Lex pulled back slightly, waiting until Amanda did the same so that they could see each other's face. She reached out and cupped the tear-stained face below hers. "I love you with all my heart, Amanda. There's not a moment in the day I don't thank God for bringing you into my life."

Amanda felt her heart skip a beat as Lex's face came closer and their lips met. *Every kiss is as powerful as the first,* her mind marveled, while her hands tangled themselves in her lover's hair and she found herself lost in the emotions.

"Stop laughing. You're next, you know."

Janna slumped in the uncomfortable chair and covered her mouth with one hand. She enjoyed watching the sales clerk fuss over her friend as Barbara tried on dress after dress. "You're not getting me into one of those. I don't care who's getting married."

Barbara's eyes narrowed in the mirror's reflection. "That's not what I meant." She gently pushed a slim hand away from the strap on her shoulder. "Could you give us a few minutes alone, please? I'll wave if we need anything."

The matronly saleswoman frowned, then sighed. "I suppose. But don't try to hang up the dresses on your own; that's what I'm here for, dear." She walked away, mumbling under her breath about young people not appreciating good service.

"Now," Barbara walked over and knelt beside Janna's chair, "what's wrong? You've been snappish all day."

"Have I? I certainly don't mean to be." Janna felt her hand grasped and looked down into the concerned face. "I'm sorry. I don't know what's wrong with me lately."

Barbara had a pretty good idea what the accountant's problem was. *She's been like this ever since we got the invitations to*

Lex and Amanda's wedding. Their own relationship had been moving along slowly, and she couldn't understand what was holding Janna back. *A few kisses, a little snuggling. Why is she so reluctant to go any further?* "Maybe we should wait and finish shopping another day."

"No, that's okay." Janna glanced around to make sure no one was looking at them, then ran her fingers through her friend's light brown hair. "You know, I really liked that last dress." The pale yellow silk had draped across Barbara's body, accentuating the bank teller's soft curves and bringing out her brown eyes.

"You did, huh?" Although she hated to admit it, Barbara enjoyed the way Janna's eyes lit up when she had stepped out of the dressing room in the outfit. She was just afraid the dress was too sexy for a small wedding. "You didn't think it was too much?"

"On the contrary." Janna leaned closer until they were inches apart. "I thought it was perfect." Suddenly realizing where they were, she sat back quickly and cursed herself for her cowardice. *Why can't I just tell her how I feel?*

The spell of the moment broken, Barbara sighed. "All right, then. Guess I'll take the yellow dress." She started to stand, but was stopped by a pull on her hand. The anguish in Janna's eyes tore at her heart.

Tired of fighting her feelings, Janna was determined to tell the other woman what was in her heart, before she lost her nerve. "Can we go someplace quiet and just talk?"

"Sure. How about my place? It's not that far from here." Barbara stood up and smoothed the dress she was wearing. "C'mon, you can unzip me." She tried to lighten the mood, while her heart worried at what Janna needed to talk about.

Janna watched as Barbara straightened the magazines for the third time. "Why don't you come over here and sit down? The coffee table looks fine." She knew that her own reticence was the main reason her friend was so nervous, and vowed to herself to make it up to Barbara any way she could.

"I'm sorry. It's just—"

"No." Janna pulled Barbara down to sit beside her. "I'm the one who should be apologizing. We really need to talk."

Here it comes, Barbara thought to herself. *The old "it's been fun, but let's just be friends" speech.* She willed herself not to cry.

"So, talk."

Confused by the brusque tone, Janna mentally shook off the hurt Barbara's words caused. "These past few months have been some of the best of my life, Barbara."

"But?"

"Huh?"

"But? These little talks always have a 'but'." Barbara jumped up and started to pace the floor. "Am I not attractive enough to you? What is it about me that you find so repulsive? I've tried and tried, but every time I want to go further, you stop us." She stood at the opposite side of the room with her back turned, angrily wiping away the tears that fell down her cheeks. "Do you find me that hard to like, Janna?"

Janna rose quickly and crossed the room, reaching out and lightly placing her hands on the quaking shoulders. "Hard to like? God, no." Her voice cracked on the last word. "I love you, Barbara," she whispered, wanting so badly to take the hurt away. She was surprised when Barbara spun around in her arms.

"You what?" Barbara searched the other woman's face for any indication that she had misheard her. "Did you say..."

"I love you," Janna repeated, louder this time. She reached up and brushed the dampness away from Barbara's face. "I'm so sorry I didn't say it sooner."

"I love you, too." Barbara linked her hands behind Janna's neck and pulled her face closer, pressing their lips together.

At Martha's insistence, the entire family gathered at the ranch house for dinner. The new dining room held everyone comfortably, with a couple of leaves removed from the formal table allowing everyone to sit closer together.

"The ham was wonderful, Martha," Jacob exclaimed at the end of the meal. "I'm going to harass you unmercifully for the recipe to the glaze, you know."

Amid the laughter, the proud cook glowed. "You'll do no such thing, Jacob. I'll write it down for you before you leave tonight." Emboldened by the company with which they were surrounded, she decided to have a little fun. "Lexie, when do you want to go shopping for your dress?"

"What?" Lex's fork clattered noisily on her plate, as all conversation stopped and every eye focused on her.

"A dress. You can't get married in boots and jeans, you know."

Lex looked at Amanda fearfully. "We hadn't really discussed what we'll be wearing."

"Oh, Lexington. I know the most chic little boutique in Austin. I'm sure we can find you just the perfect thing," Anna Leigh added, picking up on the game.

"A...but...um..."

Amanda was trying hard not to spray iced tea through her nose, as she had just taken a sip when Lex began stammering at her. She quickly swallowed, and patted the nervous woman on the back. "I'm sure you'll look beautiful, honey. Why—"

Shaking her head, Lex tried to speak, but only a squeak came out of her mouth. She leaned back in her chair, and would have fallen backwards except for Travis's hand against her back.

"Settle down, child. I think they're pulling your leg," he laughed, as the other three began to laugh as well.

Lex glared at her partner. "I am *so* going to get you back for this, Amanda."

"I can't wait." Amanda looked across the table at her grandmother, then at Martha, who was sitting near Charlie at the other end. "Gramma, speaking of what to wear, I really do need to go shopping. Martha, would you like to go with us?"

"I'd love to. When are you thinking about going?" Martha smiled at her husband, who, with the other men at the table, had stood up and begun to clean off the table. "Thanks, Charlie."

He leaned over and kissed the top of her head. "No problem. Since you cooked this fabulous meal, how about letting us guys do the cleanup? You ladies can discuss wedding plans."

Jacob stood up. "That's a great idea, Charlie." He and Travis picked up several items from the table and followed the sheriff into the kitchen.

Ronnie, who had been quiet up until that time, shook his head at Lex's expression. "Good luck," he mouthed to her.

Lex got to her feet as well, picking up her plate. "Maybe I should just help in the kitchen."

"Oh no, you don't." Amanda took the dish away from her financee. "You're going to listen to the wedding plans, and you're going to participate, too." She looked around the room at the other women, who watched the scene with amusement. "Why don't we go into the den, and the guys can join us there later?"

Anna Leigh stepped around the table to link her arm with Lex's. "That's a splendid idea, Mandy. We can also talk about the sleeping arrangements for the guests coming in. I'll save your old bedroom for you, so you can stay with us the night before the wedding."

"What?" Amanda stopped in the doorway, causing Martha to run into her.

The housekeeper patted her on the back. "You said you wanted a traditional wedding, dear. One of the traditions is not seeing each other before the ceremony." She gently pushed Amanda through the hallway and into the den. "Anna Leigh and I agreed, that it would do you both good to spend a little time apart. It's only for one night."

Later that same evening, Amanda and Lex were snuggled in bed, a solidary candle cutting through the darkness. Amanda's head was pillowed on Lex's shoulder. "How on earth did we let them talk us into that?"

"Don't blame me. I was ready to elope days ago." Lex really wasn't upset, the happy glow on Martha's face more than making up for any discomfort the wedding plans might cause. "I don't think Mada ever thought she'd be getting to do all this."

"They are having fun, aren't they? I just don't see why we can't go shopping together, though."

Lex kissed the head beneath her chin. "Another one of their silly traditions. We can't see each other dressed for the wedding until it's time. Bunch of hooey, if you ask me." She thought for a moment, then swallowed heavily. "Do you really want me to wear a dress?"

Knowing her lover was serious, Amanda held back her laughter. "No. It was fun to tease you about it, though." She rolled off the sturdy body beneath her and leaned over Lex. "This is as much your wedding as mine, love. You can't enjoy it if you're uncomfortable the entire time."

"Are you sure? Because I'd do anything to make it perfect for you—even wear a goofy-looking dress." She unconsciously reached up and tangled her fingers in Amanda's hair.

"The only thing you have to do to make it perfect for me is be there. I don't care if you're in your boxers and tee shirt." Amanda chuckled at the mental image. "As long as it wasn't those horrid black boxers with the red lips on them. Those are scary."

"You shouldn't have bought them if you didn't want me to wear them. Teach you to try and mess with me." When Amanda had joked about all of Lex's cartoon shorts, Lex told her if she wanted to see her in more "grown-up" clothes, she should buy her some. The black satin boxers had been a gag gift, which Lex had worn regularly ever since.

"I know, I know. Never dare you to do anything, right?" Amanda leaned down until their lips were almost touching. "I bet you won't kiss me," she whispered.

Lex raised up and covered Amanda's lips with her own. She kissed her slowly, deepening the kiss and rolling Amanda over onto her back. "You lose again," she mumbled, bending down and kissing Amanda again.

Nuh-uh, Amanda thought happily. *I win again.*

Chapter 22

"I'm not coming out," Lex yelled. "I look like a complete idiot."

Martha rolled her eyes and shook her head. "God grant me the patience to get through this day," she muttered, trying to ignore Anna Leigh's laughter. Since they knew she would be the harder of the two to outfit, the two women had decided to take Lex shopping first. They left Amanda at work, her pleas for them to take pictures of the event falling on deaf ears.

"Lexington," Anna Leigh called from outside the dressing room door, "it's only the two of us out here. I'm sure you look lovely." She watched under the door as one athletic-socked foot stomped childishly.

"No."

Martha knocked on the dressing room door. "Lexington Marie Walters! You get yourself out here this instant, or I'm coming in after you."

Damn. Lex glared at her reflection in the mirror. *She would, too.* She unlocked the door and stepped out, wanting to be anywhere but where she was. *This just sucks.*

The ivory dress had multiple ruffles, the two largest circling the sullen woman's shoulders and knees. Both older women suddenly covered their mouths with their hands, attempting to hold back their laughter. "Oh my," Anna Leigh finally choked out, understanding why Lex had refused to step out of the dressing room.

"Who the hell picked this one out?" The lower ruffle looking even more absurd against Lex's white socks.

"I believe it was that last saleslady," Martha offered. "The one you told to go to—"

"Okay, okay. I get it." Lex waved one hand in a dismissive gesture. "Can I please get out of this monstrosity?" Her patience was wearing thin. She had been trying on dresses for the past several hours, each one more ridiculous than the last.

Martha patted her arm. "Of course you can. You go on, and we'll send something else over in a minute."

Muttering about elopement and jeans, Lex slunk back into the dressing room and slammed the door.

"Excuse me, ma'am." A young woman holding a light-colored garment tapped Anna Leigh on the shoulder. "I hate to interrupt you, but I accidentally overheard your conversation." She handed the hanger to the older woman. "Try this." The sales clerk looked around, hoping that no one was listening. "I'm new, so I'm only in charge of hanging up the clothes, but this looked like it would fit." She rushed away before either woman could thank her.

"Well? I don't suppose we have anything left to lose at this point, do we?" Anna Leigh asked Martha, who shrugged. She handed the garment to her co-conspirator, who quickly draped it over the door.

A loud groan followed its appearance. "Not another one," Lex pleaded.

"This is the last one, I promise."

"Okay. But I'm gonna want that in writing."

Moments later, Lex stepped out of the dressing room, a thoughtful look on her face. "I think I can handle this." She held her arms out wide. "Well?"

Martha stood speechless. She glanced over at Anna Leigh, who had a similar look on her face. The three-piece outfit appeared to be tailor-made for the tall woman, the soft ivory silk contrasting nicely with her tanned skin. Wide-legged pants, a sleeveless blouse, and a matching lightweight jacket complimented Lex's broad shoulders and slim hips. Finding her voice, Martha finally declared, "You look beautiful, Lexie."

"She certainly does." Anna Leigh reached out and touching a silk-clad arm. "What do you think about it, dear?"

Lex shrugged. "It's not that bad. At least it's not some slinky dress." She stood in front of Martha, concerned. "Are you sure it's all right, Mada? You look kinda upset."

Martha gave Lex a hug, then pulled back. "You look perfect. I guess it's just finally hit me that you're getting married, that's all. My little girl has really grown up. It's a hard adjustment."

"It's not like I'm going anywhere, you know." Lex reached out and caressed the older woman's cheek. "We live a few yards away from you; nothing's gonna change."

"It's not that, Lexie. You've got your own life, now. You don't need an old woman bogging you down."

"I'll always need you, Mada. Getting married doesn't change that." Lex leaned down and kissed the housekeeper on the head. "I love you." Deciding to lighten things up, she grinned. "Think my boots will look okay with this suit?"

"Boots? Oh no you don't, Lexington Marie." Martha swatted Lex on the rear. "Go get out of these clothes before you ruin them. We'll find you just the right shoes, won't we, Anna Leigh?"

"We'll certainly try. I hope the shoe store is ready for us."

Muted conversation mingled with the normal sounds of a busy restaurant. Silverware against china and the tinkling of ice in glasses blended in well with the sounds of hurried footsteps as servers rushed from one table to the next. At one particular table, a beautiful young woman sat down next to an older man, then placed her purse under her chair.

"You didn't have to buy me lunch just to see me," Amanda chastised. "I've missed you too, you know."

"Well, between both our busy schedules lately, this was about the only time we had free." His photography studio was constantly busy, and he was seriously thinking about hiring an assistant. "You about ready for the big day, sweetheart?"

She nodded. "Almost. I'm supposed to go shopping for a dress with Gramma and Martha tomorrow. Although, after today, I don't know if either one of them will be ready to go shopping ever again."

"Why's that?" he asked, raising his glass of water and taking a drink.

"Because they're shopping with Lex today." She laughed at the look on her father's face.

He struggled to keep from spraying water all over the table, and coughed several times after swallowing. "You're going to put Lex in a dress?" Michael gasped, wiping his chin with his napkin. "I don't mean to sound tacky, but people would pay to see that."

"Excuse me, folks. What can I bring you to drink today?" A teenaged waiter stood at their table, notepad in hand.

Amanda smiled at the earnest young man. "I'll have iced tea, please." Her father nodded, indicating he wanted the same. Once the waiter had taken their order and left, she responded to Michael's question. "I told Lex that I wanted her to be comfortable for the ceremony. She could wear boots and jeans for all I care."

"I'm sure she appreciates that thought, Amanda. But knowing Lex like I do, I'll bet that she wants to dress in keeping with the occasion. Although I do feel sorry for Mom and Martha."

"Me too."

Michael's expression sobered as he reached across the table and took Amanda's hand in his. "Sweetheart, I want you to know how proud I am of you. It does my heart good to see you so happy."

"Thanks, Daddy." She looked down at their linked hands, and then back up at him. "I never thought I'd be getting married."

"To tell you the truth, neither did I. Especially after you told us you were gay." Michael took a deep breath and gazed intently into his daughter's eyes. "It wasn't the life I wanted for you, Amanda. I hoped that you would find some nice fellow who would look after you, so that you could settle down and start a family." When she opened her mouth to interrupt, he shook his head and squeezed her hand. "No, wait. Let me finish. I've come to know Lex well these past few months, and now I can honestly say that I'm glad you've found each other. The way she looks at you lets me know that I don't have to worry about my little girl any more. And that's all a father can ask."

Amanda closed her eyes for a long moment. When she opened them, tears of happiness tracked down her face. "She's the best thing that has ever happened to me, Daddy. Thank you for understanding."

Michael choked back tears of his own. "Thank you for giving me a second chance to try, Amanda."

Plates being set down in front of each of them broke the emotionally charged mood. "Here you go. Is there anything else that you need right now?" the waiter asked, not realizing the moment he'd interrupted.

"Ah, no. We're good," Amanda answered, pulling her hand back and wiping at her eyes. "Right?"

"Yes. We're great," Michael agreed, his smile almost as broad as his daughter's.

Lex rubbed her eyes, the small words on the computer monitor beginning to blur. She had closeted herself in the office after returning from the shopping trip, deciding that she might as well look over the information Janna had e-mailed her the day before. The ranch was prospering under her firm guidance, with the previous quarter showing more earnings than she'd anticipated. She gratefully stretched her legs out under the desk. Her denim jeans were a pleasure to wear, especially after spending all of the morning and part of the afternoon trying on clothes. "Thank God for boots." A soft knock at the door caused Lex to look up. "Yes?"

The door opened slightly, and Travis's gray head poked inside. "Lexie? Are you real busy?"

"Not a bit, Grandpa. Come on in," she invited, standing up and walking around the desk. Wrapping her arms around the taller man, Lex squeezed him as tightly as she dared. She held the embrace for a long moment, then released him and pointed Travis to a chair. "Have a seat. What's up?"

"What makes you think something's up?" he asked, bending his long form to fit into the comfortable chair. "Can't a man just want to see his granddaughter?"

Duly chastised, Lex sat down in a chair close to his. "Um, sure. I didn't mean—"

Travis laughed. "You're just too adorable, Lexie." He reached across the small space and placed his hand on her arm. "Actually, I did want to talk to you. Have you girls decided where you want to go for your honeymoon?"

"Honeymoon?"

"Yes, honeymoon. The trip you take after your wedding ceremony," he explained with mock seriousness. "I plan on sending the two of you someplace nice to start your life together. Maybe somewhere in Europe? Paris, perhaps?"

"Paris? France?" Lex was having a terrible time absorbing the conversation.

"Of course, France. Although Paris, Texas, is a lovely place, I don't think it's quite honeymoon material."

Lex paled. "B-b-but, that would mean we'd have to fly," she stammered weakly. A sudden feeling of helplessness washed over her as she flashed back to when she was much younger.

Eight-year-old Lexington was so excited she could barely contain herself. Her father had agreed to let her accompany him on a cattle-buying trip to Colorado. She sat next to him in the seat of the pickup truck, her eyes taking in the scenery as they drove to the small airstrip a few miles north of Somerville.

"How long will we be gone, Daddy?" she asked, her left foot enthusiastically thumping back and forth against the door of the truck.

Rawson took his eyes from the road for a quick moment to look at his daughter. "Just overnight. Did you remember to bring a notebook? I want you to really pay attention to what we're doing, Lexington. Some day you'll have to buy the cattle for the ranch." He turned his attention back to the road, not seeing her nod.

"Yes, sir," she assured him, pulling a tattered spiral notebook from her backpack on the floor in front of her. "I've even drawn a cow on the front, so I'll know what's in it." Although she was no artist, the rendition on the cover did resemble a cow, at least in her own mind. "Are we driving all the way there?"

"Nope. A fella I went to school with owns a small plane. He's offered to fly us up there and back, for half a rack of beef in trade." He turned the truck on to a small dirt road.

"A plane? We get to go in an airplane? Neat!" Lexhe sat up higher in the seat, peeking over the high dashboard of the truck to see ahead of them. "Are we almost there?"

The rancher shook his head at her childish enthusiasm. "Almost." He spotted a small hangar to the right of the road, and parked the truck behind the metal building. "Okay, we're here," Rawson announced, almost laughing as the girl fought with her seat belt. "Take it easy, girl. The plane ain't goin' anywhere." He stepped out of the vehicle and pulled a large duffel bag from the rear of the truck. "Don't forget your bags, Lexington."

"Yes, sir," she acknowledged respectfully, climbing out of the truck and hefting her backpack over her shoulders. She grabbed a smaller duffel bag from the floorboard of the truck, slinging the strap over one shoulder. "I'm ready, Daddy."

"Good girl," Rawson commented, reaching her side and rubbing the top of her head playfully. "C'mon. Let's go meet Buck." He directed her to the front of the hangar, where a small white

plane was parked. The wings ran across the top, braced on the sides, and rust was showing through in several places on the frame. A slender man was walking around the vehicle, puffing heavily on a large cigar. "Buck," Rawson yelled, waving as the man turned around.

Buck met them halfway, holding out his hand. "Rawson, you old son of a—" He noticed the young girl with the rancher and paused before finishing, "gun. How the heck are ya?"

"Doing all right, Buck. I see you got that old rust-bucket cleaned up some," he joked, pointing towards the plane.

The tall man released his friend's hand and slapped him on the back. "Hey, talk nice about my baby. All she needs is a paint job, and she'll be good as new." He leaned down to look the young girl in the eyes. "You must be Lexington." The pilot held out his hand. "I'm Buck Dalton."

"Nice to meet you, Mr. Dalton." Lex shook his hand and stared past him at the aircraft. "Is that your plane?"

"Sure is, kiddo. C'mon, I'll show it to you." He winked at Rawson and put a companionable arm around her small shoulders, leading the excited girl to the plane.

Lex's eyes were as round as saucers as she took in the small aircraft. The single-engine propeller looked huge to her untrained eyes as Buck opened the side door. "Wow! This is so neat," she exclaimed, trying to take it all in at once. "What kind is it, Mr. Dalton?"

"I'm glad you asked, Lexington. She's a 1957 Cessna 182A. I've been working on her for almost five years now." He took her bags and lifted the youngster through the door. "Go on up to the cockpit and sit in the left-hand seat."

"Yes, sir!" Lex climbed into the front of the plane and sat down where she had been directed, her hands in her lap.

Almost an hour later, much to her father's dismay, Lex was buckled into the co-pilot's seat. "Buck, are you sure she won't be any trouble up there?" Rawson sat in the rear seat with his arms crossed over his chest.

"Nah. My new co-pilot and I have already gone over the rules, haven't we, Lexington?"

"Roger, Captain." Lex saluted, smiling.

"All right. But if she's a bother, send her back here to me, all right?"

Buck ruffled the girl's hair affectionately. "I don't think there'll be a problem." He turned around in his seat to look at his friend. "She's a lot like my Amy, Raw. Thanks for letting her sit up here with me." His fourteen-year-old daughter lived with her mother in Boston, and Buck hadn't seen her for almost three years. The young girl sitting next to him brought back fond memories of a time long ago, when Amy would fly with him.

The flight was uneventful, and the initial excitement had worn off for the youngster. Lex had fallen asleep, and her dark head lolled to one side as she slumbered. She was awakened by Buck's colorful curse as the small engine began to sputter.

"Damn it all to Hell!" He flicked several switches and studied the gauges in front of him. "Lexington, why don't you go back and keep your daddy company? Don't forget to buckle in tight, okay?"

Confused, she did as she was told. Lex looked up into her father's face, which had paled considerably. "What's wrong, Daddy?"

"Nothing you need to worry about, Lexington. Just buckle up and stay quiet, so that Buck can concentrate on what he's doing." Rawson felt his heart begin to hammer in his chest. He knew that they were only a couple of miles away from their destination, and he closed his eyes and said a quick prayer.

"C'mon, baby. Don't let me down," Buck pleaded, working feverishly at the controls. The engine continued to complain as the small plane began to descend. He could see the airstrip up ahead, and hoped that he would be able to bring the plane in smoothly. His hope was in vain; the engine shut down completely, the only noise now coming from the pilot. "Fuck!" He continued to struggle with the controls, but held no hope of them coming back to life in time for the touchdown. "Rawson, you two need to brace yourselves. I'm afraid we're in for a bit of a rough landing."

Lex heard the fear in the pilot's voice, and couldn't understand why everything was suddenly so quiet. "Daddy?" She looked up at her father, who had his eyes closed. "What's going on?"

"Just you be quiet, girl," he ordered. "We should be landing in just a few minutes. I hope," he mumbled to himself.

Lex was even more confused when she overheard her father mention something about going to the bathroom before they left the hanger. She didn't have time to ask him what he meant, because everything started happening at once. The plane was losing altitude; and without the whine of the propeller, the silence was frightening.

"Here we go," Buck yelled, seconds before the wheels began to bounce unevenly on the blacktop. The small plane tilted to the right, and suddenly flipped onto its side, the metal of the wing screaming before shearing off. The plane was still moving too fast, and cartwheeled over onto its nose, gyrating several times before coming to a stop.

Terrified, Lex began to scream as the plane rolled down the runway. Once the rolling stopped, she found herself hanging upside down from her seat belt. Tears fell freely from her eyes as she looked over at her father, who appeared to be asleep. "Daddy!" The door wrenched open, and large hands reached for her as the small girl finally gave in to her hysterics and mercifully fainted.

"Of course you'd have to—" Travis stopped when he saw the look on her face. "Lexie?" *Why on earth would flying upset her so?* He slid out of his chair and knelt next to his granddaughter, putting one arm around her shoulders. Realizing that she was dangerously close to hyperventilating, he rubbed her back encouragingly. "Take slow, deep breaths, Lexie. It's going to be all right."

Several moments later, Lex found herself in her grandfather's arms, tears streaming down her face. She blinked several times and looked around. The flashback to the accident seemed so real to her, as she struggled to remember the rest of the details. "What happened?" she asked Travis, who was wiping the tears from her face.

"I'm not sure, honey. You zoned out on me for a few minutes there. Are you all right?" His own hands were shaking in response to the look of terror that had crossed her face.

"I think so." She paused while her heart rate slowly went back to normal. "I don't like to fly."

"I pretty much figured that out on my own, Lexie." His voice had taken on a teasing tone, in an attempt to lighten the mood in the room.

Lex shook her head and chuckled at herself. "Yeah, I suppose you did." She swallowed hard and tried to fight the feelings that threatened to overwhelm her again. "When I was eight, Dad took me on a buying trip with him. We were in a friend's small plane, and had to make a crash landing. Guess I blocked it out for all these years."

"Dear God! Was anyone hurt?" Travis squeezed her tighter, feeling the strong body he held shiver slightly.

Accepting the comfort, Lex wrapped her arms around him and held on tight. "No. The pilot was good and managed to get us down safely, but I completely freaked out. At least now I know why I don't like to fly."

"I don't blame you, sweetheart." Travis gently rocked his granddaughter. "I'm sorry I brought it up."

"Don't be, Grandpa." Lex pulled back and took a deep breath. "We could never figure out why I wouldn't fly. I guess Dad never told anyone about the accident."

"Why on earth would the man keep such a terrible thing a secret? He should have known how traumatized you were."

Lex laughed. "I think he was embarrassed." She remembered the threat of a beating if she ever told anyone about Rawson's shame. "He kinda had his own accident, if you know what I mean."

Travis threw back his head and laughed along with her. "Oh Lord! I would have paid to see that!" Realizing he was still kneeling on the hardwood floor, he slowly stood up. "How about we go raid the kitchen for some cookies? We can talk more later about sending you on your honeymoon."

"All right. As long as you don't mention flying." Lex stood up and followed him out of the office, both of them still chuckling.

"I just wish we had known before now," Martha groused as she took her place at the dining room table. She had been extremely upset when Lex and Travis had related Lex's sudden onslaught of memories from long ago. "Why on earth wouldn't Mr. Walters have told me? Poor Lexie was so upset after that trip, and I never could figure out why."

Lex looked up from her plate, where she had been using her mashed potatoes to dam up the rich brown gravy that covered her roast. "I was? I don't remember."

"You most certainly were. After you got back, you suffered from horrible night terrors, and slept in my room with me for nearly a month. 'Til your daddy found out and threw a nasty fit." At that time, Martha had lived in a small room next to the kitchen, which had been converted into a mud room when Lex built her a house nearby. After the ranch house had recently been gutted by fire, that same room had made way for the dining room they were all sitting in.

"Did he ever give you any explanation for why I was so upset?"

"No, I'm afraid he didn't. All I could get out of the man was that you'd had a bit of a scare. He never would go into any detail for me." Martha reached across the table and patted Lex's hand. "I think he felt responsible, and was ashamed to admit what had happened."

Amanda squeezed the strong thigh on which her hand was resting. "That sounds like your dad, Lex. He was a proud man, and I bet it really bothered him that he couldn't help you get through something like that. When he realized that you had blocked the whole incident out of your mind, I'm sure he was relieved."

"Maybe."

Charlie, who had been quiet up to that point, decided to change the subject. "I hear you went shopping today, Lex. Did you have a nice time?" His wife laughed, and the only response he received from Lex was a low growl. "What did I say?"

"I'd have had more fun getting my fingernails removed—without anesthesia."

"It wasn't that bad," Martha argued. "Especially after Miss Grumpy Gus over there left the poor salesladies alone."

Lex glared across the table. "That last woman had it coming, Mada. She was a complete horse's a—"

"You watch your language, young lady," Martha interrupted. "You're not too big to have your mouth washed out with soap."

"Yes, ma'am." Lex pointedly ignored the giggling woman beside her. "Anyway, Uncle Charlie, a good time was not had by all. It was sheer torture."

The housekeeper moaned. "Oh, puhleez. It wasn't half as bad as you make out."

Lex snorted her disagreement. "Two words for you, Mada." She smiled evilly. "Shoe store."

Martha rolled her eyes. "I'd almost forgotten about that."

"What happened?" Amanda asked, her curiosity getting the better of her.

"That clerk shouldn't have tried to cram my foot into that goofy-assed pointy shoe." Lex looked at Travis and Charlie, expecting sympathy. Both men appeared to be trying to contain their mirth. "What was I supposed to do?"

Martha shook her finger at Lex. "Certainly not kick the poor woman. On the chin, of all places."

Lex leaned back in her chair with a satisfied smirk on her face. "She left me alone after that, didn't she?"

Charlie couldn't hold back any longer, and guffawed loudly. "Good grief, girl! It's a wonder I wasn't called in to file an assault charge."

"She probably would have, if we hadn't bribed the poor woman with more sales." Martha looked over at Amanda. "I hope you'll be needing shoes tomorrow."

Amanda laughed. "If not, I'll buy some anyway if it will keep Lex out of jail so close to the time for our wedding. You will be going with us tomorrow, won't you, Mada?" She smiled as the housekeeper nodded. "Good. I promise to be a little easier to shop with." A hard poke to her leg under the table caused her to look at her lover. "Well? It's the truth."

"Brat."

"Grump," Amanda retorted, sticking out her tongue. "I'm really looking forward to tomorrow. I just love to shop."

"Smartass." At the glare from Martha, Lex rolled her eyes. *Damn woman has the ears of a rabbit.* "Well, I'm glad all I have to do tomorrow is take Michael riding. He's really coming along great with his lessons. My day should be a piece of cake."

Chapter 23

"How about this, Mandy?" Anna Leigh pulled a pale yellow dress from the rack. "I believe it would look quite lovely on you, dear."

A very unladylike snort came from behind Amanda. "She's getting married, Gramma. Not going to the prom." Jeannie and her husband, Frank, had arrived late the night before, and she had practically begged to be included on the shopping trip to Austin.

"Jeannie!" Amanda slapped her older sister on the arm and smiled apologetically at their grandmother. "It's a beautiful dress, Gramma. But I was hoping for something more...traditional."

Anna Leigh brightened and exchanged knowing glances with Martha. The housekeeper had been standing by quietly, enjoying the by-play between the two sisters. "Excellent! Then we have just the shop," Anna Leigh exclaimed. She gathered up their other bags and led the small entourage from the store.

Half an hour later, the foursome stood outside an exclusive boutique. Amanda gazed at the doorway, then shook her head vigorously. "Oh no, Gramma. I can't go in there."

"And why on earth not?" the older woman asked, crossing her arms over her chest.

"Because it's too expensive, that's why. I can't afford to buy stockings in there, much less an entire gown." Although she had been given the ability to withdraw money from her trust fund at age eighteen, Amanda lived off her wages from the real estate office. Out of sheer stubbornness, she refused to touch the money that had been bequeathed to her upon the deaths of her maternal grandparents, except to donate large sums to her favorite charities.

Jeannie grabbed her sister by the arm and began to pull her into the shop. "You are so pathetic, Mandy. Unless you've gone on one heck of a shopping spree in the past year or so, I happen to know that you've got more money than you know what to do with."

"Hey! Leggo." Amanda struggled to break free of the older woman's grasp. "Jean Louise! Let go of me!"

A frowning woman, who appeared to be near the same age as Martha, met them just inside the door. She watched with disdain as the two younger women argued, the smaller of the two finally throwing up her hands in defeat. "May I be of some assistance to you, ladies?" she asked. Her demeanor changed when she spotted one of the older women behind the quarreling siblings. "Martha Rollins?" The round face of the clerk softened as she recognized her friend.

"Deborah Sue Fosselmeyer. I can't believe it's you!" Martha easily maneuvered around Jeannie and embraced the other woman. They hugged for a long moment before pulling back and looking at each other. "Actually," Martha waved her left hand under her friend's nose, "it's Martha Bristol, now."

"Really? That's wonderful!" Deborah looked behind the smaller woman. "Are those your daughters?"

"Not exactly." Martha turned and waved to the other women. "Although this cutie," she pulled Amanda over, "is about to become my daughter-in-law. Amanda Cauble, I'd like for you to meet my closest friend from high school and college roommate, Deborah Sue Fosselmeyer. We haven't seen each other for over twenty-five years, I'd imagine."

"It's very nice to meet you, Ms. Fosselmeyer," Amanda acknowledged, taking the other woman's hand and shaking it. "Let me introduce you to the heathen I was fighting with when we came in." She held out her free hand and motioned her sister over. "This is my sister, Jeannie Rivers. And," a proud smile lit up her face, "our grandmother, Anna Leigh Cauble."

Anna Leigh stepped forward after Jeannie. "Lovely to meet you, Ms. Fosselmeyer."

"Please, call me Deborah." She looked back at Martha. "You mentioned that Amanda is about to become your daughter-in-law? Then I'm sure that means you're here for a wedding dress," she surmised. "Do you have any pictures of your son?"

Martha looked at Amanda, who shrugged. "Why don't you

and I go have a quick little chat, while these girls look around a bit?" she suggested to her old friend. "I'm sure Anna Leigh can keep them out of trouble for a short while."

Deborah nodded. "I'd like that, Martha. Come to the back room with me, and I'll show you pictures of my children from my last three marriages."

"Three marriages?" Martha exclaimed, following her friend. "You never could make up your mind, Debbie."

Jeannie, who had been quiet up to that point, looked at her sister. "Do you think she'll be okay?"

"Martha?" Amanda asked. "I'm sure she'll be fine. It's her friend we should be worried about. Heaven help her if she says anything bad about Lex."

"Or you, dear. Martha is very protective of you both." Anna Leigh rubbed her hands together and looked around the boutique. "Well? Shall we get started?"

"Yes, we shall." Amanda allowed her grandmother to lead her to the corner of the store that held the wedding gowns. "I hope Lex is having a good time."

"Damn it all to Hell! Keep your smelly carcass still, you stupid fool." Lex tried to get a better grip on the mud-covered body, but it slipped through her fingers again. "Don't move, dammit!"

"Are you sure there's nothing I can do?" Michael asked.

The rancher slipped a bit further, coming dangerously close to being buried in the muck. "No. Stay put. One of us in this mess is more than enough." Giving up on trying to stay clean, Lex wrapped both arms around the neck of the bawling calf. It had somehow fallen down a steep embankment and into a spring-fed section of the creek, its tiny hooves unable to scale the slippery six-foot walls.

Michael stood above the creek, holding the reins of the horses. The photographer almost pulled his camera from the saddlebag, but changed his mind. *I don't think that Lex would appreciate a shot quite that candid.* He grimaced as the calf suddenly began to struggle more vigorously.

"Calm down," Lex commanded, even as she was pulled further under the thrashing animal's body. One sharp hoof dug into the fleshy part of her thigh. "Son of a bitch," she cried, getting madder by the moment.

Michael stepped closer to the edge. "Are you okay?" He had heard the pain in her voice and was becoming concerned. A loud buzz suddenly sounded from the creek, and the two horses that Michael was holding shied, dragging him backwards.

Lex felt her heart begin to pound furiously. "Damn." She looked around slowly, trying to locate where the noise was coming from. As the steady buzzing continued, she spied the source on a rocky ledge, three to four feet away from her and the calf. *Rattler. No wonder this calf was going nuts.* "Michael?"

"Whoa," Michael crooned, trying to get the wild-eyed animals back under control. He had been dragged several yards away from the creek, and now both horses refused to follow him back. "Come on, guys, give me a break here. I'm new at this sort of thing," he pleaded, pulling on the reins. Both horses pulled back, almost sending him tumbling to the ground. He heard his name called from the creek, and glared at the stubborn equines. "Hold on, Lex," the agitated man called over his shoulder as he gave up and tied both animals to a sturdy looking tree.

"Not too close." Lex's voice suddenly became very quiet. "We've got a little problem."

Jeannie held an ivory, intricately laced gown across her body. "Oooh, Mandy. Look at this one."

Her eyes widening, Amanda looked to her grandmother for support. "Um, well..."

"For goodness sake, Jeannie. The ceremony is being held in our back yard, not in the cathedral." Anna Leigh smiled slyly at her eldest granddaughter. *Teach her to be smart with me.*

"Gramma." Jeannie put the dress back on the rack, eyeing it sadly. Seeing her sister staring over her shoulder, she turned around. "What?"

Amanda pointed with one finger. "Over there," she said, walking in the direction she had just indicated. She turned and looked at her grandmother, who had seen what she did and nodded her approval. Amanda pulled the dress down and held it close to her body. "Maybe I'll just try this one on."

In the backroom of the boutique, Martha smiled at her old friend as Deborah Sue brought them each a cup of coffee. "It's been way too long, hasn't it?"

"That it has. After your mother's funeral, we lost touch." Deborah took a sip of her coffee. "Did you end up as a teacher somewhere after all?"

"Not exactly. You remember the job I took at that ranch, helping that poor woman who became bedridden during her pregnancy?" At her friend's nod, she shook her head sadly. "I'm afraid that Mrs. Walters passed away, shortly after delivering her baby."

Deborah gasped. "Oh, my. That's just horrible."

"It certainly was. Those three children, left without a mother. Anyway, I stayed on to take care of them."

"Oh! And you married their father," Deborah exclaimed.

Martha waved her hands in front of her in negation. "No, no, nothing like that. I did care for the children as if they were my own. After a while, I was so attached to them, I couldn't have left if someone had tried to make me." She reached into her purse and pulled out a small photo album. "Amanda is going to be exchanging vows with the middle child, Lexington."

The chair she was in squealed in protest as Deborah scooted it around near her friend to look over her shoulder. The first picture was of three young children, ages four, eight, and fifteen. The oldest, a scowling teenage boy, glared at the camera while digging his fingers into the shoulder of the girl sitting beneath him. She was holding the four-year-old in her lap, happily smiling. "Gracious. Look at that dark hair and eyes. He's quite handsome."

"Yes, he is. But Hubert is just plain ornery, I'm afraid."

"He's got to have some redeeming qualities, to get a sweet girl like Amanda." Deborah paused. "Oh, the oldest boy's name is Hubert. Then, that means that—"

Martha turned the page, to a smiling young woman, standing next to a large black horse. The animal's head was draped over her shoulder, and the black hat on her head couldn't shade her bright blue eyes. "This is my Lexie, Deborah Sue, my pride and joy," she added strongly, daring the other woman to say something derogatory. To her surprise, Deborah laughed.

"You're kidding me." Deborah stood up and walked over to a cabinet to remove her purse. "That pretty young girl out there is getting married to another woman?" She stepped back over to the table and sat down. Seeing the angry look on Martha's face, she patted her friend's arm in a placating manner. "Wait, I've got something you need to see." Deborah dug through her purse and pulled out her wallet, opening it up to show a small photograph of two handsome young men. One of the men was sitting in a wicker chair, while the other leaned forward and had his arms wrapped around the first. Both were smiling at the camera. "This is my son, Donald and his partner, Lloyd. Don is the one sitting down."

"Goodness," Martha exclaimed, looking back up and into her friend's eyes. "Looks like we've more in common than we thought."

Peering over the edge of the embankment, Michael felt the blood rush from his head. "Oh, God." The rattlesnake was coiled and looked ready to strike at any moment, its attention solely on the tall, mud-covered figure a few feet away. It was at chest level to the still woman, who cautiously looked up at Michael out of the corner of her eye.

"Attached to my saddle is a small shovel," Lex told him evenly. She carefully raised her left hand, until it was slightly higher than her body. "Would you mind bringing it to me?"

"Sure." Michael slowly backed away. Once he was clear of the creek, he ran back to the horses and struggled with the leather tie that secured the folded shovel. *What the hell is she going to do with this? Dig her way out? I probably don't want to know.*" After getting the implement free, he jogged back towards the creek, stopping before he got to it and slowly stepping to the bank's edge. "Everything okay?"

"Just ducky." Lex stared at the snake, which continued to rattle ominously. "You wanna hand me that shovel? Open it up first."

"Okay." Michael fought the latch before the shovel clicked open. "You're not going to try and kill the snake with this, are you?" he asked, turning the tool around and slowly placing the handle in her gloved hand.

"You got a better idea? Step back, Michael. If I miss, I don't want him coming after you."

Doing as he was told, Michael swallowed nervously. "You'd better not miss, Lex. I'm looking forward to welcoming you into my family in a few days, and I don't like to be disappointed." He watched as the shovel was raised slowly over her head, and the buzzing sound grew in intensity. Michael closed his eyes for a short moment, opening them just in time to see the implement swing down suddenly. The black hat disappeared from his view, and he rushed to peer over the edge of the embankment.

Lex was lying back against the muddy wall, her eyes closed. Bits of pink flesh clung to the shovel that was still in her left hand, and half of the snake could be seen hanging from the rocky wall where it had been perched. "Damn, that was too close." Lex opened her eyes and looked up at the frantic man. "You okay, Michael?"

"Am I okay? Have you lost your ever-loving mind? You could have been bitten," he ranted, shaking a finger at the laughing woman. "What the hell are you laughing about?"

She wiped a smudge of the snake's blood from her cheek. "You know, a few months ago you probably would have cheered for the rattler."

Michael dropped to the ground, swinging his legs over the side of the creek. "Unfortunately, you're probably right."

"We've come a long way, haven't we?"

"That we have, Lex." Michael jumped down into the mud beside her. "I think between the two of us, we can get this little guy out of here."

"Probably so." Lex bent down and pulled the calf's rear feet free. "Put your thumb and index finger together, and make a ring in his nose. Once I get him free, he should follow you out without any problems."

Looking at his hand, and then the calf, Michael frowned. "You want me to put my fingers in a cow's nose? Is this some sort of payback for that punch in the face I gave you when we first met?"

"Nah. It's just the easiest way to lead him out of here," she assured him. "Trust me."

I do, Lex, Michael thought, as he followed her instructions. *Otherwise I'd never let you marry my daughter.*

Martha and Deborah Sue returned to the dressing area just as Amanda stepped from the small room, wearing the dress that she had picked out. They stood beside Jeannie, who clapped her hands with joy.

"I do believe we have a winner, folks," she exclaimed, rushing over to her sister to ooh and ahh. "Gosh, Mandy. You look beautiful."

Amanda ducked her head and smiled. "You really like it?"

She turned around and glanced at herself in the mirror. The sleeveless ivory satin accentuated her body well, and the scoop neckline showed off her heart necklace. She turned back to her grandmother. "Do you think it's too short?" The hem came to just above her knees, and the small scar where her leg had been operated on after the accident was partially visible. Amanda scowled at her reflection. "Maybe I should go with a floor length."

"I think you look perfect, dearest." Anna Leigh stepped up behind Amanda and placed her hands on her shoulders. "Remember, this is a casual, outdoor afternoon affair. I think this dress would complement Lexington's outfit perfectly."

"Oh? And what's she wearing?" Amanda asked, turning around to stare at her grandmother.

Martha stepped forward. "Oh no, you don't, young lady. We're not going to spoil the surprise for you." She looked Amanda over carefully. "You really are beautiful, honey. I love the dress."

"Thanks, Martha. I hope Lex thinks so, too."

"I know she will. My Lexie always looks at you through love's eyes, Amanda. You could wear a flour sack and she'd think it was a ballroom gown."

Jeannie stood next to her younger sister and put an arm around her waist. "Isn't that the truth? I know that Frank loves me, but sometimes I wish he'd look at me like Slim looks at you."

"Aw, Jeannie, stop it," Amanda sniffled, waving one hand in front of her face. "You're going to make me cry."

Deborah Sue tapped her friend on the back and waved Martha away from the other women. "She certainly makes that dress look good," she whispered, pointing back to where Amanda was still fending off the compliments from her family.

"That she does," Martha agreed proudly. "And she's just as beautiful on the inside, too."

"After just being around her for a short time, I believe you. I want her to have the dress, Martha." Deborah held up her hand to forstall Martha's arguement. "Please, consider it a wedding present. Look at this place. My second husband was quite well off, you know. This boutique is just something to keep me from getting bored in my old age."

"You're not getting old, because that would mean that I'm getting old, and I refuse to accept that." Martha wrapped her arms around her friend and pulled her close. "If you can get Amanda to agree to accept the dress, then thank you, Debbie. Would you like to come to the reception? I'd love for you to meet my girl."

"With an invitation like that, how can I refuse? From the pictures you showed me, she looks like a beautiful young woman to be proud of."

"Damn, I reek." Lex flicked another clump of mud from her jeans. "Amanda's going to kill me." She stretched in the saddle, fighting the tightening of her overused muscles. "I thought we'd never get that calf out of the mud."

Michael scratched the back of his neck, feeling the skin tighten where the mud was. "I'm sorry about that, Lex. If I hadn't let go when the little devil sneezed, he wouldn't have dragged you down like that."

She looked over at her future father-in-law. "That's okay. You look as bad as I do." It was true. Michael had tried to help Lex out of the mud. But when he reached down to give her a hand, the calf half-butted him and caused him to lose his balance, causing Michael to fall face first right next to his daughter's partner.

"Do I?" He scratched his head, the drying clumps of mud tumbling away. "Well, it's only fair, I suppose." Trying to get his mind off of his itching skin, Michael decided a change of topics was in order. "I know this isn't the best of circumstances, Lex, but I'd really like to talk to you."

"Sure. Do you want to stop somewhere, or keep riding?" Lex tried to put on an unaffected air, but her hands shook slightly at his serious tone.

"Let's keep going. The sooner I get this mud off of me, the better." Pulling his horse closer to hers, Michael looked into the worried woman's face. "I thought about asking Amanda, but she'd probably just tell me what she thought I wanted to hear. I'm sure she's told you that my divorce was final not too long ago."

"Yeah. Congratulations."

"Thanks. I feel one thousand percent better, knowing I'm not legally connected to that viper any longer." He shrugged his shoulders. "I've, um, been dating recently, and I was wondering if I could bring Lois to the wedding."

Surprised, Lex almost fell from her horse. She reached out for the saddle horn to keep astride Thunder. Pulling the animal to a stop, Lex looked at Michael for a long moment. "Is this the lady from the bar?"

He nodded. "Yes, Lois Compton. I wasn't sure if you'd remember her or not."

"I was pretty tanked that night, wasn't I?" Lex admitted. "She's also the woman who did the interior design work on the ranch house. Yeah, I remember her. Is it serious between you two? Or is it really none of my business?"

"Uh, well," Michael suddenly found the mud caked on his saddle fascinating. "I wasn't looking for anything serious," he admitted, "but she's just the most incredible person. I can't stop thinking about her, Lex."

Oh, boy. I'm sure that listening to Amanda's father talk about his love life wasn't on my list of today's things to do. What am I supposed to say to the man? Lex began to panic. *What if he asks me...*

"Can you fall in love with someone in such a short amount of time?" Michael asked, unaware of the internal conversation Lex was having with herself.

"Huh?" She didn't see the tree Thunder walked under, and was almost swept off the horse. "Damn!" Lex pulled him to a stop, then climbed down from the saddle and took the reins. "I think I'd better walk for a bit."

"I think I'll join you." Michael stepped down and began to walk beside her, leading his horse behind him. "I'm sorry, Lex. I didn't mean to upset you."

"No, no. I'm not upset, really. Just thinking about how to answer you." They walked for a couple of minutes in silence before she spoke again. "You asked if I thought you could fall in love with someone in just a few weeks, right?"

"Right," he agreed. "This is all very new to me. I've never been in love before, Lex."

Amanda is going to owe me big time for this one. "Neither had I, before I met your daughter." Lex kicked a rock with her boot, unable to look at him. "It's hard to explain, but the moment I saw Amanda, I knew I loved her. There we were, walking along during a thunderstorm after I had fished her out of the creek. Both of us were drenched to the bone, and every word, every touch from her was like a healing balm to my soul." She blushed when she realized what she had said. *Jeez. He's going to think I'm some sort of lunatic.*

Feeling the emotions that accompanied the words, Michael

stopped in his tracks. He reached out with his free hand and grasped Lex's arm, turning her to face him. "That has got to be one of the most beautiful things I've ever heard, Lexington Walters." Tears shone in his eyes, as well as a new respect for the woman standing next to him. "I'm damned honored that you've chosen to share your life with my daughter." Not caring about the mud covering them both, Michael pulled her into a bone-jarring hug. "You're going to make a damned fine daughter-in-law, Lex."

"Thanks, Michael," she whispered, overcome with emotions herself.

"You can call me Dad, if you'd like."

Lex pulled back from the embrace and smiled, her teeth shining through the dirt liberally coating her face. "I'd like that a lot, Dad."

"I really appreciate you coming with us today, Martha. It made the shopping trip much more fun," Amanda commented to the older woman. They were walking from Martha's house after parking the Explorer. "I still feel guilty for letting Deborah Sue just give me that beautiful dress. It wasn't cheap, you know."

Martha laughed as they climbed the back steps to the ranch house. "Don't you fret any over her, honey. Debbie has more money than she has good sense." She stopped when she saw two heaps of mud that appeared to have once been two pairs of boots. "Oh, lordy. What has that child gotten herself into now?" She pushed the door open and shook her head. Clumps of mud and grass formed a distinctive trail down the long hallway. Martha knew that if she looked, the route would lead up the stairway and into the master bedroom.

Footsteps could be heard jogging down the stairs. Amanda watched as Martha stepped further into the house and stood in her usual "Lexington is dead meat" stance. To both women's surprise, the person rounding the corner of the staircase wasn't Lex, although he was wearing a set of her sweats.

Michael skidded to a stop, his socked feet sliding on the hardwood floor. "Oh! Uh, hi there." His hands were full of muddy clothes, and the expression on his face caused his daughter to burst out laughing.

"Oh, Daddy! You look like you got caught with your hand in the cookie jar." Amanda had to lean against the housekeeper to keep from falling on the floor, she was laughing so hard.

He looked down at the pile of clothes in his hands. "Um, I didn't..."

"Hey, Dad. Did you—" Lex stopped at the foot of the stairs, also carrying a large pile of mud-covered garments. "Oops." She broke out into a huge smile, and tried to hide the clothes behind her back. "I didn't hear y'all drive up."

Dad? What went on this afternoon? Amanda walked over to her father and shook her head. "Just what were you two doing today? I thought you went for a ride."

"We did. But there was this calf stuck in the creek, and—"

"My Lord. You sound like one of the kids, Michael." Martha reached out and tried to take the clothes out of his hands. "Give me those, and I'll put them in to soak."

Michael turned around and looked at Lex, who shrugged. "Better do as she says, Dad. You don't want Mada chasing you around with a spoon." Lex pulled the mess from behind her back and walked up to the housekeeper. "Want me to carry these for you?"

"No, I don't." Martha took the bundle from Lex and turned around. "Blasted kids, always getting into trouble," she muttered, as she walked back down the hallway and into the laundry room.

"Is she mad?" Michael asked as he watched Martha walk away.

Lex stepped up beside him and put a companionable arm around his shoulder. "Nah. She wouldn't know what to do with herself if it wasn't for me."

"I wouldn't have as many gray hairs," Martha yelled from the other room.

Amanda shook her head. "One of you is almost as bad as the other," she lamented, her heart secretly proud of the two people standing in front of her. "Who's going to tell me what you got into today? It's got to be a great story."

"Not much to tell," Lex replied, backing up slowly. "Things were going just fine until that damned rattlesnake caused such a ruckus." She grinned and ran.

"Rattlesnake?" Amanda's face grew pale. "She didn't say—"

Michael patted his daughter on the back. "It wasn't really that close to her head, honey. And she was able to kill it with a shovel."

"Shovel?" Amanda watched as the rancher disappeared in the

den. "Lex!" she yelled. "I'm going to have to hurt her," she grumbled, following her lover. She tried to shut out her father's laughter as she walked away. *He's next, she decided.*

Chapter 24

Lex watched Amanda place her makeup in the overnight bag. "Tell me again why you have to go so early? The wedding is tomorrow, and it's only," she looked at the clock on the nightstand, "ten-thirty in the morning." She stood up from the bed and followed her lover into the bathroom. "I can take you over to your grandmother's later this afternoon."

"Honey, please. It's only for one day. We'll see each other tomorrow." Amanda turned around and almost ran into Lex. "Just pretend that I'm at work. You probably won't even miss me." Although she was having just as rough a time at the thought of leaving, she tried to put on a brave front. *One of us falling apart is enough,* Amanda thought as she reached around Lex to grab her toothbrush. "You know how Gramma and Martha are. If I don't get downstairs soon, one of them is going to come up here and get me."

"I miss you already." Lex stepped behind Amanda and wrapped her arms around her waist. "You know," she bit gently on a nearby earlobe, "I'm sure we can find something to do up here." One hand snaked its way under the light-colored tee shirt that her partner was wearing, and Lex began to trace a gentle pattern across Amanda's skin. Hands reached up and tangled themselves in her hair as Lex continued to nibble on Amanda's neck.

The sound of a throat being cleared caused both women to look to the doorway, where a red-faced Jeannie stood. "Don't you guys ever get enough?" she blustered as she tried to ignore the blush that stained her face. "Gramma sent me up here to get you, Mandy. She said you two can pick up where you left off tomorrow after the reception."

"Give us just five more minutes," Lex asked, hating the pleading tone in her voice.

"Oh, no. Gramma said that you might beg. But I'm not supposed to show you any mercy." With her hands on her hips, Jeannie glared at her soon-to-be sister-in-law. "What's the big deal, Slim? It's only for one night."

Not able to even explain it to herself, Lex stayed quiet for a moment. *She's right. I spent plenty of nights alone before Amanda came into my life. I can do this.* She watched as Amanda gathered up the rest of her things and closed the small suitcase. "I'm being silly, aren't I?"

Feeling sorry for her, Jeannie reached out and placed one hand on Lex's arm. "Actually, I think it's incredibly sweet." Jeannie leaned closer to whisper into Lex's ear. "I'm glad my sister has you to love her, Lex." She wrapped her arms around the startled woman and squeezed.

Lex felt a feather-light kiss on her cheek before Jeannie pulled away. "So am I." Picking up the suitcase, Lex grunted. "Good grief, Amanda. Did you pack your favorite bricks or something?"

"No, silly. Just the things that I'll need tomorrow." Amanda linked her arm though Lex's free one. "Walk me downstairs?"

"Sure, if I really have to."

Jeannie quietly followed the couple, amused at their loathing to separate, even for one day. *They'll probably be just like this on their fiftieth anniversary.*

Two frowning faces met the trio at the foot of the stairs. Martha had her hands on her hips as she glared at Lex. "It's about time you dragged yourselves down here. We were just on our way up."

"C'mon, Mada. It's not like we're on a time schedule today." Lex stepped past the older woman and yelped at the slap she received on the rear. "Hey! What was that for?"

The housekeeper shook a finger at Lex. "For sassing me, that's what. You know that tradition says you're not supposed to see each other before the ceremony. So yes, we are on a schedule. Neither one of you would get ready on time if we didn't do things this way. One day apart won't kill either one of you, Lexie."

Lex fought to keep the pout off her face. "Yes, ma'am." She looked down at her lover, who was fighting a losing battle to hold back her giggles. "What's so funny?"

"You look like a little kid when you pout like that," Amanda chortled, shaking her head. She leaned up and kissed Lex on the cheek. "Walk me out to the car?"

"Yeah." Lex led her fiancée down the hallway.

Travis, Charlie, and Jacob all stood up as Anna Leigh made her way through the lunch crowd at The Crossing and stepped up to their table. She gladly accepted the chair her husband pulled out for her. "Thank you, dearest."

"We were afraid you wouldn't make it," Martha commented, catching their waitress's eye and waving her over.

"I almost didn't. Mandy kept wanting to follow me around. I think she misses Lexington already."

Martha laughed. "I know what you mean. If it wasn't for Morris and Kevin staying out at the ranch, I don't know how I would have gotten away from Lexie. She's just as bad. Although she finally took off on that monstrous horse of hers, so maybe she'll come home in a better mood."

A heavyset older woman stood by the table, waiting until they had finished talking. "Excuse me, folks. I hate to interrupt, but is there something I can bring you, ma'am?" she asked Anna Leigh.

"Yes, please. I'll have tea and the fajita salad." She handed back the menu that had been lying on the table. "Thank you, dear."

"You're welcome, ma'am. I'll bring your tea right over, and it'll be just a few minutes for your salad." The server left quickly, bringing back the glass of tea and retreating silently.

Anna Leigh looked at the happy grin across the table. "All right. It looks like you've got something to share. Travis? Care to tell me what I missed?"

"Well, like we had agreed to on the telephone, I think all of us were concerned that the girls hadn't made any plans for a honeymoon." Seeing the nods from everyone, he rubbed his hands together. "Since Lexie doesn't like to fly, we were extremely limited as to where we could send them."

"That certainly leaves out some of the more typical honeymoon spots. We don't want to send them by bus," Jacob interjected. "Maybe a cruise?"

"That might have worked," Martha agreed. "But I can tell you from experience, those cabins on board ship are tiny. And since they'd probably spend most of their time in their room, the poor things would probably go nuts. So, Travis and I put our heads together, and came up with something I think everyone will like." She nodded to the older man. "Why don't you tell them? It was your idea, after all."

"Certainly." Travis looked around the table to make sure he had everyone's attention. "As you know, I still have my limousine and driver from my home in Dallas. Well, Martha and I were talking the other morning, and we were trying to figure out some place close that we could send Lexie and Amanda. She mentioned that she had always wanted to see New Orleans."

"Of course! What a splendid idea." Anna Leigh reached over and clasped Martha's arm. "Absolutely wonderful, dear."

"Thank you," the housekeeper blushed slightly. "But I can't take all the credit. Charlie and I have been discussing going to New Orleans for a while now. We both would love to see Bourbon Street and the French Quarter. I just thought it would be some place close that the girls could take a car ride to."

Charlie put his arm around his wife's shoulders and hugged her. "Don't be so modest, honey. I know you spent half the night on the Internet, searching for hotels. Martha's a whiz on the computer. She can find just about anything."

"She sure is," Travis agreed. "We found this wonderful old hotel, the Hotel Monteleone, right in the French Quarter. With a quick phone call, we were able to get their nicest suite for the week. I think the girls will be pleasantly surprised."

Anna Leigh's eyes widened. "I've heard of the Monteleone, Travis. It's quite elegant. I can't imagine what a suite would cost for an entire week, especially on such short notice."

"You don't want to know." Martha pointed a finger at Travis and shook it. "But you're going to let us know how we can pitch in, aren't you?"

Although he had more money than he could ever spend, Travis understood where Martha was coming from. They had all agreed to pool resources for the girls' honeymoon, and he knew that if he offered to pay for everything, the rest of the family would be terribly upset. "Well, the room is already paid for, but I think we can come up with something."

Jacob jabbed him in the ribs with an elbow. "Good answer, my friend," he whispered.

Before another word could be spoken, the waitress returned,

bearing their meal on a large tray. "All righty, everyone. Here you go." She placed the appropriate plate down in front of each of them and then scuttled away.

The morning and afternoon dragged along for Lex, who had spent the majority of the day on horseback. Morris and Kevin had each offered to ride with her, but she preferred to spend the time alone, to cover a larger portion of the ranch. She had found herself at the creek, not too far from where Amanda's Mustang had been thrown into the water. Lex stared into the slow-moving stream, her mind drifting back to several months before, when torrential rains had swollen it to a dangerous level. The animal beneath her stretched out his neck and shook his head, snorting. "I hear you, Thunder." She stepped down from the saddle and dropped the reins, allowing the horse to walk away and graze.

It looks so peaceful now. Lex bent down and picked up a rock to toss into the water. She stood on the bank, fighting the sudden onslaught of memories.

The small car washed into the raging creek and she raced to pull the unconscious woman from the vehicle. She could almost feel the pain of the debris slamming into her as she swam back across, carrying the young victim on her back. Lex dropped to her knees as she thought about how that day could have turned out. If she hadn't been repairing the fence at that exact place, that very moment, they could have just as easily pulled Amanda's body from the car days later. "Dear God." Lex wrapped her arms around her body and bent forward. She felt tears of loss fall from her eyes as she imagined a life without her lover.

Lex had no idea how long she had knelt there, but was brought back to the present as Thunder butted her in the back with his nose. Wiping her face with her shirtsleeve, she stood up and scratched the curious equine between the eyes. "Thanks, buddy. Guess I'm on emotional overload today, huh?" Lex checked her watch and sighed. "We might as well head back to the house. Mada will give me a whipping for sure if I miss dinner."

After brushing the stallion until his coat gleamed, Lex slowly walked back up to the main house. She knew that she was still early for the evening meal, so she continued to walk around the large wraparound porch. The new swing was in place along the front of the house, and Lex dropped her weary body onto its padded surface. Stretching her long legs out in front of her, the tired woman leaned back and pulled the front of her black cowboy hat down over her eyes. Quiet footsteps alerted her to someone else's presence, but she stubbornly refused to acknowledge them.

"Uh, Lex?"

Damn. She sat up and raised the brim of the hat back. "Hey, Morris. What can I do for you?"

He looked at her uncertainly. "I saw you ride back to the house, and when you didn't come inside, I was worried. Are you okay?"

Lex rubbed her eyes with one hand and exhaled heavily. "Yeah, I'm all right." She patted the empty space next to her. "Have a seat."

"Thanks." Morris accepted the rancher's offer and sat down beside her. They sat in silence for several minutes before his hands began tapping a nervous tune on his thighs.

"What's on your mind?"

Morris looked at her innocently. "What makes you think something's on my mind? Maybe I just wanted a bit of fresh air," he theorized, his hands continuing their rapid thumping.

Rolling her eyes, Lex reached over and grabbed his hands. "Yeah, right." When she thought it was safe to release him, she removed her hands and leaned back against the swing. "C'mon, Morris. You're as nervous as a nun in a whorehouse. Spill it."

"God, you're something else, Lex." Morris turned so that he could look directly into her eyes. "I was wondering if I could bring someone else to the wedding tomorrow."

"Oh? Friend or family?"

He bit his lip. "Family, actually."

Confused at his nervousness, Lex studied him carefully. "Family?" Her eyes narrowed. "Just what part of the family are we talking about?"

"My sister."

Amanda watched through the back door glass as several workmen puttered around in the back yard. Since the weather forecast called for clear skies, they were already setting up everything for tomorrow's ceremony. She didn't hear the footsteps behind her, and almost screamed when a large hand grasped her shoulder gently.

"Sorry, squirt. I didn't mean to frighten you," Frank apologized. He peeked over her shoulder. "Looks like they're about done, huh?"

"Yeah."

He had just come from the living room, where Anna Leigh had asked him to talk to her granddaughter. She told him how Amanda had moped around the house all day, not even showing any interest in arguing with her sister. "Want to go for a walk? I have it on good authority that dinner isn't going to be ready for another half-hour or so."

Why won't everyone just leave me alone? Although she felt like snapping at her brother-in-law, Amanda couldn't think of a plausable excuse to get away from him. "I guess."

"Try and contain your enthusiasm," he teased, taking her hand and leading her through the house. "I'm not that bad of company, am I?" Frank opened the front door and bowed. "After you, ma'am."

Amanda walked slowly down the steps, never releasing his hand. "You're fine, Frank. I guess I'm just not in much of a mood for company."

"You should be bouncing off the walls, Mandy. I thought you'd be more excited about tomorrow." Frank led her down the sidewalk, gently swinging their linked hands. "Are you having second thoughts?"

"No!" Looking at her feet, Amanda shook her head. "I love Lex with all my heart. I can't wait until tomorrow."

Frank stopped. He reached down and lifted her chin with his free hand. "Then why have you been so sad today, honey?"

"You'll laugh."

"Try me, squirt. We've been friends for a long time, haven't we? Have you ever known me to laugh at something that was important to you?" Frank shook his head. "I'd never make fun of you, Mandy."

Looking into his earnest face, Amanda knew what he said was true. Unlike her sister, he had never broken a confidence, and had never teased her when she spoke her heart. "I hurt inside," she whispered, tears pooling in her eyes. "I miss Lex so much, and we've been apart for less than one day." The feel of his gentle fingers wiping away her tears caused Amanda to fall against the big man and burst into sobs. "I feel like such an idiot."

"Shh. It's okay, sweetheart." Frank wrapped his arms around

her. "You're not an idiot, Mandy." He gently rocked the crying woman. "I think it's nice to see someone so much in love."

"You do?" she sniffled, leaning back and wiping her face with one hand.

"Sure." Pulling a handkerchief out of his back pocket, Frank took a moment to wipe the tears from his sister-in-law's face. "I hope Lex realizes how lucky she is."

"I'm the lucky one." She accepted the handkerchief from him and gently blew her nose. After placing the cloth in her pocket, Amanda took his hand and began walking again. "You should see the way she looks at me, Frank. Those gorgeous blue eyes practically sparkle with love."

"I've seen that. When you came out to California, and we were in that bar. She looked across the room and practically glowed. After I saw who she was looking at, I knew that you were in good hands."

"Yeah. And her voice can just melt me. Lex can say the sweetest things." Amanda continued the walk, feeling her spirits lift as she talked about the woman she loved.

"Are you out of your ever-lovin' mind?" Lex jumped up from the swing. She clenched her fists, fighting the urge to gather Amanda's uncle up and toss him over the porch railing.

Morris held up his hands. "What do you...oh, no!" He reached up to touch her arm. "Wait, Lex," he pleaded, as she turned on her heel to leave.

The angry woman felt his hand pull at the back of her shirt, and she spun around and slapped him away. "Don't touch me." Lex could feel her control slipping, but she couldn't stop the words from leaving her mouth. "Of all the people in the world, you should understand why I don't want to see that woman. You know how much Amanda means to me, and yet you want to bring the woman who almost killed her to our wedding?" She raised one fist and held it close to his face, her entire body trembling with the effort of holding back.

"Wait, Lex, please," Morris begged, taking his life in his hands and gently wrapping his fingers around her fist. "That came out all wrong. I'd never invite Elizabeth to any family gathering, unless it was her own sentencing. I was talking about one of my other sisters, Christina."

"Christina?" Lex echoed as she blinked several times to get her bearings. "You have other sisters?"

"Yes. Two others, as a matter of fact. Paula and Christina."

Lex looked at her fist, which was still held tightly in his. "Oh jeez, Morris, I'm sorry. I should have let you explain before I threatened you like that." She sat down on the swing, even more exhausted than before. *I can't believe I went off on him like that. I've got to get myself under control.* Ducking her head, Lex stared at her boots in shame.

"Hey, don't apologize." Morris sat down next to her and patted Lex on the leg. "I should have been a bit more clear. I didn't know that you hadn't heard of my other sisters."

"Yeah, well. I could have just asked, instead of almost knocking you off the porch."

"Well, no blood was shed, and no punches were thrown. I'd say we both survived just fine." Morris draped one arm around the back of the swing, pulling Lex close. "Let me tell you about my family, so we won't have any more misunderstandings, all right?"

"Sure." She still wouldn't look at him.

"Once upon a time, in a land far away...let's call this land Los Angeles," he decreed. "Anyway, there was this king and queen." Morris leaned over and whispered in her ear. "Actually, he was a shipping tycoon, and she was a society matron, but I digress."

Unable to help herself, Lex laughed.

"Good. Now, where was I? Oh, yes. The king and queen were very happy. Or, at least as happy as two people could be, that were told they had to furnish a male heir to their wealthy and very nasty sovereigns. So, just a scant six months after they were wed, a child was born to them. Paula was a very sickly baby, and soon drove all the hired help wild with her demanding ways." He covered his mouth in feigned shock. "Imagine the surprise of all when another child was born, a little over a year later."

Lex laughed again and shook her head. "You're crazy."

A happy smirk was her only answer. "Elizabeth was the surprise child. You'd think people with that much money would know what causes such things, but..." He shook his head sadly. "Since they still had no son, the couple waited a few years before trying again. I suppose two royal brats were more than a handful for them, for a while. Anyway, several years later, another daughter was born. Christina was the sweetest of children, yet constantly tormented by the evil older siblings. She soon learned how to hide in plain sight, or better yet, go along with whatever the others asked of her." His face saddened at the thought.

"That's a shame." Lex knew exactly what Christina had gone through. Her own brother had treated her like his personal punching bag while they were growing up. Lex learned to either stay away from him or pick something up to use as an equalizer, such as a large stick or rock. "Since you're sitting here, I see that they finally succeeded in producing a male heir."

"So true, dear lady. But, alas, by the time the son they wanted came along, he was no longer needed. Another branch of the family tree had the requested male heir, and I was but an afterthought." He laughed. "Not to mention that the son looked better in heels than the eldest daughter. I swear, my sister Paula is what you would call a handsome woman."

Snickering, Lex leaned back in her seat. "Handsome?"

"Oh, yes. Believe me, she'd look much better pulling a hansom cab than dressed in a ballroom gown." Morris broke out in laughter at his own joke. "She looked just fine before her last face lift. But now her eyes are pulled so far back on her face, she has to turn her head to see something with both of them."

Lex laughed so hard she fell off the swing. "Damn, Morris," she wheezed from the ground, "next time warn me before you say something like that." She looked up in surprise when the front door opened and Martha looked out.

"Lexington Marie, whatever are you doing lying on the porch like that? Get yourself up and go get cleaned up for dinner." Martha turned around and stomped back to the kitchen, muttering under her breath about crazy kids.

"Where on earth have you two been? We've been worried sick." Jeannie had been sitting on the front steps reading a magazine, and jumped to her feet when her husband and sister walked across the lawn.

Amanda bent down and picked up the magazine. It was one of those women's rags that had tips on how to keep your husband or boyfriend happy, and was opened to a "rate your mate" quiz. "I can see you've just been beside yourself." *Hmm. Looks like old Frank has his work cut out for him. Better not tell my sister how Lex would rate—she'd be jealous.*

Jeannie saw what her sister was looking at. She blushed and jerked the paper out of Amanda's hands. "Gimme that!"

"What's the matter, honey?" Frank asked, knowing how his

wife loved to take the quizzes. He'd caught her shredding her answers one time, and learned that she was always too embarrassed for anyone else to see them.

"Nothing!" Jeannie stomped into the house.

The two people left standing on the porch looked at each other and burst into laughter. "Sisters. Can't live with them, can't kill 'em." Amanda linked her arm through Frank's and followed the upset woman inside.

"You two are just in time," Anna Leigh greeted from the kitchen doorway. "Jacob just put the finishing touches on dinner."

"Thanks, Gramma. We'll go upstairs and get washed up." Amanda hurried up the stairs with Frank on her heels, both of them still laughing.

During dinner, Jeannie continued to glare at her sister. Her sullen attitude kept Amanda in high spirits, and she couldn't help but tease her. "You know," Amanda said in between bites of food, "Lex and I took one of those magazine quizzes one time." She looked across the table at Frank, who almost choked on his food.

"Which quiz was that, dearest?" her grandmother asked, glad for the conversation. She couldn't understand what was wrong with Jeannie, but was thankful that Amanda seemed to be in a better mood.

"You know, the one in last month's edition of the magazine Jeannie reads. To see how compatible we were in bed."

Jacob sputtered, having just taken a drink from his water glass. "Are you sure you want to share that bit of information with us, Peanut? I'd think that would be a little personal, don't you?"

"Yeah," Jeannie agreed, glaring at her sister.

Amanda laughed again. "Aw, c'mon. It's all in fun." She winked at her brother-in-law. "You're curious, aren't you?"

"Sure," he agreed. "Ow!" The sharp pinch to his thigh caused Frank to cut his eyes to his wife. "Whatcha do that for?"

Jeannie huffed and tossed her auburn hair back over her shoulder. "No reason, big mouth." She looked at her sister and sighed. "Okay. So go ahead and tell us how compatible you two are, like we don't already know."

"Well," Amanda put her fork down and looked around the table, "Lex took the test first, and scored almost a perfect high score. It said that she shouldn't be too close to combustible materials, because she's so hot." She winked at Frank. "I'll have to agree with them on that one."

"Oh, for God's sake," Jeannie moaned, "spare me the details."

"You're just jealous."

Frank looked up from his plate, indignant. "Hey!"

Amanda shrugged and cast him a pitying glance. "No offense, Frank."

"None taken, I guess."

Anna Leigh stifled a laugh at the antics of the younger people. "Children, please. No fighting at the dinner table." She waved a hand at Amanda. "Go ahead, dear."

"Thanks, Gramma." She gave her sister a snotty look. "As I was saying, before I was so rudely interrupted, Lex rated so high on their scale, she should be encased in ice to protect everyone else around her."

Jeannie made a gagging sound, but didn't say anything.

"What about you?" Frank asked, his curiosity piqued.

"Me?" Amanda blushed, suddenly very shy. "I did all right."

Her sister tossed a pea across the table at her. "Oh, no, Miss Smarty Pants. You've gone this far. Finish your story."

Amanda bit her lip and looked down at her plate. She could feel her face growing redder by the minute. "I scored..." The last few words were mumbled and unintelligible.

"What's that? I didn't quite hear you," Jeannie insisted, cupping one ear with her hand and leaning over. "Speak up."

"I said, I scored one point below Lex," Amanda almost yelled, then looked around the table in horror as her words fairly echoed in the quiet room.

Frank smiled broadly. "No wonder Lex is so happy. You go, girl."

Amanda jumped up from the table and fled the room in embarrassment.

Jeannie slapped her husband on the arm and jumped up as well. "Now look what you've done," she chastised, following her sister from the room.

Kevin looked across the table at Lex, who was picking at her food. He leaned over and whispered in his partner's ear, "So? Did you ask her?"

"Sorta. We were called in for dinner before we got finished."

"I'm not deaf." Lex glared at the two men across from her. "Tell me more about your sister, Morris."

"Sister?" Charlie exchanged glances with his wife, who

shrugged her shoulders. She looked at Travis, who appeared to be as confused as they.

"Yes. I asked Lex if it would be all right if I asked my sister, Christina, to the wedding. Although she hasn't seen Mandy since her high school graduation, we've kept in touch." Morris placed his fork beside his plate and looked around the table. "I was pretty much kicked out of the family that day, and both Elizabeth and our oldest sister, Paula, threatened to make life miserable for Chris if she went against their wishes."

"Why now? Isn't she still afraid of them?" Lex asked, still trying to decide if it would be in Amanda's best interests for another family member to suddenly show up.

"You all know how Liz was. She and Paula ruled over our family like they were some sort of royalty. Christina often bore the brunt of their tyrannies, and over the years she found that it was just easier to go along with them. But now that Elizabeth is locked away, she really wants to get to know Mandy again." He smiled at Lex. "And you, too. When she found out that you owned a ranch, she practically begged me to get permission for her to visit. Chris just loves horses."

She can't be all bad, then. "How does she take your relationship with Kevin? I don't want another homophobic woman harassing Amanda."

"Uh, well, considering her inclinations, I don't think you'll have much of a problem." Kevin gave Lex a moment to understand what he said. "Although their marriage was pretty much on paper only, finding her husband with the gardener really upset her. After she divorced the bum, Christina moved to Boston, presumably to start over. But she actually stayed with us for a while, until she met Samantha. I think Chris was as surprised as we were when she realized she was gay."

"Samantha, huh?"

Martha patted Morris on the arm. "Does she want to bring Samantha to the wedding with her? I'm sure we have enough room for two more."

"That would be great! Let me give them a call. They're staying in a hotel in town, just in case." Morris jumped up from the table and hugged Lex. "I can't wait to see the look on Mandy's face." He hurried from the room to use the phone.

"Me neither. I can't wait to see her, period."

Finding Amanda's door closed, Jeannie paused for a moment. *Maybe she wants to be left alone.* Hearing her sister's sobs, she knocked lightly on the wood. "Mandy? C'mon, let me in." The door was unlocked and opened slightly at her knock.

"Go 'way."

"No." Feeling like a first-class heel, Jeannie pushed the door open and stepped inside. The room was dark, but she could just make out her sister's form lying across the bed. "Mandy, please, talk to me." Without permission, she sat down next to Amanda and placed her hand on the crying woman's back.

The gentle touch only made Amanda cry harder. "I don't think I can do this, Jeannie," she sobbed, her face partially buried in a pillow.

Oh, God. I was afraid of this. She wants to back out of the wedding, but doesn't know how. "Oh, Mandy. Let me help." She stroked her sister's hair tenderly. "Do you want me to break it to Lex for you?"

"No, I don't want to upset her." Amanda sniffled and rolled over onto her back. "She'd probably drive over here in the middle of the night."

Jeannie's pulse quickened. *I didn't think that they had that kind of relationship. It's worse than I thought.* "Are you afraid of her, Mandy? We can always have the whole family with you, if you want."

What? Amanda reached over and turned on the bedside lamp. She looked up at her sister in confusion. "Jean Louise, what on earth are you babbling about? Why would I be afraid of Lex?"

"You said you can't do this. I thought you were talking about the wedding."

"Oh, for Pete's sake!" Amanda slapped her sister's leg and began to laugh. "I meant that I didn't think I could go until tomorrow without some contact with Lex."

Jeannie laughed along with her. "I didn't think you two had a relationship like that, but you've been acting really weird today. What was I supposed to think?"

Amanda sat up and pulled her sister into a hug. "Thanks, sis. Even though you're misguided at times, I still love you."

"Thanks, I think." Jeannie leaned back to get more comfortable on the bed. She crossed her legs and bounced, glad to see her sister in a better frame of mind. "So? What are you going to do? Sneak out of the house like a teenager?"

"Probably not. But if I don't at least talk to her tonight, I'll lose my mind."

Lex stared up at the ceiling, unable to sleep. After dinner, she had gone back down to the stables and brushed all the horses, stacked fresh hay in the barn, and even polished her boots. She had been wandering around in the den after midnight when her grandfather found her and sent her to bed. "Treating me like a child," she grumbled, crossing her arms over her chest. Whipping the bedcovers off, Lex was about to get up when the phone rang. A quick glance at the clock showed one-thirty, and she hurriedly grabbed it before it woke anyone. "Hello?"

"Lex?" a small voice whispered.

"Yeah. Amanda? Is that you?" Lex sat up in bed and leaned back against the headboard. "Why are you whispering?"

"Because I don't want to wake anyone up. I was afraid Gramma wouldn't let me talk to you, and I missed you."

"I miss you too, sweetheart," Lex admitted, lowering her voice for no reason other than to match the other woman's whisper. "Are you okay?"

A sniffle came from the other end of the phone. "I'm fine. Just missing you like crazy. I've almost driven my family insane today with my mood swings. I think Jeannie was on the verge of having me committed."

Lex closed her eyes and soaked up her lover's voice. "I've been just as bad. I rode out to the bridge today, remembering when we met."

"Oh Lord. That was pretty wild, wasn't it?"

"Yeah. It was the best day of my life."

"Really? Even with your injured ribs?"

"Uh-huh. I wouldn't change one second of our time together, love." Lex felt a lump form in her throat. "Every minute with you is precious, Amanda. I treasure them all."

There was a quiet throat clearing on the other end of the phone, as Amanda tried to control her emotions. "I love you, Lex."

"I love you too, Amanda. Do you think you can get some sleep now?" As much as she wanted to keep her lover on the phone, Lex knew that tomorrow's events would be tiring. "You wouldn't happen to know what happened to my nightshirt, would you? The last time I saw it, I had left it on the bed this morning."

"I accidentally packed it." A smile could be heard in the quiet voice. "I'm wearing it, as a matter of fact."

"Well, at least I know it's being put to good use." Lex looked at the silky gown that was wrapped around her own pillow. "I'll take good care of yours, too."

"Thanks. Goodnight, honey. I love you."

"Goodnight, love. I'll see you tomorrow." Lex waited until she heard the phone click before she hung up. With a satisfied sigh, she pulled the nightgown up against her cheek and drifted off to sleep.

Chapter 25

The morning sun struggled through the window shade, inching its way across the down-filled pillow in search of eyes to shine into. Hitting its mark, the bright streak showed no mercy. With a disgusted groan, Amanda grabbed her pillow and rolled over. Minutes later, a gentle knock on her door disturbed her again. "Go 'way."

"I'm sorry, Mandy. But you asked me last night to wake you this early." Anna Leigh opened the door and stepped inside. She was swathed in a colorful cotton bathrobe, the lavender flowers that covered it going well with her beautiful silver hair. Sitting down on the bed next to her granddaughter, Anna Leigh pulled the pillow away from Amanda's face. "You don't want to miss your wedding day, do you?"

"Of course not." Amanda rubbed her eyes and sat up. "What time is it?"

"Almost nine. Since you were up so late last night, I did let you sleep in this morning." Her hand reached up and began to comb through Amanda's unruly hair. "How was Lexington?"

Amanda's eyes widened in alarm. "How did—sometimes I swear you have the house bugged, Gramma. I never could hide anything from you." She hugged her pillow to her chest. "She wasn't doing any better than I was. But we had a really good talk before we went to sleep."

Anna Leigh chuckled and placed her hand on Amanda's cheek. "I'm glad, dear. You could have called her earlier, you know."

"But I thought we weren't supposed to—"

"The tradition is to not see each other before the wedding, Mandy. I don't think it meant you couldn't talk on the phone." Feeling sorry for her granddaughter, she patted her on the leg. "Come downstairs for breakfast. I'm sure your intended will be calling again soon."

"She's already called this morning?"

"Oh, yes. Around seven, if I remember correctly. Jacob told her that as much as he valued true love, he wasn't about to wake you up before nine."

"She's so thoughtful." Amanda couldn't keep the dreamy look off her face.

"She's impatient, I think." Anna Leigh started to stand, but was pulled back down by Amanda.

"Thanks, Gramma. For everything." Amanda gave her grandmother a fierce hug and kissed her on the cheek. "I love you."

Anna Leigh pulled her out of bed. "I love you too, Mandy. Let's go downstairs and see what your grandfather has whipped up for you on your wedding day."

"Lexie, quit your pacing around and sit down." Martha was tired of watching her stomp around the kitchen. She carried a plate full of food over to the table and set it down.

Lex turned away from the window and checked her watch. "It's almost nine. Maybe it's okay to call now." She started to leave the room when her belt was grabbed from behind.

"You'll do no such thing, young lady." The agitated housekeeper dragged Lex across the room and pushed her into a chair. "Now eat your breakfast before it gets cold."

"But—"

Sitting down next to the nervous woman, Martha placed a hand on her arm. "No buts, honey. Today is going to be crazy, and this may be the only time you have to sit down and eat."

Lex lowered her head and stared at her plate. "I know you're right, Mada, but I don't know if I can keep any food down right now. It feels like a team of horses is stampeding through my stomach."

"Honey, that's just nerves talking. I felt the same way on my wedding day."

"Really?" Lex raised her eyes, silently pleading for reassurance.

"Oh, yes. As a matter of fact, if you hadn't had such a strong grip on me when we were walking down the aisle, I probably would have fallen flat on my face."

Lex relaxed, feeling relieved. "It's good to know I'm not losing my mind, then. I wasn't this nervous the first time I tried to break a horse."

"Well, of course not. You weren't going to spend the rest of your life with the horse." Martha stood up and patted Lex on the shoulder as she walked by. "Just remember why you're doing this, and you'll get through the day just fine."

"God, I hope so." Lex dutifully began to put food in her mouth, not tasting a thing. *I hope Amanda is doing better than I am.*

Amanda glanced down at her plate. "Tell me again why I'm doing this?" When she had come downstairs a short time earlier, she had gently refused any type of food, telling her grandfather that she was afraid it wouldn't stay down.

"Because if you don't eat now, you'll pass out during the ceremony," Anna Leigh admonished her. "Just try a few bites, dear. You really do need to put something in your stomach."

Frank, who was sitting across the table from the two women, studied Amanda carefully. "You look kind of tired, Mandy."

"I didn't get much sleep last night."

Jeannie nodded knowingly. "Ahh. Scared?"

"No."

"Nervous?" Frank asked, helpfully.

"Lonely, actually." Amanda picked up a forkful of scrambled eggs and stared at them. "Do I like these?"

Jacob stood behind her and put his hands on her shoulders, rubbing them gently. "Normally you do, Peanut. Would you rather I make you something else?"

"No, this is fine, Grandpa. I just don't have much of an appetite." Amanda began to slowly bring food to her mouth, chewing automatically. When the phone rang, she dropped her fork and jumped from the table. "I'll get it!" She raced from the room and headed to the den, where she could have more privacy. "Hello?" Amanda answered, breathless.

"Amanda? Are you okay?" Lex's concerned voice poured over her like a relaxing balm.

Curling up in a large chair in the corner of the room, Amanda felt her world finally right. "I am, now. Let's never do this again."

"What? Get married?"

"No, silly. Sleep apart. I'll marry you every day for the rest of our lives, as long as I don't have to leave you."

There was a short silence on the other end of the line. "That's the best idea I've heard in a long time, sweetheart," Lex finally said, her voice soft. "God, I miss you."

Amanda closed her eyes. "I miss you, too." She was content to sit and listen to her lover breathe. "Only a couple of more hours, Lex. Think we'll make it?"

"Of course we will. The wedding will be a cinch. It's the reception afterwards I'm not looking forward to."

"Why not? It's just a little party for the people who won't be at the wedding itself." Amanda couldn't understand Lex's reluctance.

"Exactly. And we'll have to stay, and visit, and make small talk, and..."

Oh. "And we won't be alone until later this evening, right?"

"Yeah."

"Don't worry, love. We'll have some time alone if I have to sneak you out the back door and make out in the truck." Amanda smiled at that thought. Before she could say anything else, the front door opened and she heard her father's voice.

"Where's the beautiful bride-to-be? I've got something for her." Michael didn't see her in the den, and walked into the kitchen to search for his youngest daughter.

"Was that your dad?" Lex asked, knowing that their phone call was about to be cut short.

"I'm afraid so, honey. I guess we'd better start getting ready, huh?"

Silence from the other end of the phone, then Lex cleared her throat. "Yeah."

Amanda could almost picture the pout on her intended's face. *I wish I were there to kiss those pouty lips.* "Lex? C'mon, hon. In just a couple of hours, we'll see each other again. And after that, I don't intend to let you out of my sight."

"Okay, I guess I'll see you then." Lex paused for a short moment. "I love you so much, Amanda."

"I love you too, Lex." She waited, but the other end of the line was still open. "You need to hang up, honey."

"You hang up first," Lex said childishly.

Good grief. "I love you," Amanda whispered, gently pushing the button on the phone to disconnect the call. *I hate being the grownup, sometimes.* Wishing the day was all ready over, she stood up and went in search of her father, wondering what he had brought for her.

After she hung up the office phone, Lex leaned back in her chair and closed her eyes. She could almost feel Amanda's gentle touch, and she ached with the need to see her lover. "God, help me get through this day," she whispered, swallowing the lump that seemed to have taken up residence in her throat since yesterday. A quiet knock at the door caused her to open her eyes.

Martha stood in the doorway with a worried look on her face. "Lexie? Are you all right?"

"Yeah." Lex yawned, then stood up and stretched her arms over her head. "Just having a bout of self-pity." She reached out and pulled the startled housekeeper into a bear hug. "I don't know what I'd do without you, Mada."

Martha returned the hug. "No place else I'd rather be."

"How can a person become so dependent on someone else in such a short amount of time?" Lex asked. "I don't feel complete without her here."

"That's what love is all about. As much as it hurts sometimes, there's no greater feeling in the world." Martha turned and placed one arm around Lex's back. "C'mon. Let's go get you dressed for this shindig."

"Good idea." Lex leaned down and kissed the top of the Martha's head. "I love you, Mada. Thanks for always being here for me."

"I love you too, honey. Let's get you upstairs," Martha directed, leading the way out of the office.

Her sister caught Amanda outside of the den and proceeded to pull her upstairs. "Hey, wait! I heard Daddy come in." Amanda struggled to break the grip on her arm.

"Yes, you did. Gramma told me to get you upstairs and dressed, and he'll be up in a little while to see you." Jeannie stepped into Amanda's room and closed the door behind them.

"You wasted a lot of time on the phone, you know."

"It wasn't a waste of time," Amanda defended, finally shaking off the death-grip Jeannie had on her. "What's the big hurry?" She looked at the clock next to the bed and her eyes widened. "That clock isn't right, is it?"

Jeannie nodded. "Yep. You two sat and listened to each other breathe for almost an hour. And you haven't even had your bath yet." She began to untie the bathrobe that Amanda wore, pulling her hands back as they were slapped away.

"Stop that. I'm perfectly capable of undressing myself. Blast it!" Amanda struggled with the heavy tie, finally giving her sister a pleading look. "Well, don't just stand there. Help me!"

Downstairs, Michael sat at the kitchen table with the rest of the family. He kept turning around and glancing back into the foyer, while playing with his coffee mug. "I never thought I'd see this day—my little girl getting married."

Frank bristled at the comment. "Why? Because she's gay?"

"No, no." Michael waved his hands in front of himself. "Because she just never showed any interest in anyone." *How would I have known? I was so wrapped up in myself, she probably could have gotten married and had several children before I realized it.*

Seeing the distant look on his father-in-law's face, Frank reached out and touched his arm. "Hey, Mike. I'm sorry. I didn't mean to upset you."

"You didn't. I was just kicking myself for being out of touch with my family for so many years."

"That's all in the past, son." Jacob patted Michael on the hand. "You're here now, that's the important thing. Why don't you go on upstairs and see your daughter? I'm sure she'd like to share this day with you."

Standing up, Michael reached out and squeezed his father's shoulder. "Thanks, Dad." He reached into his pocket and pulled out a small jewelry box. "If you all will excuse me, I'm going to go give my daughter a present on her wedding day."

Halfway up the stairs, Michael almost ran into Jeannie. "Hi, honey." He wrapped her in a firm hug, which she happily returned. "After we get your sister married, I hope you have plans for spending time with your old man."

"Of course, Daddy. We don't have to be back in California until next week, so we thought we'd just take a mini-vacation while we're here." She kissed his cheek and pulled away. "Go on up. She's dressed already."

"Thanks, sweetheart." He continued his trek up the stairs, until he found himself standing outside of Amanda's door.

"Would you just look at you?" Morris gasped, as he walked around the quiet woman. He and the other men had been waiting downstairs in the den while Martha helped Lex get ready. "Honey, you look positively radiant."

Lex's eyebrow raised at the older man's words. Her dark hair shone. Hanging loose around her shoulders, it spilled gently onto the ivory jacket she was wearing. At her request, Martha had taken the slacks up slightly, but they still draped delicately on her slender hips. She held her arms out while Martha continued to fuss over the fit.

"Lexie, these pants are loose. I swear, if you don't start eating better, I'm going to—" The housekeeper's words were stopped by a gentle hand to her mouth.

"Mada, please. They fit fine, really. Don't worry so much." Lex looked down into her concerned eyes. "You know I can't eat when I'm nervous. After today, you'll probably have to let out all of my pants."

Travis chuckled as he stepped closer. "Especially if you eat everything Martha cooks. I swear I've gained several pounds since I moved in here." He put his arm around his granddaughter's shoulders. "It's about time we leave, Lexie. You ready?"

"As ready as a person can be, Grandpa." Looking around the room, Lex counted heads. "I don't think we can all fit in the truck, though."

"No need to worry. I've already taken care of that." Travis led the way to the front door, opening it and gesturing ahead. "You first, Lexie."

Travis's large white limousine was parked in the driveway, the uniformed chauffeur holding the rear door open. Lex turned to her grandfather and shook her head in disbelief. "When did...how...what..."

He guided her down the steps slowly. "You don't think I'd allow my only granddaughter to drive herself to her own wedding, do you?" He turned around to the others who stood on the porch gaping at the long car. "There's more than enough room for us all.

Come on."

The bedroom door opened, and Michael became speechless. His youngest daughter stood in the doorway, her hair pulled up on top of her head with tiny tendrils falling against her neck. "You-you look, beautiful, sweetheart," he finally uttered as she pulled him into the room and closed the door.

"Thanks, Daddy." Amanda sat down on the bed and patted the space beside her. "I'm so glad you're here."

Michael sat down and took one of her hands in his. "Me too, angel. I, uh, brought you a little something for today." He reached into his pocket and pulled out the jewelry box. "I saw these in a window, and they looked like something you'd like." He handed the box to her and held his breath, hoping he'd done the right thing.

"Oh, Daddy, you didn't have to get me anything." Amanda opened up the box and peered inside. The light hit the earrings and caused them to sparkle. "They're beautiful."

"They're half-carat channel set diamond hoops. I was afraid that anything bigger would pull your ear off."

Amanda looked up into her father's eyes. "Thank you."

"I know they're not much, but—"

"No. Thank you for being here," she said, wrapping her arms around him and burying her face in his neck. "I love you, Daddy."

Michael fought back his tears. "I love you, too." They sat holding each other for a few minutes before he pulled back. "Why don't you put your earrings in, and then we'll wait for them to call us. I thought I heard a car door slam a couple of minutes ago."

"What's taking so damned long?" Lex paced back and forth in the den. "I'm here, I know Amanda's here. Why can't we get this show on the road?"

Travis watched his granddaughter in amusement. He had already chased everyone else out to the back yard until it was just the two of them. "Calm down, honey. They have to make sure everyone is seated before the ceremony begins." A timid knock on the doorframe caused them both to turn around.

"I'm sorry to disturb you," Ronnie stammered, "but the reverend says he needs the rings."

Lex looked down at her hand, where her ring rested on her finger. "Oh, yeah. I forgot all about that." She took a deep breath and pulled the white gold adornment off. *That's the last time I'm letting this ring leave my finger.* She wordlessly handed it to her grandfather, who in turn gave it to the young man at the doorway. "Thanks, Ronnie."

"Thanks for having me here, Lex. I know how important today is to you." Ronnie turned to leave when his arm was grabbed from behind. "What?"

"You're right. Today is probably the most important day of my life. That's why I wanted to be surrounded by my family," she told him. Lex put one arm around his shoulders. "You're a part of this family now. I'm proud to have you here."

"Thanks, Lex." He fought back tears of happiness and wrapped the rancher in a bone-jarring hug. "Being a part of this family is the best thing that has ever happened to me." Pulling back, he held his fisted hand up near his face. "I'll just get these out to the reverend now." Ronnie quickly scurried from the room, leaving behind a much calmer Lex.

Travis put his hand on his granddaughter's shoulder. "That was a nice thing you said to him, Lexie."

"I meant every word, Grandpa. He's a good kid."

Another knock and Morris stood at the doorway. "They're ready for you." He immediately turned and headed back outside.

Lex hugged her grandfather and took a deep breath. "Thanks for not giving up on me, Grandpa. I just wish Grandma Lainey were here, too."

"She is, honey," he said, leaning back and tapping her gently on the chest. "Right here. Now, let's go get you married."

Ronnie stood at the back door, looking both nervous and handsome in his navy blue suit that Martha had bought for him. He nodded at Lex and Travis then stuck his head outside and waved one hand. The signal given, the small quartet that the Caubles had retained began to play a soft medley of classical music. Lex and Amanda had both decided they didn't want the traditional wedding march played, but instead agreed to a subtle string melody. Since neither wanted to play the male role, it had been decided that each would be escorted separately to the minister by a member of their family.

Lex held on to her grandfather's arm tightly, now understanding what Martha had meant about nearly passing out. *I can't believe I'm this nervous. This is ridiculous.* She gave Martha a shaky smile as she made her way up to the front of the aisle. Travis kissed Lex gently on the cheek. "Be happy, Lexie." He turned and sat down next to Martha, while Charlie stood up beside Lex as her best man.

All eyes turned back to the door, as Michael began to escort Amanda down the steps. Lex felt her breath catch in her throat as she caught sight of her partner for the first time. It only took Lex a moment to realize that they had both picked out similar outfits, except that hers were slacks while Amanda's was a knee-length dress.

Michael stopped when he reached Lex, tears of happiness causing his eyes to sparkle. "Take care of her." He gave Amanda's hand to Lex, then kissed his future daughter on the cheek. "I love you," he told Amanda, kissing her and going back to his seat.

Amanda handed her bouquet of flowers to her sister, who stood off to her left as her matron of honor. She looked deeply into Lex's eyes before they both turned to face the minister.

"Friends and family, we are all gathered here today, in the sight of God, to celebrate the union of these two people." Reverend Hampton smiled down on the couple. They had requested an abbreviated ceremony, and he was more than happy to oblige. "To make my job easier, they've decided to recite their own vows. Lexington Marie." He handed Lex her grandmother's ring.

Lex cleared her throat nervously. Her mind went blank for a frighteningly long moment before she looked into Amanda's eyes and felt her nerves melt away. "Amanda. You're my best friend, and I love you with all that I am. I promise to cherish every moment we have together, to listen to and encourage you, to be there beside you in good times and in bad times. I promise to take care of you if you're sick, and laugh with you when you're happy. I promise to always put you before anyone else, and never take you for granted. These promises and more I give to you always, now and forever." With a shaky hand, Lex placed the ring on Amanda's finger, looking back up into her lover's watery eyes. "I love you."

Amanda could barely contain the tears of happiness that were threatening to cascade down her cheeks. As Lex withdrew her fingertips after the wedding ring was in place, Amanda began to speak. "If someone had told me a year ago that I'd be standing here, feeling what I do now, I'd never have believed it. But here I am, and I feel wonderful. When I look at you, I see every dream I've ever had come true. You are the love of my life, Lex." Amanda lifted Lex's hand to her mouth and kissed her ring finger, then slowly began to place the wedding ring there. "I promise you," Amanda began, nearly too choked up to continue, "I promise you my heart, my love, and my life—because you are all those things to me." The tears that she'd been holding back ran freely down her face. Lex was overcome as well, and Amanda concluded her vows in the comfort of her partner's arms. "Forever, Lex. I will love you forever."

"Forever." Lex's whispered promise caused Amanda to cling to her even more tightly. After a moment, Amanda pulled back and allowed Lex to wipe at the tears on her face. Lex took Amanda's hand again, and they both turned to face the minister.

Reverend Hampton smiled broadly at the couple. "That was beautiful, ladies. Now the fun part. Go on, seal it with a kiss."

Lex reached out and cradled Amanda's face in her hands. "I love you," she whispered, leaning forward and gently touching their lips together. She pulled back after a moment, but was surprised when Amanda captured her face and pulled her back for another kiss.

"I love you too, Lex," Amanda murmured after they broke apart. Both looked back up at the minister, who began to laugh.

He looked out at the couple's family and close friends and held his arms open wide. "You have all witnessed the beginning of their lives together. May I present the happy couple, Lexington and Amanda."

The string quartet broke into song, playing their version of the Corrs' *Runaway.* Their families immediately surrounded both women, as everyone began to talk at once. Congratulations and celebratory hugs were shared amid laughter and happy tears.

Morris tapped Amanda on the shoulder. When she turned around, her eyes grew big. "Aunt Christina?" she cried, embracing the woman next to her uncle. "I can't believe you're here."

Christina accepted the embrace happily. "You can thank Morris for that." Her once plump figure had been replaced by an almost athletic build, and her light brown hair had been colored and was short and neatly styled. She reached beside her and grasped another woman's hand. "I'd like for you to meet my partner, Samantha Moore."

"Congratulations, Amanda. It's really nice to meet you," the other woman offered, holding out her hand. She was a few inches taller than Christina, and her shoulder-length blonde hair was streaked with gray. "I've heard a lot about you from your uncle."

Partner? All right, Aunt Christina! She accepted Sam's hand, then pulled her into a hug. "Welcome to our family, Samantha. I hope we'll get to know you a lot better."

A few feet away, Janna shook Lex's hand and wrapped her arms around her. "Congratulations, my friend. I hope you both enjoy the best life has to offer, for many years to come."

"Thanks, Janna. So, when are we going to be invited to your wedding?"

"W-w-what?" Janna's eyes widened in alarm. "I don't know what you're talking about."

"Uh-huh. Just remember, I want an invite." She was about to torment her further, when Michael interrupted.

"I'm sorry, Lex, but Mom wants to go ahead and get all the pictures out of the way before you two go and change."

"Me? Change? Nah. You're stuck with me just the way I am, Dad." She wrapped an arm around his shoulders and winked at her friend. "Remember what I said, Janna," she said as Michael led her away.

Barbara walked up beside Janna and grasped her hand. "What was that all about?"

"Huh? Um, nothing. She's just giddy with relief, I think. Want to go watch them cut the cake?"

"Sure," Barbara agreed, a confused look on her face.

After all of the pictures had been taken, Jacob stood next to a large table and waved his hands over his head. "Excuse me, everyone! If I can have your attention, please." Once the guests had gathered around, he pulled Lex and Amanda forward. "We thought you could cut the cake here, and that would leave you free to socialize more at the reception." Handing them a large knife, he placed both women behind a large, three-tiered white cake.

"It looks almost too pretty to cut." Lex looked at her partner, who smiled up at her. "You ready?"

"Yep." Amanda's hands were entangled with Lex's on the handle of the knife, and together they brought the blade down in slow motion.

Cheers and catcalls were heard from the people watching, as

the couple was encouraged to feed each other a piece of cake. Amanda took a slice first, raising it slowly to Lex's mouth. With an evil grin, just as she was about to place the cake on her partner's lips, she smeared it all over the bottom portion of Lex's face.

Lex licked her lips slowly. "Not bad," she smacked, reaching down for her own piece. With cake still falling from her face, she raised a portion up to Amanda's face and gently fed her. When the crowd booed, Lex smirked and leaned down to kiss her wife, making certain that her face rubbed Amanda's thoroughly.

"Cheater." With bits of frosting and cake falling from her chin, Amanda reached up and swiped at Lex's face. Then, using her most sultry voice, she teased, "We'll finish this later," and gave Lex a lascivious grin and a wink, much to the crowd's delight and Lex's embarrassment.

Feeling hands grab her from behind, Amanda almost screamed as she was pulled into the darkened kitchen at the Ladies Auxiliary Hall and pinned against the wall. Warm lips covered hers, and she raised her hands to run them through her captor's hair.

"I've been wanting to do this for hours," Lex gasped once they broke apart to breathe. "If one more guy tries to dance with you, I'm gonna start breaking legs!"

Amanda dropped her head to rest on her lover's chest. "I know what you mean. Nobody said that half the town would show up." After her eyes adjusted to the semi-darkness, she reached up and caressed Lex's cheek. "What do you say we tell our family goodbye and go home? I really want to get our honeymoon started."

"That's the best idea I've heard all day. But first..." Lex leaned down and once again covered Amanda's mouth with her own.

Ten minutes later, both women stepped out of the kitchen, their faces flushed and their clothes in partial disarray. Lex tucked her blue cotton shirt back into her jeans, while Amanda ran her fingers through her hair to straighten it. They spied the majority of their family at a nearby table and headed towards them.

"I bet I know what you two have been up to," Jeannie teased.

"Grow up, Jean Louise. You're just jealous." Amanda looked at Frank. "No offense."

"None taken."

His wife tossed her hair over one shoulder in disgust. "Why would I be jealous?" Lex leaned down and whispered something in her ear, causing Jeannie to blush furiously. After Lex stepped away, Jeannie fanned her face with one hand. "Never mind."

"What did you tell her?" Amanda asked in a whisper.

"I'll tell you later." Lex stood behind the seated Travis and placed her hands on his shoulders. "Folks, as much fun as we've had today and this evening, I think Amanda and I are about to leave."

Jacob exchanged grins with Travis and looked up at the happy couple. "So soon? But it's only six o'clock. You know the party has just begun."

"We know." Amanda stood next to Lex with her arm around her partner's waist. "But to tell you the truth, we just want to be alone for a while."

Anna Leigh stood up, as did the rest of the table. "We can certainly understand that, can't we?" She waved to get Martha and Charlie's attention from across the room. The other couple made their excuses and headed to the table.

"Don't tell me," Martha said, walking up and standing next to Lex. "You two newlyweds are ready for the honeymoon."

Lex blushed. "Mada, please."

"Well, if you girls are that set on leaving, at least let us walk you out," Travis offered.

Not seeing a reason to argue, Amanda nodded. "Sure."

As the group stepped outside, the long white limousine stood by, the driver holding the rear door open. Lex turned to her grandfather and smiled. "Thanks, Grandpa. I kinda forgot how we got here. It's a long walk back to the ranch."

"About that, Lexie. We all got together and decided that you girls needed a proper honeymoon."

Lex shook her head. "Now, Grandpa—"

"It's not completely his fault, dear. After such a beautiful wedding, don't you think the two of you deserve a week to yourselves?" Anna Leigh interrupted. She prodded her husband, who pulled something out of his jacket pocket.

Amanda accepted the envelope tentatively. "What's this?"

"That's your confirmation page that I printed off the computer," Martha added proudly. "You shouldn't need it, but we wanted you to have it just in case."

"Confirmation?" Lex looked at her grandfather. "We're not flying, are we?"

Travis shook his head. "No, sweetheart. We wouldn't do that to you. Or Amanda."

"Then what?"

Jacob stepped in. "You're staying a week in a suite at the Hotel Monteleone, in New Orleans. It's all taken care of."

The newlyweds looked at each other in shock. "New Orleans?" Lex asked. "How are we supposed to get there?"

"In the limo, of course. Room service is included, and the driver's cellular number has already been programmed into your phone." Travis handed the phone to Amanda. "He'll be at your disposal for the entire week. You'd better keep up with this, Amanda. We know how Lexie is."

"But," Lex stammered, "what about our clothes?"

Charlie put his arm around his wife. "All packed, in the trunk."

Amanda began hugging everyone individually. "Thank you so much! I don't know what to say," she sniffled, while Lex followed behind her and also gave everyone a goodbye hug.

"Say goodbye." Jeannie pushed her sister at the car. "I want to go back inside and dance."

"Goodbye, brat," Amanda yelled good-naturedly from the doorway of the car, pulling Lex in behind her.

The driver closed the door and saluted the family, hurrying around and climbing in behind the wheel.

Once they were on the road, Amanda leaned back in Lex's arms as they snuggled together on the back seat. She had her eyes closed, but wasn't sleeping. "Whatcha doing?" she asked, knowing that her lover had been quiet for several miles.

"Just thinking." Lex watched the passing scenery through the window. The sun was beginning to set, and the red and orange sky was soothing.

"About what?"

Lex tightened her hold on Amanda, rubbing her cheek against her lover's hair. "I was just thinking how much I wish Dad could have lived to see today."

Amanda shifted slightly, so that she could look up into Lex's troubled eyes. "I'd like to think he did, love."

"What do you mean?"

"These past few months, you two had really gotten closer. He knew how important this day was to you. I'll bet you anything that he was looking down on us today, probably with your mom and grandmother."

Wanting to believe, Lex swallowed the lump in her throat. "Do you really think so?"

"I certainly do." Amanda brushed the hair away from Lex's eyes. "Why don't you close your eyes and think about your dad? It'll make you feel closer to him."

Lex placed a gentle kiss on her wife's lips. "I will. Thank you." She leaned her head back and closed her eyes, picturing her father as he was when she was younger—tan, fit, and riding the old dun gelding that he was so fond of.

They had ridden for a while in silence, Amanda dozing lightly on her partner's chest. Lex opened her eyes and gazed out at the sunset, blinking when she saw a rider in the distance. The man was riding a dun-colored horse, the way he sat achingly familiar to her eyes. As she watched, he raised one hand to her and spurred the horse on over the horizon. Lex felt herself at peace at last. *Thanks, Dad.* She buried her face in the hair beneath her chin and fell asleep as the limousine drove them to their future.

Other books in this series available from

Yellow Rose Books

Destiny's Crossing

(Destiny's Crossing contains two stories)

Destiny's Bridge

Rancher Lexington (Lex) Walters pulls young Amanda Cauble from a raging creek and the two women quickly develop a strong bond of friendship. Overcoming severe weather, cattle thieves, and their own fears, their friendship deepens into a strong and lasting love.

Faith's Crossing

Lexington Walters and Amanda Cauble withstood raging floods, cattle rustlers and other obstacles to be together...but can they handle Amanda's parents? When Amanda decides to move to Texas for good, she goes back to her parent's home in California to get the rest of her things, taking the rancher with her.

ISBN 1-930928-09-2

Hope's Path

In this next look into the lives of Lexington Walters and Amanda Cauble, someone is determined to ruin Lex. Attempts to destroy her ranch lead to attempts on her life. Lex and Amanda desperately try to find out who hates Lex so much that they are willing to ruin the lives of everyone in their path. Can they survive long enough to find out who's responsible? And will their love survive when they find out who it is?

ISBN 1-930928-18-1

Love's Journey

Lex and Amanda embark on a new journey as Lexington rediscovers the love her mother's family has for her, and Amanda begins to build her relationship with her father. Meanwhile, attacks on the two young women grow more violent and deadly as someone tries to tear apart the love they share.

ISBN 1-930928-67-X

And Coming in 2003 from
Carrie Carr
and
Yellow Rose Books

Something To Be Thankful For

Randi Meyers returns to her hometown to attend the funeral of an uncle she barely knew. During the graveside services, she's beseeched by a young boy to follow him into the woods to help his injured sister. After coming upon the unconscious woman, Randi realizes that the boy has disappeared. She brings the woman to the hospital and finds out that the woman's name is Kay, and that her brother Jared was killed five years earlier by a drunk driver. Kay has a broken ankle, but is otherwise fine.

Although the two women quickly become friends, circumstances and job loyalties force them apart, sending Randi back to her home in Ft. Worth, while Kay starts a new job to support herself. Phone calls back and forth aren't quite enough, and after a vision of Jared, Randi rushes back in the middle of the night to see Kay. An ex-girlfriend has been harassing Kay, begging her to take her back, but Kay finally realizes that her life is with Randi. After saying goodbye to her ungrateful relatives, Kay and Randi leave the small town to start anew.

Carrie is a true Texan, having lived in the state her entire life. She makes her home in the Dallas/Ft. Worth metroplex with her partner A.J. and their teenage daughter, Karen. She's done everything from wrangling longhorn cattle and buffalo, to programming burglar and fire alarm systems. Her spare time is spent writing, traveling, and collecting television memorabilia. She can be reached by email at carrie_carr@hotmail.com. For personalized bookplate information, go to her website at http://cbzeer.home.attbi.com.